BETWEEN EARTH AND SKY

Olivia Woods

First published 2021
by Rowanvale Books Ltd
The Gate
Keppoch Street
Roath
Cardiff
CF24 3JW
www.rowanvalebooks.com

A CIP catalogue record for this book is available from the British Library.

Paperback ISBN: 978-1-913662-27-1

Contents

A sacred place exists. It is where beauty and a peaceful solitude prevail. You can find it in the distance where gentle breezes blow, where sweet, aromatic scents fill the air, and where falling waters cascade down rocky slopes. It dwells in that tranquil space where the sun falls at sunset, and lingers briefly for a moment in time. Reserved for those who have endured much and loved purely, it exists in that tiny slice on the horizon, between earth and sky.

FOREWORD

I regret not knowing my father better before he passed away. After his death, I came to realise how very historically significant his life had been. As a young child, I lived in fear of him much of the time. He was a strange man who spoke with a foreign accent. He had come from a faraway land I knew little about. He demonstrated strange behaviours I could not understand, and his stern ways embarrassed me around my friends. He was quick to temper, and it seemed he was filled with frustration that was always waiting to boil over. He was a man who always demanded the best of you, a strict disciplinarian, and he would be more apt to criticise than praise. As a teenager, I avoided him as much as possible. Sadly, as an adult, I never felt completely comfortable in the company of my father.

I anguished over these things after my father was gone. Many of my friends had that special connection that exists between fathers and daughters. Why had it been so difficult for me to reach my father, and for that matter, who was this man I called *Dad*?

He was never one to hug or kiss his children, nor tell them he loved them, but my father did care about us. It was evident in the sacrifices he made to ensure that we always had a roof over our heads and food on the table. He was a hard worker, toiling away at three jobs in his effort to elevate us out of the rat- and bug-infested shacks we lived in as new immigrants to Canada. In addition to that, he cultivated and maintained a huge vegetable garden that was the envy of all the neighbours. Those vegetables sustained us during the early years of struggle in a new country. Because of my parents' strong work ethic, they were able to purchase our first house in a nice residential neighbourhood within five years. My father would make time in his busy schedule on Sunday afternoons to take his family fishing and picnicking by the water at the lakes nearby. Long drives in the country seemed to mellow him out, and he would be kinder during those times. He was a good husband to my mother for fifty years, loving, faithful, and caring.

When I was a child, I asked my mother why my father was so quick to temper and so mean. She told me it was because *life had not been kind to him*. I asked her what she meant, and she said it was in the sad history of his family and where they had come from. This sparked an interest and a genuine curiosity in me. When I was older and he was gone, I researched that history. I set out on a quest to learn more about my father and the place he was from. I needed answers to all my questions. I had no idea this journey would lead me down a path of intriguing discoveries and horrific revelations as I stumbled over a little-known piece of history. I knew the Polish peoples' story needed to be told, not just for the sake of telling it, but because it must find its proper place in history. In the end, I would gain a deep respect and understanding of my father, and I would come to recognise the hero in him.

I am left with so many things I would like to discuss with my father now, if only I had known his story sooner… if only he were here.

***

When I started writing *Between Earth and Sky*, the story was intended to chronicle my father's life. However, as my research led me further into the history of my father's people, I discovered there were many more layers to this tale that needed to be told. My father's narrative turned out to be the paradigm of so many young Polish men who were arrested on trumped-up charges by the Soviet occupiers in Eastern

Poland at the start of WWII, and who were then exiled to forced labour camps across Siberia. All that they suffered, and all that history forged for them afterward on their long walk across a frozen continent to an army that saw them fighting on the frontlines of battle, is only part of the tragic tale. This story needed to include the harrowing details of what happened to the other Polish citizens in Eastern Poland who suffered at the hands of the Russians when the Soviet Red Army marched in and occupied their land in 1939. It is a sad story of suffering, horror and hardship that the Soviets tried to keep hidden. Consequently, it was many years before this chapter of Poland's devastating history came to light.

The two main characters in *Between Earth and Sky,* Jozef and Lilyana, are fictitious. Jozef is not my father, but his story is based on my father's life. The character of Lilyana was developed to recount the devastating realities of civilian life in Poland during WWII, and aspects of the massive deportations that occurred at that time. Yet, amid all the gloomy circumstances and despair, moments of joy, humour, and hope continued to persist among the Polish people. Jozef and Lilyana's love story bears witness to the fact that good triumphs over evil. Unlike Jozef in this narrative, my father did not marry a Polish girl. He met my mother in England a few years after the war had ended.

Between Earth and Sky chronicles a piece of history that needs to be woven into the fabric of time. I only hope I have done the story justice. I dedicate it to all the Polish people who suffered through reprehensible atrocities during WWII. Their strength, courage and endurance are an inspiration to mankind. May their story be told, never forgotten, and never replicated.

PROLOGUE

An early morning sun filled the air with warmth, replacing the bitter cold winds that had swept across the frozen lake throughout the winter months. The last of winter's snow had left the ground, and fresh new growth of green was beginning to carpet the earth. Buds were starting to form on the forest branches, while crocuses and daffodils burst forth from the ground following a long winter's sleep. Robins were busy gathering dead grasses and bits of twigs for their nests. Thoughts of new beginnings had taken hold and embraced this lovely spring day.

Lily leaned heavily against the railing on the deck and drank in the early signs and smells of springtime. In the welcome breeze, wisps of greying hair brushed against her cheeks as they fell from the bun pulled tight at the nape of her neck. She was an elderly woman of small stature, yet her resolve remained surprisingly strong, considering all she had been through in her lifetime. The memories of Jozef came flooding in as Lily braced herself for what lay ahead: how her dear husband had loved to feel the warm breath of spring against his face, to hear the murmuring of the wind as it whispered among the treetops, and to take in the scent of fresh pine needles and wildflowers as he walked the surrounding woodlands. Jozef had spent many evenings standing right here in this very spot with Lily, watching the sun fall behind the distant hills. Together they would scan the horizon across the lake to where the hills rose to meet the sky. They would muse that it was through this tiny slice on the horizon that they found their new beginning. It seemed like a lifetime ago now. How blessed they felt to have survived and to have built a new foundation together in a brand-new land. Their story would transcend the boundaries of continents and time.

Lily's thoughts were abruptly interrupted when she heard a car crunching against the gravel as it slowly made its way down the long laneway toward the house. Looking out beyond the garden, Lily saw that her eldest daughter, Anna, and Anna's husband, Martin, had arrived. She turned slowly and went down the steps to greet them in the yard. With hugs and only a few words, Lily, Anna and Martin solemnly walked toward the car. Martin helped Lily climb into the back seat. Composing herself with stalwart determination, Lily resigned herself to the sombre event that was about to unfold. All her family and their friends and neighbours would be in attendance this morning. It would be a long drive into town, and Lily did not want to be late for Jozef's funeral.

They had chosen to move away from the city when Jozef retired fifteen years earlier. He and Lily had purchased a large plot of land in the woodlands along the shoreline of Halistar Lake, where they would construct their final home themselves, with help from their grown children. It was a small, four-room, rustic cabin primarily comprised of wooden logs taken from the encompassing forest. Large picture windows had been placed in every room so they could look out at the wildlife and enjoy views of the lake and woodlands. The deck outside surrounded the entire cabin. They loved their tiny waterfront home, and it brought them the peace and happiness they were so deserving of in their fading years. The serenity of the place was in sharp contrast to the turmoil and upheaval they had endured as young adults in Europe.

Now the family gathered in a small chapel to say their final farewells to Jozef. When Anna and Martin escorted Lily into the chapel, a reverent silence fell upon the place as the family matriarch made her way to the front where Jozef lay. She stood there momentarily, gazing on his sleeping form. She tenderly stroked his face and leaned into the casket to kiss his cheek one last time. She could not help thinking how handsome her husband looked even now as he lay there in his final rest.

In their native Polish, Lily whispered into Jozef's ear, "Goodbye, my love. May you find your way into Paradise on the wings of the angels and wait for me there."

She gently laid her hand on Jozef's chest and smiled down on him. For more than fifty years, they had shared a strong, loving bond, and she clung to it now. As she ran her index finger over the pin firmly in place on the lapel of Jozef's jacket, she could not help but think it was symbolic of all she and Jozef had lost and gained. Now darkened and stained with the passage of time, it was the pin awarded to Jozef for his military service so many years ago.

In her fragile state of bereavement, Lily was suddenly overwhelmed by her grief at Jozef's passing. Indelible images of the past began to play in her mind. Her thoughts wandered back to the darkness of those traumatic years she and Jozef had survived in a different place so far away.

ONE
FEBRUARY 1940

He made his way toward the barn, as he had done every morning for as long as he could remember. It was barely 5:00 a.m., but already early morning shadows were dancing across the frozen landscape like ghostly forms in the distance. Despite the impending uncertainty, Jozef was determined to keep pace with the rhythm and the flow of life on his family's farm for as long as possible.

His boots made deep imprints in the fresh blanket of snow that had fallen during the night. This winter was proving to be an extremely inclement one. Snowfalls were heavy and deep, and the temperature index was averaging -30 °C. Even though it was before dawn, Jozef could tell that a grey sky would hang low over the wintry countryside this day.

The air seemed charged with a sense of foreboding. Rumours had been circulating throughout the surrounding villages for days now. All through the night, the relentless barking of dogs at neighbouring farms had alerted Jozef to the soldiers' imminent approach.

A lingering moon cast a beam of light across the surface of the snow, allowing him to catch his first glimpse of them coming for him. They were moving quickly toward the farmstead with the precision of determined hunters. Their entourage stirred the snow into a fury and made it appear like a mystical vapour swirling in the wind. Despite the ambiguity of shapes and form, Jozef could clearly identify the NKVD men poised in the backs of the lorries. The pointed tops on their hats and the long bayonets at the ends of their rifles made the Soviet secret police easily discernible. In recent weeks, he had observed them roaming the streets in town and around the countryside, searching for people to shoot or send far away from home.

All Polish citizens were living in fear. Communist Russia had allied itself with the Nazi Third Reich in a secret pact designed to restructure Central Europe. The treaty ensured that the Soviets would aid Germany in its war effort against Poland and the West. In September 1939, World War II had dawned in Poland. Hitler's troops struck from the north, west, and south at the beginning of September. Poland had little chance to defend herself against the organised and formidable Nazi forces, and the ensuing battle was short-lived. Hitler authorised his troops to kill all men, women and children of Polish descent so that Germans could take their territory.

The Soviet Union crossed into Eastern Poland in mid-September. Russia attacked with a huge force of infantry, tanks and planes, and quickly claimed the area, as the Polish Army was unable to muster a counteroffensive against such a power. The combined forces of Germany and the Soviet Union caused the military defeat and collapse of Poland.

At the end of September, new borders were established, dividing Poland in half. By October, the western half of Poland, occupied by the Nazis, became new German territory, and the eastern half, occupied by the Soviets, was incorporated into the adjoining Russian domain. The new eastern border forced Soviet citizenship on the Polish inhabitants and their lands, to take away the Polish people's identity and incorporate them into the Communist realm.

The mutual goal of the Nazi and Soviet conquerors was to destroy the Polish people's existence forever by terrorising them into submission through murder, enslavement, deportation and extermination. All Polish people, Jews and non-Jews, were subjected to special legislation and stripped of all their rights. Rationing had been set up, allowing for only the bare minimum of food and medicine to be distributed to the Polish people. All traces of Polish art and culture were obliterated, and Polish history was wiped away. Libraries and bookshops were burned, and the Polish press was shut down. The Polish language was forbidden. Secondary schools and colleges were closed. Hundreds of Polish community leaders, senators, mayors, lawyers, judges, local officials, doctors and teachers were publicly executed or deported, targeted because the invaders knew that extermination of the elite would make it easier for them to control the country. The Soviets took over Polish businesses and factories, destroyed churches and religious buildings. Most religious authorities were arrested and sent to concentration camps. Polish banks were closed, and savings accounts were blocked. The Polish currency was removed from circulation.

By December, street roundups and mass executions had begun. Multitudes of Polish men, especially those with any affiliation to the Polish Armed Forces, were taken without warning from their homes in the middle of the night to be shot. Hopes of a resistance died with them. Thousands of other Polish men, women and children were forced from their homes and assembled at railway stations for deportation.

Jozef would be deemed subversive to the Soviet Union and its interests. His crime was his nationality, his gender, his age, and the fact that he was living on his family's land. He had also carried out his military training at the age of eighteen, as all young Polish men were expected to do. Thus, his name would be listed in the index of anti-Soviet elements the Russians felt needed to be dealt with. If Jozef resisted arrest, the soldiers would hunt him down and kill him without hesitation. Gossip had already been circulating throughout his village about people being shot in the streets without any explanation or mercy on the part of their Soviet captors.

His thoughts immediately turned to his younger brothers. Had he prepared Tobias and Marek well enough to assume operations of the family farm once he was taken away? They were merely twelve and ten years old, and it would have been a daunting task during the best of times for two small boys to conduct all the work required to keep the farm running smoothly. His mother, Emilia, was a strong woman and familiar with the farm operations; Jozef knew she would help the boys. His sister Katerina would step up as well and his baby sister, Zofia, only eight years old, would do what she could. However, Jozef was concerned for his family's future on the farm. If the Soviets seized their land and holdings, what would become of them? Infinite numbers of Polish citizens were being eliminated through the Soviet's ethnic cleansing, and multitudes were dying from starvation, disease and the frigid cold.

It was Jozef who had managed the running of the farm since his father, Stanislaw, died in a plane crash three years earlier. Stanislaw and his two business partners had been on route to England to attend an exhibition where farm modernisation and the latest innovations in machinery and mechanisation were to be demonstrated. The plane went down halfway across the English Channel, and although a lot of the plane's wreckage had been recovered, none of the bodies were ever found. The tragedy had deeply impacted Jozef's family and the surrounding community. Stanislaw had been a strong voice in representing the farmers for miles around. As a member of the local Agricultural Board, he oversaw farm operations and had stood up for many local farmers through his commitment to fair practices and economic stability throughout the area. He had been looked upon with much respect as a staunch and steadfast member of the farming community. His sudden death had been a tragic loss for everyone.

Following their father's death, Jozef's older brother, Lukasz, had become a professional boxer and moved to the city in order to earn some income to keep the farmstead operating, with their father's earnings gone. Lukasz was a good fighter. He often won consecutive rounds at boxing rings in the larger cities where the pay-out was substantial.

Jozef was only sixteen years old when he'd had to take over management of the farm, in addition to attending high school in the local village. He was a bright young lad with an affinity for nature and animals. He loved his family's land, and under his supervision the annual yield of wheat and oat crops had been of high quality. All the farmers from the surrounding countryside agreed Jozef had a certain way with plants and livestock, and said that his father would have been proud to see the way his young son had assumed responsibility for the workings of the farm.

Now, with the NKVD rapidly approaching, Jozef stood motionless on the land that had been passed down through the Nowakowski family for generations. Trying to remain calm, he breathed in the early morning air through his nose, pressed it deep into his lungs and held it there for several seconds before allowing it to disperse slowly from between his lips in a snow-white vapour. The soldiers were advancing at an alarming rate. A flock of winter fowl flew overhead, having been disturbed and rising from their snowy blanket on the forest floor nearby. This reminded Jozef of the time his father had taken him into the forest as a young child to teach him how to hunt. Stanislaw had taught his sons all the skills that he himself had learned as a young boy growing up on a rural farm. No lad could get by without knowing how to hunt, so Lukasz and Jozef were taken into the woods and swamplands at a young age, and their father had trained them in the safe use of a gun for hunting small game like rabbits and wild birds. When the air turned colder and the wild ducks and geese flew high overhead on their southward journey, Stanislaw could bring down many birds in a good day's hunt. He showed his boys how to gut and remove the feathers from the birds right there on the spot so the meat would not rot before they brought it home for Emilia to cook. Jozef was a quick learner, and he was able to shoot down wild birds before his older brother managed to get off a first shot. This enraged Lukasz, who'd accused his younger brother of taking shots at birds that were rightfully his, but had Jozef waited for his older brother to shoot first, no wild game would have been harvested. When he was a little bit older, Jozef often went hunting in the woods by himself. He'd return home with wild rabbits, grouse or partridge for his mother to throw into the stewing pot, much to the chagrin of his older brother.

Jozef remembered a day when he had accidentally stumbled over a family of wild partridge in their snowy lair and roused the birds into a sudden ascent with wings flapping, beating on their chests, snow flying, and confusion ensuing all around him. That day, Stanislaw had taught his son a lesson on the importance of vigilance. Jozef learned how significant that lesson was now, as he faced losing everything he had ever known and loved. Following the moment of his arrest, the trajectory of young Jozef's life would be altered forever.

The lorries slid to an abrupt halt just short of where Jozef stood. Many Red Army soldiers, a few members of the local Communist Committee and some from the local militia accompanied the NKVD men. The soldiers had rammed through the surrounding wooden fence that Jozef, Lukasz and their father had erected on a hot and sunny day several years earlier. Jozef had only been eleven years old at that time, but he had caught on to the art of fence-posting much more quickly than his older brother. Lukasz had been fifteen then and the lad had always been very tall and muscular for his age. Their father often said that Lukasz was as strong as the family's ox, Borys, but what he boasted in physical strength was lost on him when it came to intellectual perception. Jozef remembered how the difference between their ideas of how to build the fence had caused a fight to erupt between the two brothers. In a vain attempt to impress their father, both boys had insisted their technique was the more cost effective and efficient. Words between them had escalated into a clash of anger and swinging fists. Jozef was much shorter than his older brother, but his agility and speed guarded him from Lukasz's long reach and swift, strong punches. Eventually, Stanislaw had to separate his brawling sons, and it was agreed that Jozef's method of engineering the fence was the more practical way to go, much to the frustration of the older boy.

Now, Jozef could not help wondering where his older brother was. Had Lukasz been arrested in some faraway city and taken captive for being a son of Poland?

A Russian soldier approached, his long rifle aimed at Jozef's head. A member of the NKVD searched Jozef for any weapons he may have hidden on his person. Then they ordered Jozef to go into the farmhouse, followed by the NKVD men and several soldiers. More soldiers and members of the local militia surrounded the lorries and stood guard over the young Polish men who had already been arrested at surrounding farms. Jozef recognized a few of the captives. He had attended school with them, and a few were his closest friends.

The soldiers thumped loudly on the door of the house, and then they forced their way inside, dragging Jozef with them. His family were huddled together in the front room, the younger ones still clad in their pyjamas. Zofia clung to Mother with fear written all over her little face. Katerina stood next to Mother. Her hands were covered in the flour she had been using to make the morning bread. Tobias moved closer to Marek to restrain the younger boy, fearing he may run over to Jozef and cause the rifle to fire. Each family member was thoroughly searched for hidden weapons, and then they were ordered to line up along the wall and remain quiet. Jozef was forced to sit on the floor a good distance away from the other family members with his hands behind his back. A soldier's rifle remained squarely aimed at the side of Jozef's head. No sudden moves would be tolerated.

Some of the soldiers began searching the Nowakowskis' house for hidden weapons, for people in hiding, for any anti-Soviet literature, foreign currency or large amounts of valuables. An NKVD member took inventory of everything on the property, making notes, listing the items and filling out a report in the small notebook he carried with him. The names of Jozef's family members were checked against the list that had been drawn up for their location. Members of the NKVD unit became extremely agitated when they discovered that Lukasz could not be found anywhere on the property. Several soldiers were dispatched to search the grounds and outbuildings. The house was torn asunder as they rooted through all the nooks and crannies that Jozef's brother could possibly have hidden in. The animals in the barn had become very unsettled, and Jozef worried that the soldiers might shoot them if they got in the way of the Soviets' search. Several times Emilia, Jozef, Katerina and Tobias were asked where Lukasz was hiding. Each time, the NKVD men became more aggressive and adamant in their desire to discover his whereabouts. Jozef was interrogated mercilessly.

Lukasz had been traveling from town to town on the boxing circuit, helping the family by sending home some of his winnings, before the Soviets came and occupied Poland. The family tried to make the Soviets understand that they had not heard from him in several months. Eventually, one of the officials from the operative group overseeing the interrogation stepped forward and mentioned that he had heard about Lukasz's boxing wins in nearby Minsk. A couple of men from the local militia were able to confirm that, and finally the NKVD let up in their quest to find Lukasz at the farm.

The identities of all family members present were verified. With the exception of Jozef and Lukasz, the Nowakowski family were not considered to be persons of interest, and they were no longer detained.

The Russian soldiers surrounded Jozef. His hands were yanked behind his back and bound as one of the Soviets read out an official order to lay grounds for his arrest. The officer concluded by stating that Jozef was sentenced to five years in the interior of the Soviet Union, Siberia, for being an untrustworthy citizen in the eyes of the Soviet government.

Emilia gasped in horror at the official decree. Tears began to well up in her and Katerina's eyes. Little Zofia pushed her face further into Mother's apron as though she could make this terrible moment disappear if she did not watch them take Jozef away. The family knew this was really a death sentence. In the past, several generations of Polish people had been enslaved by Russia. Those unfortunate souls were deported to the barren wastelands of Siberia, bordering the Arctic Circle, a place known among the Poles as 'the inhuman land'. The fate of those deported had always been the same. Slave labour was forced on them amidst the cruellest conditions in which to survive, with only the barest of necessities for supporting life. Most died from the hard work, cold, hunger, disease and heartbreak. People banished to Siberia were never heard from again.

Jozef was pushed outside into the barnyard where the lorries were parked. With little regard for her own wellbeing, Emilia ran out and grabbed onto her son. Tears streamed down her rosy cheeks. She hugged Jozef so hard that he nearly fell over on the icy, uneven ground. Katerina, Tobias, Zofia and Marek were not far behind. They surrounded Jozef with a heartfelt embrace. The soldiers quickly pushed aside Jozef's mother and sisters. The NKVD men teasingly prodded at young Tobias with their long bayonets and grabbed little Marek's curly locks to pull him back when he refused to let go of his older brother.

The brave, little lad yelled at the Russian soldiers, "You can't take Jozef away! He has done nothing. Leave us alone!"

Emilia scrambled to get up from the ground where the soldiers had pushed her. She reached out to pull her youngest son away from the menacing assailants. One of the soldiers still held fast to the tight curls on Marek's head. The little boy screamed in pain as the soldier pulled him back by his hair, away from the outstretched arms of his mother. Another soldier made a joke in Russian about the little resistor, and all the NKVD men and soldiers laughed loudly. Marek, enraged, lashed out with a sudden, swift kick that connected squarely with the boot of the soldier holding onto his hair. The soldier looked down at the scuffmark little Marek had left on the calf of his tall boot. Suddenly, the laughing ceased.

Then the soldier lifted Marek up by his hair and, using both of his hands, threw him a good distance across the farmyard. The little boy landed on the frozen ground near the barn with an audible thud. Emilia let out a scream and ran over to where he lay, stunned and demoralised. Again, the soldiers erupted into fits of laughter, and they joked among themselves as they re-enacted all that had just transpired. Tobias eyed the assailants with a threatening stare, and he would have lashed out in his own way if Jozef had not given him a stern look, warning him to stand still.

The Russian soldiers surrounded Jozef once again. Tobias put on a brave face and told his older brother not to worry. He said that he and Marek would do a fine job operating the farm, wanting Jozef to believe the farm would still be there running smoothly whenever he returned home to them, even though in his heart he knew no one believed a word of what he was saying.

Zofia could not say anything. She just cried and clung to Mother in utter despair.

Marek shouted above the din of the rumbling lorries, "You must run, Jozef! Run into the woodlands and hide so the Russians cannot find you!"

Jozef remained stoic and tried to sound confident telling his smallest brother, "It will be alright, Marek. The Russians may mock us and imprison me, but I will return to this land and farm again another day."

Despite the stabbing pain inflicted on him by the rough treatment of the soldiers, Jozef found himself more concerned about the way some of the soldiers were ogling Katerina. One of them boldly walked up to her and ran his fingers across her neck and down her shoulder, which was scantly covered by the thin shawl she had thrown on as she ran outside. Jozef felt anger rising inside, but dared not act on it for fear of what the soldiers might do to his family if he vented that resentment. If the soldiers thought throwing a ten-year-old boy against the barn was amusing, they would probably have no qualms about assaulting his sister right there in the cold barnyard in front of him.

A sudden disturbance from inside one of the open lorries interfered with Jozef's troubled thoughts. It was Katerina's fiancé, Jakob, who stood up and protested the manhandling of Jozef's sister. He and Katerina had been romantically involved for over a year now. Jakob worked on his own family's farm close by, and had also been working diligently at a shop in the village to save up enough money so he and Katerina could be married the following summer. He was a kind young man well suited to Katerina. Jakob's family and the Nowakowski's were happy about the forthcoming marriage, and it was obvious to everyone in the village that the two young people were very much in love. Jakob doted on his beautiful bride-to-be. Katerina was indeed a lovely young lady. She possessed an air of elegance and graceful refinement that matched her radiant beauty. Her fine features and long, silky hair set her apart from many of the other young ladies in the surrounding countryside. Everybody remarked on how beautiful she was.

The Russian soldiers struck poor Jakob across the head with the butts of their rifles. They knocked him down and, not caring to avoid injuring the other men huddled next to him, viciously kicked him with their heavy boots until he lay bleeding and unconscious in a crumpled heap on the muddy floor of the lorry.

The prisoners had been forced to sit on the floor of the lorry in rows. The first row was ordered to put their backs up against the wall of the driver's cab with their knees up and their legs open. The next row sat between the legs of the first, their backs pressing against the chests of the men behind them. Each consecutive row of prisoners was seated in this same manner, fitting thirty to thirty-five men in each lorry. Two armed soldiers stood in the space between the last row of prisoners and the closed tailgate facing them. It was amazing that Jakob had managed to rise from among the tightly packed mass of humanity to voice his objection when he observed the Russian soldier manhandling his precious fiancée in the Nowakowski farmyard that morning. Jakob and several disgruntled young prisoners around him now bled openly into the cold, winter air.

It was all too much for Katerina to bear. She fell into the snow shaking and sobbing, screaming Jakob's name and reaching her arms out to him as though he would come to her with a loving embrace. The Russian soldier who had been fondling her instantly felt disdain. He backed away and left her there wallowing in heartbreak and despair. Another Russian soldier called her a cheap Polish whore, while kicking snow in her face. More jeers and insults were hurled her way. Some of the soldiers even spat at her and cursed in Russian before they finally climbed back into the parked lorries by the barn.

As they pulled away from the Nowakowskis' farm, Jozef knew this might be the last time he would ever see his family, his home and their land. People were already speculating that those who were sent far away were never meant to return. He knew many thousands would disappear into the fabric of war-torn tragedy, never to be heard from again.

Katerina lay prostrate in the snow, beating at the frozen ground until her fists were red and bleeding. Jozef's mother sobbed uncontrollably as she tried to console her terrified children. The younger ones clung to her cloak, shaking. Tears streamed down their little faces. Zofia reached out and wrapped her arms around Katerina as though she could infuse enough love into her older sister to stop the pain piercing through Katerina's heart. Unabashed by his tear-stained face, Tobias managed to turn and offer Jozef a brave salute as the last of the lorries crept away, and despite his fear, little Marek courageously shouted out one last thing for Jozef to hear.

"You must escape, Jozef! Escape, and return to us to sow seeds when the next planting season begins!"

The Russian soldiers did not understand what the little boy had called out in Polish, but they sneered and pointed their rifles at the farm to show their dominance one final time. They pretended to shoot at Jozef's family until the farmstead had faded far into the distance. Jozef would be haunted by those final sounds and the suffering images of his family until the end of his days.

***

He closed his eyes and tried to erase the bitter scene that had just transpired, reflecting on the happy years he had spent growing up on the farm. Visions of the small, clapboard farmhouse in which he had been born, with its decoratively carved framework around the windows, the huge barn overshadowing the house and the stone structure known as the cold shed on the opposite side of the barnyard, would be forever etched in Jozef's memory. So too, would the images and smells of green fields alive with hearty crops blowing gently in the summer breeze, and the bustling activities of his family members all around him as they went about their daily chores. His thoughts gradually drifted beyond the boundaries of the farmstead to the surrounding landscape, which transformed into a richly forested area and beyond that, the Neman River. This was where Jozef had grown up, and this domain breathed life into all the happiness he had known throughout his brief nineteen years.

When he was born, in 1920, the village was known as Kuczkuny. It existed as it had done for generations by the banks of the Neman River. Although the region had previously been embraced as a part of the vast Russian Empire for over one hundred years, it had been taken back as a partition of Poland following the Russo-Polish War just prior to Jozef's birth. It was a small hamlet located southwest of Minsk, comprised of farmsteads. The farmers would bring their goods to the market square at Stolpce by horse and wagon on market days for sale and trade, and life continued as it had done for centuries in this quiet, rural area.

Jozef's family was self-sufficient, depending on themselves to raise most of what they ate, make most of what they wore and to keep warm with the wood they gathered from their land. They prospered well, and they had operated an organised farm right up until the war began. In the barn, a small row of box stalls housed their livestock. An old workhorse named Matylda was used for pulling the wagon, the harrow and a sled in wintertime. Matylda and Borys the ox occupied neighbouring stalls for many years. Borys was used to pull the harrow as well, but his primary duty was to pull lumber from the forest and ice from the river in winter. There would always be a couple of cows residing in the barn stalls for milking, and one cow was taken for slaughter every autumn. Beyond the stalls was a henhouse at the end of the barn. Jozef could not remember a time when there was ever a shortage of eggs or roasting chickens during his years growing up. A large hay-bay was positioned on the opposite side of the animal stalls, and a pen in the far corner of the barn housed the hogs during wintry weather. The large barn doors opened out into the barnyard, allowing the loaded hay wagon to come in to fill the hay-bay. In the large barn were many tools and farm implements, including the harrow, the winter sled, and the farm wagon.

From a young age, the children had been taught the many jobs required for running a farm, and they were put to work performing the more menial tasks in helping with the chores. By the time they had begun school, all of them were rising early to feed and water the livestock, milk the cows, collect the eggs from the henhouse and clean the hay mangers and the stalls before they set off on the long hike to school in the village square at Stolpce. The schoolhouse was a far enough distance from the family farm to afford the boys an opportunity to run and tumble, and play fight along the way. During the warmer months, the children stopped to skip stones across the surface of the river. In winter, they had snowball fights and frolicked in the snow as they skied across the hilly countryside into the village. Katerina tried in vain to keep her brothers neat and tidy and to have them arrive at school on time. The children were expected to hurry home from school after their lessons were done, in order to do their evening chores at the farm.

As the lorries bumped across the frozen landscape and on toward another farmstead, Marek's final words kept reverberating inside Jozef's head.

"Return to us to sow seeds when the next planting season begins!"

That would be next spring, when the frost had left the ground. Jozef could not help feeling amused as he remembered how much Marek had enjoyed working with him and Tobias during planting season earlier that year. Jozef had thought then that young Marek would follow in his family's footsteps to become a fine farmer one day. While Marek's little friends played in the woodlands or down by the river, Marek insisted on keeping up with his older brothers, and he worked from early morning until late into the evenings helping to prepare the soil and seed the crops. He helped Jozef hitch Matylda to the harrow and had the animal drag the iron teeth across the chunky soil time and time again to break up the clumps of earth until the soil was finely tilled and ready for planting. The seed crops had to be planted quickly before wild weeds took root in the soil. Jozef marked the field with a log that had a row of wooden pegs driven into it at even intervals. He had the horse draw the log behind her crosswise, causing the pegs to make small trenches in the soil. Then the field was marked lengthwise in this same manner so that the trenches turned into little squares. The planting could then begin. Jozef felt satisfied to have passed this technique down to his younger brother before he was taken away from their farm.

His father, Stanislaw, had made a game for the children of planting seeds. That was when Lukasz, Katerina and

Jozef were much younger. Father strapped small sacks filled with seeds to each of the children and had them walk along separate rows to establish which one of them could plant the most seeds in the least amount of time. At first, Lukasz was always the first to complete all his rows as he had the longest legs and the fastest gait. However, in a few years' time, Jozef took over as the leader in this competition with his nimble little hands and his hurried pace, never once missing a single square.

A wide variety of crops were grown on the farm, including potatoes, onions, garlic, carrots, beans, peas, cabbages, beets, turnips, radishes, tomatoes, horseradish root, cucumbers and a vast array of herbs. The seeds sown for the grain crops needed to be turned into the soil, so the horse was hitched to the harrow and the soil was tilled in the grain fields again. Then the boys began the constant battle to stave off the weeds that tried to take hold before the young seedlings had a chance to develop into plants large and strong enough to hold their own. This kept the boys occupied with continual weeding and hoeing for many weeks, but life was good back in those days.

Now, circumstances were quite different, and it would be left to two small boys to carry on. As much as Tobias had tried to reassure him, Jozef knew the tasks would overwhelm his younger brothers. He worried how his family would fare during this difficult time. Being self-sufficient was good so long as everything was going well, but if the farm failed to produce, their livelihood would be seriously compromised. Jozef was also aware that the Russian soldiers were hungry, and they would take whatever food they could find from the local farms, leaving the Polish farmers with nothing. NKVD troops would shoot livestock for food, and sometimes just for sport. Without the livestock to help farmers work their land, production on the farms would cease. Jozef knew it was going to be difficult for his family to survive. Tragically, there was nothing he could do to help them now.

A bitter wind gusted from the northwest, and in the back of the open lorry, Jozef realised how fortunate he was to have been wearing his winter coat, hat, gloves and boots when the NKVD came to make his arrest. Days before, he had heard stories of his friends in town being pulled from their beds in the middle of the night and forced out into the wintry elements clad in nothing more than their pyjamas and bare feet when the Russians came for them. Jozef had been prepared and slept in his winter clothes for the past two nights, certain the soldiers would come to apprehend him soon. There was no escape. The only feasible route to flee from Eastern Poland was through Romania, and those who had tried were arrested at the border. All the would-be escapees had been violently interrogated, deported or shot.

It was a miserable ride in the lorry on this grey, cold morning. He looked around the lorry and recognised a few sullen faces from the nearby farms. Nobody dared to speak a word. All these young men were afraid of the Russian soldiers. The NKVD troops had a reputation for being extremely cruel and violent. It didn't take much for them to lash out at those they viewed as agitators. Some of Jozef's companions already bore the brunt of the Soviet's brutality. He wondered how poor Jakob was faring. He knew he must find some way to help his future brother-in-law when they arrived at wherever the Russians were taking them.

***

Jozef's thoughts drifted back to a happier time several months earlier. It was when the long summer days had arrived with a warmer sun and the plants had begun to grow very quickly, keeping Jozef and his brothers busy with hoeing, watering and weeding. Mother sent Katerina out into the fields every couple of hours with a large bucket of cold water drawn from the well by the house to cool the boys down while they worked.

They stopped briefly to rest as they drank refreshing water from the ladle, and Katerina chattered away, telling them about all the women's work going on inside the house where she and Mother, and little Zofia were busy with domestic chores.

"We are preparing your favourite raspberry pie for you, Marek," she would say.

Then Marek would reply, "Well, you had best prepare a lot of it. I'm as hungry as a horse today!"

She would tease Tobias because he was always so serious, and he did not take the teasing very well. It would take him a little time to realise it was all just in fun.

"Mother says we won't make that old meat pie that you enjoy so much anymore, Tobi. She believes that because you're the only one who likes it, it's not worth the effort."

"Ahhh! That's not fair!" Tobias would blurt out, before realising that she was just joking.

"And Mother thinks that you look silly with your hair so long and scruffy," she would continue. "She thinks it's time we shaved it all off."

Not willing to get caught a second time, Tobias would blurt out, "Get out of here, Kat! We are busy with men's work! And it's not nice to tease me all the time!"

Jozef would chuckle over his siblings' sparring. He would ruffle young Tobias' hair or push him down, making the younger boy jump on top of him and a play fight ensue right between the neatly manicured rows of wheat and oats. Without hesitation, little Marek would join the fray as well.

With her water bucket emptied, Katerina would turn around and stomp back to the kitchen, shaking her head and saying, "You boys are impossible!"

That was how each warm, sunny day passed. However, there was one special day during that last summer in Kuczkuny that stood out in Jozef's memory. On that day, the sun had risen high in the sky. Jozef, Tobias and Marek had ceased working in order to tuck large, fresh green leaves into their hats so the tops of their heads and the backs of their necks would stay cool and not burn in the blazing sun. It was an old farmer's trick that Father had taught Jozef many years before. Jozef's eyes scanned the field of crops as he checked Marek's hat to ensure that the little boy had satisfactorily secured his leaves. He noticed Zofia struggling toward them with a heavy jug of drinking water that was now overdue.

Never were two sisters so unalike as Jozef's were. Where Katerina was tall, thin, fair and delicate, little Zofia was short, dumpy and dark in complexion, with an unruly tuft of curly, black hair on top of her head. Her chubby, dimpled cheeks made her appear much younger than her eight years, but she was a tough little girl. She was able to keep up with Tobias when it came to the daily chores, and Tobias was much taller and older.

"Where is your sister?" Jozef called out to her.

"I cannot tell you," Zofia yelled in response. "There is a surprise you will find out later."

"Has Kat gone into town *again*?" Marek demanded to know.

Attempting to sound equally rude, Zofia answered in an obnoxious voice, "*No!* And stop asking me questions! I am not supposed to tell!"

Jozef could only conclude that Katerina's absence implied something good was happening, because Zofia's little face glowed with a kind of hidden, joyful secret that she was bursting to tell.

It was later that day when the boys returned to the farmhouse for supper that the good news was divulged.

Mr and Mrs Jozwicki sat at the dining room table across from their son Jakob. The two younger Jozwicki children, Henryk and Rowena, were seated next to their parents and Zofia. Katerina was sitting beside Jakob, radiant as ever, and beaming with excitement in the ray of sunlight that streamed in through the window that evening. All of them were dressed in their Sunday church clothes, and Mother had laid out her best tablecloth and fine china. A mixed aroma of Mother's delicious cabbage rolls and pierogi stuffed with bacon, onions and mushrooms filled the air, and Jozef spied three freshly baked fruit pies set on the shelf by the kitchen window. He was so hungry he wanted to dive into the food straight away. However, Mother insisted that the three boys wash up and change before they dragged their work-weary bodies to the table.

During the evening meal, the good news of Kat and Jakob's engagement was announced. Jozef was given the distinct honour of making a toast to the young couple on behalf of the Nowakowski family. Mother had suggested that Father's special brandy be used for the toast. That bottle of brandy had not been touched since the last time Father shared a drink with his business partners, when they had departed on that fateful journey more than three years earlier. Jozef had difficulty stifling the wave of emotion that overcame him at Mother's suggestion, but he managed to reverently pour a small amount of the brandy into each glass. Realising the significance in that moment, he had managed to raise his glass and make an impressive toast for his sister and his future brother-in-law.

"Jozef, when will you and Lilyana be getting engaged?" Tobias teased between his mouthfuls of raspberry pie and cream.

Then Zofia chimed in, "Yes—let's make it two weddings for next summer!"

"There is nothing going on between Lily and I!" Jozef kept insisting.

However, it was obvious to everyone that Jozef and Lilyana had taken a liking to each other. Every time he went into Stolpce, Jozef made a beeline for the hardware store that Lilyana's father ran because he knew she would be there helping her father. Jozef always had some excuse for having to frequent Prawoslaw's Hardware Mercantile. Some longer nails might help to secure the boards at the back end of the barn, or perhaps a better length of rope might improve the hoisting mechanism to the hayloft. Lilyana always hurried over to help Jozef with his purchases. With her father peering on from behind the service counter, Jozef and Lilyana blushed awkwardly as Jozef dawdled over deciding what to buy, giving himself enough time to flirt a little with Lilyana and to see if she returned his sentiments.

Being the same age, they had attended school together in the village. They had known each other for most of their lives, but it was not until that final year in Kuczkuny that they had developed their mutual attraction. Whenever Jozef went to the counter to pay for his purchases, Lilyana's father questioned him about circumstances on the Nowakowski farm. Had Jozef managed to get all the planting done yet? How were the crops doing this year? Was all the harvest taken in and stored properly now? Was the barn secured for winter? On and on Mr Prawoslaw's questions went as the seasons passed. It did seem as though he was testing whether Jozef was a worthy suitor for his only daughter.

Lilyana had lived all her life in Stolpce. The Prawoslaws' stately house was situated along the main road, not far from the family's hardware store. It was a tall, red-brick structure with enormous windows in the front room overlooking the street. As a young child, Lilyana would sit cross-legged in the window seat and watch people milling about outside as they tended to their daily business. Mrs Prawoslaw was an immaculate housekeeper. All the windows were hung with fancy curtains made from exquisite lace tatted into intricate patterns by the nuns at a convent in Belgium, imported by special order. The shiny hardwood floors reflected images of the sturdy oak furnishings in every room. An elaborately adorned chandelier dripping in tear-shaped pieces of crystal hung above the enormous dining room table. The kitchen was massive, and there were always wonderful aromas coming from pots cooking on the stove. An impressive, stone-faced fireplace stood in the centre of the front room. Lilyana would sit by the hearth on cold winter evenings, warming her fingers and toes. Her life was comfortable and blessed.

***

An abrupt jolt caused all the prisoners to sway in a singular motion as the lorries came to a halt at another farm closer to the river. Jozef recognised it as the Borkowskis' place. His father, Stanislaw, and Mr Borkowski had been good friends, and both he and Lukasz had been acquainted with two of the Borkowski's older boys, Jon and Antoni, for many years. The Borkowskis had six sons, but only the two eldest were of the appropriate age for arrest on this day.

The NKVD men in the front lorry jumped out and banged very loudly on the farmhouse door. More troops poured out of the remaining lorries and surrounded the convoy with their rifles poised and aimed to shoot at any prisoner who might try to escape. None of the young lads were foolish enough to try.

Mr Borkowski had just begun to open the door when the soldiers forced their way into the house, and some time afterwards, Antoni and Jon emerged with their hands tightly secured behind their backs. The soldiers pushed and hurried them along to where the lorries were parked. Through a foggy veil of snow that danced around the Borkowskis' doorway, Jozef managed to see the outline of Mrs Borkowski, standing there in her nightclothes. Her four younger sons surrounded her as tears streamed down her face.

She cried out after her two eldest boys, "Be good! Take care of yourselves, and we will see you again soon!"

Jon and Antoni were pushed into the back of the lorry beside Jozef. He gave them a subtle nod of recognition as the lorries sped off in the direction of the village.

***

Rumbling along the snowy terrain next to the Neman River, Jozef thought about the many happy days he had spent with his family and friends along these banks during his boyhood years. His father allowed the children some time to play away from the farm on hot summer afternoons, despite the heavy workload. When they were younger, Lukasz, Katerina and Jozef ran through the cool depths of the forest playing hide-and-seek. The boys chased after the wild birds, butterflies and rabbits that dared to scurry across their path, while Kat stopped to poke at wild mushrooms, ferns, wildflowers and other plants that inhabited the woodlands near the farm. When they finally made it through to the other side of this stretch of forest, they would arrive at the lush, green banks of the Neman River. The boys hurried and stripped down to their underwear, then raced each other into the temptingly cool water. It felt so refreshing against the warmth of their farm-tanned skin, and they floated there for ages, enjoying the reprieve from all their chores. The natural beauty of their surroundings was intoxicating.

Sometimes a few boys from the village and neighbouring farms would arrive at the riverbank and join them in their water sports. Jon and Antoni were often there on those lazy summer afternoons. They splashed each other and tried to dunk one another deep into the water, only to resurface gasping for air and bent on retaliating at whichever boy it was who had done the dubious deed. The boys competed in races to see who could swim the fastest or the furthest, playing boisterously on the water. It was amazing that none of them were ever injured or drowned during those summertime frolics in the mighty Neman.

The children would arrive back at the farm later in the afternoon on those sunny days. They would often find their father in the shade of the barn, keeping things in order—sharpening tools, repairing implements or whistling as he carved useful gadgets from wood. He would teach the boys how to make magnificent fishing poles, using only the straightest of tree branches stripped down to a smooth finish. A length of fishing line would be attached at the top end of the pole, and a piece of cork from an old wine bottle threaded through and pushed a good distance down the line, then secured in place with a firm knot on both ends of the cork. A fishhook would be fastened to the bottom end of the fishing line, and a small weight of metal would be attached to the line to sink it in the water. The fishing poles were then complete.

The boys and their father loved to go fishing. The young lads would dig up a few earthworms and catch a few frogs and minnows down by the river to use for bait. Father and sons quietly lined themselves up under the trees along the banks of the Neman and dropped their baited hooks into the river. They were familiar with a spot where some old trees had fallen into the water, providing a haven for the larger fish to hide beneath. Jozef loved seeing how the fish poked their heads out from their secret lair deep in the pristine water. Then cautiously, the fish would approach his baited hook, and before long his cork was bobbing on the surface of the water as the fish nibbled at the bait.

Jozef, Lukasz and Father caught many fish. They would return through the forest to the family farm with a string-full of fresh catch. Immediately, they took the fish behind the house where the fish heads were cut off, the scales scraped away and the fish guts removed. The dressed fish were taken into the house, where mother rinsed them in clean water, and dredged them in a mixture of flour, salt and pepper. Then she fried them in butter for supper. There was nothing better than a meal of crispy, fresh-fried fish on a hot, summer evening.

***

Several times the lorries became caught up in the deep drifts of snow that had accumulated along the roadway. The men from the local militia had to jump out and dig the vehicles free. Progress was slow, but the convoy pressed onward.

They were passing the outer fringes of the forest when the sun began to rise. Jozef and his siblings had loved going berry picking in those woodlands during the long summer months. Wild berries grew in abundance in the forest and along the banks of the river. Jozef had learned very quickly that the best berries grew under smaller, leafy bushes between the taller trees. The children spent hours picking the red raspberries and purple loganberries that burst into ripeness in the forest, and the wild strawberries that grew close to the ground along the banks of the river. They filled their mouths and small buckets until they were overflowing with berries. Large buckets were not used because they became too heavy to carry once they were filled, and the weight of the berries on top crushed the ripe berries underneath.

The children ran back and forth between the woodlands and the farmhouse, delivering pails full of fruit to their mother. Emilia sat at the kitchen table sifting through the berries, removing any bits of stems, leaves or small twigs the children had overlooked, and tossing the clean berries into the large stewing pot.

After all the strawberries and raspberries had been picked, blueberries would be ripening around the rocky exterior that lined the riverbank on the perimeter of the forest, and the quest to pick the best of the blueberries began. Each child hurried to fill their pail the quickest, but the blueberries were a little bit smaller and it took longer to pick a full pail.

There would always be many delicious pies baked at berry-picking time. The girls would help their mother make enough jars of jellies, jams and berry preserves to last for an entire year. Jozef would scarf down huge pieces of pie drenched in fresh cream from the larder, and in winter his favourite treat was to slather his mother's home-baked bread with a thick layer of her butter, topped off with a thick layer of her berry preserves. His mouth watered at the memories of his mother's delicious treats.

While he was still young, Jozef had enjoyed helping his mother and Katerina with the culinary chores inside the house. One of his favourite things was to make butter in the wooden barrel churn. The barrel would be half-filled with the cream that had risen to the top of the cow's milk after it was left out to separate in his mother's large pans. The barrel churn stood on wooden legs, and there was a handle that spun the barrel over and over. When you turned the handle, the cream inside splashed around until the churning caused the fat from the cream to form bits of butter that floated in the remaining milk. Mother drained the buttermilk away and stored it in jugs for drinking, then she washed the bits of butter in a bowl. The butter was then salted and pressed into tubs. Jozef enjoyed spinning the barrel churn and making butter, but he never let his father or older brother know. It was considered women's work, and if they had known, he'd have been teased relentlessly.

A commotion erupted inside the lorry at the front of the line and returned Jozef to his dismal reality. One of the young prisoners must have done something to irritate the soldiers. There was much shouting, and the convoy slammed to a squealing halt. A young man was tossed like a sack of potatoes from the back of the front lorry. Several soldiers jumped down and pummelled the man with their heavy boots and rifle butts. A flood of blood quickly engulfed the prisoner, who lay still and silent in the snow. The soldiers continued to kick at the lifeless form. They spat at him and shouted obscenities in Russian so loudly that their words could be heard echoing across the frigid surface of the river. One was so angered that he lifted his rifle high into the air and brought it down heavily, goring the victim through the abdomen with his long bayonet. Without hesitation, the soldier jerked the blade free from the prisoner's belly. Then, raising the blood-stained weapon high for everyone to see, he proceeded to taunt the young Polish men, daring any of them to step down and take him on.

A stillness prevailed above the din of the idling lorries lined up along the frozen bank. Not a single soul dared to move or make a sound. All were numbed into silence. Then, just as quickly as it had happened, the Soviet soldiers hopped back up into the lorry without any remorse. The convoy resumed its course, leaving the dead victim frozen to the ground in his own blood and entrails.

As the lorry Jozef was riding in passed the spot where the unfortunate man lay, he and many of the other prisoners felt compelled to look down and see if they could recognise whom it was. The face of the young man was bloodied, and his jaw broken and distorted. Nevertheless, Jozef could distinguish it as that belonging to Dyzek Orlowski from one of the farms much further down the river. Dysek was the same age as Jozef's older brother, Lukasz. Quite often Dyzek and the lad's sisters met up with Jozef and his siblings on their way to school, making the long hike together. One of Dyzek's sisters was very friendly with Katerina. They knew Dyzek was a quiet, ordinary man. Jozef could not imagine him having done anything intentionally to aggravate the NKVD men or the soldiers. Much later, Jozef learned from another prisoner who had shared the lorry with Dyzek that Dyzek had dared to hum the Polish national anthem in front of their Russian captors. This so enraged the soldiers, they brutally murdered him for his patronage to Poland.

Jozef worried that Dyzek's parents or sisters might find his butchered body left there in the snow on this crude roadway. He hoped and prayed that the wolves or other wild animals would drag it away into the forest before they had the chance.

He found himself recalling the many times when Dyzek and Mr Orlowski had helped work on his family's farm. The Orlowskis made their business in the raising and the selling of livestock, and it was from their farm that the Nowakowskis purchased their cows and pigs each year. The Orlowski farm was located further down the river, where the forestlands dwindled and transformed into a vast meadow area that produced perfect pasturelands for grazing animals. The Orlowskis were known far and wide for their fat, healthy cows and prize-winning hogs. Dyzek and his sisters helped their father raise the animals and prepare them for sale and trade at the market square in Stolpce.

Just before winter arrived every year, it was butchering time on the farm. Mr Orlowski and Dyzek would go to several of the neighbouring farms to help the farmers at slaughter time. In return, the Orlowskis were given enough hay and other feed crops to see their own livestock through the winter months in their large barns, when their pasturelands were covered over by deep snow.

Jozef remembered Dyzek and Mr Orlowski coming to his family's farm at slaughter time every year since he was a little boy. Mr Orlowski was a jolly man who joked with all the farmers and the boys as the butchering was carried out.

Jozef's parents got up before sunrise on butchering day in order to prepare for the long day of work that lay ahead. His father built a large bonfire in the farmyard, and Mother set her huge metal tub on top of the framework of stones that Stanislaw made. Emilia filled the tub with water and brought it to a boil.

The fattest cow and two of the family's largest pigs were butchered every autumn. The men began by slaughtering the cow. The carcass was then dipped into the boiling tub, hoisted out, and laid on some boards. Jozef and his brothers watched as all the hair on the outer skin was scraped away and the animal was hung up by its hind legs in a nearby tree. The men cut the animal's belly open, took all the internal organs out, and dropped them into mother's large basin. The boys brought the basin into the kitchen, where their mother and sisters washed the animal's edible organs, such as the heart, kidneys and liver, and cut off the fat from the internal organs for later use. The cow's hide came off in one piece. It was to be cured later and put to good use. After the men butchered the meat, some of it was put away while the rest was prepared in a variety of ways. The pigs were butchered the same way, and the gruelling task was made easier when Mr Orlowski and Dyzek were there to help. They were swift and effective in their method, and all the local farmers said the Orlowskis were exceptionally clean in their butchering techniques.

Large pieces of pork fat were packed in salt and put into barrels for storage in the cellar by the house. Emilia boiled a mixture of brine made from water, salt, pepper and brown sugar, which was used to pickle the pork shoulders and the hams. They were stored in the brine inside barrels and put into the cellar.

The family's stone-built cold shed was located on the north side of the farm. At slaughter time, it was filled with all the meat, including the roasts, spareribs, steaks, chops, hearts, livers, kidneys, tongues and sausage meat. The meat froze in the cold shed, and remained frozen all year long. Emilia boiled the smaller pieces of pork fat in big pots and strained the hot liquid through pieces of cloth into heavy ceramic jars. This hardened into lard once it was cooled. She boiled the pigs' heads until the meat fell away from the bones, then she chopped it up, seasoned it and mixed it with the broth in the boiling pot. The mixture was then poured into pans to cool. It formed like jelly because of the gelatin that came from the animals' bones, resulting in delicious headcheese. The pans were covered and stored in the cellar.

Big pieces of meat were put into the meat grinder. When he was a small lad, Jozef had loved to turn the grinder handle until a stream of ground meat came out through the holes in the front. Emilia salted and seasoned the ground meat with her selection of special spices and herbs and stuffed it into sausage casings taken from the cow's intestines. The casings would be turned inside out, methodically cleaned, scrubbed with soap and water and thoroughly rinsed before being packed with the prepared sausage meat. A twist of the casings every four or five inches along the length separated the sausages, and the prepared sausage links were then taken to the cold shed where they froze until they were needed.

Emilia scrubbed her big pots after the lard was made, and then she filled them with the pieces of cow fat. This turned into tallow after it was boiled and cooled. It was used to make smooth, waxy candles. She and Katerina strung the tin tubes on the candle moulds with candlewick as the cow fat was boiling in the pots. The candle tubes were set close together in rows. They opened at the top and tapered to a point at the bottom end of the mould. Each pointed end had a small hole to thread the candlewick through. The wicks were tied to a stick that lay across the top end of the tubes, and they had to be pulled tight and held in place with pieces of potato on the tapered bottom end of each candle tube. The hot tallow was poured into the tubes at the top end of the moulds, and then they were put outside to cool. When the tallow was set, the moulds were brought back into the house, the pieces of potato were pulled off, and Emilia quickly dipped the set of moulds into boiling water. This released the tallow from the sides of the tubes so the candles could be pulled out when she pulled the stick up. Emilia and Katerina cut the candles off the stick and trimmed the wicking at the larger end of each candle. A small piece of wick was left on the pointed end so the candle could be lit. Jozef sometimes helped his mother and Kat in this process as the lovely candles began to take form.

The slaughter of animals was a fact of life on the farm, and it did not bother Jozef in the least. However, it was an entirely different thing viewing Dyzek as he lay there in the snow like a butchered animal, encased by his own blood with his intestines spilling out. Jozef was suddenly overcome by a wave of nausea. Many of the other young men in the lorry seemed to be experiencing the same feeling. It was the first time they had witnessed a man being brutalised like that. Unfortunately, it would not be the last they saw of man's inhumanity to man. From the onset, they inherently knew that Soviet arrests of innocent people were the start of a painful road of adversity.

Jozef closed his eyes and breathed in the cold morning air. He tried to blot out the image of Dyzek's bloodied body, but memories of times shared with the lad kept flooding in. He found himself revisiting many occasions when Dyzek had come and spent time with Lukasz on the Nowakowski farm.

One memory stood out very clearly. It had happened at the end of summer when Jozef was about seven years old. Father was demonstrating how to sharpen a scythe on the grindstone in the barn in preparation for cutting hay. He allowed Lukasz and Dyzek to take turns spinning the stone and pouring water on it while he held the steel edges of the scythe against it. The water prevented the scythe from getting too hot while the stone ground the sides of the blade to a very sharp edge. Jozef wanted to have a turn spinning the stone and pouring the water. Lukasz told Jozef he was too young and he best go away, but Dyzek was quick to offer Jozef his own turn after he noticed how desperately Jozef wanted to try.

Father had then taken the boys out into the field and shown them how to cut the hay by swinging the scythe back and forth in the tall grass. Lukasz and Dyzek were instructed to follow behind Stanislaw with pitchforks and spread out the hay that had fallen, allowing it to dry evenly in the sun. Lukasz told Jozef to go into the house and help their mother and Kat with the women's work. Jozef protested and insisted that he wanted to help with the haying. Father finally said Jozef could stay and help the older boys, but there were only two pitchforks available. Seeing the disappointment in young Jozef's eyes, Dyzek took pity on him and shared his pitchfork. They took turns spreading hay throughout that entire day.

On the second day, Dyzek returned with a pitchfork from his own farm. The work progressed quickly as Jozef, Dyzek and Lukasz each had their own tool to work with. Jozef recalled that Dyzek had shown him how to rake up the laid-out grass into piles the next morning, so it could dry some more. He remembered the smell of fresh-cut hay rising from the sun-warmed earth. Later, when the hay was completely dry, Father and the boys tossed it up into the wagon until the wagon was full. Matylda pulled it into the barn, and then Father and the boys pitched the hay into the hay-bay. Father had to hoist Jozef up on top of the wagonload of hay so Jozef had enough height to reach up with his pitchfork and toss the hay into the bay like the older boys were able to do. This entire process was repeated over again until all the hay had been brought in, to feed and keep the livestock warm through the winter months. This was Jozef's first experience at haying, and it was because of Dyzek that he had been able to help.

Dyzek had also helped the Nowakowskis for several years when it was time to harvest the grain crops. The oat stems had to be cut and tied into bundles or sheaves the same day so the oats would not rot. If they were left to lie in the field overnight, they would spoil in the dew. The sheaves were stood on their stem ends close to each other in rows, with the heads of the grain facing up. The whole Nowakowski family was out in the field at harvest time bundling the oats into sheaves. The older children assisted the younger ones as they struggled with the tall stems. The wheat crop had to be cut and tied the same way, but because the wheat was heavier and harder to handle, only the older children assisted in harvesting it. Dyzek had provided an extra pair of hands during those busy times, and his assistance earned him a generous share of the harvest to bring home to his own family in the form of flour milled from the grains.

Jozef thoroughly enjoyed helping his father and Lukasz thresh the grain crops on a clean area set aside at the centre of the barn. Father taught him how to evenly spread the grain crops out a few inches deep onto the threshing floor. The wheat crop was threshed first, using a flail that was swung high above their heads and brought down heavily on the wheat. This caused the grains to fall away from their shells on the husks and filter down through the straw. A pitchfork was used to lift the straw, shake it and toss it aside. The wheat grains dropped to the threshing floor, and more and more sheaves of wheat were spread over the top and flailed the same way. When the shelled grain piled up on the floor, it was swept aside with a wooden scraper, then shovelled into the hopper on a fanning mill. The handle on the fanning mill was turned, and the fans spinning inside separated the skins from the clean kernels of wheat. The wheat poured out the side into a heap on the floor and was shovelled into grain sacks.

Once all the wheat and oats had been threshed, there was a full wagonload of grain sacks to be transported to the mill in Stolpce, where the grain was turned into flour. There was plenty of straw left over in the barn from the threshing for the livestock to enjoy through the winter months. Emilia always had plenty of flour to use for her breads, cakes, pies, biscuits and other delectable treats. Dyzek's mother was most appreciative of the sacks of flour the Nowakowskis sent her in return for Dyzek's help.

Jozef could not stop thinking about how tragic Dyzek's brutal demise was. He had been such a good friend to Jozef's family throughout the years. The Orlowskis had lost a wonderful son. What a horrible waste of a young man's life!

***

In the summer of 1939, every day had brought news over the radio and in the newspapers about Germany's latest demands. Hitler was threatening to move into Poland, and he expected to take over the Polish state with little opposition, as he had done earlier in other parts of Eastern Europe. Polish politicians were expecting help from France and Britain if Germany demonstrated any aggression, due to the Polish/ French/British coalition. The Polish people were optimistic and believed there was not any way the Germans would take control of their land. Some thought war might be inevitable, but they were not too worried about that prospect. The ruling class felt Poland was a stable state, and they believed Poland's army was mighty enough to defend the country from any attack triggered by Hitler.

In Poland, it was generally accepted that each generation would go to war twice. While people in Eastern Poland remained vigilant to the sporadic reports coming over the radio from other parts of the country where the Nazis had pounced, they had no idea their Russian neighbours were ready to attack and occupy their land in the east.

Amid this political crisis, vegetables had to be gathered and stored for winter on the farm. Autumn always transpired into a flurry of activity. Usually the work was carried out with much joy and enthusiasm as another successful harvest came to fruition. However, following the aggressive advance of Hitler and the Soviets into Poland, autumn was clouded as life became very uncertain for Jozef and his family. There was much debate as to what the future held for people throughout Eastern Europe. Mother and Kat had refrained from their rounds of singing while they braided the onion and garlic tops into bunches to be hung from the overhead beams in the kitchen. The customary zeal that usually accompanied the cutting and bundling of herbs for drying had disappeared that year. Yet, despite the uncertainty, they went through all the motions for gathering and storing the year's bountiful harvest.

Under normal circumstances, the family would have been looking forward to enjoying these things all winter long as Emilia seasoned her delicious recipes with her dried herbs and spices. Some of the herbs would also be used for medicinal purposes, along with specific weeds and other things collected from the woodlands. The knowledge of natural remedies and therapies was something that had been passed down from one generation to the next and was still widely practised. Most people knew what type of root, weed or bark was needed or what concoction to prepare for clearing runny noses or chests, suppressing a bad cough, stifling aches and pains, eliminating rashes and bringing down a fever. Nothing gathered from the fields or forest was wasted.

Although the usual rounds of gathering, preparing and storing for winter had been completed, an oppressive feeling of worry and anxiety sucked the joy out of the harvesting season that year.

Shortly after the Russians arrived in Poland, Kat took the three younger children into the forest to scour for the usual assortment of wild mushrooms that grew in abundance there. They picked the large, puffy-white umbrellas that popped up in bunches, dotting the forest floor. The children were trained to distinguish the edible mushrooms from the poisonous varieties by recognising features on the underside of the umbrella tops. They filled their pails to the brim, picking enough mushrooms to last into the following summer. Mother spread the wild mushrooms out on a cooking sheet inside her large oven and dried them before putting them into sacks to be stored on shelves in the kitchen larder. The larger mushrooms were sliced before being dried inside the oven. Those ones were to be used in Mother's soups and stews.

As Jozef's siblings returned from their foraging in the forest that autumn day, Kat was seen dragging little Marek by his ear all the way along the pathway toward the house, and scolding him. Marek was sputtering and complaining about the harsh treatment Kat was inflicting on him. Jozef was in the barnyard mending some boards on the fence. He chuckled at the sight of his sister so flustered and dragging their smallest brother home that way. Marek had always been known for his playful mischief, and Jozef wondered what the little imp had done this time to irritate his sister. He tried to stifle his amusement, but a hearty laugh erupted from his chest and echoed across the yard.

"Oh, so you think this is funny, do you, Jozef?" Kat snapped, and pushed Marek in front of her. "Tell your brother what you have done then, Marek!" she demanded.

"Ahh!" The younger lad sighed. "I just wanted to gather some poison mushrooms to feed to the Russian soldiers if they come! What is so wrong with that?"

"Good thing I caught him before he finished filling his pail with poison!" Kat stammered loudly.

There was a moment of quiet, and then Jozef burst into a fit of hysterical laughter once more.

"Leave it to Marek to try and sort out the problems of the world!" he managed to say. "Hey, Marek, does Mother have a good recipe for poison mushroom stew?"

Jozef's laughter became infectious at that point, and it wasn't long before all the children were giggling and snickering at the thought of young Marek standing up on a stool hunched over Mother's large oven as he boiled up a poisonous concoction for the Russians to indulge in.

A couple of weeks later, carrots, beets, turnips and potatoes were being dug up from the fields and buried inside large bins filled with earth for storage inside the cellar. The family was still musing over Marek's devious plan when the cabbages were collected. The thick, outer leaves protected them from winter's chill inside the cellar. The younger children gave the cabbages Russian names as they lined them up on shelves, and Marek and Tobias pretended to shoot at the large, green heads, imagining they were Red Army soldiers assembled in rows. The boys wanted nothing more than to destroy the Russian troops before they had a chance to move in and take over their family farm.

Mother and Kat would shred some of the cabbages and pack them into large crockpots with salt and spices. The shredded cabbage was then left to rot in its own juices while being pressed down under planks of wood with heavy rocks placed on top. The rotting cabbage was turned over with a large wooden spoon inside the crockpots every week or so while continuing to be pressed. After several weeks, the shredded cabbage would turn into sauerkraut. In Marek's mind, the cabbage was every Russian soul who would dare invade his family's farmland, dead and rotting.

Emilia and the girls were busy preparing many pickles and preserves. Despite life's uncertainty now, wonderful aromas continued to waft from the kitchen as endless jars of pickled beets, pickled red cabbage, scrumptious relishes, spicy tomato juice, pickled carrots, beans and an assortment of other delicacies were produced. The packed jars would be stored on shelves next to the sweet jams and jellies in the kitchen larder. Horseradish root took three years to come to fruition, but there was always some root in the garden mature enough to be shaved down and preserved in jars as a side dish. Sometimes Emilia would mix in mashed beets as a variation.

Her prize-winning recipe for dill pickles was famous for miles around. She began by preparing the cucumbers in her signature brine made from water, vinegar, salt, garlic, dill weed and a secret combination of select pickling spices. The pickles were then packed tightly in the brine inside large wooden barrels that were sealed and left to cure in the dark recesses of the cold cellar. Emilia's dill pickles were always crisp and delicious.

When the harvest was in, the kitchen rafters, the larder, the cellar and the cold shed were well stocked with food to last through the long, cold winter months.

Jozef ploughed the empty fields and covered them over with the manure that had been collected from the animal stalls and piled behind the barn. The boys helped Jozef replace some boards that had rotted in the barn, and they hammered down the ones that had come loose. They kept themselves busy tightening the wooden windows in the barn in preparation for winter's onslaught. They put mounds of straw against the barn walls and set large stones on it to hold it in place. This prevented the winter winds and snow from entering the barn so it would remain warm and dry. They put heavy storm windows on the farmhouse. The timber that was dragged from the forest was chopped into manageable pieces to burn in the fireplace and was stacked into tidy piles between the farmhouse and the cold shed.

In the back of his mind, Jozef had known his family's toil that autumn would be pointless. As much as he hated to admit it, he had realised the Russian soldiers would eventually come to claim the Nowakowskis' land and all that came with it. The Soviets had been focusing on businesses and people in the larger towns, but it was only a matter of time before they would come to confiscate everything from the countryside as well.

***

The lorries were moving more quickly now as the snowy trail running through the forest and along the riverside merged with a more heavily trodden path entering Stolpce. A huge wooden bridge crossed over the Neman, and beyond the bridge, the streets of the small town lay. The bridge rose high above the river, and from the top you could see for miles across the countryside. Jozef looked back towards home. One final time he gazed upon the marvellous, panoramic view that encompassed a splendid landscape dotted with rolling hills, forestlands, ponds and distant farms. With the snow falling that morning, the countryside looked like a winter wonderland. From this vantage point atop the bridge, the sky was magnificent and large. It stretched without bounds into infinity.

Jozef was swept up by a strong sense of attachment to his homeland. He vowed to never let go of his patriotism to Poland. Despite the abject circumstances, he was determined to survive, and to return to this land and his family one day.

Snow was falling fast and furious by the time the convoy reached the town. They crawled past the massive Greek Orthodox church that Jozef's family had attended before the Russian soldiers arrived. He was horrified to see that some of the lovely stained-glass window panels had been smashed in. Hatchet marks appeared across the wooden doors on the front of the church, where the Red Army had taken axes and butchered their way into the sanctuary without any regard for the holiness of the place. The large wooden cross that normally stood outside the church had been burned to the ground and lay in ashes.

Some of the town's shops and businesses had been vandalised and were strewn in ruins. Others had vanished altogether. Heaps of ashes and debris marked the spots where they once stood. Some of the town's larger buildings appeared to have been taken over by the Russians to be used as a headquarters and munitions stores. They were heavily guarded by soldiers.

NKVD men and soldiers were seen freely coming and going throughout the town, and the smell of burning wood permeated the air. Jozef came to realise that some of the soldiers were tearing apart people's homes and businesses in order to keep warm by burning wood taken from furniture and whatever else they got their hands on.

Evidence of anything Polish had been wiped away. Road and business signs had been torn down and replaced by hastily erected boards covered in Russian propaganda, painted with words and slogans. Jozef had studied the Russian language in high school and understood it well enough to see how much the Soviets were glorifying their homeland while making a mockery of Poland through their campaign to eliminate everything Polish.

An eerie feeling prevailed throughout Stolpce now. Other than the Soviet soldiers milling about the town, the streets remained strangely quiet and deserted. How peculiar it seemed, on a day that normally was a market day. Before the occupation, Stolpce would have been bustling with farmers bringing in wagonloads of goods, and villagers and townspeople would have been coming in and out of the shops and businesses along the streets. The usual din of chatter and horses clopping along the roadways had vanished. All the familiar sights and sounds were replaced by the deep droning of the lorries echoing along the abandoned streets toward the train station at the edge of town. The broad, muddy roads usually froze in winter and became lined with ruts left by horses' hooves and farmers' wagons leading to the cobblestoned market square. Now they were matted down by large tracks left by lorries and army tanks.

Jozef's heart sank as the convoy swept past Prawoslaw's Hardware and Mercantile. The two storefront windows had been smashed in. As the lorries pushed on through the snow, Jozef could see that the store had been ransacked. Empty shelves had been overturned, and it appeared that nothing remained in the store except for the emptied cash register that stood open on the counter by the front door. Even the wood stove that normally sat in the middle of the shop had been ripped from its foundations and carried off. Further down the road, Jozef strained his neck to see if he could catch a glimpse of the Prawoslaws' tall, red-brick house. It appeared that the beautiful home had met with the same fate as the family business. Signs of vandalism and plundering were evident.

Jozef had gone to Prawoslaw's Mercantile at the end of August hoping to find Lilyana there. He was enamoured with her following a lovely afternoon they'd shared by the river, and he was anxious to ask her out again. From behind the service counter, Mr Prawoslaw had noticed Jozef looking around the store in search of his daughter. He informed Jozef that Lilyana was visiting with relatives out in the countryside. Jozef thought it odd that Lilyana had not mentioned this to him—they had spoken about getting together again soon. Her father said he did not know when Lilyana was to return. Jozef found Mr Prawoslaw's details rather evasive, and he was curious why the man seemed intent on steering the conversation in another direction, talking about things on the farm. Soon after that day, the Germans and the Russians had invaded Poland, and everything changed.

He had prayed his dear friend Lilyana was safe from the evil outreach of the Russians, but now he realised his worst nightmare had come true. Jozef had heard the rumours about the town's leaders and businessmen being thrown out onto the streets and shot in the middle of the night. Whispering waves had drifted from the town across the Neman and out into the countryside.

Immediately, when the Red Army had entered Stolpce, lists of the most prominent men in business, politics, trade unions and professional, cultural and social organisations had been drawn up. Arrests of those men had been carried out during the first few days of the Soviet occupation. Many of the arrested men had been sentenced to forced labour in concentration camps, while others had been dragged from their homes into the streets and publicly executed.

Seeing the state of things in the town with his own eyes, Jozef believed all the rumours he'd heard were true. He feared Lilyana's father had been shot. Had Lilyana prevailed against these horrific conditions, and if so, where was dear Lily now? Jozef trembled as a confusing mix of emotions ran through him. He closed his eyes and prayed more fervently for Lily's safety and wellbeing.

TWO
JOURNEY INTO HELL

The train station loomed ominously in the foreground as the lorries turned the corner and approached the main building. Jozef was shocked to discover the multitude of people emerging from village trails in the surrounding wooded areas. As they arrived, entire families were being ushered out from their horse-drawn winter sleighs that the Soviet troops now laid claim to. All were escorted by the NKVD and herded into the building.

Jozef's friend Wladyslaw, who worked as a labourer at the railway station, had previously told him about preparations being made for trains that were destined for the Soviet Union. At the time, it had not made sense why these preparations were being carried out on such a massive scale. Jozef knew groups of arrested men had been deported by train to the furthest reaches of Russia's uninhabitable interior since the Soviets came and occupied their land several months earlier, but now, pieces of Wladyslaw's puzzle were beginning to form an entirely different picture. With whole families being detained at the train station, he realised an even greater tragedy for his fellow Polish citizens was unfolding.

This would be the first of several massive deportations of Polish people from Soviet-occupied territory to Siberia. Russian authorities would proceed to systematically deport Polish people living in the eastern regions, village by village. The first deportation would include administrative workers from the towns, forestry workers and entire villages of farmers and working-class settlers from the countryside. Further deportations would occur in April and June, and in June of the following year. A secret registration by the NKVD of people deemed to be socially dangerous, such as anti-Soviets and social undesirables, preceded the deportations. The deportation lists included many people active in political, social, and economic life. Registrations and deportations would also include family members of people on those lists, and friends and associates of people who had escaped abroad. The Soviet Communists believed an individual was the product of his or her environment, and if that environment was producing criminals—anti-Soviet elements—then it must be destroyed. Consequently, the registers of deportees included many women and children considered to be enemies of Communism. The sick and elderly, poor peasants and farm labourers with many small children would soon be wiped out by the onslaught of typhus, measles and whooping cough epidemics. Severe winter elements and slave labour conditions would later eliminate thousands more who reached the Siberian wasteland.

At the railway station, the young Polish men were pushed out of the lorries and onto the ground. With their hands bound, those who were unable to keep their footing in the packed snow and accidentally slipped or fell on the icy path took the brunt of the soldiers' hostility. A huge commotion ensued around the entranceway of the station as the men were forced into the building by unforgiving soldiers. With rifles poised in readiness, the Red Army closely guarded the arrested prisoners and corralled them into the farthest corner of the station's lobby.

More people were continually arriving, and all were being packed tightly into the station building. Fearing what was in store for them, chaos ensued. People gathered in groups amid shouting and sobbing. The Soviet soldiers lashed out blindly in a futile attempt to regain control of the masses amid the confusion. Mothers were hugging terrified children, babies were crying, some people were praying, while others stared blankly off into space. People were yelling out names of family members or friends they spotted in the throng. Soviet troops were pushing people along, threatening those who could not keep up. Individuals who appeared to oppose the soldiers in any way were beaten.

Everywhere Jozef looked, he saw an endless sea of frightened faces. For generations, the Poles had refused to let the Russians enjoy the suffering they inflicted on the Polish people, and he wouldn't give them that satisfaction now. He was determined to remain brave and strong in the face of all the adversity the Communists subjected him to. He was infuriated by the loss of control over his own life, but there was little choice other than to accept his fate. Shots could be heard behind the railway station. Some of the elderly people, some of the sick and those who had challenged their Soviet captors were being dragged outside and shot.

While Jozef scanned the mass of humanity, he overheard many villagers sharing the stories of their sudden and unexpected removal from their homes in the middle of this freezing cold night. Their stories resonated with familiar details. Many had been awakened in the middle of the night by loud banging and soldiers shouting, "Open the door!" The NKVD men, Russian soldiers, members of the local Communist Committee and the militia had barged into their houses and forced everyone out of bed, then lined them up while they searched the family members for weapons. All the villagers spoke of how brutal the armed invasion was as their homes were searched and ransacked room by room. Many said the soldiers had taken things thought to be of value. Fathers or heads of households had been arrested while wives and children broke down into tears. There seemed to be some discrepancy as to how long the sentencing for those men arrested was to be. Some were saying it was five years. Others had understood it to be as much as a fifteen-year sentence to exile into the interior of the Northern Russian wasteland. In any case, most Poles realised that so-called political offenders rarely came out of those concentration camps. Even if one managed to withstand the lack of food, the heavy work, the inhospitable climate and the horrific conditions, the NKVD courts often extended their sentence if they were due to be released.

In many cases, whole families had been removed, and their properties had automatically fallen into Soviet ownership. With heads of households arrested, the remaining family members were told they had from ten minutes to an hour to pack up some of their belongings and get ready to be moved out. Family pets were shot or left behind to fend for themselves. Everybody was overcome with fear. Many did not know where their family members would be taken. Some had been told that the Russians were moving them to another region for their own safety, while others instinctively realised they were headed for Siberia.

The villagers had been loaded into their sleds and driven to the train station through the dark, freezing cold night in a state of confusion and fear. Everyone mentioned the heavily snow-covered roads, the howling wind and the bitter temperature outside when the NKVD men came and uprooted their lives.

Thousands of people from nearby towns and surrounding villages were brought to the train station in Stolpce that night. All shared a common bond of terror and despair. Jozef realised how fortunate it was that his family had somehow managed to avoid being taken away from their home for deportation. He could only assume that it was because the Soviets considered his older brother to be the head of household in his family's situation. His home would be watched until Lukasz was found. Jozef prayed his mother and his siblings might be spared.

Amongst the huge crowds, Jozef observed that no class was exempt from the Soviet's list of deportees. From the very wealthiest of Stolpce's elite down to the poorest of peasants from the countryside, all blended into this mass of misery now. From the tiniest infants to the most elderly of citizens, pregnant women, the sick and even those on stretchers, all were included in a single fate.

"Jozef… Jozef Nowakowski! Over here!"

A distant voice was faintly calling out Jozef's name from somewhere in the masses. He scoured his surroundings to determine where the voice was coming from. Peering above numerous heads and bobbing winter hats, he caught sight of his friend Alexi fervently waving as he tried to get Jozef's attention. Alexi attempted to strike up a conversation with Jozef, but his words were muted and mingled with the undertones of many other voices and noises in the station. Jozef could only nod in Alexi's direction, acknowledging that he could see him. Alexi was holding up his little son, who looked to be about two years old. Alexi's wife, Mila, was standing beside him. Jozef's heart sank when he saw she was noticeably pregnant, and it appeared that the new baby was due very soon, judging by the roundness of Mila's belly. He could only imagine how Alexi's poor young wife would fare with what lay ahead now. He could see she had been crying, and did not appear to be very well. The little boy in Alexi's arms was coughing and flushed; the child and mother must have fallen victim to one of the many sicknesses rampant in the area. No doubt the family's ride through the cold winds and snow to the station that night had aggravated their condition.

Jozef's heart went out to this young family, and to so many others who were suffering in the station. He overheard stories being told about children and elderly people who had frozen to death in their sleighs and on foot while being herded to the station through the wintry night. Bodies of those who died were being piled up somewhere behind the station on their arrival. Family members were ordered to leave their loved ones there with no time to bury them, and no time to grieve. The situation was appalling.

***

Many agonising hours passed before the rumbling of an approaching train was heard above all the noise and commotion. Jozef recognised the sharp, howling whistle of the coal-burning locomotive as it hissed and groaned to a stop at a siding outside in the railway yard. The Red Army had now surrounded the entire station. Heavily guarded by the soldiers, Jozef and his fellow captives were escorted out of the building. He was increasingly concerned that he had not been able to see Katerina's fiancé, Jakob, among the large gathering of prisoners. He feared that Jakob may have been one of those young men deemed an agitator and shot by the soldiers behind the building.

A stream of black smoke was expelled into the air as the steaming locomotive started up and moved from the siding onto the tracks behind the station, pulling an endless line of wooden cattle cars meant for transporting animals. The men were herded toward the waiting boxcars. An operative group carrying out the deportation orders arranged to have the prisoners assigned to one portion of cars along a large section of the train, to be distributed to labour camps across Siberia. A copy of the names of deportees who were to be loaded into the cattle cars was handed over to the chief of the deportation train. He then called out the names and herded men into their allocated cars. People who refused to get on the train were severely beaten by the soldiers. Several brave souls attempted to escape and started running away. They were shot on the spot and left lying where they fell, trampled by the frightened masses.

The arrested heads of households were suddenly separated from their families without any warning and were loaded into the special railway cars designated for the prisoners. Their families were loaded into other cattle cars further down the track, causing much distress and panic. They were to be sent to special settlements in distant regions. People were begging the Soviets to allow their families to stay together. There was a lot of shouting and pushing. The soldiers were saying that things would be better where the families were being taken, but that did little to calm the women and children. History had taught them to never trust the Russians. They were in tears, feeling lost, and dreading what awaited them.

Some of the boxcars were tightly packed with more than fifty individuals unable to move or sit down. All the people were forced to stand crowded up against each other. Once the car was fully loaded, the sliding side door was slammed shut and locked from the outside. There was no way to escape. Tiny barred windows at the top of the cars allowed for the smallest sliver of light and fresh air to enter. The bitter wind wound its way into each boxcar through the barred windows and between the cracks in the slats of wood.

It took hours for all the deportees to be checked and crammed onto the train. More groups continued to arrive and were herded into the boxcars. Jozef's group stood in the cattle car at the railway station in the freezing cold for hours. Much crying, sobbing and praying could be heard coming from the cattle cars that contained the families down the line as they were being loaded. Finally, after the tiny beam of sunlight had faded away from the barred windows, the long train began to pull away from the station in darkness. The train's infernal whistling noise only aggravated the tense situation. The feet and ankles of many men in Jozef's boxcar were badly frozen as a result of standing there in the biting cold for such a long time. As the train started to move, a sudden jolt caused the standing mass inside the car to fall over, one on top of another. The Soviets had untied the prisoners' hands when they were loaded onto the train, but that did little to mitigate the situation as the train's engineer made a sport of causing the train to shake severely every time it started up or stopped.

It was an arduous journey. The deportees found themselves being lulled to sleep, supported in the upright position by the sheer volume of bodies packed tightly against each other in the boxcars. Conditions were very primitive. With no facilities available, people in some of the cattle cars finally relieved themselves where they stood. In other cars, some of the men ripped up a board from the floor of the boxcar to create a hole to relieve themselves in.

Urine and faeces would freeze around the hole, the severe cold causing a cone of excrement to develop and protrude underneath the car. The stench was overwhelming.

A metal drum with a pipe for a chimney sat in the middle of each car, but with no wood or coal available, fires could not be lit. The crude stove only served to torment the people because of their desperate need for heat. Exhaustion, starvation, thirst, the bitter cold and pain became constant companions on this horrific journey.

***

Two days after the journey had begun, the train finally came to a stop in an isolated area of track. The cattle doors were opened, and the people were ordered to get out. All the deportees were stiff and numbed from the cold and from standing in the same position for so long. They had difficulty getting down from the boxcars, with their floors so high above the ground. People had to slide down backwards on their stomachs over the rim of the doorway to lower themselves, the Soviet guards laughing at the ones who fell while trying to get out. Squad guards, NKVD soldiers and vicious guard dogs were everywhere.

Jozef rubbed his legs and stretched them out, trying to get the circulation going as the Russian soldiers patrolled along the open side of the cattle cars. Other guards assumed their positions on the opposite side of the train. A frozen wind swirled around, taking Jozef's breath away whenever he tried to inhale. It ripped right through the flimsy clothing of many underdressed prisoners as they shivered and complained. The prisoners were ordered to squat in front of the cattle cars, and each was given a piece of black bread. The water offered to them was dirty, but because they were so parched, they drank it anyway. They were permitted to walk in a designated area far away from the family cars.

At this and every other stop to follow, railway men were seen going along the train tapping on the wheels with hammers. Defects in the wheels would create serious problems. Sometimes repairs were necessary and the train would sit for extended periods while the railway men replaced the wheels that were worn or defective.

The soldiers called for volunteers to clean the cattle cars. Several men volunteered to get out of the biting wind. It was a revolting job and the smell was sickening. The volunteers were often seen sticking their heads out from the car doors to breathe in fresh air. Once the debris had been cleared from the boxcars, all the prisoners were ordered to get back into the train.

The further they travelled, the colder it became. The men on the outside walls of the car found it increasingly difficult to endure the numbing cold. The next time the train stopped and was reloaded, those men were placed in the middle of the car where some warmth could be absorbed from the tightly packed bodies around them.

Initially, detours were taken so more deportees could be added to the train at various stations along the way. There were many stops, and deportees were frequently forced to change trains. They were ordered out of one train and marched over to other trains waiting on frozen sidings nearby.

Deportation trains could stand still on sidings for long periods of time before their journey resumed. Sometimes huge snowdrifts blew across the railway lines, stalling the trains and causing them to stand idle for days, frozen in place. The trains moved through larger towns and junctions at night when the townspeople were sleeping, and they hid on branch lines in the countryside during the day. The soldiers and train officials tried to prevent prisoners and other deportees from having any contact with civilians at railway stations.

The deportees had nothing to eat or drink for extended periods. Rations of food and water were always small, when they did come—a piece of bread and a ration of salty soup. Occasionally, a bucket of dirty water was offered. This had to sustain them for two or three days. Some of the deportees took handfuls of snow from the top of the boxcars by putting their fingers through the barred windows and reaching up. Even though the snow was dirty and tasted of soot, it took the edge off the endless thirst.

***

The train came to a halt at the Russian border. Barbed wire three layers thick marked the boundary, and a wide strip of freshly raked soil was prepared to reveal the footprints of anyone who dared to cross it. A collective groan and moaning came from the family cars further down the track. The deportee families knew their worst fears were being realised. They too were heading into Siberia.

The Soviet railway tracks were built on a wider gauge than the Polish tracks. Russian trains were huge, and their engines were enormous. Soviet cattle cars were twice the size of the Polish boxcars, so more deportees were crowded into each one when they transferred to the Soviet lines. A third engine was coupled onto the Russian train.

It was impossible to jump up and crawl into these higher cattle cars. When the deportees were ordered to get in, the men had to clasp their hands together to create steps for other deportees to climb up into the cars. The ones who got inside first pulled up the others. There was always a dash for the best spots toward the centre of the boxcars where it was warmer, and away from the toilet hole.

Some of the family boxcars had narrow ledges along the side walls. The two-tiered side decks were cleaner than the floor of the cars. Many people pushed to get onto the decks when the cars were loaded again. With the massive Russian cattle car doors opened, the deportees only saw the heads and shoulders of the armed guards standing in the snow below.

Older people, children, women and the weaker men began to die in great numbers along the journey. Many froze to death, and many others died from starvation and illness. Every morning, the Soviets would open the cattle car doors and tell the deportees to throw out their dead. At first the frozen bodies were stacked like cords of wood on top of a flatbed car midway along the train. Jozef viewed the snow-covered bodies stacked on the death car through cracks between the slats of wood in his car every time the train rounded a bend. Eventually, there were so many people dying, the Soviets just left the dead bodies lying by the tracks where they landed when the deportees tossed them out.

The number of deportees perishing in the family boxcars increased daily. Prisoners in Jozef's car who had family members in those cars worried how their wives and children were coping. When the cattle car doors were opened in the mornings, the husbands and fathers pushed and shoved at the opening to get a better look at the line of corpses spread out beside the railway tracks outside. While they struggled against each other to see beyond the side doors, the Soviet guards thrashed at them, pushed them back into the boxcar and slammed the doors shut. The prisoners then peered through the cracks in the boxcar walls, attempting to see the dead bodies lying in the snow outside. Some deportees in the family cars would take clothing and things of value from the corpses before their dead bodies were discarded. Thousands of unidentified, naked, family remains littered the sides of the railway tracks all the way from Poland to Siberia. There were no graves dug, nor any signs made to mark the final resting places of the dead. No prayers were offered for them. They simply disappeared into the unknown.

At one point, Jozef clearly saw the lifeless body of Alexi's little son frozen on the ground. The child's tiny coat and hat had been removed. Jozef was saddened and could only hope that the boy's clothing had been given to a desperate child somewhere along the endless line of cattle cars. Alexi was not in the same prisoners' car that Jozef had been herded into, but he could not be far away. Had Alexi noticed his little son's lifeless form lying there in the snow? Every so often, men could be heard joining in the sobbing and moaning coming from other sections of the train when the horrific discovery was made of a dead wife or child, frozen by the side of the railway line.

Conversations between the prisoners flowed freely when the train was moving. All agreed to defy the Communists' secret plot to annihilate them through hard work and harsh conditions at the labour camps.

It was not long before various personality traits began to emerge among the men. Some demonstrated leadership qualities, and one in Jozef's car organised a rotational movement of bodies and positions by intermittently telling all the prisoners to shift together in one direction. This way, each man had a turn standing near the tiny barred windows to breathe in fresh air and get some sooty snow to drink. The leaders tended to set rules for the others to follow and instructed their peers on how to behave and function to remain alive. These men were the ones with the strongest desire to survive.

Another group of prisoners was quick with witty comments and jokes. These men managed to raise the morale of prisoners in Jozef's cattle car during the darkest times along their journey. It was a stressful situation, being locked up together in horrendous conditions for hours on end. Sometimes they travelled for two or three days before the train stopped and the guards came to open the doors so the men could be given some rations and stretch their legs. The comedic prisoners did not seem to let the circumstances weigh them down. They had the uncanny knack of turning the worst situations into something laughable. The other men laughed wildly at their antics. They hated the Russians, and they despised Hitler and the Nazis. They made a mockery of all things Russian. Their language was often coloured, and their wisecracks could be downright vulgar. Nevertheless, they were credited with encouraging many prisoners to survive who might otherwise have given up.

There were a few prisoners who did lose faith in their own ability to persevere. They were the ones filled with a spirit of doom from the very beginning of the journey. A few of those men perished in the night when their turn came to stand against the frigid corners of the boxcar walls. Their bodies would keel over on top of other men. When the cattle doors were opened in the morning, as the car was being unloaded, they would be tossed into the snow, stiff and cold. The Russians would remove their clothing, and their names would be removed from the official list. Their mortal remains lay lost forever somewhere in the barren wastelands of Russia.

There were also a few antagonistic prisoners in Jozef's car. These were the men who always had some derogatory remark or criticism to express. They had little control over their irrepressible urge to argue with the opinions and thoughts of other prisoners. At times, the antagonists wore down the tolerance of other men trapped inside their small confines. Irritation frequently escalated into violent arguments. With nerves already frayed, it did not take much for the argumentative prisoners to explode into fits of rage and make threats against others in the car. It was a good thing they were so tightly crowded, otherwise those who quarrelled may have wound up in vicious fist fights.

The men frequently talked about their families during the long, cold, dark trek into the frozen hinterland. There was speculation that the Soviets were moving the families to the Russian interior because they were looking for a labour force to fill their empty camps, villages and collective farms for economic purposes. The Poles brazenly swore that the Communists would not be able to populate those regions in Siberia with Polish slaves. The previous Russian governments ruled by the Tsars had tried to do that for one hundred years, and it did not work.

One unfortunate prisoner inside Jozef's boxcar caught sight of his elderly father and then, a few days later, his young wife dead by the side of the tracks. He was very affected by the horrible reality. He blamed himself for their demise. They had been deported because of his involvement with an anti-Communist group when he was a teenager. As the train came screeching to a halt a couple of days later, the young man pushed his way to the side of the car where the guards unsealed the doors. No longer able to cope with the insufferable truth, he leapt from the boxcar and started running the moment the doors were opened. He knew the Russian guards would shoot him dead. Within seconds, his wish was granted.

There was another prisoner inside the boxcar whose feet had become badly frostbitten. While the Soviets were slamming the cattle doors shut, the man was seen bending over and trying to pull on the boots that one young man had left behind. Several of the prisoners in the boxcar began to reprimand him for taking the dead one's boots. Accusations and arguments quickly ensued. Things started to become heated until one of the older men in the car whistled very loudly to get everyone's attention.

"Listen to us now!" he shouted. "Have we lowered ourselves to the measure of our oppressors already? We have yet to reach our destination, and already there is discord and petty fighting amongst us. Let us not forget that our Polish parents raised us to a higher standard than this. We cannot and we will not allow the Russians to reduce us to their level and create a divide among us."

A long moment of silence followed the man's admonishment. It seemed to have a calming effect that washed over the entire boxcar. All the men settled down as the train jerked and pulled further ahead into the barren, snow-laden land of the Soviet interior.

Confined in such close quarters, and dealing with suffering and uncertainty, conflict was bound to occur among some prisoners. If too much commotion erupted when the train was sitting at frozen sidings, the guards went along thumping on the sides of the cars with the butts of their rifles ordering the prisoners to be quiet and threatening to open the doors and shoot everybody inside if they did not settle down.

Close bonds were also created from the suffering these young Polish prisoners endured. A sense of camaraderie began to develop among the men in Jozef's car. Solidarity and compassion grew between those who had come from similar backgrounds. Those bonds would help to protect and support the men through all the intolerable hardships they would have to endure daily in the places they were being deported to.

Passing the endless hours, prisoners sometimes broke into song. They sang old Polish folk songs that had been passed down from previous generations exiled to Siberia. The Soviet guards prohibited the songs, so the men only sang while the train was in motion. The singing helped to pass the time in the dark coldness of the boxcar. The words to the ballads were filled with history and sadness. Jozef's favourite song spoke of prisoners chained together on their way to Siberia, and here he was, following in those tragic footprints!

Eventually, all the boxcars containing the women and children were diverted onto other routes while the train continued further north. After one final transfer, Jozef leaned up against the frozen slats in a small area of the cattle car, and between the chinks of wood he watched endless kilometres of snow-covered land fleeting by outside. They passed the Ural Mountains and went on further across the endless expanse of Russia along the Trans-Siberian Railway lines. The journey seemed like an eternity. Jozef observed an uninterrupted depth of forest in the distance that spread far off into the unknown. Now and then, the train would blow by railway location signs indicating that the deportees were being driven further and further into the Siberian heartland. Sometimes small hamlets were sighted, with aged, thatched-roof houses. When the train passed by main roads in small towns, it was common to see military vehicles. Sometimes, villagers travelling in horse-drawn sleighs were spotted. Sadly, all the horses looked old and haggard with their ribs protruding as they trotted across the open countryside.

At the beginning of this harrowing journey, Jozef had difficulty sleeping due to the horrendous circumstances. The incessant, sharp, howling whistle of the train woke him up whenever he did manage to catch a few fleeting moments of sleep. However, somewhere along the line, sleep finally overcame him, and in his mind he was transported back to his childhood home in Poland.

He dreamt about the frosty winter days he spent growing up. As a young lad, Jozef had loved playing outside in the snow. In wintertime, there were fewer jobs that needed to be done on the farm, so there was ample opportunity for play. Jozef built snow forts and had snowball fights with his siblings and his friends. They skied and snowshoed into the woodlands and along the riverbank, sometimes meeting up with their young friends from the village school. All the children became good cross-country skiers. They fabricated crude ice skates and glided along the frozen river. Often, the boys raced each other to see who could go the fastest on the flimsy skates before they fell apart. The bitter cold winds and inclement conditions did not deter them from having hours of winter fun.

As the snow fell heavy and deep, Stanislaw and his sons would have to keep the area in front of the barn free and clear of snow so they could get inside to do their chores and tend to the livestock. The horse, Matylda, pulled the winter sled, fitted with wide runners that could pivot and turn easily across the surface of the snow. It was difficult for the horse to get a running start after a fresh snowfall, but with some coaxing and pulling, Stanislaw could usually get the strong animal up and over the deeper snowbanks onto a course where the snow was less challenging.

Father and the boys used Borys the ox to haul large logs from the nearby forest on the sled to the woodpile behind the farmhouse, where they were chopped into firewood. The boys ran behind in the tracks made by the runners on the sled. Sometimes they needed snowshoes to keep on top of the wintry blanket during their treks back and forth from the forest, but due to the frequency of hauling logs, a well-worn path was always quickly trampled down in the snow.

Sometimes the boys accompanied their father to a neighbour's pond to help cut ice. They'd go out to the middle of the frozen pond and clear snow off the surface, then watch as their father and the other farmer used axes to chop an enormous hole into the ice, creating a large space of open water. The two men carefully knelt a short distance apart at the edge of the hole and used long saws to cut crack lines through the ice, working their way out from the open hole. With their axes, they broke the ice across the crack lines. Large chunks of ice broke free and floated to the surface. The men then used long poles with a spike attached at the end to push the chunks of ice along to the open hole. Together, they grappled with the huge pieces of ice as they pushed them up and out of the hole onto the surface of the frozen pond. They sawed off smaller blocks of ice, which the boys would load onto their family's sled and the neighbour's sleigh. The loaded sled was brought home to the Nowakowski farm, and the blocks of ice were packed in sawdust and stored in the icehouse next to the cold shed.

The icehouse was raised above the ground on wooden blocks. The roof and floor were solid, but the sidewalls had large spaces between the boards. The floor was covered with a few inches of sawdust, and each block of ice was placed a few inches apart on the floor. Every space between the ice blocks had to be packed tightly with more sawdust, and then the whole layer of ice was covered with a few more inches of sawdust. The blocks of ice remained frozen in the sawdust, and were dug out one at a time as needed.

Jozef's deep sleep persisted as the train rolled on, and images of his boyhood days in Poland continued. He dreamt he was venturing out onto the frozen river to do a little ice fishing with his father and Lukasz. Father hacked a deep hole into the surface of the ice with his axe, and then Jozef, Lukasz and Father stood around the opened water and dropped their baited fishing lines into the hole. Their ice-fishing rods were considerably shorter than the poles they used in summertime to fish along the riverbank. They had a much longer length of fishing line attached and wound around the rod, allowing it to be loosened off according to the depth it needed to be dropped in the water to reach the fish below the ice. Every so often, the surface of the water in the fishing hole needed to be punctured again as the water quickly froze over in the frosty air. A variety of fish were pulled up and out from under the ice as the hungry creatures nibbled at pieces of bread and oatmeal on Jozef's baited hook.

In his dream, Jozef's childhood memories recaptured feelings of safety and happiness he had known as a young boy. How he wished he could know that joy and contentment again.

THREE
SIBERIA

He was wakened from his slumber by a sudden jerking of the train as it hissed to an abrupt stop somewhere in the northern reaches of Siberia. Assuming this was another one of the many locations where the train's crew would take on more coal and water for the locomotive and provisions for the guards, Jozef was surprised when the soldiers removed the lead seal and unbarred the side door of the cattle car. A flash of daylight burst into the dark confines of the boxcars as doors were unsealed along the full length of the deportation train. Having travelled across thousands of miles of territory, the challenging and torturous journey was finally over. The train reached the end of the railway line on a frozen morning in March 1940.

Russian soldiers ordered the prisoners to get out of the boxcars, and they inspected each car to ensure all the men had complied. Guards carrying rifles fixed with bayonets were evenly dispersed along the length of the train.

Prisoners were blinded by sunlight hitting the snow when they were forced outside, their eyes poorly adjusted following weeks locked up inside the unlit cattle cars. More and more frail men emerged from the frozen cocoon that had transported them to their location. Surrounded by Russian soldiers, they were ordered to form a line.

Prisoners began to converse with each other until the Soviet soldiers ordered the men to stop talking. A few were beaten when they did not obey the Soviets' order. Gunfire could be heard a short distance away. Jozef dared not turn to see who had met an unfortunate end.

He heard the commandant yelling out orders in Russian further down the line. Jozef had difficulty deciphering what was being said, but he quickly fell into place in a single row with the other prisoners along the side of the train. A vicious Siberian wind fanned by sub-zero temperatures tore at his flesh. Some men had trouble breathing as the cruel elements froze their lungs. Tears formed in Jozef's eyes because of the bitter wind, further clouding his vision. He felt his nose and ears freezing over.

The prisoners were then ordered to remove their clothing. Humiliating body searches were conducted as the men stripped down naked in the snow and cold. They were ordered to remove their socks and shoes as well, and to put all their clothing in a pile in front of them. The captives shivered uncontrollably, and tried to find refuge in the little bit of shelter provided by the side of the cattle cars. Soldiers were now shouting out orders that were repeated down the long line of men. Prisoners were forced to raise their arms, bend down, squat, turn around and show the guards the soles of their feet. Their nostrils and ears were examined as well. The guards searched the insides of their shoes and pockets, the bands on all hats and caps, and they carefully examined the seams of all the prisoners' clothing with their fingers. These procedures took a considerable amount of time to complete while the naked men were slowly freezing to death in the frigid cold. When they were finally allowed to put their clothes back on, the clothing was frozen and stiff, and it was difficult to do up frozen buttons with numbed fingers. While the guards paraded around in their heavy overcoats, warm boots and tall fur hats, they laughed at the suffering prisoners.

Holding his revolver up in the air threateningly, the commander blew a whistle to get everyone's attention. He ordered the prisoners to form an orderly line once again. Jozef lowered his head in a futile attempt to keep the harsh wind out of his face as thousands of men fell back into the long row. Hundreds of armed soldiers grouped around them.

Some of the weaker prisoners collapsed from exposure to the inclement weather conditions. They had to be helped by the men beside them to remain standing.

There were no signs of any railway stations, villages or inhabitants in this desolate place. Endless miles of deep, wind-swept snow and inhospitable, barren countryside stretched out before them.

A convoy of army vehicles suddenly appeared. Their transport commander became engaged in conversation with the deportation train's commandant. Jozef noticed the convoy commander attach a leather map case and a bag to the belt on his overcoat.

Murmurs travelled down the line of men as the convoy soldiers began to issue a Russian winter jacket to each prisoner. The jackets were padded and buttoned up from the neck down to the thighs. Padded winter trousers and laced-up, canvas boots were also distributed. The fit was better for some men than others. The clothing did provide extra warmth, but it was still inadequate for the arctic conditions of the Siberian hinterland. The soldiers also distributed two pieces of cloth to every prisoner. These were for wrapping their feet in, to prevent frostbite inside their boots. The men were instructed not to roll the wraps too tightly around their feet. Some did not heed the advice, and they paid for their lack of compliance when their feet froze very quickly.

The soldiers who arrived with the convoy of lorries were clad in heavy sheepskin overcoats and warm sheepskin gloves. Their heads were covered by hooded balaclavas. Each one of them carried a sack on their back that was tied tight with a thick string. The lorries were spread out at regular intervals, each bearing a large, mounted machine gun. One lorry served as a field kitchen, transporting a wood-fuelled steel boiler and oven.

Prisoner names were checked, and heads were counted. The long line of prisoners was divided into groups with many soldiers assigned to guard each division. The men were ordered to form columns, two-abreast, and each group lined up behind one of the army vehicles. A long length of greased and heavy chain was pulled out from a huge coil on the back of each lorry, and the soldiers laid it out along the middle of the line between each pair of men. The prisoners were ordered to pick up the frozen chain with their hand closest to where it lay. The soldiers then handcuffed each prisoner's wrist to the length of chain attached to a lorry. The organising took some time to complete, but once everything was in order, a column of prisoners was formed on each side of the chain and the command was given for the men to start marching at a rather fast pace.

The same warning would be uttered repeatedly: *The guards will use their weapons on any man who steps out of line! A step to the left, a step to the right will be considered an escape! Get going! March!*

***

The prisoners set out silently across a large field at a quick pace despite the depth of snow that lay ahead. They had no idea what was going to happen to them, and fear was written on every face. As their chains were continually pulled along by the lorries ahead of them, they were forced to continue marching at a steady stride. Jozef knew he and the other captives were being driven like cattle to a diabolical place.

Though the men had been snow-blinded by the stark contrast when coming from the darkness inside the cattle cars, their eyes gradually adjusted to the outside light. Looking toward the west, Jozef caught sight of the Ural Mountains far in the distance. The sun sat low on the horizon, confirming his suspicion that they had been deported to the far reaches of the north. He remembered learning in school that the sun never appeared high in the sky near the Arctic regions, and that it set only a few hours after rising. With the sun sinking quickly now, Jozef bemoaned the harsh reality. He trudged on across the frozen landscape viewing the silent shapes marching in front of him. A short while later, darkness fell and made the crisp winter air feel even colder. Out in the wintry elements, with bodies undernourished and weakened by all they had already endured, the cold winds cut through frail bones like icy knives.

A few Russian soldiers marched along each side of the columns at carefully spaced positions. The remainder of the soldiers in each section rode in the back of the army vehicles that the chains were hooked onto. The commander of each section rode in the cab of the lorry with the driver. Soldiers in the back of the vehicle dropped out every couple of hours to relieve the guards marching alongside the prisoners, and the spent guards then jumped up and rode in the lorry. With bone-chilling polar winds continuing to batter them, the prisoners sank to their knees in the snow and struggled on. The convoy of vehicles forged ahead in a long procession through the endless snow and gloom.

The vehicle and men marching at the front had the most difficult task of breaking the surface of the snow and blazing a trail for the others to follow. The lorries took turns at this duty. Every couple of hours, the lorry at the front moved out of the line and allowed the others to pass by. The lead lorry waited until the end of the column appeared, then moved into position behind the last lorry, giving each section of the entourage a turn to work its way to the front and take over the lead position.

The convoy steered away from inhabited places so the Russian population would not see the prisoners. The chains continually pulled and tugged the prisoners along as they struggled to keep up in the interminably thick blanket of snow. Sometimes the vehicles became stuck in the deeper drifts, and all the lorries and prisoners scrambled on until the quick pace of the march could be resumed. As they marched in perpetual darkness, the vehicle at the front of the column emitted a beam of light with glowing lamps, but it was not enough to allow the men at the back of the procession to see where they were going. They blindly stumbled onward in the tramped-down snow left by the prisoners who had moved on ahead of them.

All the men were frozen and hungry. The difficult march had drained what little reserves they had. Many suffered severe frostbite along the way, some losing fingers and toes. Others were ill and dying. Numerous prisoners froze to death. Older men began to drop in greater numbers. Jozef overheard a man somewhere in the line behind him mumbling that the dead were the lucky ones, to have escaped from the hell they found themselves facing.

The weaker ones fell and were jerked back up by the soldiers, who kicked at them forcefully, making them continue to march until they could march no more. Some were literally kicked to death. The healthier ones tried to help those who were struggling, but it was difficult enough keeping themselves on their feet. Prisoners called for the walking soldiers to come and help those who could not keep up, but the guards seldom did anything to assist them. Dying prisoners collapsed into the snow and begged the soldiers to unchain them so they could die where they lay.

Whenever one of the captives toppled over, unable to go any further, the soldiers marching alongside him shouted out a message that was relayed along the column until it reached the transport commander in the leading lorry. The entire convoy would then halt, and the unfortunate prisoner would be unshackled. The name of the victim was passed along to the soldiers in the lead lorry, and his identity was checked on the prisoners' list. The age of the prisoner sometimes determined his fate. On rare occasions, if the man was still young and deemed viable, he might be released from the chain and helped to the lorry, where he would ride with the soldiers for a couple of hours before being chained to the marching column again. Otherwise, his boots and clothing were removed, and his body was covered over under a thin mound of snow where he was left to die. His identity was then removed from the long list of prisoners' names.

The Soviets were undertaking huge projects in their northernmost regions. New roads, railway lines, mines and ports along the larger rivers needed to be established. They were also trying to meet increasing demand for gold and timber in the west. Free forced labour was an economical way to help them meet their need for increased manpower. They did not want to feed anyone who could not work and generate income for them. Any prisoner too weak or too sick to work would be left to die. Few men over the age of thirty would survive. Their journey ended where they dropped. The guards had been given orders not to help any of the older or sicker captives. Thousands of marching prisoners perished across unknown stretches of the Siberian wasteland.

There were no roads to follow as they trudged across the snowbound countryside. However, the Soviets had placed large stakes about eight feet tall with twigs, dried hay or rags attached to the tops of them to serve as route markers. The posts were spaced at intervals across hundreds of miles of snowy fields, steep hills, deep valleys and thickly forested areas. They directed the entourage across frozen rivers, where the wheels on the vehicles did nothing but spin; soldiers riding in the backs of the lorries had to jump down and push them along. Often the prisoners were called upon to help push as well.

The commandant had the convoy stop the first night in a sheltered woodland space, primarily for the benefit of the soldiers, but also to preserve as many prisoners as possible to fill Russia's free workforce. It afforded the men a little bit of relief from the constant winds and kept them out of sight from the Russian civilians.

The prisoners were unchained at their rest stop in the forest. Each group of men quickly started to pile up snow and build enclosures with their numbed, bare hands to get out of the cruel elements. They crouched down inside their ringed windbreaks away from the frigid winter blast. The transport commandant allowed volunteers from each group to gather bits of wood under armed escort so they could build fires inside their snow forts. They were also permitted to collect small tree branches to put down on the ground. Laying low behind their walls of snow, the prisoners managed to escape the worst of the icy wind, but little could be done to alleviate the discomfort caused by the sub-zero temperatures. They huddled close together to share body heat as they lay on branches near their small fires.

The mobile kitchen managed to produce a small ration of bread for each man, and a tin mug filled with a bland, steaming hot liquid. The prisoners did not care how awful it tasted; they relished the warmth the drink provided them. Most of the men did not talk. They reserved their energy, trying to remain alive. For some, the distribution of Russian winter coats, trousers and boots did little good. The next morning, many stiff and frozen bodies were taken from inside the snow forts. Clothing was removed from the corpses, and the names of the deceased were struck from the list.

The march continued through open, challenging terrain and thickly wooded areas. The snow had drifted into a series of deep gullies where the prisoners found themselves floundering waist-deep in the drifts. They remained chained together, and the guards constantly surrounded them, picking off anyone who could not keep up with the pace or who fell out of line. Occasionally, they were given rest periods for the benefit of the guards. All the men were physically and mentally exhausted. Some of them no longer cared whether they lived or died, and they gave in to the impossible conditions by purposefully throwing themselves out of line into the snow so the Russians would end their misery.

The Siberian winter lived up to its reputation that year. For two weeks, cruel winds gusted, and increasingly deep snow accumulated across the desolate landscape as the convoy plodded on. Toward the end of March, a blizzard blew in. Howling winds and freezing snow battered the procession as they tried to keep marching. With their heads bowed against the forceful snow, it was impossible to keep their eyes open. Snow built up on their scruffy hair and beards, and their shoulders slumped under the weight of the heavy build-up. Everything was shrouded in a thick layer of white. The convoy slowed down to a crawl. Huge snowdrifts held up the vehicles time and time again, and they continually had to be dug out when they became stuck. Soldiers and prisoners had to help dig the wheels free with their bare hands whenever the vehicles bogged down in the snow.

Finally, the lorries stopped altogether. The ever-increasing depth of snow had made it impossible for them to move or to be dug out. Swirling snow reduced visibility to nothing. Soldiers removed the prisoners' chains and forced them to march on ahead, forging a pathway for the vehicles to creep along in. They managed to continue struggling slowly through the deepening snow and unforgiving wind until they reached a wooded area where the commandant ordered them to take shelter.

The surviving prisoners immediately piled up mounds of snow and built their fortress walls high. It was difficult to light fires until their snowy walls were tall enough to keep out the blustery winds and swirling snow. They had to tend their fires carefully to keep them burning as the snowy gales continually threatened to snuff out the flames. The field kitchen was unable to operate while the blizzard continued, and the suffering men did not get their desperately needed rations. They huddled close together around their fires, rotating their bodies as sides facing away from the fire would freeze quickly in the blizzard's fury. Sleep was prohibited; the men would freeze to death in these conditions if they drifted off. They continually nudged each other awake when any of them started falling asleep. They tucked their numbed hands inside their coats, and they stomped their feet to keep their circulation going, trying to avoid frostbite. Vicious winds howled and whistled among the trees in the darkness.

It took two days for the storm to diminish. Everything became calm and quiet as the snow and winds gradually abated. It was still very cold, but now the prisoners could see across the endless expanse of windswept land. Heaps of snow had appeared by a cluster of trees where the vehicles had come to rest. Buried beneath several feet of snow, they were barely distinguishable. It took an entire day for the soldiers and prisoners to dig out all the lorries. The vehicle housing the steel boiler and oven had to be persuaded back into operation, but once it was up and running, the men were revived by a small portion of bread and a hot drink while they rested next to their fires. Guards' food rations were much better than what the captives were given, as they were fed canned meat and vegetable soup with their bread. The soldiers' clothing was better than the clothing issued to the prisoners as well, making them better prepared to cope with the inclement conditions. Nevertheless, the march was starting to take its toll on the soldiers too. They were beginning to show signs of fatigue, and a few perished during the punishing trek across Siberia.

When the march resumed, the prisoners were chained together in their groups once again. The columns of men were ordered to march ahead of the lorries to create a pathway for the vehicles to follow in. Each group of prisoners would march a certain distance, and then the group at the head of the procession would fall back to the end while the others all moved forward. The lead groups had a tough job breaking open a trail in the fresh, thick snow and deep drifts. For those following behind, it grew easier with each consecutive group of prisoners and vehicles that passed through. All the soldiers were marching now as well, except for the commandant and the drivers. They struggled through the deep snow alongside the captives, scrambled down deep riverbanks and fought their way up the other side.

They continued to march across open countryside, away from inhabited areas. Cold, hunger, exhaustion and illness continued to claim many prisoners as they crossed the frozen land. Each time a prisoner perished, the man behind the empty space was moved forward. A length of chain started to drag in the snow behind each group as more and more men died. The two prisoners at the end of the line took turns tucking the extra length of chain under their arms to stop the dragging.

They eventually marched into a vast forest where they were better protected against the unrelenting north winds. It was easier to locate suitable places for setting up their nightly camps in the woodlands.

After several days of trudging through this thickly wooded area, a labour camp suddenly appeared in a large clearing. Jozef could see lights, and he heard the distinct barking of guard dogs. A series of bright searchlights fell upon the column of prisoners as they marched toward the encampment. Armed guards were seen observing the captives from tall watchtowers built high above the compound. Machine guns were mounted in each watchtower, and were aimed at the marching prisoners as they approached the camp. Jozef distinguished the outline of a very tall fence made from thick, roughly chopped logs. On top of the fence, barbed wire glistened menacingly beneath the canvas of a starry night sky. Deep growls and the snarling of vicious guard dogs sounded as they approached. NKVD agents and guards kept the dogs on tight leashes next to them. Large and trained to kill, they were the most ferocious dogs Jozef had ever seen.

It was a smaller contingent of prisoners that arrived at the main gate of the fortress than had originally set out from the deportation train. The convoy commander rang the bell, and a gatekeeper opened a hatch to share a few words in Russian with him. Above the entranceway, a sign indicated that the fortress was an NKVD Corrective Labour Camp. A tall iron gate opened, and each group of prisoners moved up to the gate under scrutiny as their names were checked against the endless lists. They were then led into a closely guarded courtyard area where they were unshackled from their chains. Another gate beyond this area directed them into the labour camp compound. Fires were lit, and the prisoners sat around piles of blazing logs as they received a bread ration and some watery soup. All were exhausted and weak from the long and difficult march. Many were frostbitten and ill. Every part of Jozef's body ached, but he was still alive.

Some of the captives never recovered from their ordeal, and they died within days of reaching the camp. The men who had marched beside them carried their bodies under escort to an area a short distance away. Volunteer burial parties would chop away at the frozen ground, and the dead would be buried in shallow graves.

FOUR
SIX MONTHS EARLIER
SEPTEMBER 1939

Lilyana's family was prosperous by Polish standards at the start of the war. Prawoslaw's Hardware and Mercantile was thriving, and her family was in want of nothing. Mr Prawoslaw was an astute businessman. Despite other people's confidence regarding Poland's stability, and optimism in the power of the Polish Army, he had foreseen a time ripe with political strife approaching long before the Nazis and the Soviets breached Poland's borders. Unbeknown to the rest of the townsfolk, Mr Prawoslaw was secretly arranging with a distant cousin in England to relocate the family business there. He had no qualms about packing up and moving overseas.

Poland had a long history of wars with neighbouring countries seeking to expand their own borders by confiscating Poland's territory. The Polish people had been fighting to maintain an independent state for hundreds of years. Their land had been occupied by and divided among neighbouring countries for centuries. Poland was viewed as a prime location situated at the crossroads of Eastern Europe. Mr Prawoslaw wanted something better and more stable for his family. He knew that the time had come to carry out his plan.

When the Germans invaded Poland, the Polish Armed Forces were shocked by the speed, extent and malevolence of the German assault. German infantry, armoured and artillery divisions fought as a coordinated team, while the

Luftwaffe destroyed Poland from the air. They attacked with a multitude of troops backed by tactical aircraft and mobile armour on the ground. The Polish military could do little to counter the invasion with their outdated defences. At the time, the Polish Army did have some armed tanks, but they were still in the process of changing over their horse-mounted cavalry, which comprised the majority of the army, into armoured units. The outclassed Polish Air Force was quickly obliterated by the speed with which the Germans struck, and by the number and manoeuvrability of the German Luftwaffe.

The Poles had a tough time defending their territory, but Warsaw did manage to hold out for a few weeks against the German invasion. Early street fighting for the capital city proved more difficult than the Germans had anticipated. Despite strong resistance from the Polish Armed Forces, continual waves of fierce air bombing and ground combat by German artillery finally caused the city to fall in late September, and Warsaw surrendered to the Nazis.

The remaining Polish troops had planned to hold out through winter in the forests and marshes of Eastern Poland. Large amounts of armaments were being stockpiled, and reserves of the Polish Army were focusing on preparations for a counter-offensive. However, that prospect was dashed by the Soviet invasion of Eastern Poland in mid-September. Already weakened by the Nazis' aggressive attack, Poland's remaining army was no match for the advancing Red Army, which struck with thousands of soldiers fully equipped with tanks and planes. A small number of Polish soldiers continued fighting into October, when they were forced to succumb and lay down their guns. Guerrilla fighters resisted into winter.

At the end of September, the two conquering powers divided Poland in half, with Germany controlling the west and the USSR laying claim to the territory in the east. Most Poles found it difficult to believe their country had fallen in less than a month, but Mr Prawoslaw had known long ago, the demise of his beloved nation would be inevitable when the Germans advanced. He'd been aware that Poland's outdated military defences and small number of troops would not be able to withstand the more advanced and powerful military forces the Nazis could bring to bear. His feeling of uneasiness had been greatly amplified in August when rumours began circulating about a pact signed between Germany and the Soviet Union.

Having foreseen this time of anarchy approaching, Mr Prawoslaw had sent his wife, Olisia, and daughter, Lilyana, away from Stolpce in August when Hitler's guns started pointing at Poland with demands and threats. Olisia and Lilyana were visiting with relatives in the countryside when the Nazi incursion commenced. Mr Prawoslaw's original plan had been to meet up with his family in the countryside and then to travel with them to his cousin, Tadeusz Prawoslaw, in Britain by train and ferry. However, it took him longer than he had estimated to complete his business in town, and by the time he had everything in order and was prepared to take his family overseas, it was already mid-September. By then, the Germans dominated half of Poland's territory, as well as several surrounding nations.

Eastern Poland lay sandwiched between a large area that was now controlled by the Nazis to the north, west and south, and Poland's long-time enemy, the Soviet Union, which stretched far into the east across the border. All Poles knew the Russians could not be trusted.

Britain and France had honoured their sworn alliance with Poland, and they declared war on the Nazi regime a couple of days after Germany's invasion of Poland began. Consequently, they were caught up in the hostilities. It was now impossible for Mr Prawoslaw to bring his family safely through territories at war and reach England.

He had no choice but to revise his plan of escape. Before the Soviets invaded Eastern Poland, there was a small area of retreat through the Romanian border in the south-eastern corner of the remaining Polish territory. Mr Prawoslaw decided that the safest thing to do would be to travel south to the Romanian border, then continue through Romania and Bulgaria into Turkey. His main concern was to get his family safely away from Eastern Europe, where the major conflict was being waged.

By the middle of September, the road leading to Romania had become congested with refugees from the north, west and south attempting to escape the country after the Germans had swooped in and appropriated their homes, their land and their livelihood. A continuous stream of automobiles, horse-drawn carts and civilians on foot proceeded south toward the border. The refugees were already exhausted by the time they arrived in the eastern region of Poland. They came with frightening stories of how the Polish Army was being wiped out by the German Luftwaffe and Panzer Division tanks in the west. They said that entire towns, railway stations, military and non-military targets were being flattened. All the roads and bridges leading into and out of Warsaw had been destroyed in the Nazis' effort to capture the capital. Rumours spread about poisonous chocolates and candies dropped by German planes, and about water sources poisoned by saboteurs. Some of the refugees spoke about Polish-speaking German soldiers dressed in Polish uniforms creating further disorder, confusion and problems. All of them relayed stories about their hellish escape and passage to the east while continually being bombed along the roadways and railway lines.

With his wife and daughter safely distanced away in the countryside, early in September, Mr Prawoslaw took some of the family's best silverware and other prized possessions from their house in linen sacks to his brother, Jerzy's country home. Those items would come in handy when trading or bartering with people along the family's route to freedom. Mr Prawoslaw knew there was little time left to settle his remaining business matters in town before securing the house and heading off to accompany his family to the border. He would work frantically throughout the next couple of weeks, attempting to tie up his business at the hardware store, and continuing to secretly purge the house so nothing of value would remain for any assailants to steal or destroy. Under night's cloak of darkness, he would bury many sacks filled with personal items deep in the ground behind the house, where Olisia's vegetable garden was. If the invaders arrived, they would believe the earth in the garden area had merely been turned over in preparation for the next planting season. Mr. Prawoslaw felt sure this would not rouse any undue suspicion. He would return to this place after all the hostilities had ended, as his father had done following the Russo-Polish war twenty years earlier, and reclaim his land and the family heirlooms.

Unfortunately, when the main bank in Warsaw was shut down after the Nazis began their vicious attack on the city, it became difficult to conduct business, as Mr Prawoslaw's financial affairs had to pass through that central branch. Desperate to conclude his business in Stolpce, Mr Prawoslaw decided to withdraw some currency from his local bank. He realised that if the Polish state should fall, the Polish zloty would be rendered valueless; therefore, he requested that his funds be paid out in foreign currencies, providing him with legitimate money to use when the family travelled abroad en route to a safe haven. His apprehension increased daily as the endless line of refugees coming from the west passed by with their lives in ruins, their properties lost and their businesses and bank accounts gone. He prayed it was not already too late to put his escape plan into action.

Olisia and Lilyana waited anxiously for Mr Prawoslaw to come and join them at Jerzy's home in the countryside. When they'd left in August, Mr Prawoslaw had promised to be there as soon as he'd finished shutting down the mercantile store and seeing to his remaining business in Stolpce. With the Germans now occupying a large portion of Poland, Olisia and the rest of the family worried about why Mr Prawoslaw had not yet arrived to begin their retreat abroad as planned.

A dismal mood of nervous caution swept across Eastern Poland that September, and the local townspeople and villagers flooded into Prawoslaw's Hardware and Mercantile. They feared the Nazis would soon move east and come to take their land as well and were desperate to get whatever merchandise they could to help see themselves through the anticipated difficult time ahead. Mr Prawoslaw did not have the heart to deny any of his friends or neighbours the opportunity to purchase items they required to shore up their homes in readiness should the Germans choose to broaden their territorial demands. He delayed closing the store in order to be there so his fellow citizens had a chance to get the housewares, tools, utensils and hardware items they needed. Many of his customers walked away without putting down any payment for their purchases. Mr Prawoslaw simply told them they could make restitution for the merchandise once Poland had freed itself from the Nazis and returned to a free and independent state. He understood that all was lost for Poland, but he encouraged his fellow countrymen to remain hopeful and optimistic.

Finally, in mid-September, Mr Prawoslaw packed the family car with necessities and the sacks of family valuables for trade and barter. Then, in the middle of the night, he locked up the house and headed out toward his brother's home in the countryside. If all went well, he anticipated being reunited with his family later that afternoon. Mr Prawoslaw estimated the family's journey along the road to the border would be slowed by the mass of people, carts, animals and other vehicles attempting to reach the Romanian frontier, but he still held on to hope that it was not too late to escape. Judging from the scattered reports that were reaching the east, the Nazis were still fighting in the western regions of the country and had not set foot inside Eastern Poland.

By daybreak, Mr Prawoslaw was well on his way to his brother's home. He relaxed in the hope of seeing his wife and daughter again, and in the knowledge that their flight to freedom was about to start. The country road leading to Jerzy's farmhouse was riddled with potholes and rough terrain, and had to be navigated carefully by automobile. As he passed by one farmstead after another, the crude road gradually narrowed into a horse-trodden laneway, along which the farmers would bring their teams of horses and carts to Stolpce on market days. He cautiously traversed the bumpy tract of land, swerving to avoid the larger rocks and the deeper ruts left by wagons. Occasionally, he had to pull over in order to allow local farmers to pass by with their horses and loaded carts. One farmer stopped briefly to chat.

"Good morning, Mr Prawoslaw. Where would you be headed to in that fine automobile of yours today?"

Mr Prawoslaw recognised the man as Vladimir Glowaki, a poor farmer who had often traded foodstuffs grown on his farm for hardware and other goods at Mr Prawoslaw's store.

"Good morning to you too, Vladimir," Mr Prawoslaw replied. "I am going to visit my brother Jerzy and his family out here in the countryside. Maybe take in some fishing with my brother on the river."

"Would have been better to come out on horseback, Mr P. The pathway is very rough, and I wouldn't want to see you spoil that nice automobile of yours!"

"Yes, yes. You are correct, Vladimir. I'll keep that in mind the next time I venture out this way."

Mr Prawoslaw hated having to lie. However, he wanted to be careful not to divulge any details concerning his forthcoming travel plans to the local villagers. The fewer people who knew about his escape plan, the safer it would be.

As Vladimir squeezed by Mr Prawoslaw and the automobile on the narrow pathway in his wagon, he turned and said, "Hope you and Jerzy have a nice time fishing then."

Mr Prawoslaw was only eight kilometres away from his brother's farmstead when a major setback occurred. As careful as he had been in avoiding perils along the trail, one of the front wheels on the car rode up onto a large rock jutting out from the side of the path, covered in grassy weeds. Having surveyed the situation, he realised he could go no further without lifting the car up and away from the cumbersome boulder. He worried whether any damage had been done to the under carriage of the automobile, and if it would be possible to continue in the car once it was freed from the obstacle. Being the analytical man that he was, Mr Prawoslaw stood back for a while, deep in thought. In his mind, he played out all the possible scenarios to extricate the automobile, and concluded that he needed help. Planning to ask his brother to bring him back in his horse and wagon and assist in raising the car up and off the huge weatherworn stone, he had no choice but to walk the remaining distance to Jerzy's home.

Carefully checking to ensure that everything was securely hidden and locked up inside the boot of the car, Mr Prawoslaw then set out on foot. He was a rather large man, unaccustomed to walking any great distance. Now, feeling the strain as he plodded along the pathway leading to Jerzy's home, he was wishing he had heeded his wife's persistent nagging for him to drop a few pounds from his rotund belly. Mr Prawoslaw was most unsettled about the situation concerning the car. He had already experienced enough delay in his attempt to bring his family safely across the border into Romania. The window of opportunity was getting smaller and smaller with each passing day.

By the time Mr Prawoslaw arrived at Jerzy's home, the sun was already beginning to set. He caught sight of his daughter and one of her cousins bringing the cows into the barn from the surrounding field. It was not long before Lilyana noticed him in the distance. As soon as she realised it was her father who was coming up the trail, she dropped the stick she had been using to direct the cows into their nightly shelter and ran toward him, shouting, "Mother, Mother! Come quickly! It is Father! He is coming! I can see him coming to the farm!"

Within a matter of seconds, Jerzy's head popped out from behind the large barn door where he had been pushing the cows into their stalls. The farmhouse door suddenly tore open, and Olisia was seen lifting her long skirts as she cautiously hopped and jumped across the length of the farmyard, all the while trying to avoid colliding with any of the chickens or goats that roamed around freely. Not far behind his wife, Mr Prawoslaw saw Jerzy's wife, Janina, in fast pursuit. Her progress became impeded as she lifted her youngest child up and continued running across the uneven ground with babe in arms. Soon all five of Jerzy's children had joined the entourage as Lilyana led them down the laneway to greet her father.

There were words of welcome exchanged, many hugs and kisses all around, and then the family made its way toward the farmhouse as excited chatter and questions ensued: *Why had it taken him so long to come? Where was his car? Was the family still going to attempt their emigration plan to cousin Tadeusz's home in England? How would that be possible now? Where were the Prawoslaws' belongings that they were to take with them out of Poland? Had he been listening to the sporadic reports coming out of Western Poland, and did he know how vicious the fighting was in the west?*

Mr Prawoslaw waved his hands for everyone to be silenced. Then he said, "We will talk about all these things once I am seated in the house and have recovered from my long walk. Janina, would it be too much trouble to ask you if I could have a cold glass of water? It has been a long and difficult day."

"I was beginning to worry whether you would ever arrive!" his wife, Olisia, murmured. "I feared something bad may have happened to you. I believe it is only a matter of time before the Germans march into Eastern Poland now. We must leave quickly before that happens!"

"Yes, yes, my dear Olisia," Mr Prawoslaw said as he tried to calm her.

It was obvious she had grown anxious during the weeks while she waited for her husband to come. Olisia Prawoslaw had always been a high-strung, emotional sort of woman.

"And how will we manage to escape the Nazi soldiers if we are to reach England?" she continued. "The Germans are all around us in the north, west and south. It will be impossible to make our journey safely now!"

"Dear wife, I have a plan," Mr Prawoslaw interjected. "Let us sit down around the table, and I will propose what I believe we must do now."

Mr Prawoslaw carefully divulged the details of his new plan, explaining the alternate route and destination he felt the family should follow if they were to find safe passage out of Poland. He asked Jerzy how he felt about the revised plan. A few months beforehand, Mr Prawoslaw had visited his brother at the farm and sworn him to secrecy as he disclosed his plan to leave Poland, taking Olisia and Lilyana with him to England. He had strongly suggested that Jerzy and his family should join them. His brother had been shocked and had insisted he would remain in Poland on the family farm with his wife and children. Like so many others, Jerzy had failed to see the harbingers of war that had been sadly adding up. Mr Prawoslaw had warned his brother that war was inevitable and advised him to leave the country before Hitler came marching into Poland. He had cautioned Jerzy, saying that the Nazis would intrude upon their farm and their land would be lost to Germany. Jerzy's older sons would soon be of age to be called up into the army, and they would be forced to fight. Mr Prawoslaw urged his brother to seriously consider the consequences of remaining in Poland, when there was a way to avoid what he considered to be a catastrophe ahead.

Weeks later, when the Germans attacked Poland, Jerzy realised his older brother had been right. He went into Stolpce to meet with his brother at the hardware store, and they had secretly agreed to leave Poland together with their families.

Everyone listened intently as Mr Prawoslaw told them what things they should take with them, and what should be left behind. He said they should prepare to leave early the next morning. At first light, he and Jerzy would go to collect the car from where he had left it, and once they had released it from the huge rock, he would drive back to the farm to collect his wife and daughter. Jerzy would return with his large wagon to gather up his family and their belongings. Then they would make their way out to the main road leading them south to the Romanian border.

Jerzy's main concern now was for the farm animals that would be left behind to care for themselves. Two of his younger children began to cry at the thought of abandoning the animals they were fond of. Lilyana was able to quiet her cousins, Larissa and Michal, by telling them that their animals would instinctively migrate to where they could find food around the neighbouring farms. She said the neighbours would eventually be happy to adopt their cows, chickens and goats when they realised nobody was living at the Prawoslaw farm any longer. Lilyana had always been good with younger children, and her logical solution for their animals' predicament seemed to satisfy Larissa and Michal.

One of Jerzy's older sons came up with the notion that they should ask the neighbouring farmers to watch out for their farm and the animals while the family was away. The farm had never been left unattended before. Either Jerzy or Janina would always be there to oversee the farm work and care for the livestock; even on market days when one of them drove the wagon into Stolpce, the other would remain at the farm. Jerzy pointed out that the surrounding farmers would intuitively know the Prawoslaws were making a dash to the Romanian border to escape. Reluctantly, Mr Prawoslaw informed the family that nobody else could know about their plan. He believed many of the people among the minorities in Eastern Poland could not be trusted, and if any of them got wind of what the Prawoslaws were about to do, they would not hesitate to inform the authorities, as long as there was something to gain for themselves in the process. There were many people from ethnic minorities who farmed in this area, and he didn't want to take a chance on any of them revealing his family's plans before they were able to escape.

It did not take long for Jerzy and Janina to pack up their things that evening. They had prepared their belongings long before Mr Prawoslaw arrived, as they had been waiting in readiness for him to come. Guided by his instructions, they needed to eliminate some of the bulkier items from their load and replace them with more essential necessities, including the flour, salt, sugar, tea and lard that Janina had been storing in great amounts inside sacks and jars since the war began. Jerzy was not a wealthy man like his older brother, so he did not have much of value to offer for trade or barter along their journey. However, Mr Prawoslaw said he had many items stowed away in the boot of his car to assist all the family in securing safe passage away from Poland. Jerzy and Janina's generous supply of food would be quite sufficient.

***

It was an unusually warm and sunny September. Normally the autumn rains transformed the country roads into mud, but that year the rains arrived later than usual. Mr Prawoslaw took this as a good omen. Even though time was running out, conditions were still favourable for his family to flee.

Early in the morning, Jerzy helped his older brother step up into his horse-drawn wagon, and together they set off to retrieve Mr Prawoslaw's automobile. The women remained at the house clearing away the breakfast dishes, packing a few last-minute things and preparing the children for their journey. Jerzy and Janina's two oldest children, fifteen-year-old Wasyl and thirteen- year-old Aleksander, went about their usual morning chores around the barn, trying to make things appear normal in case any of the neighbouring farmers should happen by. Then they turned the cows out into the open field one last time.

Lilyana stayed inside, helping her mother and her aunt. She washed up little Danuta's chubby hands and face. She loved her baby cousin very much. One day, she hoped to marry and have lots of babies just like Danuta. She had fancied marrying Jozef Nowakowski. What a handsome young man he was, and well-mannered too! Even her father, who was a difficult man to please, approved of Jozef. Father had often remarked on how hardworking young Jozef was, and mentioned how impressed he was with the way Jozef had taken over managing his family's farm following Mr Nowakowski's tragic accident. Her father and Mr Nowakowski had been good friends. They both had served on the Agricultural Board in Stolpce years before.

She could not help feeling heavy-hearted now. Lilyana had grown very fond of Jozef, and she knew he cared very much for her as well. Just a month or so earlier, they had taken a walk together to the wide bridge that spanned the Neman River. It had been a glorious afternoon. They had taken in sights of the boats putting along the water, some with sails billowing in the warm breeze and others gliding along to the rhythm of splashing oars. The sound of the paddles hitting the water seemed to move in unison with the melody of birdsong coming from among the trees lining the riverbank. From the top of the wooden bridge, they could see where the bustling town gave way to fields and wooded valleys in the distance. It was one of the most picturesque spots in the region. The view from the river had always been breathtaking as unspoiled scenery full of beauty and history came into view.

Jozef had taken to calling her *Lily* on that day. He had stolen her heart with a gentle kiss on the lips by the bridge, then whispered in her ear that he loved her. He was the only young man Lilyana could ever imagine marrying, even though there had been others who had tried and failed to get close to her heart. She blushed now at the memory of how Jozef's brother Tobias had teased the two of them upon their return to the mercantile store that afternoon.

"Oh, I see. Another Nowakowski wedding may be in the offing!" Tobias had yelled from behind the bins of nails stacked neatly by the door of the store as Jozef and Lilyana approached hand in hand.

Jozef had looked mortified, and Lilyana had put her head down and started to scrape at the floor with her shoe, as if trying to push some invisible debris out of the way in the aisle where she and Jozef had stood. She dreaded Jozef noticing how rosy her cheeks had become at his brother's off-handed remark.

Now, all Lilyana could think about was the fact that she would never see dear Jozef again... not even to say goodbye! Sadly, her father had unexpectedly insisted she and her mother be taken to Uncle Jerzy and Aunt Janina's farm the next morning, where they were to wait for him.

Her heart ached, and she found herself brushing away uncontrollable tears. Shortly after arriving at her uncle's farm a few weeks earlier, Lilyana had climbed up into the hayloft in the barn, and she had cried silently for hours. She grieved having to leave Poland, and more so, she mourned leaving behind the young man who had taken hold of her heart and enveloped her with feelings of love. She hated being so vulnerable and upset, but now that her family's exit from Poland was becoming a reality, all she could think of was Jozef. She had not even had an opportunity to speak with him and explain her sudden disappearance from Stolpce. What must he be thinking of her now?

"Lilyana... Lilyana... when are you going to help me get my dolly ready for our adventure?" eight-year-old Larissa begged as she tugged at her cousin's apron. "Why are you crying? What is wrong?"

"Oh... it is nothing," Lilyana managed to stammer as she hastily dried her eyes and attempted to refocus on the task of helping the younger children.

Just then, Wasyl came rushing into the farmhouse. Beads of sweat were forming across his brow, and he was breathing very heavily. He had obviously come running in from the fields a good distance away.

"Just heard about it," Wasyl blurted out. "The Russians. They have declared war on Poland! Farmer Lachowicz rode in to tell Father. He saw me in the field, and he told me to go and tell my family!"

There was an instantaneous and audible gasp of horror that came simultaneously from Olisia and Aunt Janina.

"What does it mean?" Olisia questioned. She clutched her breast and demanded, "Where is my husband? He must know about this immediately. What are we to do about our travel plans now?"

"How does Mr Lachowicz know this?" Aunt Janina snorted.

Still flushed and breathless, Wasyl continued, "He said that his son heard the news on the radio broadcast coming from the south just now. The Polish guards at the border patrol are saying the Romanian border guards told them the Soviets have declared war! Russian planes have started to drop bombs in the southeast, and they report that Russian tanks are moving toward our border, followed by machine guns and the Red Army!"

Olisia steadied herself as she made her way to a nearby chair and sat down.

"Well, this news could all be a mistake!" she exclaimed. "Perhaps they have it wrong! Rumours of that pact between the Germans and the Russians have put all Poles on edge… but I think it is not probable that the *Russians* will attack us!"

A degree of panic was notable in Olisia's voice despite her confident words.

Meanwhile, Mr Prawoslaw and Jerzy had reached the spot where the car had run aground and they were working to lift the automobile off the massive rock. With a great deal of manoeuvring they finally managed to free it. Jerzy crawled underneath the car and gave it a good inspection, looking for any consequential damages.

"Seems good to me," he called out. "Just a small dent below the front fender, but nothing leaking, nor any mechanical problems that I can see."

"Good!" Mr Prawoslaw replied. "Then I shall start the engine and see how it is running."

Jerzy was more familiar with the trail leading to his farm, so he went in front of his brother in the wagon, steering Mr Prawoslaw's car away from the remaining danger areas along the path. As they passed by the other farmsteads, Jerzy noticed that things appeared unusually quiet. This was a busy time of year for the farmers, with a lot of work that needed to be done. Something did not feel right, and Jerzy became increasingly apprehensive. As soon as they reached the farm, Wasyl came running into the yard to tell his father and uncle the news that Mr Lachowicz had delivered.

"The *Russians!*" Mr Prawoslaw and Jerzy both exclaimed when they heard what Wasyl had to say.

"Never could trust those Communists!" Jerzy muttered angrily. "We should have seen this coming when they supposedly signed that pact with the Germans!"

"We must move quickly," Mr Prawoslaw declared. "Jerzy, collect your family and cram as much as you can into that wagon of yours. Olisia and Lilyana, get into the car. We will pack as much as we can in the automobile as well. We must leave immediately before the Red Army has a chance to come marching in!"

Loaded down with everything they could possibly manage to take along, the family started out toward the main road leading them to the Romanian frontier. They gradually became swept up in a procession of people hurrying to the border. Everybody was talking about the unexpected turn of events that day. The one-way traffic was jammed with everything imaginable. Cars, lorries, buses, horse-drawn carts and wagons, tractors and even a few vehicles loaded with weapons and mounted with heavy firearms rolled toward Romania. Military men had joined the procession. A Polish soldier rode past them on horseback and announced that he had received official word the Red Army was already advancing toward Poland. From what little information he had gathered, he believed the Soviets were not far away, across the river in the southeast. Polish troops had blown apart the only bridge in that area, and he reckoned that would hold off the Red Army from entering Poland until the following morning.

Mr Prawoslaw and Jerzy cautiously glanced at each other upon hearing the news. Neither one said a word, but both knew what the other was thinking. If what the soldier had told them was correct, there was no way to reach the border before the Russian troops marched into Poland. The border was a few hundred kilometres away. Even if they were to travel all that day and through the night, it would be impossible to get there in time. Progress was slow in the heavy traffic, and Jerzy's two horses wouldn't cover that distance in such a short time.

"Brother, if you hurry you may be able to reach the border with your family in that car before the Russians arrive. You could move more quickly if you passed along some of the extra baggage my family has burdened you with to others who may need it along the route. You could reach the border before morning, ahead of the Bolsheviks charging in."

Mr Prawoslaw lifted one hand off his steering wheel and waved it in the air.

"No, no," he told Jerzy. "Brothers stick together, always. You and I will look out for each other and for each other's families. I will not hurry to the border without you, your wife and your children. Do not even suggest such a terrible thing!"

"But wouldn't it be better to have some of us safe, than none safely across the border?"

Jerzy spoke the truth. Mr Prawoslaw may have been able to rush ahead of the crowd along the shoulder of the road and arrive at the Romanian border before sun-up the next morning in his speedy automobile. However, he refused to break ranks with his only brother. They would stick it out together, no matter what uncertainties the future held for them.

Mr Prawoslaw began to question his recent actions. Why had he taken so long to tie up his affairs in Stolpce instead of going to fetch his family earlier as he had originally planned? If he had left in mid-August when he sent his wife and Lilyana to his brother's farm, the family would have had ample time to escape from Poland. If he had not dragged his feet in closing the store, he could have slipped away much sooner and the family would have been miles away from Poland already. Why hadn't he taken care of his banking affairs sooner when war clouds had begun to gather on the horizon? These questions, and a great deal of self-doubt, began to eat away at Mr Prawoslaw as the family continued their journey south. However, he knew the situation was what it was, and now there was nothing he could do to change it.

"What will we do when the Red Army troops approach us on the road?" Jerzy asked. "If it is true they are already close to the border, they surely will be crossing over and marching up this road some time tomorrow. We will be travelling straight into their path!"

"Yes, my brother," Mr Prawoslaw said as he drew in a deep puff on his cigarette. "I have been pondering that question as well. We must make our way back to your farm through the forest."

Jerzy said nothing for a long time, but after due consideration, he replied, "Then that is what we will do. Once we have safely returned to the farm, we will do whatever it takes to keep our families safe!"

"The hunting trails we used to walk along when we were boys are somewhere around the woodlands here, are they not, Jerzy? Do those paths still weave among the trees and underbrush from the farm to this location? If they do, we must circumvent the Russians by moving away from this traffic on the road. It will do no good to continue south to the border. As you say, the road will direct us straight into the waiting arms of the enemy. We have no choice but to change our plan, and return home."

"The boys and I still hunt out this way every year," Jerzy replied. "There is a passageway through the forest a short distance ahead. If we continue south for another couple of kilometres, we will arrive at an area where the densely wooded growth becomes sparse. We will be able to make our way onto a woodland trail there, but we will need daylight to see our way through. It is rather dark in the dense woods."

"We should make camp at the location you are referring to," Mr Prawoslaw said. "If we leave at daybreak tomorrow morning and find our way north, we should be able to arrive back at the farmstead before evening. My automobile and your wagon will have to be hidden in the forest as they cannot be driven through the thick foliage and the hilly terrain. Perhaps we can load up the horses with some of our belongings and coax the animals through the forest with us? We have the axe and other tools to force a wider trail through the denser parts if we need to."

Giving the plan further thought, Jerzy again insisted that his older brother should make haste with his family toward the border in the car before the Russians had a chance to march into Poland. He suggested that perhaps Mr Prawoslaw take Janina and the three youngest of his children to safety in the automobile as well. He and his two older sons, Wasyl and Aleksander, could venture into the woodlands and return to the farm tomorrow... but once again, Mr Prawoslaw refused to rush on ahead. He would never leave his brother and his two older nephews behind.

Progress remained slow as many assorted vehicles, animals and people continued to creep along the road in a southerly stream. When the afternoon hours merged into evening and the sun began to fall, many people in the endless procession started pulling over to the sides of the road. Some families prepared small meals over open flames in pots and pans they had brought with them. There was a strong sense of comradeship among the ethnic Poles now. Some offered tea and food to those who had rushed away so quickly from their homes that they neglected to bring any rations with them.

The Prawoslaws pulled over at the location where Jerzy indicted the woodland trail was located. It was a pretty spot among the trees with a small creek that trickled nearby. Olisia and Aunt Janina made up a quick flatbread with the flour, salt and lard that had been stowed away in preparation for their journey. Lilyana set to work cutting up pieces of the sausage and cheese they had brought along.

The smaller children played by the creek with some other youngsters they met at the impromptu camping area near the roadside. Baby Danuta seemed to sense something ominous was brewing. Being too young to grasp what was happening, she refused to settle down for the night, no matter what Aunt Janina tried. Eventually, the baby was passed along into Lilyana's arms, and she managed to quiet the infant as she rocked her to sleep.

Throughout the night, shadows of passers-by continued in an endless flow toward the south. Silhouettes of automobiles, noisy lorries, soldiers on horses clopping by and wagons loaded with people and their belongings fluttered past like apparitions. Their outlines were etched in the lights of vehicles and lanterns people carried to light their nightly passage along the road.

Lilyana forced herself to stay awake all night. She hoped to see some sign of Jozef making his way south, but by the time the sun began to rise the following morning, there had been no sign of her dear friend.

The sun had barely risen when the Prawoslaw family prepared to pull away from the roadside into the forest. Mr Prawoslaw had long since given up his hunting days, but he was happy Jerzy still ventured out with his sons and was familiar with the forest here. Jerzy would be responsible for leading the family back to his farm.

Before they made their way into the woodlands, they needed to sort through all the baggage they had brought along. Some of the linen sacks were emptied and their contents evaluated to determine what should be taken back to the farm and what could remain locked up and hidden inside the car in the forest. Some passers-by questioned what they were doing. Mr Prawoslaw explained that it was no longer possible to escape across the border before the Russians came marching into Poland up the road they were travelling on. Some scoffed and insisted that it would be a few days yet before the Bolsheviks arrived, if indeed the news regarding the Soviets was even true. Others considered what Mr Prawoslaw said and debated the issue among themselves as they continued toward Romania.

The uncertainty of those who doubted disintegrated quickly when a Soviet reconnaissance plane flew overhead and let out a shattering explosion of gunfire. Bullets hit the ground along the side of the road. As the plane circled around, people travelling on the road were terrified. Russian red stars illuminated on both wings of the plane clearly came into view, and at that pivotal moment, those who had been in denial suddenly realised that the vague reports concerning the Soviets' declaration of war on Poland were true.

Panic and chaos followed. Many people tried to take cover in the tree line along the roadside. Others scattered and ran further to hide among the larger trees in the nearby forest. Spooked horses reared up, tossing some soldiers and civilians from their mounts. A couple of wagons were overturned, throwing their contents and their inhabitants out onto the road. Women screamed, and children clung to their parents in horror. Babies cried, and men reached for their rifles and other weapons they had brought with them. As the yelling and stampeding continued, the Russian plane lifted higher and flew off in a northerly direction. More machine gun fire could be heard in the distance.

Mr Prawoslaw helped Jerzy calm his two horses and gently coaxed them into a thicket of underbrush near the road. His voice was barely audible above all the noise and confusion.

"Those were merely warning shots!" he yelled. "The Russians are sending us a clear message. They want us to know they are here, and if any of us think it is possible to reach the border now, they will shoot us down like sitting ducks!"

"You are quite right," Jerzy responded. "We must make haste if we are to arrive back at the farm safely. Help me unhitch the wagon in those trees over there. We will fill the sacks with the necessities we need to take and load them onto the horses. We should head off into the forest quickly."

Lilyana's voice was faintly heard as she called for her father to come and help calm her mother. Olisia Prawoslaw sat rigid in the front seat of the car, hyperventilating. She clutched at her throat as sweat poured from her flushed face and she made loud gasping sounds. Olisia had always been prone to nervousness and panic attacks. The sudden appearance of the Soviet plane and brief burst of bullets raining down was more than she could handle. Mr Praowslaw was the only one who could ease her episodes of neurotic fright.

Lilyana noticed that Wasyl and Aleksander were busy helping her uncle handle the horses, so she went quickly to assist Aunt Janina with the younger children. The baby was clinging so tightly to her aunt that red marks were forming on Janina's arms where Danuta had latched on. Larissa and Michal were hanging on to her legs tightly with tears streaming down their cheeks. It was the first moment of real terror they had known in their young lives.

With the wagon and car hidden among a thick outgrowth of trees set a good distance back from the road, the Prawoslaws made their way into the forest trail on foot. Many other families seemed to have come to the same conclusion now, and it was a large group of people that began the difficult trek back to their farms through the woodlands. Each family gradually disappeared into the tangled mix of trees and forest growth as they went their separate ways. Jerzy and his older sons chopped and hacked at the trees and bushes that hampered their progress. Though more challenging, the route back to the farmstead through the forest was shorter and safer than having to wind their way around the entire region along the main road that remained cluttered with a procession of people and animals heading south.

***

Lilyana never forgot the difficult trek back to her uncle's farm that day. The woodlands were riddled with winding streams, sharp drop-offs from rocky ridges, and steep inclines that had to be climbed. She struggled to help her younger cousins make their way back to the farm. Larissa and Michal fell several times as they tripped over large tree roots buried among drifts of dead leaves and underbrush. Their knees and hands became badly cut and bruised, small bits of twigs and dirt embedded in their wounds. They cried and sobbed as the family continued deeper into the forest. Olisia, still very shaken by the machine gun fire, did little to help the children. She required just as much encouragement and coaxing to keep her going through the web of trees and wooded vegetation. Mr Prawoslaw had to carry his wife across the stony pathways over the flowing creeks, and he had to pull her up all the hilly rises they encountered along the way. He grew tired from the exertion, and several times they had to stop and rest before he could continue. The horses protested at several points where the declines to lower ground became rather steep, and they stubbornly refused to get going again every time they came to flowing water and wanted to drink. Baby Danuta had to be carried the entire way, and as her weight became progressively more difficult to manage, she was passed around between Aunt Janina, Lilyana, Wasyl and Aleksander. She shrieked and screamed each time she was taken from her mother's arms, and due to the unsettling circumstances, she developed a bowel problem that needed to be dealt with.

However, despite all the obstacles, before the sun fell behind the tree line, the Prawoslaws made their way out of the forest and into the valley of meadowlands and fields where Jerzy's farm was located.

***

A few days later, the Prawoslaws learned the Polish government had gone into exile in France, having fallen to the invasions by Germany and Russia, without surrendering. The Soviet soldiers arrived at Stolpce swiftly, as the town was positioned not too far from the Russian border. The Red Army seized Stolpce with little effort. Within hours of capture, Russian tanks had moved in and the Soviets were in control of the town. Stolpce was the heart of business and commerce for all the surrounding villages, but now extensive damage had been done to many of the town's businesses and her commercial core was annihilated. Persons of interest were being rounded up and brought into the hastily prepared headquarters of the NKVD for questioning. The first days of military occupation initiated many atrocities and war crimes against Polish military personnel and civilians. Rumours of these things quickly echoed from the town and across the countryside.

At the end of September, after the Germans and the Soviets had declared new borders in the former Polish state, they promised the people living there a peaceful life. Nevertheless, instead of practising peace and order, both Germany and the Soviet Union inflicted horror on the Polish inhabitants. Their mutual goal was to completely eradicate the Polish people forever. Their reign of terror continued with increasing oppression and persecution as the days, weeks and months passed.

The Prawoslaws tried to resume their daily activities back at the farm, but they worried about the atrocious things they heard were happening in Stolpce. It was difficult to carry on as normal. The men and the boys picked up where they had left off and tried to proceed with work around the farmstead. Aunt Janina, Olisia and Lilyana reluctantly began the usual rounds of pickling and preserving as the men and children brought in the seasonal harvest.

Mr Prawoslaw felt awkward and out of place on the farm. He had left his days of manual labour far behind when he moved into Stolpce and became a practising businessman many years before. He found himself frequenting Farmer Lachowicz's home, where the man's son had a radio he could listen to. Sporadic reports continued to flow in at intervals, and Mr Prawoslaw was curious to keep informed about what was happening in the world beyond the confines of the farm. He was never one to sit idly by and do nothing when things of a serious nature occurred. He grew increasingly restless as the days went by, and finally he could bear it no longer—he needed to go into town and see for himself what was happening. He was a well-respected and prominent businessman; perhaps he could be of some help to the townsfolk, rather than hiding at his brother's farm and waiting for disaster to reach them.

Knowing his family would do everything they could to dissuade him from returning to Stolpce, Mr Prawoslaw managed to talk Farmer Lachowicz's son into secretly taking him to the town by horse and wagon. It did not take much for Mr Prawoslaw to persuade the young fellow to help him carry out their covert mission. The boy was most enthusiastic, and he looked forward to the adventure. Being a lad of sixteen years, the intrigue of sneaking off into town and seeing the Red Army soldiers in command was most appealing.

One morning in early October, the man and the boy skulked off to Stolpce while their families slept. It was a relatively uneventful trip into town, but once they arrived, things changed dramatically.

From atop the wide bridge leading into Stolpce, Mr Prawoslaw and the lad viewed a couple of Soviet tanks and many canvas-covered lorries parked along the main road.

One of the open-backed lorries was occupied by a few soldiers who were smoking and playing a round of cards. They were laughing loudly and poking at each other as a bottle of vodka was passed around. Russian words and personal insults could be heard freely floating from the lorry into the air above the river.

Mr Prawoslaw and the lad had hardly left the bridge into town when several members of the newly formed Communist Militia suddenly appeared and surrounded them. They ordered the wagon to stop. At first, the young boy was elated. He had never encountered an event of this magnitude before. He even recognized a couple of the militiamen as older boys from the school he attended in town. They were still dressed in their civilian clothes, but they wore the distinct red armbands that identified them as members of the Communist Party. These militiamen had formed the new civil or policing force whose job it was to maintain order, and to report any discrepancies to the Russian secret police. The Polish police force had been dissolved, and its members had been arrested. All former Polish policemen were now enemies of the socialist system and the working classes, according to the Soviets.

Within seconds of being stopped, Mr Prawoslaw and the boy were ordered to get down from the wagon with their hands in the air. One of the militiamen had alerted an NKVD officer who began coming toward them. Mr Prawoslaw and the boy were thoroughly searched for hidden weapons, and when Mr Prawoslaw's rifle was removed from the wagon, both he and the lad were arrested. They were promptly marched along the road and held captive in the school gymnasium, which had quickly been made over into a prison. Several other captives were also being held there.

Mr Prawoslaw was in shock. Although he'd known the Soviets had taken hold of the town, he had not anticipated that he and the boy would be denied access to venture along the road in an open horse-drawn wagon. He had not only put his own wellbeing in jeopardy, but he had also put a stain on the young Lachowicz boy; he knew from historical record that this boy would be marked as an anti-Soviet conspirator for the rest of his life. Wherever the boy's life would lead, his wellbeing would always be in question if the Bolsheviks were in command.

"Mr Prawoslaw! I wondered what had happened to you and your family. I hoped you had escaped to Romania!"

Calling out to him inside the gymnasium/prison was Mr Riznyk, a lawyer friend whom Mr Prawoslaw knew from his business dealings in town. The lawyer's usual tidy appearance left somewhat to be desired now. His hair was matted, his shirt wrinkled and askew, his face unshaven, and large, dark circles surrounded his puffy red eyes that sorely peered out at Mr Prawoslaw.

"Oh, Mr Riznyk, my dear man… What has happened to you?" Mr Prawoslaw blurted out. "You are not looking well!"

"Soviets!" Mr Riznyk replied. "They arrested me in my office after they seized the town. I was preparing to leave the country. I had paid a Romanian citizen to smuggle me across the border, but before I could get to the pre-arranged meeting location, the NKVD barged into my office and took me captive. Lousy conspirators! I am sure it was the Romanian who took my money and then reported me. The Soviets found me with my passport and foreign currency on my person. Now they torture and interrogate me every night, demanding that I give them the names of other collaborators. We are all doomed, my friend. There is no escape now. Our plight lies in the mercy of their hands!"

"But they have not shot you!" Mr Prawoslaw hastened to point out.

"It is only a matter of time, my friend. For whatever reason, the Russians insist that I have information on anti-Soviet subversives in Stolpce. When they finally believe I do not, I will be marched outside and shot." The dejected look on Mr Riznyk's face cast pain on his words as he spoke.

"What is going to happen to us then?" the young Lachowicz boy dared to ask. Only now was he beginning to realise the seriousness of the situation.

"What is going to happen indeed!" a gruff voice yelled from a distance across the gymnasium. "How naïve can you be! Unless we escape from this infernal prison, we are going to die, of course… like all the others who have been led from this place out into the field… to be shot… DEAD!"

"What is this lunatic talking about?" the boy asked defensively. "They're not going to shoot us! We've done nothing to them. Surely, they will just question us and let us go on our way. I will be back at my father's farm long before nightfall this evening!"

Low groans and snorts echoed throughout the gymnasium as the captive men offered up a variety of opinions and conclusions. The Lachowicz boy started asking himself why he had allowed Mr Prawoslaw to convince him so easily to drive him into Stolpce. For a sense of adventure, his very life was now in peril! Farmer Lachowicz had told all his children to stay far away from the town. He had warned them they would meet with danger and uncertainty if they ventured out this way. Why hadn't he heeded his own father's words? More than anything, he wanted to believe he would be returned to his family… and then he would welcome the belting his father would certainly give him for having disregarded the warning!

Seeing how distraught the lad was, Mr Prawoslaw put a reassuring hand on his shoulder and told him everything would be alright. He told the young boy that no matter what happened to the other prisoners being held in the gymnasium, the Soviets would spare him as he was so young, and he'd done nothing the Russians could accuse him of.

"They will see you are not yet a man, and they will turn you out onto the street to return home to your mother," Mr Prawoslaw assured him. "What harm can a mere boy like you do to them? The Bolsheviks will know this, and they will set you free. When you return to your farm, please get word to my dear Olisia that I have been delayed in Stolpce. Do not tell her that I have been detained in this prison. Just tell her that I will be back at my brother's farm soon… and please extend my sincerest apologies to your father. I should never have convinced you to come with me. It is my fault. What was I thinking? Tell your father I said to take it easy on you. It is I who should be throttled, not you!"

Mr Prawoslaw really did believe the boy would be freed. However, he was not so ignorant as to assume he would be granted the same liberty himself. Other prisoners were offering up all kinds of sordid details about their fates. The more facts he was made privy to, the keener his sense of impending doom became.

The other prisoners informed him that the Communists had gathered information pertaining to all Polish citizens living in Stolpce. People from the ethnic minorities had helped the Soviets compile lists of names. Any individual who had held a position of power or authority within the community was a suspect and had either been called in for questioning by the NKVD or shot in the streets.

As soon as the Red Army had entered Poland, they immediately eradicated all active politicians. The Russians had already prepared lists of the more prominent men in politics, trade unions and cultural associations, and had arrested all those individuals within the first few days of occupation. Mr Riznyk speculated it was due to the fact those people all played an integral part in the workers' movement and in the struggle for democracy against Hitlerism and fascism that many of them had been executed. Many more had been sentenced to years of forced labour in concentration camps, while the fate of others remained unknown. In all probability, they had been killed. Anyone who had previous associations with anti-Soviet organisations, people whose fathers had fought in the Russo-Polish War twenty years earlier, soldiers, anybody affiliated with the Polish military, and all the educated classes—lawyers, judges, professors, doctors, scientists, engineers, teachers, priests, accountants and businessmen—were all in jeopardy. So too were any persons who had taken part in organisations before the war, including the boy scouts, voluntary firefighters, the Red Cross, persons active in religious parishes, aristocrats, landowners, wealthy merchants, bankers, industrialists, and hotel and restaurant proprietors. Mr Prawoslaw learned that endless numbers of people, those deemed to be even remotely associated with any counter-revolutionary elements, were also being arrested in town and subjected to long, nasty, repeated interrogations. Houses in Stolpce were being searched for no reason, and people on the streets were being stopped and searched. Groups of innocent people walking on the streets were being ambushed by the militiamen and NKVD agents and then separated. They would be questioned individually and asked what they had been talking about. If their answers did not line up with what the others from the group had said, they would all be arrested and interrogated. In the middle of the night, the NKVD and militia were taking men from their homes while telling their wives and children they would be returned very shortly. The families would never see their husbands or fathers again.

Arrests had become a daily reality. Within days of the Soviet occupation, there was no class of person exempt from this occurrence. Factory workers, farmers and peasants, young and old, mainly ethnic Poles, were mysteriously disappearing in the middle of the night. All were considered suspect by the Soviet government, which did not feel secure in its occupied territory. The Russians realised that most of the population wanted to remain as a Polish state, and they knew that the Poles were not suited to accepting a Communist regime. Hence, the mass deportations of Polish people to the interior of Russia, making them disappear, their places in Poland to be taken by disciplined Soviet citizens who would comply with the Communist Party's agenda.

Mr Prawoslaw's heart sank. He had good reason to worry. He knew his name would appear near the top of those lists of so-called anti-Soviet elements. Without a doubt, he was a marked man. He had been an affluent businessman within the community, he had wielded power and authority in his tenure for many years on several committees, and he'd served as an influential citizen in the region. In addition to that, he had completed his mandatory military training as a teenage boy, his father had fought against the Russians in the war twenty years earlier, and he had been a staunch member of an anti-Soviet underground group when he was a younger man. He had not yet been interrogated, but he knew there would be no way to escape the details of his past. Even if he were to lie about who he was, where he had come from and what his intentions were, the newly appointed militiamen would trip over each other to be the first to inform the NKVD all about him. They would readily put a name to his face and give the secret police an account of his public life and political legacy in Stolpce.

The young Lachowicz boy was not returned to his family's farm that day, nor did he ever see the farm or his family again. In the middle of the night, he was poked awake by the long end of a guard's rifle and taken away to another area of the school. A painful and cruel interrogation began. Repeatedly, the NKVD officer asked: surname, given name, year of birth, place of birth, nationality, and tell me about yourself… details of your business here… your reason for entering Stolpce? It seemed that the officer was trying to wear the lad down gradually, to trip him up in some way or force a confession from him for some crime he had not committed. The questions were being asked in Russian, and the boy only knew what little of the language he had learned in school. In Polish, the Lachowicz boy kept asking the officer to repeat the questions, not fully understanding what he had been asked. This was obviously irritating the NKVD officer, who kept shouting for the boy to stop using Polish. The young fellow was nervous and frightened. With artful deception, the officer had quickly trumped up fraudulent charges against the boy and got him to sign a paper written in Russian, admitting to wrongful offenses. The young boy was deemed an anti-Soviet supporter, accused of counter-revolutionary activities. Following several months of imprisonment in many makeshift prisons, he would be doomed into exile. He rode the rails in the same prisoner cars that Jozef Nowakoski did in February, into the dreaded Siberian wasteland.

Mr Prawoslaw would not be given a chance to plead his case. There would be no privilege of an interrogation for him. As he feared, members from the local People's Militia had readily identified him and reported their findings to the NKVD. The secret police had been looking for him for a while; his name had indeed appeared near the top of several Soviet lists of undesirable persons. They had torn apart his home and his place of business in Stolpce searching for his whereabouts. In the middle of the night, two NKVD officers appeared and escorted Mr Prawoslaw outside to the field behind the school. Three militiamen eagerly verified his identity.

Before his execution, Mr Prawoslaw recognised one of the men who came to seal his fate. It was Vladimir Glowaki, the poor farmer he had spoken to on the trail leading to Jerzy's farm. Vladimir stood before him, proudly sporting the red armband.

"I see you have chosen to become a Communist, Vladimir," Mr Prawoslaw managed to state. "Have you been tricked by years of Soviet propaganda?"

"Better to be a Communist than one among the minority class in Poland!" Vladimir spat back at him. "My family has been in want and need for too long. The Soviets have jobs to offer. My family will never go hungry again!"

Vladimir, a Polish-Ukranian by birth, was speaking in very broken Russian now, attempting to make a display of his newfound position. It was obvious that the man was feeling a sense of self-importance. Being chosen as a member of the People's Militia seemed to have helped him overcome feelings of inferiority that had plagued him throughout his life.

"What would you know about these things?" Vladimir continued. "You… a wealthy capitalist! You are an enemy of the people. Now you will pay for your sins with your life!"

"Is it a sin to help your fellow citizens live better, Vladimir? Is it wrong to lend a helpful hand to people who are in need? Is it not right to attend church and to practise living by God's laws, or to pass along food and clothing to the needy through charitable means? I have practised these things all my life. Why do you turn the truth around and accuse me of being an exploiter of the working class? Has your family not benefited from my very own hands throughout the years?"

What Mr Prawoslaw said was true. There had been many times when Vladimir turned up at the cash register in the hardware store without adequate funds to pay for the merchandise he wanted to buy. Mr Prawoslaw would simply pat him on the back and tell him he could pay up the remainder the next time he came into the store. With barely a thank you, Vladimir would leave with the goods tucked under his arm. He never did pay Mr Prawoslaw the full amount he owed for the merchandise, nor did he ever have any intention to—he knew Mr Prawoslaw would not insist he pay the outstanding balance for those purchases. Vladimir's family also benefitted very much from the charity of the church, and the Prawoslaws happened to be one of the major contributors in paying alms.

Mr Prawoslaw's words weighed heavily on Vladimir's conscience. He looked around and noticed that the NKVD agents and other militiamen were occupied with several prisoners who had been taken out into the field that night.

After a brief pause, Vladimir moved in closer and murmured quietly in Polish so that only Mr Prawoslaw could hear, "It is because you have helped my family in the past that I did not alert the secret police to your location when I knew you were at your brother's house in the country. I could have turned you in. But now you have been foolish enough to return to Stolpce, and you have left me no choice but to point you out."

The NKVD men approached, and Vladimir moved back. Mr Prawoslaw was shot through the head with a single bullet. He would be buried in a mass grave together with several other prominent men from the community who were brutally executed that night. His family would be left only to imagine what had happened to him following his sudden disappearance from his brother's farm early that October morning. Vladimir Glowaki would live the remainder of his days tormented by Mr Prawoslaw's candid last words.

***

When winter arrived, it set in with a vengeance. Frigid winds blew mountains of drifting snow everywhere and made the sub-zero temperatures feel even colder. Uncle Jerzy's farmhouse was a good deal draughtier than what Lilyana and her mother had grown accustomed to inside their luxurious house in Stolpce. Lilyana bundled on layers of shawls over her heavy winter dresses, and she piled many blankets on top of her mother's bed to keep her warm. Olisia Prawoslaw had taken to her bed shortly after her husband had vanished. His mysterious disappearance had angered and frustrated her at first, but within days she had slipped into a deep depression. Now she could not get out of bed or do anything useful. Olisia lay silent and still much of the time. She had to be forced to eat and drink. Whenever she thought about her missing husband or his peculiar departure, she would start to hyperventilate and succumb to severe attacks of panic. Lilyana would have to sit with her mother for hours, stroking her hair and telling her things she wanted to hear but knew would never be true again:

"It will be alright. Father has gone on a trip, but he will return to us soon. Everything will be back to normal before long."

Lilyana had to appear strong to keep her mother's sanity intact. Nevertheless, she was hurting deep inside, just as much as her mother. The repercussions of Lilyana's loss would last her a lifetime. Vivid images of the happy life she had shared with her parents at their home in Stolpce would remain imprinted in her memory forever.

Meanwhile, the People's Militia and the NKVD had started to move their roundups of innocent people further away from town. Reports were circulating about arrests and people disappearing from their homes in the countryside. Fear and feelings of vulnerability gripped people everywhere. Then came that fateful night in February when endless numbers of people—men, women and children—were turned out of their homes into the cruel winter elements. Whispers had rippled across the countryside. Those unfortunate souls had been taken to the train station in Stolpce, and people could only conclude that they had been forced into exile. Gossip spread about people having died in the snow on the way to the station, about people and their pets being shot if they refused to comply with the Soviets' wishes, and about the endless sorrow and suffering of thousands of Polish citizens at the hands of the merciless Russians.

Two families near Jerzy's farmstead vanished that night for inexplicable reasons. They had been poor farmers with little to show for all the toil on their small farms. The Soviets were becoming less selective in their choice of people to remove. All social classes were coming under scrutiny now.

It was obvious that anyone of Polish ethnicity was no longer safe in Soviet-occupied Poland. Risk-taking became a way of life. Within weeks of the Soviets entering Stolpce, Wasyl was approached by a group of young men from the town. They asked him to come to a secret meeting at one of the boy's homes. He did not hesitate to go. There were eleven local farm boys and three older boys from the village in attendance. Together they formed a cell in a secret underground army that had developed. One of the older boys acted as leader of their group. He would receive orders from ranks above. All the boys, ranging in age from fifteen to nineteen, were sworn by oath to never reveal any secrets of their organisation to anyone outside their cell. They were to report anything of interest from within their locality to their leader, who in turn would report to their superiors. Wasyl's family had no idea he had taken up activities with the Underground Army. He executed his duties within the cell clandestinely, and around the farm he continued his daily chores as normal.

Larissa and Michal were still able to go to the village school. At first their lessons remained unchanged, but soon the new politically correct subjects and books appeared as the Soviets attempted to instil their Communist ideals in the younger students. Wasyl and Aleksander could no longer attend high school in town as the building had closed when the Russian occupation began. The Red Army had taken over the school and transformed it into a barracks. It was believed the NKVD were using it for their headquarters and a prison.

Some of the older boys who had lived in Stolpce slipped away from the town quickly after the Red Army advanced. They spread out and were now staying with relatives on farms in the countryside. They told people in the farming villages stories about what was happening in Stolpce. They said that Soviet propaganda had sprung up everywhere. Red banners now stretched across the streets, inscribed with Russian slogans. A popular theme seemed to be "Long Live the Red Army." Communist propaganda posters, books and newspapers were freely available for everybody in town, and only Soviet films were being shown at the cinema. Anything distinctly Polish had quickly been removed and erased from sight.

The townspeople complained that food had become scarce. Some of the stores in town remained open, but the Russian soldiers were buying up everything. When the Red Army first arrived, the Soviet troops had been awestruck by the amount of merchandise that filled all the store shelves. Despite the Bolsheviks' insistence there was plenty of the same merchandise in Russia, it was clear to see that there was little for sale in their own state-run stores. The Poles speculated that the free market prices in the Soviet Union were inflated for what little there was to buy there. The Soviets found the prices for food and merchandise in Stolpce to be unbelievably low. They had an unending desire for everything and anything they could get their hands on, and the stores had all been emptied of merchandise and food.

One of the older boys in Wasyl's secret cell asked him to start delivering messages to a farmhouse near his family's home. That house had been designated as a 'safe house' affiliated with the Underground Army. The cell's leader felt it would not raise any suspicion if Wasyl were to deliver messages and packages there, because he had been delivering eggs from his mother's chicken coop to that house for the past couple of years since the old farmer had given up rearing his own chickens. What better disguise than to insert secret messages into the baskets of eggs intended for the couple at the safe house farm? It was a perfect plan.

Wasyl was thrilled when the elderly farmer introduced him to a few young men who were covertly lodging at the farm. The men awaited word on where and when they were to meet a volunteer secret underground agent who would smuggle them out of the country to join the ranks of the Polish Army in France. It was the message Wasyl had hidden inside the egg basket on his first mission that forwarded those important details to the young men. Wasyl felt a great deal of patriotic pride in doing his part to assist the Polish Forces. Secretly, he fantasised about escaping abroad and joining the Polish Army himself when he came of age. Most of the young men he knew dreamt about doing duty for their country, as their fathers and grandfathers had done before them. For now, Wasyl was satisfied being a courier between the Underground Army in Soviet-occupied Poland, and the Polish Army-in-Exile.

**

While she was living at her Uncle Jerzy's house, Lilyana had become friendly with Krystka, a young lady from a neighbouring farm. Krystka was only three years older than Lilyana, and at twenty-two she had already mothered three children with her husband Andros. Sometimes, in the afternoons while Olisia slept, Lilyana would walk across the meadowlands to where Krystka and Andros' farm stood. She loved helping her newfound friend with her three beautiful babies: Melania, who was three; Jan, being one-and-a-half; and Izak, who was still an infant.

Naturally, Krystka appreciated the extra help Lilyana offered in caring for the children and with household chores, and the two young women became best friends very quickly. Krystka had a magnificent singing voice. She and Lilyana would often sing together when they worked in Krystka's kitchen making soups and stews, baking breads and biscuits, while taking care of the little ones. Lilyana loved singing, but it was her friend's voice that would ring out loud and clear across the open pasturelands.

Lilyana's visits to her new friend's farm were curtailed somewhat once the ice and snow persisted, but she would bundle up in her aunt's winter wear and take Uncle Jerzy's horse and sleigh across the snowed-in meadow to visit. Lilyana's aunt and uncle had taken pity on her sad circumstances and recognised that she needed a brief respite away from her mother every so often. Being with people closer to her own age seemed to do a world of good in lifting Lilyana's spirits. Lilyana was grateful to her aunt and uncle for their understanding and generosity.

One afternoon in March, Krystka and Lilyana were cooking pies in Krystka's kitchen. Unexpectedly, Lilyana broke out into a rendition of an old Polish folksong that her father used to sing to her mother every evening. Lilyana had loved the mellow tone her father's voice took on as the lovely words drifted out across the sitting room, making her mother smile. Krystka joined in singing the familiar tune. Together their voices blended in wonderful harmony.

"It has been a while since I last sang that song," Krystka remarked. "It is my good friend Katerina's favourite melody.

She had asked me to sing that song at her wedding this coming summer... Sad really! Andros told me that he heard Kat's fiancé was arrested and taken away by the NKVD during that horrendous night of disappearances last month. Poor Kat! She grieves the loss of her beloved Jakob."

Lilyana stopped rolling out the pastry she was forming into a pie shell on top of Krystka's kitchen table. She stared blankly ahead as thoughts rambled quickly in her head. She knew that Jozef's older sister was named Katerina, and she remembered Jozef mentioning that his sister was to be married that coming summer; he had hinted that Lilyana might like to join him at the celebration when the time came. Could it be that Krystka was still in touch with somebody from Jozef's family?

Returning to what Krystka was saying, Lilyana heard her friend remark that she did not think she would be able to cope if anything like that happened to Andros.

"We must all pray, Lilyana," Krystka said. "Pray that none of our loved ones will fall victim to the atrocities the Bolsheviks have brought upon our people!"

Lilyana could hold back no longer; she had to ask. "Is this friend of yours Katerina Nowakowski from across the river?"

"Why, yes, it is... Do you know her?"

"I know her and her brother, Jozef," Lilyana said. "Jozef and I are good friends. I do hope that I will have an opportunity to see him again soon. Life is so uncertain now, and one never knows what will happen from one day to the next!"

Krystka eyed Lilyana from the other side of the table. Lilyana's head was down, but Krystka could see a hint of rosy colour spreading across her friend's cheeks.

"Could it be that my friend's brother and you are a little more than good friends, Lilyana?" she asked. "If I did not know better, I would think that you are rather fond of young Jozef Nowakowski."

Lilyana was annoyed her body betrayed her every time her face lit up at the mention of Jozef's name.

She managed to reply, "Well, Jozef and I are good friends. I had hoped we would be seeing a little more of each other, and maybe we would go to the cinema together, or attend the young people's dances in Stolpce... but the Soviets have spoiled all that now. Jozef and I were starting to grow close, but since the Russians moved in, everybody's lives have been altered."

Now Krystka could see how deep Lilyana's feelings for Jozef really were. A coy smile emerged on her face as she told Lilyana that Andros would be crossing over the river in a couple of weeks.

"He will be going to visit his parents at their farm before the ice on the river starts to break up with the spring thaw," she said. "Perhaps Andros will take you across to the Nowakowski farm, as it is on the way to where he will be going. You will be able to call on Jozef to see how he and his family are doing. Andros and I worry how Katerina is faring since the loss of her fiancé. We will send Kat our best wishes, and let her know that she is in our thoughts and prayers after Jakob's arrest and disappearance. If you go to the Nowakowskis' farm, you will be able to relay our message while looking in on Jozef."

Lilyana fancied the idea of going to see Jozef, and under normal circumstances she would have jumped at the opportunity to do so. However, with the situation being what was, she had the welfare of her ailing mother to consider. She certainly did not want to place any more of the responsibility of caring for Olisia on her aunt and uncle. Visiting across the river would entail an entire day away from her uncle's farm. She would not take advantage of her relatives' kindness that way. She explained the situation to Krystka.

"Hmm... Well, there must be some way that we can get you and Jozef together!" Krystka insisted.

"But I don't see how that would be possible," Lilyana replied.

Krystka suddenly perked up as another idea struck her, and she declared, "I will write a letter to my dear friend

Katerina expressing our commiseration and support, and Andros can deliver it to her at the Nowakowski farm. We really do feel for her at this horrible turn of events! While he is there, perhaps Andros can tell Jozef that you are here in the countryside near our farm. We can invite both of you over for dinner. Surely it will not be too much of an imposition for your aunt to tend to your mother for just one evening?"

Lilyana stood back from the table and looked out the kitchen window. It was a beautiful day. A white blanket of winter snow sparkled in the sunlight over the open fields. Puffy white clouds floated serenely by on a spectacular backdrop of blue. Evergreen trees in the distance appeared like iced cakes trimmed in white with newly fallen snow from the night before. Lilyana saw the impressions her uncle's sleigh had left in the snow when she had ventured out across the meadow that afternoon. She wished with all her heart that circumstances had been different. What a glorious day this would have been for her and Jozef to go for a sleigh ride together across the frozen meadowlands. If the Russians had not come and occupied their land, she and Jozef would probably be courting now. The beauty of the day, and thoughts of seeing Jozef again, caused Lilyana's spirits to soar to new heights.

"Yes, that would be wonderful, Krystka. I would love to see my dear friend Jozef again," she stated with renewed enthusiasm.

***

Two weeks later, Andros set off in his horse-drawn sleigh across the Neman River toward his parents' house. During better weather, Krystka and the children would have accompanied him on the trip, but the wintry elements prevailed, and they did not want to expose their young ones to the snow and cold on that lengthy journey. Andros agreed to deliver a pie his wife had made, and the letter for Katerina, to the Nowakowski farm.

He arrived there early that morning. As the sleigh pulled into their farmyard, he noticed that part of the wooden fence surrounding the property was crushed and lay hidden beneath a drift of snow, and could not help thinking that was unusual. He knew Jozef was very meticulous about keeping up with things and doing repairs around the farm.

He climbed down from the sleigh just as Tobias and Marek Nowakowski emerged from the barn.

"So, what is it that you boys have been up to in the barn there?" Andros teased. "Not getting into any sort of trouble, I hope!"

"Trouble… Who has time for mischief these days!" Tobias replied. "We are too busy trying to get all the work done here!"

"And where would your brother, Jozef, be then?" Andros inquired as he made his way toward the boys. "Surely he is doing most of the work. You two ruffians are only getting in his way… no?"

Tobias and Marek stopped dead in their tracks and looked blankly at each other, then back at Andros.

"Haven't you heard?" Tobias said. "The Russians arrested our brother and hauled him away last month. Jozef has been banished to Siberia. We are praying for his safe return. Some townsfolk saw the long, black line of railway cars that carted off our brother and many others, like animals!"

"Yes, but Jozef will return to us!" little Marek yelled. "He is strong, and he will come back to our farm! We will grow wheat and oats together again!"

The younger boy fought to hold back a flood of tears as he thought about his older brother. Andros could clearly see how devastated both the young lads were. He kicked at a clump of snow in front of the opened barn door. He desperately wanted to say something optimistic to give hope to these hurting boys, but the fact remained, there was nothing positive that could be said.

"It was a horrible day when the Soviets took our brother away," Tobias continued. "The farm has not been the same without him. We struggle to keep up with all the work, and things will only get worse with planting season just around the corner. We will never be able to work as efficiently as Jozef did. Our sister Katerina cries all the time. She lost our brother and her fiancé on that terrible day. Our mother stays quiet, and baby sister Zofia is angry and acts up all the time… and we don't know what has happened to our oldest brother, Lukasz."

Andros sensed a heavy cloud of sadness hanging over the Nowakowski farm.

"You have had to grow up quickly," he managed to say. "I've heard that many young men and good families have disappeared in recent weeks. It is an abomination, the way the Russians are treating our people. We can only pray that there will be an end to this madness very soon. My wife, Krystka, and I will pray for Jozef and Lukasz, and for Kat's fiancé and your family. May God keep watch over your loved ones while they remain in exile, and may He return them safely to you."

Andros heard a voice behind him then, and he turned to see Mrs Nowakowski coming toward the barn.

"That has been my constant prayer since the evil outreach of the Soviets touched our lives!" she said. "We are all praying for the safe return of our young men and dear neighbours. I dare say that Hell will be overflowing one day with all the NKVD men and Red Army soldiers who are inflicting such atrocities upon innocent people!" She crossed herself once before adding, "May God have mercy on their souls!"

Andros nodded in agreement with Mrs Nowakowski's words. Then he remembered Krystka's pie, which he had left in his sleigh. While he went to fetch it, he inquired how Katerina was doing. He expressed his and Krystka's concern for Kat as he pulled his wife's letter out from his coat pocket and handed it to Mrs Nowakowski, along with the pie.

"Come… Come inside the house," she said. "You can give Kat the letter yourself. I know she will be happy to hear from her friend Krystka... And oh, what a lovely pie from your dear wife. I must thank her for such generosity in these difficult times. Tell me, Andros, how are those beautiful babies of yours doing? How are your mother and father doing? It has been some time since we have had the opportunity to chat with them!"

Following his visit with the Nowakowskis, Andros hurried to his parents' farm. Kat had indeed been cheered by the letter from Krystka and the chance to catch up with Krystka and Andros' family news. Nevertheless, the light in her eyes had dimmed. Gone were the days when he and Krystka would visit Kat and Jakob here, joking, laughing and looking forward to the days ahead when Kat and Jakob would be married and settle on a farm of their own nearby. How quickly life had changed! Now, Andros wondered how his wife's friend Lilyana would take the news he must deliver. Jozef was gone... arrested and exiled to the land of the white bears!

FIVE
FORCED LABOUR CAMP

When Joseph Stalin became leader of the Soviet Union, his aim was to turn Russia into a modern, industrial power. His forced labour prison system became known as gulags, associated with Soviet arrests, interrogations, deportations in freezing cattle cars, slave labour, torture, destruction of families, deaths and years spent in exile. The Communist Party officially labelled the system as Corrective Labour Camps and Colonies. To the rest of the world, the Soviets presented it as a progressive prison system to re-educate class enemies and reintegrate them through labour into Russian society. The Soviets viewed labour as a heroic, glorious, courageous, and honourable contribution to the state. Posters and banners were set up in the barracks and around the work camps with mottos giving glory and honour to Stalin and the Soviet Union.

The Russians had a vast network of concentration camps for forced labour throughout the Soviet Union. The majority existed in the most extreme geographical and climatic areas of the Siberian Arctic, where the Soviets were undertaking huge projects. Prisoners were put to work to create profit from Russia's natural resources, working in circumstances that exposed them to danger and conditions harmful to their health and wellbeing. Depending on the location of the camps, work varied from felling timber deep in remote, frozen forests; gold and coal mining in frozen, subarctic mines; and building the needed new railway lines, roads, factories, canals and ports along the larger rivers. It was an economical way for the Russians to meet their need for increased manpower, and raised big profits that financed the administration of the NKVD and the Red Army.

Soviet authorities tried to rationalise their abuse of deported captives by falsely stating that the gulag system was more humane than capital punishment or prison. However, instead of being helped and improved, the prisoners were traumatised and treated with brutality. The harsh treatments included not feeding anyone who could not work and generate income for the Russians. Any prisoner too weak or too sick to work would be left to die. Gulag captives continued to endure the harsh realities of humiliation, deprivation and death all around them.

The younger men from Jozef's group who persevered through the horrendous march through blizzards and endless miles of snow-covered terrain managed to reach their assigned labour camp in the forest. Upon arrival, they were stripped of all their clothing and forced to wear standard prison clothes. Their heads were shaved, and they were given prisoner numbers. They had no contact with the outside world. Their loved ones would be left to wonder what had happened to them.

The work generated in Jozef's camp made an essential contribution to the logging industry. A rectangular enclosure with watchtowers on tall stilts rose high above the barbed wire at each corner of the camp. Wooden ladders gave the guards access to the watchtower platforms. Lamps situated halfway between each tower would switch on when darkness fell, and the bright beams of searchlights would stream across the camp and along the perimeter walls. Without any electricity, the searchlights were run by a generator that had to constantly be fuelled. The guard towers were manned by soldiers with machine guns. Cabins for the administrative staff, and the soldiers' quarters were located near the main gate. The kitchen, storehouses, infirmary, punishment block and the kennels were built along one of the shorter walls.

Near the centre of the enclosure was an open area that served as a security barrier between the prisoners and the soldiers. A high wooden fence separated the two compounds. Barbed wire was rolled up on both sides at the top of the fence, and there was an open passageway with a second tall log fence on the opposite side. The space between the two wooden walls was used to get from the guard room at the main gate to all the watchtowers. It was continually policed by armed guards, accompanied by vicious guard dogs at night.

A courtyard area between the two perimeter fences was called the Zone. It was raked every day and checked for footprints. Nobody was permitted to go into the Zone, and if anyone did, they were shot without warning by guards in the watchtowers. Guards were quick to act if any prisoner got too close to the wire.

Coiled barbed wire encompassed the entire encampment. A deep trench lay in front of the tall exterior log walls that were reinforced with a stone abutment.

The prisoners' barracks were located beyond the main gate of the camp. They were long, flat dwellings constructed from logs. Many small barracks were lined up in rows of two, parallel to each other, with a wide laneway between them. The barracks' walls were roughly cut but provided warmth and shelter. The doors faced west, and a small, covered porch opened on the south side, protecting the prisoners from the snow and wind. The interiors of the barracks were comprised of many two-tiered sleeping platforms made from debarked posts, with plain wooden planks to lie on. The bunks were lined up in rows, crowded along the side walls. There were no mattresses and no bedding. Several men were forced to sleep on each one of the narrow wooden platforms together, half on the bottom tier, half on the top level. An iron stove sat in the middle, fuelled by small pieces of wood and logs that the prisoners brought in every day, with a short length of pipe to vent the smoke through the roof. The prisoners used moss gathered from the forest to line the hard planks in their bunks. The dwellings were over-crowded, poorly heated, and stank of too many smelly bodies. The stench of the sick and dying was a constant reminder of their plight. Terrible draughts seeped in through cracks in the wooden walls, and there were insufficient wood scraps to keep a fire going in the stove. The barracks remained so cold that ice formed on the inside walls. To keep warm at night, the men slept back-to-back with a couple of their jackets placed underneath them and the other jackets on top for a cover. They crossed their hands on their chests and pressed their knees up against their stomachs. There was no electricity or running water, and buckets were used for toileting in extremely unsanitary conditions. Usually, the weaker prisoners were forced to sleep closest to the festering pots that overflowed with urine and excrement.

Through all the intolerable hardships, only those men who formed bonds and learned how to help each other survived in the camp.

At night, the barracks were locked up and heavily guarded. Life was strictly disciplined. Every morning, a siren sounded before dawn as a wake-up call. A guard unlocked the barracks, entered, and yelled for all the prisoners to get up. They were forced to remain silent and stand by their sleeping platforms while the commander read out each man's surname from his list for that barracks. Each prisoner responded in turn. After the roll call, guards counted the prisoners. One guard would start from one end and move across to the other while a second guard began on the opposite side and worked his way across alternately.

Every day, the routine was the same. In the morning, the prisoners quickly pulled on the cloth coats, hats, gloves and canvas boots that had been issued to them when arriving at the camp. The clothing was inadequate for the sub-zero conditions and did little to protect them from the deep freeze in Northern Siberia. Rags on their feet didn't help prevent frostbite from working in the forest all day long.

The men lined up outside to be counted again in the area between the barracks and the main gate, and each prisoner was searched for hidden weapons. Then they were marched to the latrine trenches inside the wires behind the building site before marching to the kitchen mess hall to eat in shifts. They lined up and moved along quickly to an open window at the kitchen where their food was doled out. They sat at primitive tables and benches fashioned from logs in a mess hall area. This area generated some welcomed heat, but it also enhanced the stink of all the smelly men and their putrid rations. The cooks and guards took the best of the food and left the scraps for the prisoners. At breakfast time, they would receive a small ration of black bread and a tin mug of substitute coffee. Sometimes a thin, grey, lukewarm gruel would be served. It would not be enough to sustain them through the frigid cold and icy winds they were forced to work in. They had to eat and drink in haste to allow time for the next shift to come and eat. Mugs and bowls were returned through another window in the kitchen area on their way out.

Deep hunger pains constantly ravaged the prisoners. The lack of nutrition, hard labour and incessant cold depleted their energy and their health. Within a few weeks, most of the men were shattered human beings who only thought about getting a few food rations and a little warmth in their bunks at night.

Outside the mess hall, the prisoners would line up for another roll call, and then they were marched into the forest under escort by armed guards and attack dogs. Tools were issued from the storehouse, checked at the main gate on the way out, then carefully checked again at the end of the day when the prisoners returned. When they walked out the gate in the morning and returned at night, a record keeper would check their names against his lists.

A double row of guards formed a passageway outside the main gate. As each group of prisoners left for work, guards with bayoneted rifles fell into line alongside them for the long march to the work zone. It took more than an hour to reach Jozef's designated work area. Preceding every march, the guards shouted out the familiar refrain, "A step to the left or a step to the right is considered an attempt to escape. We will shoot without warning! March!" The guards always had their pistols and rifles poised and ready to shoot for the slightest infraction, preferring to shoot and evaluate the circumstances later, rather than have a prisoner escape on their watch and have to answer to their senior officers. Prisoners always walked a fine line between life and death.

They would make the difficult march to the work zone every day, regardless of weather conditions. For most of the year, they would fight the blinding snow and glacial Siberian 'wind of winds' that continually blew across the far north. In the early morning darkness, forest brigades would know when they were approaching the work zone from the smell of freshly cut wood and pine sap in the air.

After their long walk, they would toil all day in waist-deep snow, exhausted and starving. The only brief break in the workday would be during the noon meal. Midday rations consisted of watery soup. Sometimes Jozef would discover fish heads, eyes and scales in the foul-tasting liquid.

During the brief summer period, endless rains soaked the captives. Their jackets and pants were drenched before they even exited the camp en route to the work zone. On those rare summer days when the skies cleared, the men were eaten alive by gnats that swarmed their eyes, faces and hands. In summertime, a bowl of kasha, a porridge-like substance made from millet, buckwheat or whatever grain could be found, was sometimes doled out at midday. A couple of times, heavily salted fish were distributed, but the fish were rotten, having sat out in the sun for an extended time at a food depot hundreds of miles away.

A long march back to camp followed a gruelling day of working in the cruel elements and Arctic darkness with inadequate tools and equipment, and without proper nourishment or rest. The work brigades were stopped at the main gate outside the encampment and the prisoners were counted before the convoy guard transferred them over to the camp guards. In winter, the men returned with sullen faces etched with snow and ice. The cold winds caused their eyes to leak tears that froze on their cheeks every time they marched. Their outward expressions reflected the hopeless despair they felt inside. They entered the camp and lined up in darkness for the evening bowl of soup. The watery slop was often weaker and thinner than the midday soup because it consisted of the water used to boil the vegetables for the guards and administration staff. There was always a shortage of bowls and spoons. Prisoners fought to get to the front of the line so they wouldn't have to go without soup for lack of utensils. It was always a struggle to compete and survive.

The men would then be escorted back to their assigned barracks, and baskets of allotted bread rations were distributed to them according to the percentage of the work quota they had achieved during the workday. The bread was dark and dirty, and sometimes it was made from little more than sawdust. The texture was wet, like a rubbery sponge. Extra water was often added to the dough to raise the weight in a man's ration, making the bread sticky and soggy.

Gulag work was always physically exhausting. The lumber industry and mining operations were the worst to be assigned to. Usually the youngest, healthiest-looking men were chosen to toil in the forests and the mines. If any tools or machinery existed, they were primitive, defective and in short supply. Often, official work time regulations were extended by local camp administrators, and prisoners were forced to work extended hours in the most extreme climate, felling trees with dull handsaws and axes or digging at the frozen ground in the mines with crude pickaxes and their bare hands. Prisoners did not last long in these camps. All of them suffered. They were forced to work in conditions that would lead to injury, illness and death if they were unable to find ways of getting around the system. Every day, men died from hard labour, inadequate food rations, the extreme climate, unsanitary conditions, disease and violence. New transports of prisoners continually arrived to replace those workers who died. Younger men were more resilient, but many of the older ones tried to carry on and survive. They faced their harsh life in the camps with courage and determination.

The prisoners did not have to work on Sundays. However, instead, they were ordered to assemble in the courtyard area, where the commandant addressed them from atop his raised platform. He announced any changes that applied to their lives, talked about camp rules and violations and announced the work target for the coming week.

Most political prisoners were sent to labour camps without a trial. Nearly all were guilty of no crime, but that was of little relevance as the camp administrators extended their sentences at will. If a man proved to be a good, strong worker who laboured effectively and had a high daily production rate, his sentence was extended indefinitely.

In all the gulags, an incentive scheme was devised to motivate prisoners to work harder and faster. The size of a man's daily ration depended on the percentage of the work quota he delivered that day. It made many prisoners increase their production, but also caused the deaths of many who were unable to fulfil the expected high quota. They worked long, hard hours trying to meet impossible quotas to receive a full food ration, but even full rations failed to provide adequate calories to safeguard their health and survival.

If prisoners managed to survive the constant threats, they still might become victims of random violence by the NKVD guards, whose cruelty was well known. Even minor violations of discipline were punished by severe beatings or shooting. Prisoner abuse was rampant. A guard could easily dismiss murder by saying, *attempted escape*. If an investigation into the shooting of a prisoner was undertaken, the only thing considered was the position of the dead body, which was often adjusted by guards to make sure the murder was declared justified. They arranged the body so the feet laid in the direction of the camp, while the head was positioned away. That was deemed sufficient evidence of an attempted escape. Any prisoner who refused to obey the guards' orders, no matter how demeaning, was shot. Informers constantly watched the other prisoners, always waiting for a slip-up to report to the camp authorities.

Unexpected inspections of barracks would occur arbitrarily. Everything would be thoroughly searched, including bunks, the moss on the bunks, the stove and stove pipe, the floorboards, the men and all their clothing.

The gulag system transformed prisoners into exhausted, submissive, smelly men who only thought of how to survive one moment to the next, always fighting the pains of hunger and finding ways to avoid the cold, the violence and the abuse. They would be dehumanised within the system, and for many, a natural instinct towards compassion, concern for fellow inmates, friendship and honesty disappeared quickly.

Working conditions for the guards were also difficult. Even though they had it easier than the prisoners, serving as a guard escorting a convoy of prisoners in the harsh Siberian environment was not easy. They were expected to maintain a high level of vigilance in freezing temperatures where no amount of clothing was ever enough to protect against the elements. If an escape happened during their watch, they were severely punished; they could be stripped of their uniform and become labour camp prisoners themselves.

However, fault was rarely found with a guard's brutality against prisoners. Sometimes they were rewarded for violence under the pretence of preventing escapes. Soviet authorities constantly reminded the guards that they were the strong pillar in Russia's battle against the captives. They convinced the guards that prisoners were enemies of the state who posed a danger by seeking to destroy the wonderful society being built in the Soviet Union. They attempted to prevent the guards from developing any sympathy for the prisoners, and they took great effort in stopping them from getting to know the prisoners on a personal level.

Despite the authorities' threats and warnings, a handful of soldiers did take pity on the captives. At times, a little bit of compassion was shown. A few guards established a friendly rapport with the men in the work brigades they were assigned to. As soon as they were out of sight of the guard house, they would put their rifles on their shoulders and begin friendly conversations. Those guards did not show contempt toward prisoners, nor humiliate them in ways that most of the others took pleasure in doing. They cleverly bent the prison rules by surreptitiously being polite and showing signs of sympathy. It took a while for such an understanding to develop between the prisoners and a guard, but even in the worst of circumstances, rare moments of kindness emerged. Those acts posed a danger because the Soviet authorities viewed any sign of unity with prisoners as evidence of an anti-Soviet point of view.

Russian authorities used the camps to destroy both real and imagined opposition to the dictatorship of the Communist Party. Stalin wanted to remove all elements that could threaten his political structure and ideology, and the gulag became the main element in his system of terror. Many fellow Russians were arrested and deported to previously uninhabited areas as the Communist Party became paranoid that the Soviet project was being sabotaged by an enemy within. This caused millions of perceived enemies of the people to be sent away and isolated in labour camps and colonies, to protect the state.

There were other dangers in the camps. As they evolved into the main penal system, political prisoners were held together with violent criminals. Gang violence was common, and often conflicts erupted between criminal and political prisoners. To survive, prisoners were constantly contending with each other. They stole food and clothes, took credit for labour done by other inmates and informed on each other to curry favour with the authorities. They were always subjected to violence, suspicion and jealousy because they had to fight for access to the limited basics of life. Rape and beatings were commonplace. Sometimes fellow prisoners became as powerful and oppressive as the camp authorities.

If a man was alone and weak, he wouldn't survive in the camps for long; it was crucial to readily determine whom he could trust, and to quickly judge who the informers, violent gang members and rapists were.

The Soviet Union's pact with Nazi Germany had given Russia control over new territories in Eastern Europe besides their major acquisition in Eastern Poland. Thousands of NKVD arrests took place in other newly acquired territories. Many prisoners from other areas were identified as class enemies and were deported to the labour camps alongside the Poles. Various ethnic groups often established gangs and violently opposed other groups whom they may or may not have had a grudge against due to national backgrounds. Nationalities tended to stick together. Sometimes prisoners broke out into songs from their motherlands in their barracks, and one nationality would try to out-sing another. A loud ruckus often ensued. The guards could do little to stop it, so they chose to ignore it.

Starvation alone would doom even the healthiest forest workers within weeks of entering a logging camp. Eating the full ration of bread every day would barely provide enough food for survival, and for those consistently unable to fulfil their daily work quota and receiving less food, a slow spiral of death would begin. These men would become known as goners. Their gaunt-looking bodies on the verge of death constantly reminded the other prisoners of the fate that awaited them if they did not fulfil the work quotas.

Escape from the forest or the gulag was virtually impossible. Prisoners were constantly observed by armed guards from watchtowers in every corner of the work zone and the camp. Tracking dogs were also assigned to each camp, making escape hopeless. Even if they managed to escape the guards, the harsh environmental elements prevalent in these extremely remote regions made it difficult for anyone to survive. There were no roads to follow, and resources were not available. It was unlikely that an escapee could survive walking thousands of miles to freedom in the unrelenting conditions.

Jozef was able to evaluate the camp situation very quickly. He realised that finding a few trustworthy prisoners to align himself with was crucial to his survival. He remained silent for a day or two, trying not to be noticed while he carefully observed everyone and everything around him. By the third day, he was confident that a couple of men in his barracks were worthy of his trust and friendship. One of those individuals was a tough young man named Radoslaw. Jozef had overheard conversations between Radoslaw and other inmates while labouring in the forest with his work brigade and knew they had much in common. Radoslaw had come from a farm in one of the smaller villages in Poland. He was of a similar age to Jozef, and held the same views pertaining to religion and politics. He spoke of family values that Jozef regarded as sacred, and his interests mirrored all that Jozef felt enthusiastic about. Then there was Ivan, a slightly older man. He seemed intelligent, with a higher level of education. Ivan spoke eloquently to all classes of people, and he spoke Russian flawlessly. He seemed to have an ability to calm the more aggressive prisoners. Even though he was not one of the most productive men in Jozef's forest brigade, it was obvious that his talent in discourse had impressed some of the guards, and he had helped to squash several squabbles between other prisoners. Those attributes were to be beneficial for those who aligned themselves with him.

Jozef sat across the table from Radoslaw and Ivan while the guards hurried them through their meagre rations. He acknowledged them with a nod of his head as they gobbled down small portions of black bread and foul-smelling soup. Radoslaw responded with a nod in return, but Ivan stared back cautiously, sizing up Jozef and trying to determine where the loyalties of this farm boy lay. Could Jozef be trusted, he wondered. Would he be a safe and worthy ally? Jozef understood the man's reluctance. He allowed Ivan time to make the necessary evaluation in his own way and on his own terms.

All barracks remained under close watch from the towers at night. Inside Jozef's crammed quarters, Radoslaw and Ivan slept on bunks across from his. Having made up his mind to align himself with them, Jozef initiated a conversation with Radoslaw by mentioning that he had a cousin who lived in the village where Radoslaw came from. The fact that his cousin was female instantly sparked Radoslaw's interest. He was quick to respond, inquiring what the young lady's name was and what street she lived on. Ivan listened as the two of them talked.

In the gulag, alliances tended to develop the same way that conflict did. Close bonds grew slowly and cautiously. Prisoners from the same ethnic background looked out for each other. Men from the same geographical region, political party or religion, and those who spoke the same language, shared a common cause. Criminal gangs provided protection for their own group, and favoured friends. These strong bonds supported the prisoners throughout their daily existence in the camps.

Jozef slowly developed a friendship with Radoslaw and Ivan, and a steady alliance developed between them after the men determined that Jozef was worthy of their trust.

Jozef's work crew toiled feverishly to achieve the high work quota in the forest. The Soviets believed that collective responsibility for the ration given encouraged the labourers to work more efficiently. Men were organised into teams of two, bringing larger trees down with old cross-cut frame saws. Other men cut smaller trees single-handedly using dulled handsaws and axes. Large branches from the felled trees were also chopped off with axes. Jozef and Radoslaw were able to work faster than a lot of other prisoners in the forest as they were accustomed to cutting down trees at their farms back home. They remained among the strongest and healthiest men, receiving full rations for their daily work performance.

Beams would be provided on the ground to pile the trees onto. One row would be comprised of several trees, and several more layers of trees would be piled up high on top of it. The Soviets would estimate the height a pile of trees needed to be for the minimal daily norm, and when that vertical measurement was reached, the minimum ration of bread and watery soup would be doled out. Together, Jozef and Radoslaw could fell a pile of logs high enough for the daily requirement.

Some of the men in the forest brigade would work as log transporters, moving the logs from the forest to the wood processing plant. With temperatures dipping as low as -60 °C in the deadly cold winds of winter, logs would be dragged in deep snow by many men tied together. Hampered by the snow and the ropes, they would dig their way along to the processing plant with the logs in tow.

The plant was a wooden building that contained a large circular saw powered by an old steam engine. Log transporters stacked the heavy logs outside the building, and then the plant workers inside the building pulled the logs in and loaded them onto a conveyer belt to be cut. The processed wood was then sorted and transported to storage. Forest brigade jobs were rotated every month. The wood processing plant gave the men a small reprieve from the snow and the worst of the cold winds, but the machinery was antiquated and broke down continually. With no parts available for repairs, the prisoners were expected to continue cutting wood to meet the daily quota. Those who were handy enough to find ways to repair the machinery and get it running again were lucky. If they failed to deliver the estimated daily quota due to broken machinery, the guards had no sympathy, and the men were not given a daily bread card for rations.

Most of the younger men could survive a day or two without food, but by the third day the downward spiral began. If a man was unable to get up and go to work, he was left on his sleeping platform unaided until he died. Many died in the forest, or on the way to or from their work zones.

Their corpses had to be carried back to the labour camp by their fellow prisoners, who then had to dig graves in the frozen ground to bury them at the end of a gruelling day.

Without cheating in some way, it was difficult for a forest brigade to reach the expected quota felling timber. Jozef was familiar with stacking logs as he had been doing it since he was a small boy working on his family's farm. He knew how to make a pile of logs appear bigger from the outside by leaving loose spaces between the logs on the inside of the stack while keeping the stack solid and secure.

Jozef quickly developed certain strategies in order to survive. He'd been born with a strong will and mental toughness. He devised ways to keep his mind active in order to safeguard his sanity. He was able to retreat into meditative contemplation when needed. In his mind, the stench of rotten fish and foul-tasting gruel in the gulag mess hall was replaced by the delicious aromas of his mother's kitchen. A small piece of stale bread and the disgusting gruel or watery soup were transformed into a favoured dish from home. While marching in the convoy to and from the work zone every day, Jozef conjured up images of walking back to his family farm back in Poland. At night before lights out, he made up interesting stories to tell any others in the barracks who wanted to listen. He debated history with a few who shared his interest. He kept his hands from freezing by crafting little things from tree bark and wood shavings. Some of the other prisoners managed to create pieces for chess sets, and he partook in games of chess with those he'd aligned himself with. Thus, Jozef was able to survive the intolerable conditions through a combination of skilful tactics, a lot of luck, and kindness from others.

Ivan and Radoslaw would always be his close allies. Radoslaw added his own twist in finding ways to cheat the work quota, and Ivan was grateful for Radoslaw and Jozef's assistance in reaching the required daily production quota. Without them sharing their sly methods, Ivan would never have been able to achieve the expected daily norm.

He would have fallen short, received progressively smaller daily rations and fallen victim to the downward spiral and death within a month or two. The farm boys would prove to be a valuable asset to Ivan's longevity in the camp. He reciprocated by gaining favour among the guards toward the men he deemed to be his closest friends.

Ivan was one of those rare prisoners who managed to garner partiality among the camp authorities without being an informer. He would act as a model prisoner, and masterfully strike up casual conversations with the guards. Even in the unbearable conditions inside the barracks, Ivan would craftily feign empathy toward the guards for the "difficult tasks" they had to do. He became a favoured prisoner among the NKVD men, and the fellow captives he allied with benefited equally from the perks his skilful deception generated.

There were two other prisoners who became a part of Jozef's close alliance. One was a young fellow by the name of Nikolai, who was only sixteen years old when he arrived at the camp. He'd had the misfortune of watching a group of prisoners being marched out of his town in Eastern Poland on their way to the train station for deportation. Upon arriving at the station and doing a prisoner count, the escort guards discovered that two prisoners had somehow managed to escape. Rather than risk being reprimanded by the Soviet authorities, the guards had grabbed Nikolai and another young man right off the street to replace the escapees and rectify the number of prisoners being deported that day. It was a grievous blow to the young man. He bonded with the other fellow who had been abducted along with him, and together they were thrown into a cattle car en route to the unknown. Unfortunately, Nikolai's newfound friend succumbed to the bitter cold in the cattle car and froze to death halfway to Siberia. He died leaning up against Nikolai in the night. Some of the men in the boxcar had tossed his rigid corpse out into the snow when the guards opened the side door of the crowded car the next morning.

Nikolai was traumatised by the whole experience. So frail and damaged was he when he arrived at the labour camp, the men in Jozef's barracks took him into their care and advised him of what he needed to do to stay alive. Nikolai was assigned to a work brigade that included Jozef, Radoslaw and Ivan, who had immediately taken kindly to the young lad. In many ways, Nikolai reminded Jozef of his youngest brother, Marek. Once Nikolai had settled into his torturous new reality, his outgoing disposition and personal charisma began to surface while he worked with Jozef and the other men in their work crew. The older men continually watched out for Nikolai, protecting him from the would-be rapists and abusers. They shielded him against beatings and abuse from other prisoners and the guards, and ensured he received the full ration by helping him to achieve the expected daily production quota. The men appreciated the comedic relief the lad brought to them with his lively spirit and sense of humour amidst their dismal circumstances. It did not take long for Nikolai to become a staunch member of Jozef's alliance.

A tough man named Tomasz gained favour and became the fifth individual in their group. Like Jozef and Radoslaw, Tomasz had grown up on a farm in Eastern Poland. He had been arrested in September during an attempt to flee at the border between Poland and Romania when the Russians marched in. He was quickly transported to Siberia and arrived at a gulag further south in November of that year. Being the exuberant young fellow that he was, Tomasz had got himself into trouble with one of the guards at the first camp. Fortunately for him, he was deemed a very proficient worker, so instead of being shot for disciplinary reasons, the guard had beaten him and thrown him into the punishment block for several days. Upon his release from the isolation cell, Tomasz had unexpectedly been marched out of the camp with a small line of transfer prisoners. The transfer convoy met up with the same group of prisoners Nikolai had been assigned to, and they all marched to Jozef's logging camp together.

Tomasz and Nikolai had arrived in Jozef's barracks late one evening. The two of them were already a team. Tomasz was credited with keeping Nikolai alive during their march across the frozen tundra to the labour camp. It was because of Nikolai's close bond with Tomasz that Jozef's alliance had allowed the man into their group, even though he had yet to prove himself worthy of their trust and friendship. Right from the start, it was obvious that Tomasz was a rebel who was apt to go off at any time. The last thing they needed was to be associated with a troublemaker, but Nikolai insisted that Tomasz was a loyal friend when given a chance to prove himself.

In time, Tomasz demonstrated that he was an intelligent fellow, despite his flair for nonconformity and dissidence. He strongly challenged Jozef and Ivan in their games of chess, and oftentimes, he won a match out of sheer daring and craftiness. Naturally, Tomasz came up with a whole new scheme for cheating in order to fulfil the daily work quota of stacked logs. He was even able to invent ways to keep the old saw in the wood processing plant running so their work brigade's daily ration card was filled.

Tomasz had a boisterous personality that either offended other men in the barracks or earned their admiration. He did get into scuffles with some prisoners who irritated him, and on a few occasions, he was ordered to the punishment block for unruly behaviour toward the guards. Even Ivan's close association with the prison authorities could not protect Tomasz from punishment then. He spent days in the tiny, unheated, frozen, musty punishment cell without any blanket, and only a toileting bucket to keep him company. He had to exist on the sub-starvation penalty food ration while in the cell. Many of the other prisoners shouted protests and obscenities from the punishment block, but Tomasz managed to take it reverently and while other prisoners went crazy or died there, Tomasz survived with his sanity intact; his strong determination to survive overrode the harshness of the punishment. When he was returned to the barracks and his work brigade, he told his comrades stories about the places his mind had taken him to during those periods in the isolation cell. His thoughts had wandered back to his parish in Poland. In his imagination, the village priest there had prayed over him for his perseverance and survival.

Tomasz seemed to have the ability to delve into the deepest recesses of his soul and meditate his way through the harshest of retributions the gulag camp authorities could inflict on him. Few men were able to emerge from the solitary punishment cell and avoid the downward spiral the way Tomasz managed to do repeatedly. He was tough. His strong constitution earned him respect and acclaim among the prisoners and the guards alike.

He instructed his fellow prisoners on how to avoid extra suffering while in the solitary block. He spoke of ways to distribute your bodyweight evenly over the wood on the cell's sleeping platform so that one's bony contours would not come in direct contact with the planks and cause extra pain. He also told his comrades how to chew the miniscule bread ration over an elongated time in order to trick your mind into believing you had eaten much more than was actually doled out—it did not curb the constant hunger pains, but it did help save your sanity. Tomasz believed that unless a man was able to gain the feeling that he was in control over difficult circumstances, he would never survive the harsh reality that awaited him inside the punishment block.

In his effort to continue watching out for Nikolai, Tomasz had the lad exaggerate symptoms of illness that the boy suffered in order to have Nikolai sent to the infirmary. The boy was asthmatic, and the constant cold winds in Siberia played havoc with his health.

Nikolai discovered who the best actors were among the prisoners in the work camp and found himself in the company of several men who frequently gained admission to the infirmary. The camp's hospital was a sanctuary compared to the crude contrast of life in the work zone. Some of the prisoners went to extreme measures to obtain admission to the infirmary, even mutilating themselves by cutting off fingers. Many more rubbed dirt into an open cut or wound, which quickly festered into a serious infection as they were at such a low level of physical resistance. It caused their temperature to rise to the necessary degree warranting a visit to the infirmary. However, prisoners had to be careful when appealing for admission. If the camp doctor determined that a man was not ill enough to be admitted, the prisoner could be severely beaten or sent to the punishment block.

Nikolai did not need to feign any symptoms of illness; his affliction was genuine. A few days in the infirmary out of the snow and away from the bitter cold winds did wonders to improve his physical condition.

The men in the barracks were continually encouraging Nikolai to *eat... or you will die!*, but he had trouble stomaching the disgusting fish-head soup, watery gruel and stale bread. One day, the boy was faced with a unique opportunity to steal a piece of food from a guard's bowl of soup in the kitchen. The guard had been distracted by a brawl between two prisoners lining up for their food ration. Nikolai stood beside the spot on the primitive wood plank table where the guard had placed a bowl of soup, and temptation overcame him. Quickly looking around to see if any other prisoners would notice, Nikolai decided all eyes were trained on the men further down the line where the altercation was taking place, and hastily dipped his work-worn hand into the soup and pulled out a large chunk of fish.

The delicious morsel had barely touched his lips when one of the prison informers yelled out, "Guard! Guard! The boy is stealing your food!"

Immediately, all the prisoners turned their attention to Nikolai. The guard rushed back to the spot where he had left his soup and slapped Nikolai across the back of his neck to cause the lad to expel the food he had just pilfered. However, Nikolai had gulped hard when his deception was made apparent—the piece of fish was already swallowed.

The guard then held Nikolai's head firmly in one hand while prying the boy's mouth open with the other. He forced his large hand into Nikolai's throat and probed around for the bit of food. Nothing could be seen inside the lad's jaws, except for the beginning traces of scurvy. His tongue was thick, and his foul breath covered the smell of the fish he had just ingested. The guard held on tightly to Nikolai's head and smashed his face into the butt of a log supporting the thick planks of wood used as crude benches in the eating area. The boy fell to the ground unconscious. The last thing he remembered was seeing a stream of black soot billowing up into the sky from the woodstove pipe in the kitchen.

All the prisoners realised Nikolai's fate was sealed. He would be sent to the punishment cell for a few days as a disciplinary measure for his misdemeanour. They knew the boy would never survive in the hole. With his asthmatic lungs, the freezing cold and dampness would bring on the dreaded pneumonia quickly. He would probably be dead before morning.

"What are you talking about?" Tomasz suddenly declared as he pointed to the prison informer. "It was my hand that touched the bowl… not Nikolai's!"

"No! No! It was the boy!" the snitch insisted. "I clearly saw his hand pull some fish from the guard's bowl!"

"You're delusional!" Tomasz spat back. "It was I who took the food… and I will finish this bowl of soup right now!"

With that, Tomasz grabbed the guard's bowl up from the table and began guzzling the soup down his gullet as fast as he could swallow it. He realised this act warranted him many days in the punishment cell, and he did not intend on going into the hole without some nourishment inside his belly.

As it turned out, Tomasz's endeavour to save Nikolai from his fate earned him a full week in the punishment block. Afterwards, he emerged demoralised and weakened, but his allies had prepared for his eventual return, saving up pieces of bread from their meagre rations to feed to him. They secretly stored the bits of bread inside the lining of their coats so that the other starving prisoners in their barracks didn't steal the crumbs from them.

Tomasz almost did not survive the prolonged effects of the punishment cell after seven days in the hole. The downward spiral had begun. He had already taken on the appearance of a goner. Jozef, Radoslaw, Ivan and Nikolai took turns force-feeding Tomasz the bits of bread soaked in water for easier swallowing. Tomasz was on the brink of that inevitable point where no amount of food could bring a man back from certain death. Another day inside the punishment cell may have tipped the scales and pushed him over the edge. Eventually, he lost a couple of fingers and toes from frostbite in the hole, but his resilience was amazing. He seemed to come back from his deathly encounter with more defiance and a renewed determination to beat the odds.

He told his comrades stories about duelling with deathly images inside the hole that time, painting graphic pictures of the ghostly impressions that had haunted him on the final day. It was obvious the prison authorities had intended for Tomasz to die inside the punishment block. His return to the barracks, and eventually to the work zone, was nothing short of a miracle. Even the harshest of the camp guards were in awe of this man's rise from certain death time and time again.

In the beginning, Ivan had been reluctant to share any details about his personal life with his fellow prisoners. He chose his words carefully, even when speaking with his allies. However, over time, while labouring alongside them in the forest, Ivan eventually admitted that he was a few years older than the rest of them. The others took to calling him *old man*, though he was only twenty-six.

Ivan had been raised in a small hamlet just outside of Minsk. He had attended university in the city and graduated with a degree in engineering. For two years, he'd worked as an engineer at a large company in Minsk. Recently married, he and his wife had been expecting their first child when Ivan was arrested and taken away. Ivan held on to hope that he would survive his sentence in the labour camp and return to his wife and his baby, who would enter the world without him. His comrades told Ivan he should not hold on to that hope, because if his wish did not turn out the way he wanted it to, disappointment would overwhelm and defeat him. Nevertheless, Ivan would never relinquish his aspiration to be reunited with his wife, and their child.

"How is it then, the secret police never took you out to shoot you?" Tomasz demanded to know. "All the professional men in my village and in the towns around my home were marched out into the streets and shot dead. I saw these massacres with my own eyes while making my way south during the first few days of the Soviet occupation!"

"No, not all were murdered, Tomasz," Ivan replied. "My colleagues and I were taken away for investigation and interrogation by NKVD agents. Some of us were spared and sentenced for deportation to the labour camps… and here I sit."

"All of the younger ones spared so the Russians can suck the remaining life from them with their free labour plan here!" scoffed Radoslaw.

Tomasz snorted and nodded his head in agreement.

"A few other young men were taken from my office and shot outside," Ivan stated. "There was no logic to the pattern of who was killed and who was spared!"

Radoslaw hastily quipped, "Of course there was! You were probably spared because you had not yet risen to any status of importance in the city. If you had been someone of influence, you would not be here slaving your life away with the rest of us!"

"Perhaps so, my friend. Perhaps so!" Ivan replied tentatively.

Most of the educated men in the labour camps did not do very well. They may have been intelligent, but they lacked the survival skills others were more apt to fall back on. The men who had eked out an existence as peasants from the poorer farms knew all kinds of ways to sustain themselves in the harsh camp conditions. It was obvious that Tomasz had not gone far in school, but his wealth of ingenious methods for surviving the merciless conditions in the camp was a whole education in itself. Despite his crude manners, Jozef had to admit that Tomasz's survival skills were most impressive.

Tomasz was a self-proclaimed ladies' man and loved to spin tales about his encounters with the young women from his village. He would brag about his ability to charm all the girls in the market square, at church, and during festivals and county fairs. According to him, he would have the ladies lined up, waiting for a chance to dance with him or to vie for his attention and affection. Sometimes, Ivan had to cover young Nikolai's ears when Tomasz recounted details about his experiences with willing young females. He delighted in his many conquests.

However, as much as Tomasz had enjoyed what his lady friends might have offered him, he detested those men in the camp who took to raping other men and taking advantage of the weaker ones. He defended the underdogs and came to their rescue from tormentors. He stood by Nikolai's side as his protector against the perverts, like a vicious guard dog. Any prisoner who dared even to think about defiling his young comrade would have to answer to Tomasz's firm fists.

"And what about you, Jozef?" Ivan would ask one day. "Do you not have any young ladies at home who are looking forward to your return?"

Jozef blushed a little at Ivan's question. He was not comfortable talking about things as personal as this, but he managed to admit, "Well, there is one girl I am friendly with in Stolpce."

"Ha ha! *Friendly* with!" Tomasz teased. "And what does *friendly* mean, Jozef? Have you made love to your young lady friend?"

Tomasz laughed loudly until he noticed how dejected Jozef appeared to be.

"Ah... stop teasing him!" Radoslaw bellowed. "Jozef is not experienced in matters of the heart. He is what one may call a *gentleman!*"

Ivan waved off the banter between Tomasz and Radoslaw as the two of them laughed and debated what Jozef should do to try and impress the young lady.

Jozef told Ivan, "Lily and I attended school together. However, we did not become good friends until after we completed high school. Her father runs the hardware store in Stolpce. She would often be in the store helping her father when I went into town to purchase supplies for my family's farm."

"So, you got to know her better then?" Ivan asked.

"That's when Jozef started lusting after her!" Tomasz taunted.

Ivan shook his head in disgust and resumed the chess game he and Jozef were playing.

"You will instinctively know who the right girl is when she comes along," he remarked.

Jozef was quick to reply, "Lily is a wonderful lady, and the love of my life." Then, making one final move on the chess board, he grinned at Ivan and said, "Checkmate!"

SIX
LIVE OR DIE

It was springtime, and a few weeks had passed since Lilyana learned the fateful news about Jozef's arrest and deportation. Her heart had shattered. During the long, cruel passage of time since then, she still cried herself to sleep every night. She had stopped going across the meadow to visit with Krystka and Andros. In dealing with the needs of her debilitated mother, her routine had become robotic, and she no longer seemed enthusiastic about caring for her younger cousins.

Aunt Janina could not help noticing the sudden shift in Lilyana's demeanour. She had to ask her niece what was going on inside her mind. Janina worried that perhaps Lilyana might be falling into the same deep abyss as Olisia Prawoslaw.

It took a lot of courage, but Lilyana felt the need to share her pain with someone. She could not discuss her inner turmoil with her own mother, so through tearful sobs she finally broke down and explained the sad details to her aunt.

"Oh… poor child," her aunt said soothingly as she cradled Lilyana in her arms. "You have had to endure far too much loss these past few months… and now this. Tck, tck! I can see why it has all become too much for you to bear. Poor, poor child!"

Lilyana sobbed deeply for a long time. She let loose all the pain and frustration that had been building up inside her for many months. It poured out like the rushing torrent of water that broke free when the dam upstream on the river was opened every spring. Aunt Janina let the sorrow and heartache flow from her niece, all the while hugging her and telling her to cry the pain away. She tried to assure Lilyana that things would look better once she allowed herself to have a good lament, but Lilyana knew she would never have closure over the loss of her father, and she would never be able to love another man with the same depth of affection she felt toward Jozef.

Meanwhile, Lilyana's cousin Wasyl had become more involved with the underground resistance movement. He had proven himself to be a reliable secret courier for his cell, and now he was designated as a courier for a larger group, assigned to secretly carry more important messages and packages to various destinations further afield. The Soviet authorities would never suspect he was a secret messenger. More and more of his workload around the farm had fallen onto his brother Aleksander's shoulders as Wasyl's extended wanderings away from home began to interfere with his chores.

One day, Uncle Jerzy took Wasyl aside in the barn and asked him directly if his recent meanderings had anything to do with some secret organisation. Wasyl flatly denied association with any such group, but his father knew better. He warned Wasyl that his affiliation with an anti-Soviet body not only endangered himself, but it also jeopardised the wellbeing of his entire family. As much as Jerzy favoured his countrymen fighting back against the Russians, there was just too much at risk when a man had a family to look out for. Already, whole families were mysteriously disappearing from their farms without explanation. A few farms in the area lay empty after the Russians had laid claim to those lands and to all that came with the homes, the barns and chattel on those properties. The buildings had been tightly locked up, and nobody but the NKVD could get into them. In spring, rumours indicated that many thousands more innocent people had been sent away to Siberia in a second massive deportation wave. Eastern Poland was now known as the Soviet Zone.

Uncle Jerzy was thankful his family had been spared, especially after he learned that any people who were closely associated with those listed on the NKVD's endless index of *anti-Soviet elements* were being arrested and brought in for interrogation. He knew his brother's name had to have appeared on those lists. Jerzy feared his brother had either been killed or deported, yet the NKVD had not come looking for other members of the Prawoslaw family. If Wasyl had aligned himself with some secret underground cell and was discovered, then an even larger target would be put on their backs. Jerzy felt a strong sense of doom closing in around his farm with every passing day.

Initially, people living in the country had escaped a lot of the turmoil that the townspeople were experiencing on a daily basis. Red Army soldiers and NKVD agents were constantly harassing townsfolk on the streets and in their homes. Sometimes they entered stores fully armed with rifles, shoplifted whatever they pleased and sent the goods on to Russia. Everything had quickly become scarce in the cities, and life had become difficult. Once the Polish currency, the zloty, had been removed from circulation, even those people who had savings were left destitute. As husbands and fathers were being arrested, detained and removed, mothers with small children struggled to find ways of eking out an existence in order to survive. Most of these families no longer had any source of income, and they suffered indescribable hardships. Many grappled with the lack of food and nutrition, outbreak of disease and lack of heat and decent shelter throughout an extremely severe winter that year.

During the early months of Soviet occupation, farming families remained self-sufficient and fared better. As the war progressed, shortages became more acute and the Soviets spread out into the countryside looting farms, taking whatever they wanted. Quiet country life was impacted, and security no longer existed outside the cities and towns. At first, the Soviet officials had assured the farmers they would not throw them off their farms, but very quickly families were being forced to move out. Any show of resistance cost the farmers their lives, so they left without opposition. Initially, the Russians selected the best farms with the most fertile lands and the biggest houses constructed from brick or stone. The people on those farms were usually given twenty-four hours' notice to vacate their premises. They were permitted to take some personal possessions and food with them, but all the farm's livestock and trappings had to remain as the farmers were rendered homeless. Shortly afterwards, the massive deportations began. Ordinary farmers were awakened at gunpoint in the middle of the night by local militiamen and the NKVD, who forced entry into their homes and arrested most of the men. Entire families were uprooted and taken to the nearest train stations, where they were deported in crowded, filthy cattle cars as the Soviet ethnic cleansing of Poles continued.

Uncle Jerzy had good reason to worry about Wasyl's movements. Danger existed everywhere throughout the new Soviet Zone, and nobody could be trusted. Being barely sixteen years old, Wasyl was inexperienced in the ways of the world, particularly during times of war.

On a chilly morning in early May, Lilyana's cousin went missing. No one heard or saw anything that day as Wasyl carefully took his bicycle from the barn and rode off down the laneway. He was never seen nor heard from again. Wasyl's brother, Aleksander, asked several of the older boys who remained around the farms in the area if they knew anything about Wasyl's sudden departure or disappearance. None of the lads volunteered any information. Aleksander knew that Wasyl had been waiting for an opportunity to escape to the west and join the Polish Army in France. He told his parents about this, and he held on to hope that his brother had in fact managed to do so. Perhaps Wasyl was alive, somewhere in France. However, their grim suspicions were confirmed when Aunt Janina and Uncle Jerzy searched Wasyl's room after he had vanished. Neatly stashed in the metal coils under his mattress, they discovered a bundle of leaflets intended to encourage young men to join the Polish Army. Fliers like these had been appearing on fences and walls in public areas where people gathered, left by dispatch couriers like Wasyl, who were distributing various pamphlets and pasting leaflets to walls wherever they could, under the watchful eye of the Soviet authorities. The secret cells wanted to keep the civilian population informed and make it clear to the Soviets that the Polish Underground Army was still functioning despite all the Russians' barbaric tactics to wipe it out. All tasks associated with the resistance movement were dangerous. Anyone caught posting what the Soviets deemed to be subversive propaganda was shot on the spot without warning or explanation.

A family friend living near Stolpce eventually told the Prawoslaws that he had spotted young Wasyl carrying a large bag filled with papers heading into town early on the morning he disappeared. The Prawoslaws had no choice but to fearfully assume Wasyl had been intercepted by the authorities during some covert mission for the underground movement. They were left to wonder whether he had been killed, imprisoned or if he had been sentenced and deported to a labour camp in Siberia.

When Aunt Janina found out Wasyl was missing, her whole world collapsed. She'd never dreamt her eldest son would be taken from her like that. She cried and sobbed long into the night. Days afterwards, she still trembled in her grief. She had trouble focusing on her daily work. Lilyana was shocked at the loss of her cousin, but she stepped up to help care more for the younger children and with the household chores as her aunt came to terms with the situation.

Uncle Jerzy was quick to throw all the leaflets from Wasyl's room into the fire, destroying the evidence before any NKVD agents descended upon the farm to search every crack and niche. If any so-called anti-Soviet literature were to be found on the farm, the entire family would pay the price for his son's courageous patriotism.

***

Later that month, Lilyana decided it was time to reconnect with her friends Krystka and Andros. She had not seen them since that horrible day in March when Andros told her about Jozef's fate.

The pasturelands were now dry, following the winter thaw. A vivid green carpet of springtime grasses dotted with floral blooms lay before her as she set out on foot across the open meadow.

What a lovely day it was. The sun was high and shone brightly. A chorus of singing birds accompanied her as she made her way through the feathery tall grasses and wildflowers. She had almost reached her friends' farmstead when something in the distance caused her to stop dead in her tracks. The farmhouse appeared quiet and dark. Normally, on a day like today, the sound of children playing outside and Krystka's clear, bell-tone voice echoed across the meadowlands. Andros' wagon that usually sat in front of the barn was nowhere to be seen. The barn doors, which always remained open on fine days like today, were barred up tight, and Krystka's cow and goats that freely roamed the pasturelands had vanished.

A cold, hard lump welled up inside Lilyana's throat. She did not have to venture any further. The harsh reality of what had happened here slammed her hard in the chest. It was the same story being told everywhere in recent weeks.

Tears flooded Lilyana's eyes. She stood frozen in the solitude of the meadow staring out at her friends' familiar farmhouse, remembering the happy days she had shared with them there. She shuddered at the thought of how terrified Krystka and the children must have been when the NKVD men came and took them away. It was not likely that any of the little ones would survive. They were all so small and vulnerable to the cruel climate and conditions that Lilyana knew prevailed in the northern regions of Russia. Nobody ever returned from there. Even the toughest adult men perished.

Things began to turn fuzzy then, and Lilyana fell to the ground in a rumpled heap. The next thing she remembered was waking up to the sound of buzzing bees collecting pollen from the wildflowers growing around her. The sun felt warm against her face. Her cheeks were wet from the tears that had broken free as she lay in the soft meadow. She felt safe and content there. If the ground were to open up and swallow her now, she would not resist.

How long she had lain in the meadow, she did not know. She said a prayer for her good friends Krystka and Andros and for their three children, Melania, Jan and Izak. She asked God to watch over them wherever they were, and to keep His merciful and protective hand on all of them.

She could not imagine why the Soviets had deported her friends. They were good people, hardworking, and they had done no harm to anyone. No doubt, Andros had carried out his military training as all young Polish men were expected to do at eighteen, and perhaps this was why the paranoid Russians had removed him… but why had Krystka and the children been deported? It was terrifying and unfair.

Lilyana was gaining a deeper understanding why her Uncle Jerzy had become extra vigilant in watching over the Prawoslaw family and their farm in recent weeks. Since her cousin Wasyl had disappeared, Uncle Jerzy had taken a tighter hold of the reins and was attempting to control everything around him. There was nothing he could do if the Soviet authorities were to come for them, but Lilyana understood her uncle's increased diligence. She shared in his feelings of dread and impending doom.

***

Life carried on through fear and uncertainty until June. The Prawoslaws' fateful hour came early one morning with the sudden sound of heavy pounding on the door, striking terror into all of them.

A shiver ran through Lilyana's body. She'd thought she had mentally prepared herself for this moment, but now it had finally arrived, she felt ill-prepared to handle the agony she knew lay ahead. She was being forced to leave what fragments remained of her life in Poland behind, and she was being taken to that insufferable place called Siberia to live out the rest of her days impoverished, cold and hungry, diseased and at the mercy of the Russians. A life of suffering, ill-treatment and humiliation was about to begin.

She heard yelling downstairs. An officer was shouting out orders.

"Open the door! Open the door, *now!*"

She heard the soldiers stomping into the hallway below. Her mother still lay beside her, sound asleep in the attic room they shared. If all the family were to be removed now, Lilyana knew it was going to be difficult to force her mother to leave the house. Upheaval was difficult for Olisia Prawoslaw, and Lilyana worried that the officers might shoot her mother if she refused to comply with the NKVD order to vacate the farm.

She was sitting on the edge of the bed, mulling over what to do, when Aunt Janina burst into the room, telling her to hurry and get her mother prepared for travel, and to help organise the younger children. The family had already thought out an evacuation plan in case of this tragic event, but all details of their carefully designed procedure had escaped Lilyana's memory as panic and fear took hold of her.

"Lilyana... Lilyana... come to your senses!" her aunt urged, as she gave her niece a less-than-subtle shake.

"Yes... yes. We must hurry," was all Lilyana managed in response.

Now she could hear her uncle pleading with the soldiers:

"Why us? What have we done? Take me if you must, but please leave the women and children alone. What harm can they possibly do to anyone?"

His desperate pleas fell on deaf ears as an NKVD officer shouted out an official order in Russian. Lilyana understood enough of the language to realise her uncle was being accused of various crimes, arrested on trumped-up charges. It sounded like a death sentence.

Larissa and Michal were crying in the room below the attic. Baby Danuta awoke and immediately started to scream. The infant would continue crying non-stop for several more days through all her waking hours. Lilyana got dressed and was beginning to get her mother ready for the journey when she discovered what had alarmed and frightened her young cousins in the room beneath them. Three armed and uniformed soldiers now launched into her bedroom with rifles drawn. Two of the men immediately began to ransack everything, looking for hidden weapons. The third soldier poked at Lilyana with his gun and ordered her and her mother to get downstairs and join the rest of the family in the living room immediately.

"My mother is ill, and she has difficulty leaving this bed," Lilyana tried to explain, but before she could say any more, the soldier smirked.

"Then let me help her!"

The soldier grabbed the end of the bed and flung it upside down. Lilyana gasped in horror as her mother flew across the room and landed stunned and disoriented by the door.

"Mother! Are you alright?" she fretted, hurrying toward her.

Lilyana did not even have time to help her mother up from the floor before the offending soldier was pushing her and Olisia out the door toward the stairs. Her mother half-walked and half-tumbled down the stairway in a zombie-like state, but somehow she and Lilyana managed to wind up with the rest of the Prawoslaws in the living room.

Uncle Jerzy was seated in a chair beside the cook stove in the kitchen, his hands tied behind his back. A Russian soldier held a gun to his head, demanding to know where he kept his weapons and ordering him to turn them over immediately. The bayonet at the end of the soldier's rifle glistened with the reflection of flames from the fire in the oven, making it appear even more menacing. The smell of fresh-baked bread overpowered the room and intensified above the commotion and the din. Jerzy sat motionless, trying to explain that there were no weapons to be found in the house. The soldier kept pressing the sharp edge of his bayonet deeper and deeper into Jerzy's temple. Eventually, blood started to trickle down the side of his head, but he did not give the soldier the satisfaction of seeing his fear, and he did not even flinch as the brutal interrogation continued.

Other soldiers had spread out everywhere in the house and barn, tearing things apart room by room in search of weapons, anti-Soviet literature, foreign passports or currency and anything else they deemed to be subversive or offensive to the Soviet Union. A few of the soldiers were pocketing items they thought might have some value as they continued in their relentless search.

Olisia lay in her nightdress, limp and lifeless on the sofa, next to where the children had been ordered to sit. She looked like a character taken from the *Portraits of Tragedy* that Lilyana had seen in a museum near Krakow when she'd accompanied her father there on a business trip several years earlier. One thing the Prawoslaws did not realise was that despite Olisia's feeble state, she was aware of the dangers awaiting the family now. She was cognizant enough to know that they would be transported to Siberia. The same catastrophe had befallen her grandparents many years earlier. They had lost all their property then. Her father had been a child at the time, and he was the sole survivor from that calamity. He had returned to Poland with horrific stories about life in the northern reaches of Russia. Olisia had always believed her father's early demise when she was only six years old was due to the harsh life he had endured as a boy in the Siberian tundra.

At some point during her uncle's interrogation, Lilyana realised the Soviets knew nothing about Wasyl's disappearance. They kept demanding to know where her cousin was. Why wasn't he at home? It was obvious they suspected him of being in the Polish Underground, but it appeared they had no idea Wasyl had vanished weeks before. Maybe there was still hope that he had escaped and was alive and in hiding somewhere?

A member of the secret police spat in Uncle Jerzy's face and shouted profanities at him when answers to their relentless questions were not forthcoming. The NKVD officer in charge of the investigation called him a stupid, thick-headed peasant. The officer stated that Wasyl was of age and must serve in the Russian Army as all young men living in the new Soviet Zone had been ordered to do. However, Wasyl was absent, and Uncle Jerzy was deemed to be uncooperative. The officer then declared that the Prawoslaws were anti-Soviet subversives, untrustworthy citizens toward the Soviet Union. All of them needed to be removed.

The family was ordered at gunpoint to get dressed quickly, pack only what possessions they could carry with them, and be ready to leave the farm in twenty-five minutes. Uncle Jerzy was ordered to sit on the kitchen floor against the wall while the rest of the family scrambled to gather some items of clothing and food into bundles they wrapped in sheets. Jerzy spent those fleeting minutes silently in conversation with God, praying for the safety of his family. All the while, a Russian soldier held a rifle to his head.

Olisia remained slumped on the couch in the living room. The children had scattered and were grabbing the things that Aunt Janina told them to put into their bundles. Lilyana prepared a large pile for her mother and herself. She packed mainly warmer winter clothing as she knew those items were needed in Siberia. When Larissa asked where they were going, one of the NKVD men told her they would be taken to a better place for their own safety and wellbeing, but the older family members knew that was a lie. They were being hauled off far away to a cold and unmerciful hell.

Aunt Janina had a screaming baby clinging to her side as she hurried into the kitchen to collect the freshly baked loaves of bread, some cured sausage and a few other rations to take on the journey. She used the opportunity to say goodbye to her husband, knowing the fate that lay ahead for Jerzy. She was not allowed to get near him, so she spoke loudly in Polish above the wailing of their frightened infant, telling him she would watch out for the family until they could all be reunited again when the madness ended. Jerzy tried to reply, but the soldier guarding him rammed the butt of his rifle into Jerzy's face, causing his lips to crack and bleed. The Polish language was forbidden now, and for Jerzy and Janina, no more words were allowed to be uttered. Janina longed to hug her husband, but she dared not approach him for fear that the soldier would cause him further injury.

The assailant pushed Jerzy's head to the side with the razor-like edge on the long bayonet at the end of his rifle, until Jerzy could no longer see his wife and infant daughter. Janina was ordered to go outside immediately.

With Danuta still hanging on her one hip, she managed to scoop up her items and tie the sheet into a bundle with her free hand while tears filled her eyes. Then she struggled out the door with the baby and her belongings. The children were already out in the yard, clutching the bundles they had prepared. A couple of soldiers stood by with rifles at the ready in case any of them decided to make a run for it. Janina noticed that Aleksander had taken a protective stance beside Larissa and Michal. He stood slightly in front of them, putting a defensive buffer between his younger siblings and the threatening weapons of the soldiers. What a tall, handsome, young lad he was growing into. Janina wondered why she had not noticed this before. Aleksander had just turned fourteen years old, and already he was assuming the position as leader and protector of his family.

Lilyana floundered out into the yard with one hand wrapped around the large bundle she had packed and her other arm around her mother. She was coaxing Olisia along, trying to make her come out of the house faster than Olisia wanted to move. Two Russian soldiers were pushing them out with guns drawn against their backs. Olisia was sobbing quietly and muttering something about not knowing what items would be important enough to take with her to a life she knew nothing about. Lilyana was trying to calm her mother's nerves and to get her to be quiet. Olisia was noticeably annoying the soldiers, and Lilyana was afraid they might harm her mother in some way if she did not cease her objections and her moaning.

Jerzy was pushed out into the yard just behind Lilyana and Olisia. In a futile attempt, he tried to speak one final time to Janina when he saw her standing in the yard with the children.

"Be strong and live!" he managed to shout before the soldier at his back pushed him down and started beating on him.

Jerzy fell to the ground, face bloodied and hands bound behind his back. There was no chance for him to defend himself.

The same soldier who'd guarded him in the kitchen and ordered him and Janina to be quiet was again enraged by the sound of spoken Polish. In a horrifying voice, he yelled, "Shut up! Shut up!" as he continued pounding on Jerzy's body.

All the family was terrified. Lilyana offered up a quick prayer: *Please Lord, make the beating stop! My uncle is a kind and innocent man. Make the beating stop before they kill him!*

Aleksander stood rigid, his fists clenched in anger, but he dared not move for fear of what might happen to the rest of the family if he were to go to his father's defence. Tears streamed from Janina's eyes. She shielded Danuta's eyes so that the baby would not witness the vicious attack being carried out on her father. Aleksander attempted to do the same to Larissa and Michal, but they had already seen the soldiers' assault, and their tears transformed into loud sobs and wailing.

Larissa cried out, "Please don't kill Daddy! Please!"

Finally, the NKVD officer in charge raised his hand in the air, signalling the soldier to end his brutal attack on Jerzy.

The commander called out to the assailant, "What do you say, comrade? This rebel may prove to be a strong worker, no? We will see what substance he is made of when he is sent in exile to work for our great Imperial Leader's cause in the land of the white bears!"

Uncle Jerzy was dragged along and deposited into the back of a lorry that was parked nearby. The image of his limp and bloodied body being thrown around like a sack of turnips was very unsettling. Lilyana would never see her kind uncle again.

The larger wagon the family had used in their hasty attempt to escape from Poland had never been returned to the farm. When Uncle Jerzy had gone to retrieve it, it was no longer in the spot amongst the forest trees where he had hidden it. Now, the smaller farm wagon had been moved out of the barn, and it waited in the yard with the horses hitched and raring to go. The family were ordered to climb into the wagon. It was a tight fit for all of them and their belongings.

One of the Russian soldiers took control of the reins, and the full effect of their devastating reality impacted Lilyana. Everything her aunt and uncle had ever lived and worked for on their farm no longer belonged to them. Everything had been taken over by the Russians… including their lives. Despite what the soldiers were saying, Lilyana knew they were being sent far away from home to live out the remainder of their days slowly watching each other die one by one. She had listened to her mother's stories many times over; she knew all too well about her grandfather and his parents' suffering, their torture and humiliation in Siberia at the hands of the Russians. Those years had affected her grandfather for the rest of his life… the grandfather she had never met. Although he had managed to escape when he was a young man, he had died prematurely, life in Siberia having taken a toll on his body and his health while he was growing up there.

Lilyana felt an overwhelming sense of defeat and bitterness as the wagon pulled away from Uncle Jerzy and

Aunt Janina's farm that morning. She looked out across the pastureland where she had walked many times. Long grasses waved in the gentle breeze, and wildflowers stood tall in a glorious display of colours as they reached for the summer sun. She viewed the well-worn paths she had come to know so well in the past ten months. Lilyana remembered the freedom she'd felt driving her uncle's horses and sleigh across the meadowland in wintertime. She turned to take one last look at the farmhouse, the barn and the fields. Everything still looked the same, yet in this moment their lives were being turned inside out and changed forevermore.

Lilyana was infuriated by the corrupt injustice the Soviets were inflicting on the people of Eastern Poland. She made a definitive decision to carry herself through all the hardships that lay ahead, willing herself to remain strong and not allow the Soviets to sense her inner fears. She wouldn't bend willingly to their oppressive tyranny. Lilyana needed to remain steadfast for her mother and her younger cousins—they looked to her for hope and support. She deeply desired to continue living, and to successfully overcome whatever the Soviets threw at her. This strengthened her resolve. No matter what, she wouldn't allow the Russians to destroy her.

Her mother continued her muddled rant in the wagon, believing that God had abandoned the family in their time of need. She frightened the children by saying that the coming suffering would be beyond description, now they were caught up in the horrors of this Soviet malediction. Fortunately, much of her muttering wasn't heard above the fuss Danuta was making. The noise coming from the back of the wagon was wearing on everybody. One of the soldiers guarding the family threatened to kill the baby if Janina did not stop Danuta's screaming.

Olisia paid no attention to the guards. She did not seem to care anymore. It no longer mattered to her whether she lived or died. To her, it may as well have been the end of the world.

***

The family arrived at the railway station weary and frightened. On their way there they had noticed a group of people gathering along the bridge above the river. There were many other families being escorted to the station by armed Soviet soldiers and NKVD officers.

After masses of innocent Poles had assembled at the station, the gathering of people on the bridge was heard singing nationalistic Polish songs in the distance. Their voices travelled loud and clear across the water as they expressed their patriotism for their occupied homeland. For a brief time, the songs continued. Then rounds of shots were heard being fired. Screams and sounds of chaos followed.

At the station, the Prawoslaws met up with a few good neighbours and people they recognised from nearby villages. Many were crying. All were confused and scared. Children clung tightly to parents. It was a terrifying experience for everyone. Uncle Jerzy had already been separated from the family as the lorry he'd been thrown into sped off, leaving the family in the wagon far behind him on the road. They did not know where he was now.

A freight train stood waiting at the station. Two coal-burning locomotives in the front were pulling a long line of transport cars designed to carry cattle and other goods. With little else to do, Lilyana found herself counting the number of cattle cars lined up on the rails. A few of the cars were different. One of those was positioned directly behind the locomotives, the second was in the middle of the train, and the third one was at the back. Those cars were for the guards. Conditions inside them were much more comfortable. They had windows on both sides so the guards could look out and view the full length of the train, and there were little turrets on the roofs.

After many hours standing among thousands of frightened faces inside the station, the soldiers started loading people into the boxcars. All the cars were packed tightly with fifty or more men, women and children. Many sobbing children were asking their mothers why they were being taken away from their homes, and they wanted to know where they were going. The NKVD men continued with their stories about moving everybody to another region for their own safety. They said there would be plenty of everything where they were going, and things would be better in the new place. Few people believed their lies.

Lilyana was herded into a cattle car amid shouting and pushing. She was immediately repulsed by the filth and the smell inside. There were no windows to let fresh air in, and with so many nervous bodies crammed closely together in the heat of summer, Lilyana had to force herself not to gag. She managed to work her way over to the side of the car, where gaps between the boards allowed her to breathe in some air from outside. She quickly discovered that she was able to view what was happening at the station through the spaces between the wooden slats from this vantage point. Throughout the remainder of the day, and all through the night, more carts with families sentenced to exile kept arriving. Frightened and tearful people were systematically loaded into the wretched cattle cars.

There were no comforts of any kind. There was a stove made from a large metal drum in the centre of her boxcar with a pipe that had been fashioned into a chimney. For toileting purposes, a hole had been cut into the floor. There was no screen to use for privacy, so everybody would have to relieve themselves in full view of the others. This was the first of many humiliations to come.

Olisia Prawoslaw had now lost her mind entirely. She spoke to Lilyana as though Lilyana were her mother. Lilyana had to respond as though Olisia were her child in order to get her mother to cooperate appropriately. She had her mother sit on one of the lower ledges at the side of the boxcar, and she instructed her to remain there. Many other people in the car had already laid claim to the upper and lower ledges on both sides of the boxcar. The car was so overcrowded that all the people could not sit down at once. The adults stood until it was their turn to try and sleep on the ledges. Nobody was able to sleep for some time. Those who eventually did manage to drift off into a restless sleep were continually interrupted by the screeching of the train's whistle.

When all the people at the station were finally loaded into the cattle cars, the wide doors were slid closed, and soldiers bolted them from the outside. With a quick jolt, the train started to move in the direction of the Russian border. A sickening smell of black smoke and spewing steam along the length of the train filled the air. Reluctantly, Lilyana leaned against the large bundle she had brought with her. A new life of misery and pain had begun.

Mr Prawoslaw had instilled the importance of self-worth and inner strength in Lilyana. Perhaps it was because his wife, Olisia, did not possess strong mental conditioning that he had felt the need to fashion his daughter into a woman resilient to life's troubles. As much as Mr Prawoslaw loved his wife, he did not want Lilyana to share her mother's weaknesses. Olisia was far too nervous and emotional. Mr Prawoslaw reckoned that her emotional state had been the cause for several miscarriages she had endured throughout their marriage. Lilyana was the only baby his wife had managed to bring to term. Mr Prawoslaw had always believed it was a sign that Lilyana was strong. He conscientiously helped his daughter develop her innermost strength and perseverance as she grew up. These qualities would prove to be invaluable now as a genuine test of fortitude and tenacity was unfolding.

Lilyana looked around the crowded cattle car and saw nothing but lost and helpless people. The early morning sun's rays had started to break through the barred openings at the top of the car. Everybody was overwhelmed by the personal tragedy that had befallen them.

There were not many men in the boxcar. A large number of women had been packed into the car, having to fend for their children on their own. Aunt Janina was not alone; all were overcome by grief as they worried about the fate their husbands, their fathers and their brothers faced. Everyone shared in uncertainty and fear as the train pulled away from the station.

Lilyana was surprised to discover that several Jewish families had been loaded into the boxcar. She would later learn that the two massive deportations in February and April had mainly been made up of ethnic Poles from the new Soviet Zone, but a lot of Jewish refugees had been added to the deportation list in June. Many of those were not local Jews; most had been refugees who'd fled to the east from the Nazi Zone in Western and Central Poland.

Inside the car, the smell and mess intensified. There were many small children and infants, and little order. Nothing could be done about it; the occupants had no means of cleaning the freight car. With so many bodies packed tightly inside, it was horrendous. The train continually jerked and jolted as it stopped, started and rolled along.

Many people had packed a few food rations in the brief time the Soviets had given them to leave their homes, and during the first few days, there was plenty to be shared by everyone. Once that was gone, the heat, dirt, hunger and thirst overcame them. The Soviets were inconsistent in feeding the deportees. Small rations of bread and soup were sometimes offered to them, but the salty soup smelt terrible and those individuals who did eat it just became thirstier. Sometimes, they were fed every day. Other times, two or three days would pass before being given any more food or water.

Temperatures inside the packed cattle cars rose steadily as June rolled over into July. Every day, the sun continued to beat down on the tightly packed wooden cars, and the heat became unbearable. Everyone suffered from overheating and excessive thirst. The stifling cars caused profuse sweating and eventual dehydration. Children were constantly crying from hunger and thirst. Occasionally, the Soviets provided a bucket of dirty water for all the people to drink, but it did little to quench the insatiable thirst for that number of people. When the train stopped at various stations along the way, the women begged passers-by for water. Sometimes, a person took pity on them and passed water to the suffering people.

Many of the elderly, the weak and the infants began to perish. Ironically, where people had been freezing and dying from hypothermia throughout the winter deportations, people were overheating and dying from dehydration and heatstroke during the summer deportations. Sometimes, bodies of the dead remained in the boxcars all day long. The smell of death filled the stuffy cars. Lilyana learned that it was possible to get used to something as horrific as that very quickly when you have no other choice.

One family appeared to be more distraught than the rest of the people in the Prawoslaws' car. Amid the chaos and confusion of loading the freight cars, they had been divided and did not know what had happened to their other young children. Every time the Russians opened the sliding doors at the side of the car, the family pleaded with the authorities to keep their family together in their relocation. The Soviets simply ignored their panic and despair. When the train arrived at their destination, the family would be overcome by grief when they learned that their other children had died en route to the Soviet Union. Their inconsolable pain touched Lilyana deeply.

With that many sweating bodies crammed together inside the freight cars, with clothes dirty and smelling, and without any hygiene facilities available, an infestation of lice became inevitable. Nobody remained untouched by the pesky insects. All the deportees suffered with inextinguishable itching and discomfort. Aunt Janina cut Larissa's beautifully braided hair as the child cried unstoppable tears. She trimmed back baby Danuta's locks as well. The infant put up no fuss. The baby was sick with a fever and no longer cried. She had been quiet for a couple of days now. Janina and Lilyana were concerned, knowing that Danuta required medical attention, but none would be forthcoming.

Occasionally the train stopped at stations to take on more coal and supplies for the guards. The soldiers opened the boxcar doors, and while being closely guarded, they allowed the deportees to get out and stretch their legs. People who had things to sell or exchange for bread did so during those stops at the stations. Others ran to the engine to collect hot water to drink. Many brought back boiling water to the boxcar in cups, cans or whatever they had to collect it in. However, when the train started up again, the sudden jerking motion caused people to fall over into each other, and many were scalded by the boiling water. Loud cries and groans were heard coming from many cars.

Lilyana wished the Prawoslaws still had the valuables her father had packed in sacks and stowed away in the family vehicle when the war started. Mr Prawoslaw had meticulously chosen items to sell and trade during the family's planned flight to freedom. Now she better understood the rationale behind her father's thinking and preparations. He had known what he was doing, until he disappeared shortly after the Russians occupied their homeland. Lilyana's cousin, Wasyl, had reported that her father's car had been discovered and ransacked some time after the family abandoned it in their failed attempt to slip across the Romanian border. Wasyl had seen the car during his many meanderings around the countryside before he had vanished himself. He said it appeared to have been driven down into a ravine near the dense grove of bushes where Mr Prawoslaw had hidden it. All the tires had been removed. Some of the mechanical parts were missing, and the doors and boot had been pried open. Nothing remained of the family's valuables; all the sacks had disappeared. An empty, rumpled metal shell was all that remained of the car. The family would never know whether the Red Army had discovered the car and stripped it down, or whether the deed had been carried out by desperate local villagers.

As the miserable days inside the cattle car dragged on, many people kept their spirits alive by singing religious and patriotic songs. Lilyana joined in the singing with great enthusiasm and pride. They sang with sincerity, from their hearts, as though they were offering up prayers to God in song. It reminded Lilyana of the hymns she sang in school and the church choir. It also brought back happy memories of how she and Krystka would sing together in her friend's kitchen.

Sometimes, people in neighbouring freight cars joined in and created beautiful harmonies. A few times, Lilyana was sure the entire train was singing and humming the prayer songs together. It was a harmonious offering of prayer that God must surely have heard up in Heaven. This was the only positive memory Lilyana would take away from that dreadful transport into the Siberian unknown. When she was singing, the awful conditions inside the wretched cattle car would disappear for a while.

Aunt Janina would often nudge her niece and say, "Lilyana! Stop singing! The Bolsheviks will tear open this door and shoot all who are joining in!"

Lilyana would reply, "Oh Auntie! Let the Russians try! They will have to shoot everyone on this train then. What use will our able bodies be to them if we arrive in Siberia dead! Besides, the singing is the only thing that the Soviets have no control over. We cannot let them win by ceasing in our songs."

The train was heading in a north-easterly direction. The people knew this from the names of the smaller towns and stations they passed along the way. They left Poland and crossed over the border into the vast Russian territory. The border was heavily guarded and patrolled by Russian soldiers. A massive barbed wire fence stretched along the border from the checkpoint gates as far as the eye could see.

Lilyana's cousin, Aleksander, and a few other young lads took turns climbing up onto each other's shoulders to peer out of the small grate at the top of the car. From there, they reported the names of Russian towns and villages as the train continued rolling on. Eventually, the boys announced they could see the Ural Mountains in the distance, and later they spied the mighty Volga River. The lads also mentioned that some people in more populated areas were seen coming out from their homes and making the sign of the cross in the air as the train passed by. It seemed like they were blessing the passing freight cars, knowing that the mass of humanity inside was heading into perdition.

Sounds of moaning, sobbing and prayers echoed all the way along the length of the deportation train. It took three unbearable weeks for it to reach its destination. All sense of time vanished as the intolerable days dragged on. Sometime during the second week, Lilyana was awakened to the despairing sobs of her aunt on the ledge next to her. A glint of moonlight seeping through the gaps between the boxcar boards cast a tiny bit of illumination across the forlorn mass of people inside. Lilyana was able to distinguish Janina's hunched and sobbing body cradling Danuta close to her heart. She need not ask for an explanation. She knew the baby had died. She reached out to her aunt and wrapped her arms around Janina and the babe. Together they cried silently well into the morning hours.

An old man who sat next to Olisia on one of the lower ledges nearby eventually turned to Janina and Lilyana, saying, "You will have to surrender the baby unto God. She cannot stay in here with the living!"

Janina just glared back at him with her tear-stained face. She did not want to let go of Danuta. She wanted to carry the infant all the way to their destination and give her a proper Christian burial. Lilyana understood her aunt's desperation. However, she realised that would not be possible. In the stifling heat inside the boxcar, the body was already decomposing. If her aunt did not willingly release the baby's corpse to the officials, the surviving people inside the car would force her to. Lilyana had to encourage her aunt to let Danuta go.

Janina was steadfast in her reluctance to turn the baby over to the Soviets. She had seen how they discarded the dead bodies of those who passed away, and she was not going to let anyone toss Danuta out by a railway siding somewhere as though she were yesterday's garbage. Gradually, Lilyana managed to console her grieving aunt by promising her she would speak to the authorities when they opened the boxcar doors, and she would make them allow the family to bury Danuta properly somewhere near the next railway stop.

It took a lot of courage, but in her unwavering persistence, Lilyana was finally able to convince the guards to give the Prawoslaws permission to bury the baby. While other deportees scrambled to sell their wares at the next station, the Prawoslaws stood silently in prayer over a small dirt mound where their youngest member was laid to rest. They were able to choose a quiet spot near a tree situated opposite the station platform. Aleksander dug a small hole with an old tin can he had found. Lilyana helped her aunt wrap Danuta's body carefully in her flea-infested blanket. They all sobbed as Aleksander gently placed the baby into the hole, then pushed the soil back over Danuta's tiny body. He and Lilyana helped support Janina, who was beside herself with grief. They prayed together, and Lilyana offered up a hymn. The song evoked a sense of Danuta's spirit rising into Heaven. Larissa and Michal wept without constraint. Aleksander tried to bury his grief and remain stoic, but it was obvious his heart ached just as much over the loss of his baby sister.

Throughout the Prawoslaws' makeshift service, a staunch Russian soldier stood guard over the family. His presence felt intrusive on their private moment, but they were thankful that Lilyana had been successful in getting the Soviets to allow them this opportunity.

Olisia Prawoslaw stood quiet and motionless over the burial plot. It was difficult to determine whether she understood the gravity of what had happened. She had slipped into a state of deep depression and remained unresponsive. It seemed that her mind had gone to another place. Lilyana was sure her mother was no longer aware of anything happening around them.

The surviving family members silently returned to the freight car, each one hanging onto their own special memories of the brief time they had shared with baby Danuta. Some of the people inside the car looked at them sympathetically. Others were too wrapped up in their own tragic circumstances to notice. An old, toothless man told Janina that freedom comes by death for some. Others encouraged her to take courage in the face of sorrow.

There were times when the survivors envied the dead. Some even prayed to die. Tragically, several people would put an end to their suffering by committing suicide.

Lilyana noticed that Aleksander had scooped up a handful of soil from around Danuta's grave when the family was ordered to return to the train. Once her aunt had finally settled and drifted off to sleep with Larissa and Michal, Lilyana asked Aleksander why he had put the dirt into his shirt pocket.

"I brought it with me so that I can return Danuta to our home one day. When I go back to a free and independent Poland, I will take this dirt and spill it over our farmland, where her soul will come to rest eternally."

Lilyana was impressed by her young cousin's deep, caring thought. When she considered the meaning behind Aleksander's heartfelt gesture, she grew teary eyed.

"That is a wonderful idea," she said.

Leaning in closer to Lilyana, Aleksander quietly revealed that he had also taken a fistful of soil from in front of the farmhouse when the soldiers had come and sent the family into exile. It was wrapped up in a handkerchief inside the bundle he had brought with him. He felt that by carrying a piece of their past with him, it would represent a symbol of hope for the future. He believed he would return the earth to the ground where he had taken it from when the family was free to go home and reclaim their farm.

Lilyana smiled a weak smile. She doubted that would ever be possible. However, she did admire her cousin's motive.

"If any of us survive and are able to recover the family farm, it will be you, Aleksander," Lilyana stated. "I am sure you will be the one to do it!"

Two days later, another unfathomable drama unfolded that would shake all the Prawoslaws to the core. It happened when the train stopped at a remote location to take on more supplies. Many people were milling about outside, and Lilyana helped her mother exit the boxcar to breathe in some fresh air and get some exercise. She and Olisia walked along the side of the train and reached the final one in the long line of freight cars. Another train could be heard barrelling along the rails as it approached the outpost. Lilyana turned to see the oncoming train. It appeared that the rattling locomotive was going to pass straight through without stopping. Olisia suddenly broke free from Lilyana's grasp and darted past the deportation train out onto the railway tracks. Lilyana let out a scream and, pleading with her mother to come back onto the station platform, ran toward where her mother had bolted. The oncoming train had almost reached the outpost. Lilyana was racing against the locomotive to reach her mother and pull her off the tracks. Suddenly, Aleksander appeared and was beside Lilyana, trying to outrun the train. Together they dashed toward Olisia as the roaring locomotive moved forward with increasing speed. They were covered with smoke and soot as a black plume spewed from the chimney. The train's whistle screeched a series of deafening blasts as it rumbled along the rails. Lilyana felt the thundering vibration of the train shudder through every inch of her body. The train overtook Lilyana and Aleksander, and suddenly Olisia was gone. Aleksander had to forcefully restrain Lilyana from reaching out as the roaring train sped by. When it had passed, he tried to hide Lilyana's face from searching the spot where her mother had leapt. No trace of Olisia Prawoslaw remained.

"Mother! Mother! Where are you?" Lilyana lamented again and again, as though she believed her mother could have survived by some divine intervention.

Curious people were gathering at the location now. Aleksander had to literally drag Lilyana away, kicking and screaming. A few guards moved in quickly to break up the curious crowd and forced everyone back into the transport train. Lilyana was completely numbed by shock and disbelief. It would be a few days before she would be able to speak again.

She blamed herself for her mother's death. If only she had not taken her mother outside for a walk… if only she had been more attentive in watching her … if only this, that or another thing. Her self-condemnation carried on. Aunt Janina and many others tried to tell her that she was not responsible for her mother's actions. Janina insisted that if anyone were to be blamed, the fault would squarely rest on the Soviets' shoulders. Olisia Prawoslaw had not been the same ever since the Russians had moved in and occupied their homeland. After Mr Prawoslaw had vanished, her life effectively came to a standstill. Once the family had been sent away into exile, it was too much for her to cope with. She had psychologically dismissed herself from this life some time ago. All that remained had been for her to release her body into the virtual netherworld that enveloped her.

At times, Lilyana wanted to believe her mother's demise had been an accident. Perhaps Olisia had not realised what was happening when she ran out in front of the oncoming train. Had she been cognizant of the reality? Had it been a deliberate act on her part, or was it all an unfortunate mishap? The answer to Lilyana's difficult question finally came when Aunt Janina handed over an important item Olisia Prawoslaw had left behind.

A few days before the deportees arrived at their destination, Janina opened her bundle of possessions. She handed over little Danuta's winter wrap to another mother in the freight car who had a surviving baby about the same size as her infant had been.

"I have no more use for this," Janina said. "I pray that your child will survive, and that she will be warmed in body and spirit by my daughter's cloak."

Then Janina pulled out a book from the centre of her bundle. Glancing over at her niece, she motioned for Lilyana to come closer and see what she was holding in her hands.

"Lilyana," she began. "Your mother gave this book to me a few months ago. She instructed me to pass it on to you if anything were to happen to her. She was very adamant that the book be stored in a safe place, and that I give it to you if the time should come when she was no longer with us. I believe she would want me to give it to you now."

Lilyana stared incredulously at the book as her aunt handed it to her. She immediately recognised it to be the book of poems that her father had given to her mother on their wedding day. She recalled many cold winter nights when she was a little girl in Stolpce, her mother cuddled up next to her in bed reading the lovely words from her special book of poems. Her father had inscribed a dedication to her mother at the front of the book. Lilyana knew it by heart.

To my Darling Olisia:
May our lives together be filled with
endless love and joy. I will love you
always!
Your devoted husband
xxx

Gently stroking the front cover, Lilyana pressed the book against her heart. She opened it and held it close to her face. A faint smell of her family's home in Stolpce still lingered among the pages, the familiar aroma of her mother's wonderfully prepared recipes strangely blended with the smell of polish and cleaner. Olisia Prawoslaw had been a proud housewife. Cooking, cleaning and polishing were her specialities. She was known far and wide for her beautifully served traditional Polish meals and her immaculately clean and tidy home. How difficult it must have been for her to sit in the filth and debris of the cattle car.

Aunt Janina hugged Lilyana and turned away in order to give her niece some privacy when she saw how much the book meant to her. This had been Olisia Prawoslaw's favourite possession. Lilyana would guard and treasure it forever. She prayed with faith that her mother had moved on to a better place. She fell asleep cradling the book of poems next to her heart. It was the one and only thing that remained of her parents, and it would always hold great value and importance for her.

Later, she flipped through the pages of her mother's book. The familiar words brought back happy recollections of times when her mother had read the poems to her while she was growing up. As she fanned through the pages, a strange object caught her eye near the end of the book. She turned back to see what it was. An envelope was wedged between the pages of a poem that spoke about the infinite love a mother has for her children. Lilyana's name appeared on the front of the envelope in her mother's handwriting. Was this a message being sent to her from beyond the grave? Carefully, she pulled the envelope free. A handwritten letter was inside.

Lilyana had to brace herself. Did she really want to read what her mother had written? She returned the envelope to the spot where it had been discovered and closed the book. Then, slowly, curiosity got the better of her. She went back to the marked page and carefully removed the envelope once more. She lifted the flap where the envelope had been sealed, and cautiously removed the letter. Her hands trembled as she worked up the courage to unfold the letter and read it. It had been written a few months earlier.

30th March 1940
My dearest Lilyana,
If you are reading this, my precious girl, then I must beg your forgiveness for what I have done. I could no longer bear to be a burden to you, nor to your aunt and

uncle. Although none of you have ever complained about my deteriorating state, I know it has not been easy for you to abide my hopeless condition. At first, I did believe that your father would be returning to us following his sudden disappearance last year. However, it is obvious to me now that something terrible has happened to him, and I will never see the face of my sweet and loving husband again. I find it difficult to exist without my sweet, darling man. He was my strength and courage. Only he could instil in me the fortitude required to exist in the bad circumstances that we find ourselves suffering through now.

You know, my loving daughter, how delicate I have always been. I would not have been able to bear any of life's adversities, were it not for your adoring papa. Now, without him, our life situation is too much for me to endure. Please harbour no resentment toward me, my precious child. I plead for your absolution. If God chooses to send me into Hell for my transgression, surely it will not be as bad as the hell we are suffering through in our occupied homeland now.

You are much stronger than I have ever been, Lilyana. Your perseverance is a gift passed down to you from your father. Please move forward in your life with the strength and courage dear Papa instilled in you. Pray that the persecution and oppression clouding Poland now will be lifted. Believe that you will live to see Poland free and alive again one day. Do not let the Bolsheviks rob you of your steadfast spirit or your joy, as they have done to me. Remember to live your life as Papa showed you. Be kind to your fellow citizens, help those who you can, and love God with all your heart and soul. Cling to what good comes out of the unfortunate circumstances we live in right now, and always remember the happy childhood your papa and I afforded you in Stolpce, wherever your life ends up.

You are loved, my dear and precious child, more than words could ever convey. You and Papa were the great loves of my life. Do not despair in my absence. I leave you with *only happy memories of what once was, as I release you from my encumbrance.*

Forever your loving mother.

xxx

***

Lilyana's disdain toward the Soviets would increase substantially following her mother's suicide. Had it not been for the oppressive Russian invasion and occupation, she would still be living a happy life in Stolpce with her mother and her papa. Life would have carried on as usual. Her uncle, aunt and cousins' lives would have prospered as usual on their farm in the countryside. Lilyana would have been helping her father in the mercantile store, and courting her wonderful friend, Jozef. If the Soviet's had not invaded their world, all the people who meant the most to her would still be alive and well. The Russians had taken away everything she loved and valued most.

For the first time in her life, Lilyana found herself tasting the bitter elixir of hate. There was an ache deep inside her that no one would ever heal, yet she found solace in the fact that the Russians could never steal away the loving memories imprinted on her heart of those she had lost along the way.

SEVEN
WORKING COLONY

Toward the end of the Prawoslaws' journey, the train became shorter as many cattle cars were detached and left behind at major stations along the tracks. It felt like their odyssey was never going to end. Years later, in her dreams, Lilyana would still hear the noise of the train wheels rattling along the rails and feel the constant swaying and jerking of the boxcars.

The harrowing journey brought them to an area near Arkhangelsk in Siberia where their car was uncoupled. They had arrived at their final stop and were ordered to get out. Armed guards were everywhere. Nobody dared to refuse their orders or to ask any questions. Horse-drawn wagons awaited their arrival at the station, but many people chose to walk as the carts became overcrowded with smelly, dirty, coughing elderly people and children, and all their filthy, bug-infested belongings. Filled with trepidation, the deportees were marched under guard through a few outlying villages. Lilyana walked beside Aleksander in the long line. All of them felt as though they were being treated like criminals.

It was now mid-July, but there was a nip of cold in the air. Trudging along the mucky dirt roads, Lilyana took in images of the local villages. All the small, wooden houses were capped with thatched roofs. They looked damp and uninviting.

The landscape around them was mainly comprised of hills and vast forestlands. Distant mountains were covered in snow. Further to the south, the train had passed through a large, swampy region devoid of trees. Lilyana had observed the swampy floodplains along a network of rivers and deep valleys through gaps in the planks of the cattle car. Sporadic meadowlands had been observed along the route as well.

To Lilyana's surprise, spruce, pine and larch grew this far north. Here in the taiga, coniferous woodlands thrived between the extensive, treeless plains further south and the Arctic tundra to the north. What a strange and diverse place Siberia was. She was surprised that beauty existed in this place of banishment.

The convoy of deportees stopped overnight to rest in a large, wooden barracks. They were fed a thin soup and small portion of foul-tasting bread. It was enough to tease their appetite, but not enough to stifle the hunger pains. A caretaker family was responsible for cooking and cleaning in the large house. They treated the deportees with the same distain and rudeness that the Russian guards and soldiers showed toward them. There was one long wooden table, and benches for sitting and sleeping on. Because there was not enough room for all the people to sleep on the benches, the Prawoslaws slept on the floor. It was cold and uncomfortable, but at least it provided them more room to stretch out their legs than they'd had in the cramped boxcar.

There was an outhouse behind the barracks that was closely guarded by soldiers. When the women went there, the guards would tease them by lifting the backs of their dresses with the long bayonets at the end of their rifles. Lilyana had become accustomed to the Soviets' ill manners, and she chose to ignore their insolence.

A river ran beside the barracks. Lilyana saw the caretaker family's son drawing buckets of dirty water straight out of the river to bring to the deportees. She hurried back into the crowded, dirty, noisy barracks and lay down and tried to sleep. Soon the guards were forbidding the deportees to leave the barracks for any reason, even when people who had drunk from the unsanitary water in the buckets began to experience ill effects.

The next morning, the deportees were taken to the bathhouse. Their lice-infested clothes were disinfected, a census was taken, and then they were confined to the barracks.

Every day after that, selected groups of people were taken away in wagons. Nobody knew where those individuals were being taken or what fate awaited them when they got there. Everybody worried about when their turn would come.

Several horse-drawn wagons came when the Prawoslaws' turn arrived. Many other families were driven away with them. They followed a long route across mountainous countryside that descended through narrow passageways into such steep hills Lilyana thought the loaded wagons would tumble over the embankments. They travelled by night and day with few breaks for meals or rest. Night travel was particularly treacherous. Lilyana and Aleksander opted to walk beside the wagon when the passages became narrow and the hills became too steep and slippery. Their clothes became torn and dirty, and they were exhausted from scrambling up and down the dangerous mountain slopes.

The deportees eventually arrived at a small village where the wagons and horses were changed over to different drivers and carts, but the soldiers guarding them remained the same. They rested there for a day, were given some rations to eat, and were wakened early the next morning to continue their journey.

Lilyana remained close to the wagon that pulled her aunt and younger cousins with their belongings. Another family had been crammed into the wagon with them, making it difficult to sit comfortably. Aleksander and an older boy from the other family trekked alongside the wagon as well. The other lad's name was Edward Leski. He and Aleksander became good friends. Aunt Janina and Edward's mother, Rowena, were overheard in the wagon taking note of Edward's apparent attraction to Lilyana, creating an awkwardness that made Edward and Lilyana avoid each other at all cost. However, one afternoon, the convoy of deportees and wagons were climbing a steep incline and Lilyana lost her footing on some loose gravel when the strap on her shoe suddenly broke. Edward managed to grab onto Lilyana's shoulder and pull her in close to him to prevent her from falling over the edge of the cliff. Embarrassed but grateful, Lilyana quickly thanked the Leski boy while pulling free from his lingering grasp. Aleksander smiled broadly and teased Edward about the incident. Edward was mortified. Mrs Leski and Aunt Janina chuckled about it for days afterwards.

The entourage was travelling east of Arkhangelsk. Two soldiers argued in Russian over the number of kilometres they had covered. There was some discrepancy as to how many remained between them and their eastern destination.

One of those soldiers had started showing favour toward Lilyana along their journey, frequently positioning himself close to her while she walked beside her family's wagon. Following the drama when she'd almost tumbled down the side of the hilly cliff, the Russian soldier had taken Lilyana's broken shoe and threaded a piece of string through the defective clasp so it would stay closed. These things did not go unnoticed by Aunt Janina or Mrs Leski.

Lilyana did not thank the Russian soldier for mending her broken shoe. She was afraid he might take advantage of her in some way if she validated him and did her best to avoid him.

Her mind kept going back to a tale that a young woman named Olga told her at the barracks when they were waiting to be dispersed. Olga had described what could happen to females the Russian soldiers took a fancy to. She said her sister had been arrested and exiled to a forced labour camp in the north for her participation in an anti-Soviet demonstration when she was attending university. Her sister had written a letter that was smuggled out from the camp and forwarded on to Olga. It described the horrible indignities that were inflicted on women at the labour camp, such heinous events that Lilyana found it difficult to believe the information was true. Upon arrival there, the prisoners in her convoy had been ordered to strip off all their clothes and leave their belongings in a heap inside the camp's gates. The prisoners, men and women together, were then shoved naked into enclosures made of planks. Each pen was small and held three or four shivering, frightened individuals. The cages had no roof, and the prisoners were forced to stand on top of frozen excrement that covered the ground inside. While they were being held in the enclosures, camp officials had thieves sift through all their belongings to steal the best shoes and clothing. The pens were then opened, and the prisoners were led naked across the yard into an official building where they were subjected to thorough body searches. Olga's sister had believed there would be no humiliation worse than that, but she soon discovered women suffered added atrocities in the camp. They were subjected to frequent degrading night searches when camp guards entered their barracks and ordered them to get up, get undressed, go outside with their hands up and line up against the wall. Olga's sister said these repeated episodes were terrifying. Some of the guards, camp employees from surrounding villages and even some of the male prisoners raped and abused the women.

Olga's sister wound up pregnant as a result of repeated rapes in the camp. She requested to be released in a special reprieve, but camp authorities rarely released pregnant women. Those who arrived at the camps pregnant and those who became pregnant while surviving in the gulag had little rest from forced labour in order to give birth. Camp officials took the babies from their mothers and placed them in special orphanages. Olga's sister wanted to let her know what had happened, and she wanted Olga to try and search for the baby boy she had given birth to in the camp. She had provided Olga with the name of the camp where the boy was born, the date of her son's birth and a few other details, but Olga's attempt to find her sister's son had proved futile.

Although Lilyana had not been exiled to a forced labour camp, she was being hauled away into the unknown. She did not want to be singled out by any of the Russian soldiers.

***

The final leg of the Prawoslaws' journey followed the course of a winding river through a thick forest. Boggy terrain and a pestilence of mosquitoes, gnats, horseflies and midges plagued them the entire way. Amid confusion, and feeling weak and helpless, they eventually arrived at a small village far away from any railway lines or towns.

The deportees were assembled at the centre of the remote village. An NKVD commander was in charge of the settlement here. He assigned the families to their living quarters. Lilyana held on tightly to Larissa's hand so the little girl would not get lost in the large crowd of people being shuffled around. Aunt Janina stood between Lilyana and Aleksander, who clung onto the family's bundled possessions. Michal leaned against his mother. He had become ill during the journey. Janina just wanted to get to a place where she could settle Michal down for a good sleep. She needed to mix up a concoction of her fever medicine to bring down her son's temperature. Following Wasyl's disappearance and Danuta's death, she could not bear the thought of losing another child.

Lilyana dreaded what the living quarters would look like. What would be required of them to live there?

Their belongings were thrown into a cart with those of many other families, and they were led away from the village centre. They marched for several kilometres before the soldiers started directing groups of people into a series of crudely constructed shelters in the middle of nowhere. Lilyana noticed that the soldier who had repaired her broken shoe was one of those conducting deportees to their assigned dwellings. She did her best to remain hidden among the large group of people so he wouldn't notice her.

The hovels had been built earlier by exiles who had died of hunger and cold trying to eke out an existence. The living quarters were extremely small, damp and dark. They were not insulated, and spaces between the planks of wood on the walls were so wide you could see through to the outside in some spots. The wider gaps had been stuffed with moss, which they soon discovered was the perfect breeding ground for bedbugs and other insects.

It felt like a prison cell. There was a wash basin sitting on a wooden stand, with no running water or electricity. A tiny wood-burning stove for cooking and heating in winter was situated in the middle of the room, but there was no wood or fuel of any kind.

Initially, there were eighteen people crammed into the Prawoslaws' tiny, one-roomed, wooden shack. Lilyana, Aunt Janina, Aleksander, Larissa and Michal; Mrs Leski, Edward and his siblings, Dionizy, Jolanta and Margisia; Mrs Bablak and her surviving children, Cyryl and Elzbieta; and Mrs Dobrowolski with her daughters, Marta, Lina, Maria and Helena. They worried how that many people could all fit in. Two double-tiered sleeping bunks were pressed against the end wall. The only way for all of them to sleep was to share the wooden sleeping platforms three or four abreast. A small wooden table was placed against a side wall with a wooden bench that stretched along the opposite side of the table. On the wall, across from the sleeping bunks, a series of poorly constructed shelves was roughed in.

The room was cheerless and depressing, no better than conditions inside the dark, smelly, cramped cattle cars. Two small slits for windows allowed a minimum amount of light to enter the living space. There was no food, and there were no mattresses or bedding on the sleeping bunks. They used their coats and other clothing to cushion themselves and to keep warm on the sleeping platforms. The families unpacked their belongings and tried to make the crude shack feel more like home, but they were so morally crushed, little could be done to improve their mood.

Two of the Dobrowolski girls, Michal Prawoslaw and Margisia Leski were all sick upon arrival at the settlement, and Aunt Janina and Mrs Dobrowolski set about preparing a potion to relieve their fevers. Janina had thrown her bag of herbal remedies into her bundle of possessions before she was forced out of her kitchen at the Prawoslaw farm. Mrs Dobrowolski had also brought along some herbs and medicines. Aleksander was sent outside to collect water in a bowl his mother pulled out from her bundle. There was a river that flowed nearby at the bottom of a ravine behind their shelter. Edward Leski and Cyryl Bablak were sent out to scrounge up some bits of wood to build a fire in the small metal drum that served as their wood stove. A metal pipe extruded out from the drum and vented outside. With water being boiled inside an old tin can, the herbal remedy was made. Eventually, it helped to ease the children's coughing and bring down their fevers. Unfortunately, little Maria Dobrowolski would be found dead next to her sister on their sleeping platform several days later. Her frail lungs had given out following a night of wheezing and severe coughing. Seventeen people were left crammed into their one-room wooden shack. They would live in these barbaric, over-crowded conditions for many months.

***

The day after they arrived, local authorities catalogued the deportees' names and ages and counted them again before organising them into categories of older and younger adults, and older and younger children. The older men worked in the camp sawing timber into boards, and the younger men were sent to the forest to fell trees every day. In this settlement, all people fourteen years old and up were considered working age.

Aleksander, Edward and Cyryl went to the forest and did lumbering work. At first, Lilyana, Elzbieta Bablak and Marta Dobrowolski were sent to the forest to collect resin. Shortly afterwards, the girls were transferred to a brigade of young women who were sent into the forest to cut down trees with the younger men. They were given axes and saws and were expected to keep pace with the men in their brigade.

Without any experience, the young women had no idea how to go about cutting down huge trees, or how to cut the timber into various sizes after the trees were felled. The men in their work crew wanted to reach the daily required quota, so they showed the young women how to do the job. While they were working as lumberjacks, Lilyana often spotted wild bears, wolves and reindeer in the forest.

In the local village there was a school set up for the younger children, a communal bathhouse, a couple of small, state-run shops with very few, over-priced things available for purchase, and the NKVD Headquarters. Workers in the forest were paid a meagre wage for piece work according to the same system that existed in the labour camps, except their compensation was paid in Russian rubles instead of rationed food. With their money, they bought basic products in the village shops. Those who only managed less than half the work standard the authorities demanded were subject to sanctions, and their already small pay was drastically reduced.

The major means of support in the village turned out to be from selling things they had brought with them and things their relatives or friends remaining in Poland were able to send to them in parcels, rather than their insufficient earnings.

The Soviets maintained strict control over the deportees and their lives in the remote village colonies. They were not free to do as they pleased nor to travel outside of their designated settlements. Although the death rate of deportees was lower in these cooperative villages of Central and Northern Russia than in the forced labour camps further north, the people were equally affected mentally and physically by their ordeal.

Labour settlements were the Soviets' answer to colonising and developing the more barren areas in the Russian territory. Conditions in the villages were brutal. The large gaps between wooden slats in the flimsy, over-crowded shacks allowed insects, mice and rats to get inside and run rampant. Constantly filling in the chinks with mud, turf and tree branches did little to deter frost from forming along the poorly heated walls inside. When winter came, many people died from frostbite and hypothermia.

The scant meals were comprised of a thin soup and one piece of stale bread. Resourceful people supplemented the insufficient diet with a horrible-tasting, thick porridge they made with grasses collected from the nearby fields. It did not provide much in the way of nutrition, but it helped to stave off the painful cramps that would accompany their empty bellies. Starvation claimed many lives, and illness ravished the colony because of their weakened immune systems. Scurvy resulted from lack of a proper diet.

Sickness and death constantly surrounded them. Fresh new horrors were always waiting to come and destroy their lives. Long working hours, poor hygiene, lack of medical facilities and medicines, cruelty and harsh punishments from the guards added to the toll. The Soviet secret police were unpredictable, and people always had to be vigilant of everything happening around them. If a NKVD officer took a disliking to any individual, they could easily fabricate a scenario to have that person severely mistreated or killed. Only those individuals capable of toughening themselves up in body and mind survived the savage treatment and conditions of life in the settlements.

When the Prawoslaws first arrived at the village, summer winds from the north brought long spells of cold rain with them. On the days when the sun shone, it became extremely hot and humid. Through July and August, it was not unusual for the thermometer to suddenly soar as high as 35 °C. It became unbearably hot inside the crowded living quarters with so many bodies packed tightly together. Then, just as quickly as the temperature had risen, it would abruptly plummet and become freezing cold again. Rapid changes in the weather were a part of life here in the far north.

They soon learned that in order to survive they would have to be cunning and resourceful. Aunt Janina and Mrs Leski started a small garden plot by the side of their shack and attempted growing a few vegetables from seeds Rowena

Leski had brought along with her. Constant weeds threatened to choke out the vegetables as they began to sprout.

Mrs Bablak and Mrs Dobrowolski were more refined, coming from the larger towns of Eastern Poland. Their husbands had apparently been influential men. Survival here was more challenging for them.

Lilyana helped her aunt and Mrs Leski wash clothes down in the river amidst swarms of mosquitoes and gnats. They did not have any soap for bathing with or for doing laundry, so they scrubbed the clothing on a rock down at the riverbank. Lilyana discovered wild onion greens growing along the shoreline and cheerfully brought them to the shelter for everyone to chew on.

Dionizy Leski was twelve years old, too young to be sent to work in the forest. He attended school, and it was his responsibility to bring water from the river at the bottom of the ravine and help the older boys fetch wood from the forest for the fire. The dirt pathway down to the river was very steep, making it difficult to haul full buckets of water back up the hill without spilling some, and the forest was also a good distance away from the shelter. Without a wagon to carry the wood, it took several trips back and forth from the forest every day. Often the older boys were away felling trees in the forest, and Dionizy was left to fetch the wood himself.

Mrs Dobrowolski proved to be good at bartering. She went to the shops in the village and exchanged the few trinkets she'd managed to bring from her home in Poland for small quantities of flour, sugar and lard. With her affable personality, she quickly befriended the local peasants who farmed the fields along the outskirts of the settlement. She discovered that they were primarily Ukrainian in descent. They had been deported here by Stalin during the earlier purges and abandoned in the middle of the forest to fend for themselves with nothing. Starvation and cold had killed most of them.

The peasants were delighted with the things Mrs Dobrowolski had for trade. They had never seen anything like the delightful trinkets she bartered with. She managed to trade a few of her things for some potatoes and turnips they had stored up for winter.

When merchandise arrived in the shops, everybody hurried there and fought and pushed to get something to purchase. A queue would quickly form and stretch a long distance outside the shop. All the merchandise was overpriced, but still disappeared off the shelves quickly. Unless you were fortunate enough to be near the front of the line, nothing would be left to buy. Everybody's shoes and clothes were worn out, but on the rare occasions boots and jackets arrived in the shops, they were only sold to people whose names were on lists for working in the forest. Those items were exorbitant in price, and of poor quality. They wore out very quickly.

Aleksander and Edward made fishing poles from tree branches and attached string at the top end. They found a small piece of wire and bent it into two hooks. The hooks were tied to the bottom of the string on each pole. The boys then attached a stone to the lines so the string would sink in the water. They dug up grubs from the ground to bait the hooks and went fishing down at the river in the ravine during their brief times away from working in the forest. Everybody in the shack appreciated a meal of fresh-caught fish. It helped fill their starving bellies, gave them some nourishment and lifted their spirits. One day in August, the two boys caught so many fish that Mrs Dobrowolski took part of their catch to the village. Together with a few rubles the young ones had earned from forest work, she bartered for two noisy chickens in a wooden cage. They enjoyed fresh eggs every day for a week until one morning when they found one chicken dead in the cage and the other missing. They assumed it had been stolen. The dead chicken made a delightful meal that day.

Lilyana, Elzbieta and Marta discovered some wild plums growing on shrubs when they walked to the forest for work. They often picked the sour plums and brought handfuls back to the shelter for those who could stomach them. Mrs Bablak made an herbal tea from them as well.

The girls gathered whatever was edible from the forest, the fields and the swamps. The Ukrainian peasants told them about big, juicy, yellow berries that grew in the marshes, and they discovered handfuls of grain in the fields that had recently been harvested. They gathered as much as they could find, along with edible weeds, wild fruits, berries and mushrooms. Wild cranberries flourished in the deeper swamps. The girls staved off swarms of mosquitoes and other insects to pick them. Sometimes they sank up to their armpits in the freezing cold water to reach the berries.

Despite their resourcefulness, there was never enough food to go around. They were always starving. They drank weak tea rationed from Aunt Janina's supplies and ate a small ration of dry bread every day. Sometimes they tried to make their own bread when they had the ingredients to do so, but more often they had to settle for the stale bread sold in the state-run shop, full of hair, bugs and bits of string. It was a long walk to go and get the over-priced, foul-tasting bread, and often they arrived at the shop to find the shelves bare. They rationed out the potatoes and turnips that Mrs Dobrowolski acquired in trade with the peasants, but most days there was only water and stale bread to eat. They spent their free hours trying to comb lice out of their hair and boiling their ragged clothes to kill the lice and bedbugs.

The children were ordered to attend school in the village. Those under the age of eight stayed home. Every day, Larissa Prawoslaw, Dionizy and Jolanta Leski and Lina Dobrowolski made the long walk to the village school. They constantly complained of hunger. Their clothes and shoes were worn out and inadequate for the continually changing weather. They wrapped rags around their shoes to hold them on and keep their feet warm. In winter, the snow on the rags melted at school and made their feet wet and cold. Fortunately, they did not have to toil in the bone-chilling winds and blinding snowstorms as their parents and older siblings had to do during the winter months.

In school, the children learned how to speak Russian very quickly. They were able to help the older ones translate orders and directions from the village officials. Contrary to what Christian parents had taught their children, the Soviets told them that God does not exist. They told the children that there was only Father Stalin. In some of the colonies, the Soviet teachers would use tricks to make the children believe their atheist philosophy. One popular ploy was to tell the children to pray to God to give them candies. No candies came. When the children were told to ask Father Stalin to send them sweets, the teacher pulled a string, causing candies to fall from the ceiling. They were led to believe that Father Stalin loved children and was kind to them. They were exposed to and brainwashed with Russian propaganda that conditioned them into allegiance to Stalin and patriotism to the Russian state. The Soviets moulded the children into Communists. Polish was never allowed to be spoken. Those children who challenged the Soviets were punished, and their families came under scrutiny and relentless investigation. It was not unusual for parents to be taken away and sent to forced labour camps as a result of a child's misstep at school.

During summer, the children had time away from their studies. They worked in the forest, picking berries and mushrooms that were traded for staples at the state-run shop. In this way, they contributed to the upkeep of the family while their parents and older siblings were forced to do hard physical labour. At harvest time, the craftier school children filled their pockets and their shoes with grain that was stocked outside and brought it home to their families. If the guards noticed, they turned a blind eye. They were often more compassionate toward children.

The NKVD kept tabs on everybody. They knew who everyone was, where they had been and who they had interacted with. Officials often arrived unexpectedly to inspect shelters at random. Sometimes they'd suddenly move people from one dwelling to another.

There was no sense of stability or permanence. Lilyana always worried that she would be separated from her aunt and surviving cousins. That fear was amplified one afternoon when she received orders to report to the commander's office in the village. She was terrified!

Lilyana arrived at NKVD Headquarters late in the day with a knot in her starving belly and her knobby knees shaking. She was escorted into the commander's office, and found the chubby man perched in his chair reading some papers at his desk. He scrutinised Lilyana up and down with his beady eyes, peering over the rim of his glasses.

"Name?" he queried in a flat monotone.

"Lilyana. Lilyana Prawoslaw." A faint quiver could be detected in her small voice.

The commander then shuffled through a stack of papers piled next to his messy desk.

"Lilyana Prawoslaw… from Stolpce. Correct?"

"Yes," she said, hoping she had answered appropriately.

The commander then motioned flippantly for her to take a seat across from him at the desk. She did so apprehensively. All the while, she had that eerie feeling one experiences when watched by someone or something unseen. It made goosebumps rise at the back of her neck. She shook her head momentarily to try and shake the feeling away, but it remained.

The commander eyed her with a look of disdain. "Stupid Polish wench!" he spat out venomously. "It would do us a great service if all you Poles would perish!"

Lilyana's bony knees knocked together as her fear increased with the cruel man's words, sensing his deep-seeded hate.

It was a huge relief when she learned the reason she had been called to Headquarters. She was being transferred from the group of young women collecting resin and felling trees to take charge of a women's brigade being sent deep into the forest to pick wild mushrooms. The commander ordered her to ensure the work be done quickly and efficiently. She was to report to work at 6 a.m. the next morning. The brigade would be paid according to the weight of mushrooms picked each day.

Lilyana hoped this job transfer would allow her to earn more rubles. She was used to picking mushrooms in the woodlands back home in Poland, and it was easier work than felling trees in the forest or tearing bark and collecting resin. She left Headquarters feeling relieved and grateful for this new opportunity. Her only quandary was that winter was closing in quickly. Very soon, the cold, northerly winds would bring snow. Would she have to search for and dig up mushrooms with her bare hands underneath a cold, wintry blanket of white, until she was assigned to other work? The long winter season here lasted from October until June.

The days were already growing colder, and the frequent rains were more intense and of longer duration. On her walk back to her family's shelter that evening, Lilyana encountered a heavy downpour and had to struggle through the deep mud and water that was pooling everywhere. Her shoes were already ruined. Now they became stuck in the mud each time she moved her legs to take another step. It would be easier to walk barefoot along the boggy road.

She stopped to remove her shoes and noticed a lorry coming toward her. It bumped and spun along as the thick mud began to weigh the wheels down. The motor growled and hissed as the driver coaxed it on. Lilyana could only see one Russian soldier inside. How odd! Usually there would be at least two soldiers in an army vehicle travelling along this road.

The lorry fought its way onward through the boggy mud. When it drew closer to where Lilyana was walking, she suddenly recognised the driver. It was the young soldier who had repaired her broken shoe when her family was marching to the remote settlement. Was he following her now? She spun around quickly with shoes in hand, intending to forge onward to her family's shelter. However, she slipped in the thick mire and plunged headfirst into the boggy mud. Caked in the dirty muck from head to toe, she emerged to find the driver passing by her on the road. She was filled with embarrassment and dread but attempted to keep pressing forward. The driver was now yelling something at her from inside the cab. She could not make out what he was saying. Then she saw him motioning for her to climb into the back of the lorry. It was moving along slowly enough for her to latch onto the back bumper and clamber up. She hesitated at first, but then she feared the soldier might report her for being uncooperative and resisting orders. That misdemeanour could bring untold calamity down on her entire family, so she reluctantly scrambled up into the back of the army vehicle. It was rather difficult as the lorry jerked and spun, forcing its way through the deep pools of mud and water.

When Lilyana had finally managed to settle herself in the back, the driver opened the small window hatch in the rear of the cab.

"Greetings, Miss Prawoslaw!" he said. "I thought that was you in the commander's office this afternoon. It seems as though you're always having difficulties with your footwear here in Russia!"

The soldier then let out a hearty laugh and slammed the window hatch shut.

Lilyana was very confused. Was that *Polish* the Russian soldier had been speaking to her, or was her tired brain deceiving her? The Polish language was forbidden here! Was he trying to trick her into speaking in her native tongue so he could report her to the authorities and have her punished? Why was he the only soldier in this lorry? Why was he singling her out? Was he planning to take advantage of her?

It truly angered Lilyana when she realised it had been his eyes that she had felt peering at her from behind while she was seated in the commander's office that afternoon.

She wanted to cry or scream, or both… but no… she would not allow this insolent Russian the pleasure of sensing her fear and exasperation.

She sat at the edge of the tailgate in the open lorry, as far away as possible from the cab where the soldier was situated, and lifted her face to the sky as the cold rain poured down on her. It felt good as the rain flushed away some of the mud from her face and hair, and it helped to ease the frustration and anger she felt inside.

The lorry suddenly lurched to an abrupt halt, causing Lilyana to jolt forward. She found herself only meters away from her family's living quarters. The soldier quickly slid the rear window on the cab open again. His face looked more serious this time, and he had to yell to be heard above the pounding sound of the rain beating on the roof of the cab.

"Be careful not to get lost in the deeper forest when picking mushrooms!" he warned. "It is easy to become disoriented in the dark woods where you are being sent. Some people have died out there in the forest. The guards will not care what happens to you and the other women. They will not help you. You are Polish. The Soviets wish you dead. If you want to live, you must be cognizant of your surroundings all the time. Do not become weak. Do not lose your bearings. Watch where you are!"

The soldier then motioned for Lilyana to get out of the lorry. As soon as she had stepped down, he sped off, causing the rear wheels to slosh mud and grimy water everywhere. Lilyana stood alone in front of her shelter, drenched, muddy and befuddled.

He had spoken to her directly in Polish for a second time. She had understood his words so clearly; her Russian was not that fluent. His Polish words had been well-chosen and uttered with only a slight hint of a Russian accent.

Her curiosity regarding this Russian soldier was starting to grow. Was he just teasing her, or could it be possible that he really did care what happened to her? Why had he gone out of his way to help her, a *Polish* girl? Why did he insist on coming to her rescue? Could her aunt and Mrs Leski be right? Did this soldier hold a soft spot in his heart for her?

She hoped Aunt Janina and Rowena Leski had not noticed her emerging from the soldier's lorry. She did not want to face their innuendoes and teasing.

Much later, when Lilyana was sitting in front of the fire inside the shack, drying her hair and her ragged clothes, she realised the implications of the situation. If the Russian soldier really did care about what happened to her, he was putting himself in personal jeopardy with the village officials. Speaking Polish, and any kindness or show of compassion toward deportees, was strictly forbidden and carried serious consequences for the soldiers and guards.

***

Soon after, the older boys, Aleksander, Edward and Cyryl, were suddenly taken away to work at a lumber camp deeper in the forest, where they were to remain. The camp was many kilometres further north, making it too far to walk there and back every day. They no longer resided in the settlement, or added their earnings to their dwelling's collective coffers.

Food reserves were low. Those remaining in their living quarters wouldn't earn enough rubles to buy the amount of food they needed to survive. The harvest from the garden by the shack was small. Mrs Leski's seeds had been planted too late for the short growing season here. They had no idea how to get through the coming winter.

The younger children continued to suffer during their long walks to and from the village school without warmer clothing and winter boots. The older ones had official coats and boots to wear for work in the forest, though they were inadequate for the frigid cold and deep snow that would come. Lilyana had once again been transferred to a work brigade helping the men fell trees in the woodlands.

The first deep snow arrived at the beginning of October. Thick ice formed on the window slits and the walls inside the flimsy shack, and it became increasingly difficult for Dionizy to collect wood for the fire and water from the river. With the older boys working elsewhere, the young lad had to carry out his chores alone. He nearly froze to death every time he ventured into the bitterly cold forest underdressed. The river froze over, and Dionizy developed frostbite on his hands and legs as he hacked away at the ice, trying to break it open. The steep pathway on the slope leading down to the river became very icy. The older girls also suffered when they went to help Dionizy haul buckets of freezing water back up into the shack.

Then the unthinkable happened. Dionizy did not return from collecting water at the icy river one evening. Mrs Leski and Lilyana went outside to see why he was taking so long to bring the water in. They found him frozen to death by the riverbank where he had been trying to open the ice.

With her older son, Edward, working elsewhere and Dionizy lost forever, it took much determination and inner strength for Mrs Leski to carry on. Aunt Janina and Mrs Dobrowolski had recently suffered the loss of children resulting from the deportations. These women shared a common bond; mothers should not have to bury their children. They managed to help each other through the deep grief and sadness that followed losing a child.

Nevertheless, life may as well have ended for all of them. Not only had they lost precious children, but their husbands were also gone... probably to forced labour camps further north, where torment and death were a foregone conclusion. All hope of being reunited with their spouses had faded. They felt helpless to protect their remaining children from the harsh elements and the inhumane conditions in this reprehensible place. Their lives had become obscured by dark clouds of despair. It took strength of character to overcome the nightmare that life had become for them.

In early November, many people started falling ill with typhus. The epidemic spread rapidly throughout the settlement. Everybody was affected, but children seemed especially vulnerable. Exhaustion, lack of nutrition and the severe conditions all contributed to the swift spread of the illness throughout Russia. The number of people dying from the disease continued to rise every week. More and more dead bodies were being taken from peoples' living quarters, and multiple funerals became a daily occurrence. No home was left untouched.

A couple of doctors were sent to inspect people in their shelters. Some of the ill were taken away on horse-drawn sleds to a makeshift hospital in the village school. Everybody was ordered to disinfect their clothing and their houses, but the illness continued to rage on like an uncontrolled wildfire. The interim hospital became overcrowded. Horses and sleds stopped coming. Those who were falling ill would be left to cope without any doctors or medicines. Many more continued to die in their shelters.

The dreaded day came when the children in the Prawoslaw living quarters began to fall ill one by one. A familiar pattern ensued. The sick feeling came over Lina and Helena Dobrowolski, Jolanta and Margisia Leski, and Michal and Larissa Prawoslaw. They all spiked high fevers and complained about severe headaches and pain in their bones. Then the course of the illness caused them to become delirious for the next four or five days as the sickness attacked their brains. Their delirium produced hallucinations.

In every shack around the colony, delirious children could be heard screaming out with pain and fever. Mothers could be heard crying and fervently praying over sick children. Despairing people everywhere felt abandoned by God. Some believed the end of the world had come.

Aunt Janina, Rowena Leski and Mrs Dobrowolski rotated in shifts caring for the seriously ill children. Mrs Bablak proved to be of little help. Then Mrs Leski and Mrs Dobrowolski both fell ill with the sickness. Lilyana, Marta Dobrowolski and Elzbieta Bablak stopped reporting for their forest work and helped Aunt Janina cope with all the sick ones in their dwelling.

There would come a critical point when a typhus victim's temperature would finally go down, and they would either live or die. The temperature of survivors gradually returned to normal, leaving the victim feeling completely exhausted and very weak for some time afterwards. Miraculously, Margisia Leski, Helena Dobrowolski and Larissa Prawoslaw managed to pull through that critical stage, and they survived. Sadly, Jolanta Leski, Lina Dobrowolski and Michal Prawoslaw did not.

Weakened and mourning the loss of another child, Aunt Janina fell ill with typhus herself. Mrs Leski was still fighting the sickness when Jolanta succumbed to it. She would never learn that her daughter had died, because she herself would not survive either. Mrs Dobrowolski did recover, and she grieved very deeply when she learned that another of her daughters had died.

While caring for Larissa and her aunt, Lilyana fell victim to the disease. She lost consciousness for several days as a high fever and severe pain ravished her. Elzbieta would also fall prey to the typhus epidemic. Marta Dobrowolski and Mrs Bablak were the only ones in their living quarters who remained untouched by the illness. The typhus seemed to pick and choose who its victims would be.

In her painful, fevered state, Lilyana saw shapes and lights moving around the room. She saw her mother and her father come to her as if in a dream. They encouraged her to be strong and to fight… to carry on.

It was the morning after Lilyana experienced the encounter with her parents in that dream-like state that her fever broke. She was alive. It would be a long, slow recovery, but she would live.

Aunt Janina had survived as well. However, she was in a bad state of mind now, almost reclusive. With the death of Michal, three of her dear children were gone. She had no way of knowing how Aleksander was faring at the lumber camp far away in the forest. Was he still alive, or had he met with some terrible fate as well? Maybe four of her five children had already slipped away from her.

Lilyana tried her best to comfort her aunt, but she was very weak following her own recovery from the typhus. She could hardly walk. She and Larissa lay on the sleeping platform next to Janina. Her aunt remained unresponsive for many days, having slipped into a state of depression. There was nothing anybody could do to pull her out of it. As time went on, Lilyana became more of a mother to Larissa, as Aunt Janina was never the same again.

Russian soldiers were being sent into the deportees' dwellings every day now to remove and bury dead bodies. A few days after Lilyana pulled through her close walk with death, three soldiers came into the Prawoslaws' shelter for their routine check. She vaguely recognised one as the young man who had shown favour to her in the past. He marched into the living quarters with two other soldiers, acting like any guard would, performing his duties and quickly leaving. He allowed his two comrades to exit the shelter in front of him. Then, just as he was about to go outside, he pulled a small package out from the inside of his heavy winter overcoat and quietly placed it on the table by the doorway without saying a word. The other soldiers did not notice a thing as the three of them moved ahead to the next shelter.

"It seems that your soldier friend has left you a present, Lilyana," Marta mused once the soldiers were a good distance away.

Still very weak and resting on the sleeping platform, Lilyana murmured, "What makes you think it is for me, Marta?"

"Well, it has your name on the package, dear friend!" Marta joked.

"Oh no!" Lilyana stammered.

"I am kidding!" Marta hastened to add, "But seriously, do you want me to bring it over to you, or do you want me to open it and see what is inside?"

Marta was obviously anxious to discover the contents of the package.

"It is not for me, Marta. I am not the only one residing in our living quarters. The soldier left the package here for all of us. Maybe the Russians are distributing medicine or more disinfectant in every dwelling to help us with the sickness. Open the package and see what it is!"

Marta quickly tore open the brown paper wrapping. "Oh my!" she shouted enthusiastically. "The soldier has left you a small jar of honey and a few slices of bread!"

"It is *not* for me, Marta! He left the package here for all of us to share."

"Sure! Say what you will… but if you are willing to share, I will not refuse eating some of this delicious treat!" Marta crooned.

It had been months since any of them had enjoyed a taste of *real* rye bread, and as for the honey… that was always a special treat. Where had the soldier acquired such luxuries? They had seen the soldiers' rations during dinner hours at the canteen area in the village where the forest workers and the guards ate every day. Although they enjoyed larger portions, the quality of their food was only slightly better than that of the workers. The Russian soldier was becoming more and more of an enigma as time moved forward.

It was amazing how much a good piece of bread dipped in honey improved everyone's health in the Prawoslaws' dwelling. Having relished a little bit of the treat, Lilyana felt strength slowly returning to her muscles, and soon she felt strong enough to sit up at the table with Marta, Helena and Mrs Bablak. Aunt Janina, Larissa, Margisia and Mrs Dobrowolski remained propped up on the sleeping platforms, sampling the treat. Elzbieta was still too ill to take in solids, but it appeared that she would recover as her fever was breaking.

Only nine people remained in their shelter now. The fate of Aleksander, Edward and Cyryl at the lumber camp was not yet known. They prayed that God would see the boys through this difficult time.

***

Christmas was fast approaching, and with no money and no food, it would be a dismal celebration. The remaining women were distraught. They needed to feed their surviving children to keep them alive; they could not exist without the basics for living. Janina decided to make the ultimate sacrifice and traded in her wedding ring at the state-run store. She had Mrs Dobrowolski go with her into the village because she knew the woman bartered much better than she did herself. Mrs Dobrowolski traded in Janina's ring for one hundred and fifty rubles, some flour, sugar and lard.

Janina handed over her most prized possession to the officials at the shop with teary eyes. That was the ring Jerzy had saved so hard to purchase for her years ago when they were married. How shy he had been on their wedding day when he'd placed that ring on her finger. She remembered the joy she had felt. How thrilled she had been to become Jerzy's wife! He was a good man... hardworking, honest and loving. He had been a deeply devoted father to their five children as well.

She felt that she had let her husband down. All the children were slipping away from her now. Larissa was alive, but the others... gone forever? What would Jerzy think of her in this moment? What kind of a mother allowed her children to perish like that... and now here she was, selling the precious wedding band that Jerzy had sacrificed to give her! She could not stop thinking that it was she who deserved to be dead, not the children.

Lilyana told her aunt there was nothing she did to cause the malady of circumstances that besieged them now, nor could she have done anything to prevent what had happened. The blame rested solely on the shoulders of Stalin and his Soviet oppressors. Yet, despite everything, Lilyana believed not all Russians were bad. It was their Imperial Leader who drove the forces of evil in the Soviet Union.

Aunt Janina worried that a certain young Russian soldier was beginning to turn her niece's head. When had Lilyana developed this defence for the Soviets' actions?

While Mrs Dobrowolski and Janina were in the village shop, a peasant woman approached them and offered Mrs Dobrowolski a chunk of horse meat. She had brought it in for trade, but she wanted Mrs Dobrowolski to take it. She refused to accept the few rubles Janina offered to pay her for the provision, saying it was a gift given in return for the assistance Mrs Dobrowolski had provided her grandson in the summer when the child became lost in the village. Mrs Dobrowolski had helped the lost child find his way back to the peasant's farm on the outer edge of the settlement. Speaking in a mixture of Ukrainian, Russian and broken Polish, the woman tried to explain that every good deed deserved something good in return.

Indeed, the horse meat was an unexpected blessing. The people inside their living quarters had not eaten any meat in a long time. They kept it frozen and buried deep in the snow underneath their dwelling. It would make a splendid Christmas treat when they celebrated with a holiday meal.

***

Lilyana had grown close to Marta Dobrowolski and Elzbieta Bablak as the older girls resided and worked together in the forest every day. At first, Elzbieta had remained aloof and snobbish. From the beginning, she had made a point of letting the others know her father once served as mayor of the town where she hailed from. She had been attending private school when the war interrupted her *elite* education. She was outraged that her once immaculate hair and clothing had been reduced to tatters, and she was always angry with the others in their living quarters. She spat venomous words against the Soviets behind their backs, and she conducted herself with an air of superiority. It took a while, but gradually the living conditions wore Elzbieta's resilience down. She learned that Lilyana and Marta's fathers had also been influential men in their hometowns. Eventually, she accepted the unfortunate reality they'd all been dealt and embraced Lilyana and Marta on equal ground.

Elzbieta told the other girls about her older brothers. She had arrived at the settlement with her mother and brother, Cyryl, but her eldest brothers, Max and Roman, had been arrested and exiled to Siberia before the rest of the family was deported. Elzbieta feared that they may have been killed because they'd worked closely with her father, whom the Russians had annihilated very quickly when the occupation began. There was always a trace of anger and resentment in her voice whenever she spoke about what the Soviets had done to her family. They had ruined her once prestigious life.

Marta was easy-going and, like her mother, had a big personality. She was generous and kind-hearted and could bring humour to relieve the tension in almost any situation. She had also been fortunate to experience a higher level of education back in Poland, and her mastery of the Russian language was impressive. These unique qualities allowed her to banter back and forth when joking with some of the friendlier Russian guards while the girls worked in the forest. It was obvious that the younger soldiers had developed a certain fondness for Marta. She baited them with teasing remarks, and they countered, sending Marta off into fits of laughter. The guards had to stand their ground with stoic faces, but occasionally some of the more amiable ones might crack a brief smile following Marta's comical words and antics. This reassured the girls that the Russian soldiers were human after all. Only Marta could have garnered magnanimity from the guards that way! What she lacked in looks, she made up for with her vivacious personality.

Lilyana thought that Marta must have been a larger-sized girl at one time, like Mrs Dobrowolski. Her ragged dress hung very loosely on her, giving one the impression that there must have been much more of Marta to fill out that dress before her departure from Poland. Now she was a skinny bag of bones like the rest of them.

Mrs Bablak and Elzbieta had been writing letters to their friends who remained in Poland. Many of those friends had been well-to-do citizens in their hometown before the Soviet occupation, who had buried some of their personal treasures and valuables so the Russians would not see their affluence or confiscate everything from them. When the Soviets took control of the town, the shops came to be run by the Russian state. Occasionally, the Bablaks' friends would take out some of their hidden items and use them for trade and barter at the shops, allowing them to acquire food staples and other necessities. A couple of silver spoons bought them a quantity of flour, sugar and butter, or enough rubles to purchase some candles and clothing. When the Bablaks appealed to those friends for food parcels to be sent to them at the settlement, some of them complied. Apparently, Mrs Bablak's husband had been a popular mayor due to his policy of fairness and equal rights for all classes of nationalities living there. Some of those remaining townspeople felt obligated to help his family members in return now that his wife and some of his children were forced into exile. As a result of sharing the food parcels that were sent to Elzbieta and her mother, the Bablaks managed to pull their weight in their living quarters. Elzbieta was overjoyed one day when a friend in Poland included a shimmering shawl in one of the food packages for her to wear. She wore it with pride over her ragged dress. Even though it was out of place here in their pathetic hovel, the shawl did keep Elzbieta warm.

The Dobrowolskis had some family members who remained in Poland. They pleaded with them to send food and clothing, and a few parcels did arrive with basic foodstuffs enclosed. However, their relatives back in

Poland were suffering terribly themselves and did not have much to spare. They struggled to keep their own families alive under Russian occupation.

Everyone knew that the Soviet officials were censoring all the letters being sent back and forth. Often whole paragraphs would be blacked out by the NKVD so that people in the colonies could not receive any news from the outside world. Likewise, people back in Poland did not learn about the intolerable conditions the deportees suffered while trying to eke out an existence in the northern settlements of Siberia as the authorities blacked out any detrimental remarks made regarding their living conditions. The Soviets also sifted through the parcels that were sent to the deportees, and they kept the best things for themselves.

Sometimes deportees would be called in for interrogation and mysteriously disappear if they had said too much against the Russians. The Soviets believed those individuals needed to be dealt with as anti-Soviet subversives and agitators.

The horrors did not end for those deportees who survived the typhus epidemic. Persistent plagues of bug infestations worsened. In turn, that gave rise to epidemics of skin and eye diseases. Combined with the unsanitary conditions and the lack of medical facilities and medicines, dermatitis and eye infections became rampant. Exacerbating the situation was the fact that all the deportees were undernourished, overworked and living in such primitive conditions. The mounting harsh realities increased the vulnerability of their weakened bodies.

By Christmastime, everybody in the Prawoslaws' shelter suffered with swollen, infected eyes, itchy skin and boils that leaked pus and fluid. Lilyana took ownership in caring for her younger cousin, Larissa, as Aunt Janina had drifted off somewhere into her own world after the typhus epidemic swept through their living quarters. She also helped Mrs Dobrowolski and Marta watch out for little

Margisia Leski, the sole surviving member of the Leski family. Nobody knew whether Margisia's older brother, Edward, would ever return.

Mrs Dobrowolski became hyper-vigilant in caring for her youngest child, Helena. Something had to be done if the little ones were to survive.

Daylight hours were brief now. At this time in the year, the sun rose late and only lasted for about five hours before setting again. Lilyana, Marta and Elzbieta had recently been assigned to work with another crew that pushed large cut logs brought down by the tree-fellers to the frozen river. When the ice on the river thawed and broke up in springtime, those logs would be floated to a sawmill further downstream. Without any roads or railways nearby, this was the only way to transport the logs.

One December morning as the sun was beginning to rise, the girls headed out to the forest to join their work brigade. Dark shadows hung around the outside of their living quarters. From the corner of her eye, Lilyana caught sight of something large and dark leaning up against the wall of their shelter. Then Marta noticed it too. She bent over to take a closer look.

"Look, Lilyana!" she screeched in delight. "Your Russian boyfriend has brought you a lovely Christmas tree for our shelter! Should we bring it inside?"

"Marta! I do *not* have a Russian boyfriend!" Lilyana insisted. "You must stop saying that! Perhaps Mr Orlowski has provided this fir tree for us?"

Mr Orlowski was an elderly gentleman who resided in a neighbouring shelter. He often came to visit with them in their shack, and always asked what he could do to help them. Since all the males in their assemblage were gone, he kept a watchful eye over their household. The people he lived with in his own shelter were suffering just as terribly as those in the Prawoslaws' shelter. However, having an adult male protector made the guards' intimidation toward them seem less threatening somehow.

"I don't think the old man has the means to go into the forest and chop down a tree, then drag it all the way back here," Elzbieta said, examining it. "Where would he get a saw from? Look! The trunk of the tree has been cut evenly with a sawblade. Mr Orlowski is too old to be hauling trees all the way here from the forest, and the effort required to cut it down would surely kill him before he even attempted to drag it here in the bitter cold and snow!"

Elzbieta did make a valid point. Maybe the Russian soldier had felled the tree and brought it to their shelter? Lilyana looked around for evidence of fresh soldier footprints in the snow, but she saw none. She looked across the pathway to where other shelters were located. The rising sun emitted a tiny sliver of light, giving her a clear view across the entire settlement. She did not see any fir trees outside any other dwellings. Where had this tree come from? Why had it been dropped off outside their living quarters? This was another mystery that needed to be solved.

"Maybe Mr Orlowski had the young fellow from his shelter drop the Christmas tree off for us," Lilyana remarked. She needed to stop Marta and Elzbieta from believing that the Russian soldier had taken a fancy to her and was doing special favours for her.

The younger girls were most appreciative of the Christmas tree. They gleefully decorated it with bits of cloth they fashioned into ornaments. Margisia made a Christmas elf from a ragged old undershirt. Larissa sculpted a Christmas bell out of a torn piece taken from some underpants printed with faded polka dots. Helena formed a snowflake from an old piece of lace torn off a tattered nightgown that belonged to her mother. Lilyana marvelled at how creative the little girls were. It made her feel guilty to see how delighted they were with their primitive creations as she remembered how much she had taken Christmas and all that went with it for granted when she was a little girl growing up in Poland. She became acutely aware of how deprived the children were, living here in this place of torment and horrors. Their childhood had been stolen from them as they struggled to survive. She wondered whether they realised there would be no presents under the tree on Christmas morning. She desperately wanted to bring a little bit of Christmas joy to these suffering children.

Lilyana posed a question to Marta, Elzbieta, Mrs Dobrowolski and Mrs Bablak. Did they have any suggestions on what could be done to get presents for the younger girls? Mrs Bablak and Elzbieta gave each other a knowing look. Mrs Bablak mentioned how Lilyana had a soldier friend who seemed to favour her, and how Marta had a way of winning over the soldiers with her captivating personality… but she went too far when she implied that Lilyana and Marta might be able to take soldier friends for companionship and survival. She suggested that it could be beneficial to all of them if it resulted in perks like food and other essentials being given to the people in their dwelling to share. Hadn't Lilyana's soldier friend already given them that gift of bread and honey, and a Christmas tree?

Elzbieta stood beside her mother, looking at Lilyana and Marta, and nodded in agreement with what her mother had dared to say. The others in their shelter were too shocked to respond immediately. Then Mrs Dobrowolski spoke up adamantly.

"We will not have these young ladies prostituting themselves out to the soldiers in the hope that *you* can be given more food and perks, Mrs Bablak! My daughter and Lilyana have both been raised with family values and good morals. They will continue to live by the godly standards that have been instilled in them. They will *not* compromise those values for your selfishness!"

Now red-faced and defensive, Mrs Bablak hastened to reply, "I did not mean for them to submit to the soldiers in that way, Mrs Dobrowolski! I was merely suggesting that they befriend the soldiers to win favours and extras that we *all* might benefit from!"

"How desperate can you be!" Mrs Dobrowolski shouted. "How would you like it if Elzbieta was forced to abandon her principles and sacrifice herself in that way? Do not think I am clueless, Mrs Bablak! You and I both know what it is you are suggesting. These young ladies will not be used that way… not now… not ever!"

Mrs Bablak lowered her head, and in a quieter tone, she could be heard to say, "These are times of war, Mrs Dobrowolski. Desperate times call for desperate measures. We must do what we need to do in order to survive. God understands. He will forgive and look the other way."

A silence fell upon the shelter then. Nobody knew how to respond to Mrs Bablak. Lilyana was aghast. How dare anyone imply such a horrible thing about her and Marta… and why was Elzbieta supporting her mother in this disgusting implication? Had she and her mother been plotting this ungodly scheme for a while now? Who did they think they were?

Marta reached out and gave her mother an affectionate squeeze for defending her and Lilyana. Mrs Dobrowolski pulled Lilyana close, and the three of them hugged together.

The friendship that had taken so long to forge between Elzbieta and her two counterparts suffered a serious blow that day. Things would never be the same for them again. Marta and Lilyana grew closer, and Elzbieta would always feel as though she stood on the outside of their friendship looking in.

A surprise package appeared outside their living quarters on Christmas Eve. The contents of the parcel were greatly appreciated. Who would not be thankful to receive an unexpected jar of jam, some chocolate, a loaf of real rye bread and a small amount of butter at Christmastime, when there was so little to eat? It angered the Dobrowolskis and Lilyana to see Mrs Bablak and Elzbieta giving each other knowing looks when the package was discovered. It was as though they believed what they had dared to suggest one week earlier was proven with the arrival of this parcel…

and there Mrs Bablak and Elzbieta sat, taking the largest portion of the jam and chocolate. The other ladies saved up some of their share to add to the children's portions on Christmas morning.

***

January 1941 arrived, and proved to be exceptionally frigid. Cold winds swept down from the north, packing a wicked punch. With the thermometer plummeting to -50 °C most days, the shack became ice cold. The fire did little to heat it. No warmth was felt unless you sat right up against the fire, because the heat did not circulate. Several inches of ice coated the interior walls. The ice that they gathered down at the river in Mr Orlowski's bucket took hours to thaw when placed on top of the fire for boiling. Sometimes they simply chipped pieces of ice off the walls and boiled it.

They were now paying the neighbour lad a few rubles each week to collect chunks of ice at the river and wood from the forest for their fire. The lad was older and wiser than Dionizy had been and had constructed a primitive device to drag large quantities of wood from the woodlands back to the Prawoslaw and Orlowski shelters. He was bigger and stronger than Dionizy, making him more capable of hacking away at the ice in the river using a chisel-like tool he'd made. His nose was seriously damaged and deformed from frostbite, so the people in Mr Orlowski's shelter took turns lending the lad their woollen mittens, sweaters and scarves whenever he had to venture to the forest or the river. He packed on layers of warm clothing and managed to get by with a minimum amount of frostbite to his limbs.

Sometimes at night it would become so cold that they all piled up against each other on the floor and wrapped themselves in a large quilt that Mrs Dobrowolski had managed to get at the village store in trade. Despite sharing their body heat and lying next to the fire in the metal drum, all of them still felt frozen all through the night. In early

February, little Helena Dobrowolski developed pneumonia. Her small lungs simply could no longer handle breathing in the frozen air. She died a slow and painful death.

While the eight survivors in their living quarters mourned the loss of yet another child, three NKVD officers arrived and deposited two more destitute families in their shelter. Another major shuffle was taking place. The new families were notably nervous, not knowing how they would be received. Mrs Bablak muttered something about having to feed extra mouths when there was not enough food for the people already living in their shelter... and where would they sleep? Elzbieta joined in with another grievance, implying that the new occupants appeared to have brought little with them in the way of contributions to the household. She doubted they would be able to pull their own weight. With small children to care for, these mothers did not work, and they could not provide any rubles for the household coffers.

The new families were comprised of two women, a small boy, and three little girls. All of them looked ragged and exhausted. They were as demoralised as the people in Lilyana's shelter were. At first none of them was sure what to say, but Marta broke the awkwardness by asking the newcomers their names.

One family was the Cieslaks. Mrs Cieslak arrived with three children. Her little ones' names were Eugenia, Fryderyk and Melka. The second family was the Albinskis, made up of a mother named Sabina, and her daughter, Karina. Larissa and Margisia had no problem bonding with the children. They were happy to share their living quarters with new friends. This development seemed to provide them with a bit of excitement and a reprieve from their otherwise miserable lives.

For the adults, the situation was cause for concern. How would all these extra people be fed? Mrs Albinski did provide a small amount of flour and lard, but Mrs Cieslak had nothing to contribute. Mrs Bablak's apprehensiveness regarding the sharing of food and space was justified; there would not be enough room in the large quilt for all of them to sleep. The new families would surely freeze to death sleeping on top of the platforms at the other end of the shelter against the icy walls.

Overnight, the small dwelling had become crowded again. Unfortunately, two of the Cieslak children arrived with an infection of scabies. When the officials discovered this during a routine inspection of everyone's shelters, they were quarantined. The officials gave them a small ration of ointment to treat the scabies. None of the residents in their shelter were allowed to leave the dwelling until the infection had subsided. The older girls were forbidden to go into the forest to work. No rubles were earned. They ran out of money to pay the neighbour lad for wood and ice, but Mr Orlowski said they could take it on credit until they were back working in the forest. Their meagre food supply dwindled to nothing. Mr Orlowski worked frantically trapping rabbits and other small rodents to feed all the people in his and the Prawoslaws' shelters. What a blessing the Orlowskis proved to be! Without the help that the old man and the young lad provided for them, all the people in Lilyana's shelter would surely have perished. The Orlowskis' kindness proved that even in life's darkest times, good does still exist. Lilyana thanked God every day for Mr Orlowski and the young lad. It was strange that years later she would not be able to recall the young lad's name.

Sabina Albinski had been a nurse back in Poland. Her husband was a doctor. Initially, she was deported with three children. Her infant son had perished on arrival in Siberia, and her older daughter was taken in the typhus epidemic. Only four-year-old Karina Albinski had survived. Despite Mrs Bablak's open resentment shown toward the newcomers, Sabina proved to be an immeasurable asset in caring for everyone's infections, sores, scabs, rashes, frostbite, sicknesses and other maladies. Her nursing skills became invaluable time and time again. She even managed to help draw Aunt Janina out of her downward spiral.

Mrs Cieslak originally had six children. Her husband and two oldest sons, aged twenty and eighteen, had been arrested and exiled from Poland to a corrective labour camp. The boys had refused to fight in the Russian Army when the Soviets came and ordered them to do so. Her fifteen-year-old daughter had been away visiting relatives elsewhere in Poland when the NKVD came to their home to deport her and the younger children. Mrs Cieslak did not know the fate of that daughter. All three of her children who'd arrived with her at the Prawoslaws' living quarters had survived the typhus epidemic in a barracks further away from the village. She considered that to be God's gift to her, because her three oldest children were displaced.

A deeply religious woman, she prayed the rosary continually, and she talked privately to God, asking Him to spare her and her remaining children, as well as the others in their living quarters. Mrs Cieslak would pray for each and every one of them by name. She hid a miniature statue of the Virgin Mary deep inside a seam of the sack that contained her personal possessions.

***

As winter progressed, Lilyana came to appreciate the beauty of the northern lights. Even though the temperature would register -60 °C most evenings, she and Marta would trek outside across the crunchy surface of the frozen snow every night to briefly admire the awesome sight. They would stand there looking at the colourful spectacle with scarves covering their faces. It was too difficult breathing in the frozen particles from the air.

One evening, while she stared up at the coloured waves dancing across the sky, Lilyana heard Marta's crunching footsteps come up behind her in the snow.

"Isn't it beautiful, Marta!" Lilyana exclaimed. "I have never seen anything as mysterious and glorious as this!"

"Yes. It is a magnificent sight," a male voice replied.

Lilyana turned around, expecting to see the young lad from the neighbouring shelter delivering the wood and the bucket of ice chunks to their dwelling as he did every night. She was shocked to discover the friendly Russian soldier standing just behind her.

"Oh! I am sorry. I thought you were my friend, Marta," Lilyana managed to blurt out in broken Russian.

When she thought she had been speaking to Marta seconds earlier, she had spoken in the forbidden Polish language. Now she worried that the soldier would reprimand her for such insubordination. Her head slumped. She appeared defeated and stood shaking with fear in the freezing cold.

The soldier stood tall with his rifle poised securely against his shoulder, adding to his height. Where had he come from? Lilyana had not seen any army vehicles passing by, and there were no other soldiers anywhere in sight. They always travelled in groups. She was motionless.

"It is alright, Lilyana," the soldier said in a hushed tone. "I have not come here to charge you with any crime. I am here admiring the aurora borealis, as you are doing."

Lilyana was fully aware that the soldier was speaking to her in Polish again. She did not know what to do, or how to respond.

"That is something you and I have in common," he continued. "I love the serenity and the beauty of the night sky too."

Lilyana still said nothing.

With a sly smirk creeping across his lips, the soldier then asked her, "Do you not have anything to say, Miss Prawoslaw?"

She remained uncertain how to reply, but after due consideration, she summoned the courage to ask the soldier in broken Russian, "Why do you speak to me in Polish?"

The soldier stepped a few paces back and looked her up and down. Then, with a quiet laugh, he said, "Well, you *are* a Polish girl, are you not? You certainly look like a Polish girl to me."

... and in that moment Lilyana became painfully aware of her appearance. She had not cared how she looked in a long time. Unexpectedly, and to her astonishment, it suddenly mattered that her skin was full of scabs and infected welts. It mattered that her hair was thinning and falling out in clumps. It mattered that her bones protruded through her emaciated torso. She hated the deep hollows that had formed in her cheekbones. She despised the skeleton-like body that had taken over her once-healthy physique, full of wellness and life. She did not want this soldier looking at her. How could he even stand being near the wretched, unhealthy specimen of a human being she had been reduced to?

"Perhaps it will help if I tell you my name," the soldier was saying. "Let us start over. I am Dimitri. How do you do this evening, Miss Prawoslaw?"

Lilyana was too stunned to answer.

Hoping to relieve the tension, the soldier went on to say, "I will allow you to speak to me in Polish if that will help. However, you must not speak Polish to anyone else, and you must always be careful not to speak Polish to me in the presence of any other people. Do you understand that both of us will be in serious trouble if we are overheard conversing in Polish, Lilyana?"

"Yes," she finally replied in Polish.

"Good. Then we understand each other," the soldier said. "It is true that I mean you no harm. Can you trust me enough to believe this truth?"

Lilyana was brimming with questions and curiosity. Looking around to ensure that nobody was within hearing distance, she asked, "How is it you speak Polish so well, sir?"

"Please... call me Dimitri. My mother was born Polish. She would speak to me in her native tongue all the time while I was growing up. I became fluent in the language, speaking it with her."

"But you are Russian?" Lilyana dared to ask.

"Yes," Dimitri said. "My father is Russian. He married my mother in Leningrad. That is where I was born."

All this information coming from a Russian soldier, in Polish, boggled Lilyana's mind. It sent her head spinning. There was something painfully wrong with this picture. Her stomach churned. She decided it would be best not to say anything else.

A few minutes passed while Lilyana and Dimitri continued to look at the pattern of colourful lights flickering across the dark sky. Then Dimitri explained the phenomenon of the beautiful dancing colours so Lilyana could understand what caused it.

"Did you enjoy the Christmas parcel left at your living quarters?" he asked.

Although she had willed herself not to speak anymore, Lilyana suddenly felt words starting to erupt from her lips. "Do we have *you* to thank for that package?"

Dimitri did not respond. Had she gone too far questioning him, she wondered? Dimitri put a finger to his lips, signalling her to remain quiet. Then she heard crunching on the snow as another soldier approached them from behind.

"What has this Polak done to draw you away from our search, comrade?" the soldier asked Dimitri.

Quietly replying in Russian, Dimitri told the other soldier he was just checking to see what she was doing standing outside. "She has done nothing... just wants to freeze to death outside looking at the sky!"

"Pewww!" the other soldier scoffed. "Stupid Polak wench!"

Dimitri turned around and headed off with the other soldier to re-join his comrades and continue in his duties. Lilyana was sure she saw Dimitri give her a quick wink as he spun around and marched off.

What a strange development that had been. But now that Lilyana knew Dimitri's mother was Polish, she wondered if he secretly harboured empathy for the deportees and the horrible plight they found themselves suffering through here in Siberia.

She hurried back inside her family's shack. She wanted to secretly tell Marta all about her encounter with the Russian soldier. When she entered, however, Lilyana saw Marta sitting at the table next to her mother. Both Marta and Mrs Dobrowolski were looking at her apprehensively. She realised then that Marta had seen her talking to Dimitri outside, and had told her mother about the chance encounter. She knew Marta would question her about it later when they were alone together, and she would have to provide an explanation for what had just transpired. Even though Lilyana felt she could trust Marta and Mrs Dobrowolski, she dared not divulge too much information regarding Dimitri.

"Little rendezvous with your Russian boyfriend, dear?" Mrs Bablak asked sarcastically.

Elzbieta had a smug grin on her face as she tried not to laugh.

Lilyana refused to dignify Mrs Bablak's remark with an answer. She knew the Bablaks could not be trusted. If they discovered Lilyana had been conversing in Polish with the Russian soldier, they would not hesitate to inform the authorities and have unknown misfortune rain down on both her and Dimitri. They were always looking for some perk or reward. Lilyana needed to control her own destiny by remaining vigilant. She merely told the others that the Russian soldier had approached her to see what she was doing outside staring up at the northern lights. She told them that he had questioned her and left. Marta and her mother were relieved that the soldier hadn't taken her to Headquarters for further questioning or punishment. Mrs Dobrowolski advised Lilyana and Marta not to go outside to watch the *pretty dancing lights* anymore.

***

With the arrival of winter blizzards, snow came down heavy and covered everything. Nothing remained visible. Some days, the deportees dug their way out from their living quarters. During one particularly extreme snowstorm, they lay in darkness under a covering of white, metres deep, for three days. In hunger and gloom, they melted snow and ice for drinking and washing. The primitive chimney attached to the stove had to continually be cleared of snow so the flames would not be snuffed out and the smoke could rise outside.

Eventually, they were able to emerge from their wintry cave. The snow had piled up so high around their shack that they had to walk up out of the shelter as if going up cellar stairs.

In February, the older girls found themselves fighting their way through another blinding snowstorm on their way to work in the forest. The local peasants bundled themselves up in animal furs to keep warm. Only their eyes could be seen peering out from their furry attire. The deportees did not have access to such extravagance. They wrapped their legs and feet in rags that were tied on with strings, but despite their efforts to prevent frostbite, the girls' legs and hands became ulcerated. The festering wounds did not heal, and during the summer months, mosquitoes and flies would take up residence in their open lesions.

Lilyana, Marta and Elzbieta stayed close together on the snowed-in pathway leading to the lumber camp. Visibility was very poor, and along the way one or another of them would accidently stray off the path and end up shoulder-deep in a snowbank. They had to help pull each other free from the deep snowdrifts. The horses in the camp even sank up to their necks in the deep snow, and their loaded sleds overturned when they fell away from the beaten path. The frigidly cruel winds and blowing snow surrounded the girls, and it took much longer than usual to arrive at their designated work area. Being late for work was an offense warranting a court appearance many kilometres away, and tardiness was always reason for a large deduction in wages. Unfortunately, the NKVD officer in charge of the work camp that day was the strictest and most unbending of all the Communist officials overseeing work in the settlement. As punishment for their late arrival, he forbade them from having any rest or food while working through the entire day. The girls slaved away for hours in their wet, frozen clothes. It was torturous to watch other forest workers sitting by a warm fire drinking hot soup during the regular break period while they continued to toil in the bitter winds and snow. They felt frozen, starving and dejected, their working progress hampered by the overwhelming snowdrifts continually piling up to extraordinary heights around them. Lilyana lost all feeling in her limbs, and she worried that frostbite would consume her.

At the end of that long, treacherous and anguish-filled day, the girls' work quota fell well below the required daily standard. The officer in charge chose to make an example of them, and he announced to all the workers there in the camp that Lilyana, Marta and Elzbieta would receive no rubles for their tortured efforts that day. He accused them of deficiency in work standards and effort, being late and having failed to achieve the daily quota.

This was too much for Elzbieta to bear. Beaten down by the harsh elements, over-exertion, starvation, hypothermia, frostbite and humiliation, she was enraged at the officer's cruel announcement and accusations. She began yelling at him in a mixture of angry Polish and Russian curses. The camp guards quickly subdued her and dragged her off, kicking and screaming with the last fragments of strength remaining in her body. The other workers could only stand by, frozen and numbed, looking on as Elzbieta was hauled away.

Lilyana and Marta struggled all the way back to their living quarters, fearing how Mrs Bablak would react when she learned what had happened to her daughter. When she was told the worrying news, she accused the girls of failing to protect Elzbieta. In a frenzied state of panic and dread at the thought of what might happen to her daughter now, Mrs Bablak bundled herself up in her warmest clothes and marched out the door into the continuing snowstorm. She said she was heading to Headquarters in the village to speak to the commander. The others tried to dissuade her from going. They encouraged her to at least wait until the storm abated. However, Mrs Bablak was on a mission, and she would not be deterred. She stomped out the door, saying she would be back after she sorted out the confusion at Headquarters and retrieved Elzbieta.

Neither Mrs Bablak nor Elzbieta was ever seen or heard from again. They simply disappeared into the Russian abyss. Nobody would ever know what fate had befallen either one of them. The young lad who lived in Mr Orlowski's dwelling said that some boys had seen soldiers collecting dead bodies along the roadway after the storm finally subsided, but he did not know whether Mrs Bablak was among them.

Lots of people perished walking out in snowstorms. The snow fell so heavy and thick, it was easy to lose your bearings. The icy winds caused hypothermia to set in very quickly. Drifts of snow were so deep that people could fall into them and freeze or suffocate to death, unable to get out.

The Bablaks' few possessions remained untouched in their living quarters for a long time after they disappeared. Finally, once everyone in their shelter was sure that Elzbieta and Mrs Bablak were not returning, Mrs Dobrowolski looked through their belongings to see if there was anything of value left. There wasn't. However, it was discovered that Elzbieta had been writing regularly in a journal. Unbeknownst to all of them, she'd had a secret fiancé back home in Poland whom she was pining for. Lilyana and Marta were very surprised she had not ever said a word about him to them. Perhaps it was because her fiancé turned out to be Jewish that she and Mrs Bablak had kept that secret from everybody, fearing—as many people did—openly admitting to any association with the Jewish population.

According to Elzbieta's written account, her fiancé came from a very affluent family in her hometown. His father seemed to have had a lot of business dealings with her father. Before her deportation to Siberia, Elzbieta had planned to become Jewish, and she and her fiancé were to be married in November. Instead of having her wonderful wedding as planned, she'd lain on a bug-infested platform in Siberia, fighting for her life and delirious with typhus, in November that year. The journal laid out all Elzbieta's exciting plans for her and her future husband's lives.

Her journal entries indicated that she had no idea where her fiancé was now. A letter she'd received some time ago from a friend in her hometown had apparently informed Elzbieta that her fiancé's family had been removed from their home. A large section of that letter had been blacked out by the officials, so Elzbieta did not know if his family had been deported to a forced labour camp somewhere or whether they had been killed in one of the roundups of Jewish people that were occurring.

It was clear that she really did love the young man, whom she affectionately called Poppy. Repeatedly, she professed her love for him throughout her journal. It must have been extremely difficult for her not to say anything about him to the others.

Lilyana couldn't help wondering what other secrets the Bablaks had kept hidden from the rest of them. Nevertheless, she felt she understood Elzbieta a little more now that the girl's secret was revealed. She grasped Elzbieta's ill temper and constant anguish. Every day must have been a torment for her. Perhaps in the end she had simply given up? If she could not have the life that she had dreamed of with the young man she loved so dearly and planned to marry, then what was the point of suffering through another day in Siberian hell?

***

Lilyana worked hard at keeping healthy. She cleaned and bandaged her infected skin, and with some assistance from Sabina Albinski she managed to stay on top of the swollen sores and infections that plagued Larissa and Margisia's arms and legs as well. Lice and bedbugs were eating everyone alive.

Scurvy was very common, due to the deportees' vitamin deficiency and malnutrition. The children's eyes were always swollen, red and watering. Lilyana felt swollen glands inside the little girls' necks. The children received a small ration of bread and milk at the village school, and Lilyana encouraged them to bundle up and play outside in the sunshine whenever possible. Her mother, Olisia, had always been a big proponent for the healing powers of sunlight.

In March, Margisia fell ill with a fever and bloody diarrhoea. Sabina would put rags drenched in cold water on Margisia's forehead to bring her fever down. Every time the little girl tried to eat anything, she would become ill with cramps and severe bouts of bloody discharges. Sabina feared that Margisia was suffering with haemocolitis, which was commonplace in the settlement. At eight years of age, Margisia's tiny body was withering away. She looked like a skeleton with a layer of damaged skin thrown over the top. Mrs Cieslak prayed fervently over the poor, sweet child for a miraculous healing. However, Margisia's emaciated body could no longer sustain her. After the extent of her suffering, death came as a blessing for the little girl. The Leski family had been the Prawoslaws' closest allies from the beginning in their living quarters. Now Rowena and all her younger children were gone... taken by the cruelties of the inhuman land.

Lilyana took Margisia's passing very hard. A mournful air of melancholy swept over her. She realised there was nothing she could have done to save the little girl. The child had needed to be hospitalised, fed intravenously and treated with proper medications and nutrition. Lilyana had thought she'd been prepared for the inevitable, but when it happened, she grieved the loss with great sorrow. It distressed her to think about the suffering the pretty little girl with the big dark eyes and the sunny smile had experienced, like all the children who had perished in their dwelling in recent months. Marta, Mrs Dobrowolski and Aunt Janina helped Lilyana prepare a funeral service for Margisia.

Larissa was the only one of the younger children originally assigned to their living quarters who survived the abominations of life in their colony.

**

It was springtime, but final traces of snow remained until late in May. When the snow began to melt, the roadways leading to the forest and the village were transformed into deep pools and tracts of mud. Large flows of water filtered down from the mountains to the settlement below. People were sinking in the knee-deep mud trying to walk along the roadways.

With massive amounts of snow and ice melting everywhere, the river flooded and overflowed its banks. New tributaries appeared across the Siberian marshlands, and fields of flowers began to bloom. Aquatic birds suddenly appeared and got busy building nests. Black flies and mosquitoes reappeared in great numbers and became a continual nuisance once again. Bedbugs, which had decreased due to the frigid cold inside their living quarters throughout the winter months, re-emerged from between the floorboards and the walls. A continual stream of the bugs accumulated and attacked in the night when people were trying to sleep. Mr Orlowski told the women to burn birch branches inside their dwelling to repel the pests, but that seemed to do little good.

With temperatures rising outside, the thick ice that had formed on the interior walls of the shelter finally began to melt. This caused a lot of wetness and dripping inside the dwelling. Everything got drenched, and huge puddles of water kept forming on the floor. The women were constantly mopping it up. The walls continued to thaw for several days, and sometimes crusts of ice would fall off, crashing to the floor. The shack became very damp and smelled like musty, moulding wood. The door could not be left open to air out the shack because hordes of flying insects would come swarming in, making the dismal situation even more unbearable.

At the end of May, the ice on the river finally broke up and all the forest workers were recruited to push the logs that were piled up high along the riverbanks into the water so they would float to the sawmill further downstream. The workers were given long hooks to roll the logs down into the river, layer by layer. Work crews were sent out onto the river to break up large log jams as floating chunks of ice accumulated in certain spots where the river twisted and bent. Several workers were injured or drowned in the river when they floated the timber downstream in the fast current.

One of the injured workers was Mr Orlowski's grandson. The lad was crushed between the huge logs. Another worker managed to pull him out of the frigid water, but the boy was seriously wounded. He suffered terribly for two days before he finally died from his injuries. Everyone in Mr Orlowski's and the Prawoslaws' dwellings attended the funeral. Lilyana was saddened to see how badly the ordeal affected Mr Orlowski. He sobbed uncontrollably at the makeshift ceremony.

The young man was buried on the edge of the settlement under a cluster of trees near the forest, where the deportees had created a cemetery. Maria Dobrowolski, Dionizy Leski, Jolanta and Mrs Leski, Lina Dobrowolski, Michal Prawoslaw, Helena Dobrowolski and Margisia Leski were all buried there. Other families had dug graves nearby for the children they'd lost, and for the adults in their families who had been killed or died as a result of disease or accidents at work. A small number of those buried had committed suicide.

Tools were only permitted for the workers when they went to work in the forest. Graves were dug with bare hands, during the brief summer months when the earth yielded to digging. The bodies of those who perished during the winter months, when the ground remained frozen, were buried beneath the snow until their graves could be dug.

Against the authorities' permission, the deportees fashioned little Christian crosses from wood to mark the graves of their loved ones. At first, the soldiers took the crosses down, but then there were so many graves being dug with crosses set up, they eventually ignored them.

The extended hours of toil at the river enabled the workers an opportunity to earn more rubles. They contemplated purchasing more food at the state-run shops in the village, but the authorities raised the prices for bread and other staples so high that the extra wages did not stretch as far as they should have. People continued to starve. All they could think about was food. They even dreamt about food. They tried to find ways of getting more food, and they sold the few necessities they had left until only the tattered clothing on their backs remained. Many concluded they all would face certain death. There could be no future if there were no food.

***

An unexpected event occurred in June. Some of the young lads who had been sent away to work as lumberjacks deep in the forest returned. Aleksander Prawoslaw and Edward Leski were welcomed into their dwelling with opened arms. They were soaked and covered in mud following their long march back, weary from work and other hardships... but they were still alive! Cyryl Bablak had apparently been taken by the typhus outbreak in their camp. Mrs Bablak and Elzbieta would have been greatly distressed to learn about his demise. Edward had survived the illness, and Aleksander remained untouched by it.

For Edward, it was a less than happy homecoming when he learned that his younger siblings had succumbed to the harsh realities of life in the settlement. He was devastated to learn that all his family members had met with a terrible end, including his loving mother, and that his smallest sister had died only a matter of weeks before his return.

Aleksander was sorry for the loss of his brother, Michal, and he wasn't sure what to make of the changes he observed in his mother. Taking Aleksander aside, Lilyana had to explain about Aunt Janina's spiral into depression. Even though he had hoped to find everyone alive and well, Aleksander had mentally prepared himself for bad news upon his return to the dwelling. The boys' work brigade had passed through a few villages on route back to the settlement, and in every one of those colonies there had been severe losses due to the typhus epidemic and unfortunate calamities. Aleksander said all the children in one village had been taken to an orphanage. The mothers remaining behind feared they would never see those children again, but they vowed to search for them later. The children had been starving to death, so the commandant in the village had ordered all of them to be removed. Their mothers bewailed the fact, but at the same time they prayed their children would be taken better care of at the orphanage, with clean clothes, clean bedding and food. Sadly, Polish children in the orphanages were ill-treated and persecuted by the Russian children, who stole everything from them, including their food. Polish children often continued to starve in the Russian orphanages, and Russian children sometimes tortured the Polish orphans. They were known to put smaller children down into wells and threaten to drown them if they did not give their food to them. Sometimes they even burned Polish children with blazing sticks or threw stones at them until they gave up everything they had. The cruellest children devised many ways of torturing other children into submission.

Aleksander had matured a great deal during his nine months away working in the forest. There was now a rough edge to him that hadn't existed before. He seemed older and wiser than his fifteen years. He had become a man while living and working in the lumber camp. He spoke of having to fight with other men to defend himself and had developed a toughness that Lilyana admired. Like her, Aleksander was a survivor. He had made up his mind not to let the harsh realities of life in Siberia take him down. He only wished that his mother had been able to remain more steadfast in face of all the adversities.

Together, Aleksander and Edward had saved up a lot of rubles from working in the forest. They had closely guarded their earnings all the way back to the settlement. Thieves were constantly on the hunt for money and items to steal. They would kill to get their hands on anything of value. Now, the lads cheerfully handed over their earnings to the dwelling's coffer, and the next morning, Mrs Dobrowolski, Mrs Cieslak and Aunt Janina walked to the village shops. They wanted to stock up on food staples and other essentials. As usual, there wasn't much merchandise to purchase, and the inflated prices for sugar, flour, lard and bread didn't allow them to procure as much as they had hoped. However, they did manage to make a few more reasonable acquisitions from the Ukrainian peasant farms on the outer edge of the settlement. Eggs and fried potatoes were enjoyed at dinnertime that night. It was the best meal any of them had eaten in a very long time!

Larissa was overjoyed to have her big brother back. She followed him everywhere. Aleksander gave her a few candies he had bought in a state-run store at one of the other settlements where there had been more items available for purchase. Larissa kindly shared the sweets with Karina Albinski and all three of the Cieslak children. Karina and Larissa had become good friends, even though Larissa was twice Karina's age. Larissa took Karina under her wing like a big sister.

The Cieslak children were eleven, eight and five years old. Mrs Cieslak did not permit them to play as freely as the other children did. She would make them sit with her and go through an entire litany of prayers every day when the two older ones had returned from the village school. Eugenia and Melka Cieslak didn't seem to mind that very much, but young Fryderyk would complain and fidget, quickly losing focus and concentration while their prayers continued. Once Aleksander and Edward arrived back in their living quarters, Mrs Cieslak almost had to tie Fryderyk down so he could complete the prayers with her and his sisters. Fryderyk just wanted to follow the older boys around.

On a rare day off from work, Lilyana and Marta took Aleksander and Edward with them to the swamp, where they managed to pick cranberries that had frozen in the ice and been preserved through the long winter months. They nearly froze to death in the frigid water, as ice remained at the bottom. With clothes hiked up over their knees, they stood on top of the icy-bottomed water with bare feet, scrambling to gather the berries. After some hard work, they had picked enough for everyone at their shelter. Aunt Janina and Mrs Dubrowolski made a small pie with the berries, with the small amount of flour, lard and sugar they had managed to purchase at the village shop with the rubles Aleksander and Edward had given them. Lilyana would fondly remember that as the best pie she had ever tasted in her entire life.

The deportees had now been given permission to have a small plot of land in the settlement for gardening in. However, the growing season was very short—they had to plant early. Aleksander and Edward helped Aunt Janina prepare a garden plot situated some distance away from their living quarters. Despite frost remaining deep in the ground, they turned over the soil and planted carrots, cabbages, beets and turnips with the remaining seeds from Edward's mother's supply. They also planted small cuts taken from eyes on the potatoes they purchased from the nearby farmers.

They prayed something would grow and come to fruition in their garden plot, as they would need a lot of food to sustain them through the winter. They would store the harvested vegetables under the floor of their living quarters. When frozen solid and thrown into a pot of boiling water, the vegetables would make a nice hot soup that would go a long way.

Aunt Janina was in her element while gardening. It reminded her of home on the farm in Poland. Also, Aleksander was back with her now. Nothing made her happier than that. However, Aunt Janina's joy was short-lived. The day after they helped her prepare the vegetable garden, Aleksander and Edward were ordered to attend a meeting at NKVD Headquarters in the village.

A group of young lads was being rounded up from around the settlement to be sent far away to work deep in the forest again. Their destination was not clear, but they were to report early the following morning to be marched off to another substation. The news of them being sent away to work at another camp was crushing.

Aleksander and Edward had described the horrors surrounding their living experience while working at their previous camp. They were forced to live in an overcrowded, communal barracks with numerous men. It was difficult to find a safe place to sleep, with many bodies heaped on top of each other. The lice and bedbug infestations were so bad that bugs could be seen crawling on the walls and hanging or falling from the ceiling. Aleksander and Edward had been badly bitten all over their bodies. Incessant itching and discomfort from infected welts continually interrupted their sleep at night. They would wake to find their arms and legs, and the bodies of those men around them, caked in bedbugs.

Aleksander described it as a living nightmare. They had to buy their overpriced, skimpy rations in a communal dining room. In the middle of the night, they would be awakened to march several kilometres to their worksite. The supervisor in their work zone was an evil man who took pleasure in tormenting the workers every day and dealing out terrible punishments. Local peasants in the vicinity were also hostile toward the workers, and they planned and schemed against them. The workers returned from the worksite late every night, exhausted. They could hardly find the strength to walk back to their barracks.

Many men perished in the camp. There was no guarantee that Aleksander or Edward would survive the rough existence in another work camp. Aunt Janina fell deeper into her mental slump. Mrs Cieslak could be heard uttering heartfelt prayers for the safety and wellbeing of the two boys as they reluctantly marched off into another unknown.

***

Trunks of huge pine trees were felled near the Prawoslaws' settlement, their treetops and branches chopped off by the work brigade that Lilyana and Marta were newly assigned to. The enormous logs were then pushed into the mighty river by other forest workers, and floated downstream to the new substation where Aleksander and Edward were located. The tree trunks were massive in length. It was no wonder that so many workers were injured or crushed to death in their struggle to roll the gigantic logs down and float them in the water.

Many kilometres downstream, workers at the boys' site had to snag the logs at the riverbank with anchor-shaped hooks attached to long ropes as the logs floated past, and then drag them up onto the shore. Aleksander and Edward were assigned to haul the logs up a sloping ramp made from tree trunks stripped of bark. Large groups of men were required to pull the colossal logs out of the water. A long line of men crouched low to the ground with their toes digging into the wet soil of the slope as they pulled on the rope, which cut into their shoulders. They had to keep the momentum of the giant log going so it wouldn't roll back and break the men's bones or kill those who didn't jump out of the way in time. Rows of workers carried the logs together on their shoulders and stacked them on the flat ground above the high water.

The trunks had to be cut up into more manageable sections. This took a long time to do with blunt saws that were impossible to sharpen with the useless files provided.

Cold weather made the job additionally risky because the men catching the floating logs, and those who attached the pull-out ropes, got soaked to their knees. Most of the men had wet feet all day and night. A fire lit on the shoreline did little to dry out their wet clothes and boots. In late summer, ice formed along the shoreline of the river and made the work even more difficult and dangerous.

***

Once Helena Dobrowolski had passed away, Mrs Dobrowolski no longer had any small children to care for. The commandant ordered her to join a brigade of women working in the forest tearing bark and collecting resin. When the fields opened up later in the summer, she was sent to work with some older women cutting tall grasses and raking up hay.

The fields were very mucky and dirty. Cut grasses dried and turned into hay, making the work dusty and taxing. She returned to the living quarters filthy and exhausted every night, being paid next to nothing for her labour.

Mrs Cieslak and Sabina Albinski stayed at the dwelling most of the time, caring for their young children, Fryderyk and Karina. Larissa Prawoslaw was attending school every day with Eugenia and Melka Cieslak. Aunt Janina had no little ones to care for during the day, so she was sent off to work in the fields with Mrs Dobrowolski. She performed her duties mechanically, but she did help Mrs Dobrowolski learn the rhythm of using a scythe and piling up hay. This work was second nature to Janina, as she used to help Uncle Jerzy in the fields every summer. If not for the repercussions of malnourishment and her fractured mental state, she would have been able to clear those fields by herself in a single day. However, it was difficult to carry out her work under the oppressive hand of the Russians in the tyrannical system they lauded over the deportees.

Janina's health suffered physically and mentally. She believed that even animals were treated better. At least they could be put out of their misery with a quick shot to the head. Thoughts of suicide tormented her. If Larissa had not survived the typhus epidemic, Janina had resolved to terminate her own anguish. She had lost everything else that meant anything to her, and she was pushed to the end of her rope. Janina wanted to find a means to stop the Soviets from torturing her any further.

On a rainy day in July, Mrs Cieslak walked to the village shop to pick up a loaf of bread and a small ration of milk for the children. Mysteriously, she never returned. The others would never know what had happened to her. Nobody reported having seen or heard anything. Had she met with an unfortunate accident along the way, or fallen victim to ill treatment by the authorities? The soldiers had let it be known that they did not approve of her religious fervour.

Eugenia, Fryderyk and Melka Cieslak came into care of the other women remaining in their living quarters. Mrs Dobrowolski readily embraced them. It almost seemed as though she was using them to replace the three daughters she had lost in this godforsaken land. The two Cieslak girls continued dutifully in their daily prayers and devotionals as their mother had taught them. However, Mrs Cieslak would have been disappointed to see how her son, Fryderyk, quickly and shamelessly became a backslider.

Every day, the NKVD officers came to peoples' living quarters to check on what they were doing, and assigned them to work brigades for various jobs in the forest. Aunt Janina was transferred to a work crew burning tree branches, a job generally reserved for the old and the sick. If the officers had noticed Janina's deteriorating state, they were sending her there to expire. Lilyana realised she would have to keep a closer watch on her aunt.

Daylight continued around the clock during the summer months. It was difficult to sleep with sunlight streaming in through the small windows of the shack. One clear, bright summer night when Lilyana failed to fall asleep, she slipped outside to try and find some reprieve from the stifling hot and humid air inside. She wandered down the steep slope to the river, and despite having to ward off swarms of mosquitoes, she dipped her bare feet into the water along the shoreline. She leaned back against a large tree and closed her eyes. While continuing to swat at the mosquitoes and horseflies, she imagined eating an enormous plate of delicious food. This always helped her cope with the insatiable hunger that tore at her insides. In her mind's eye, she was enjoying a large stack of carrot pancakes topped with fresh whipped cream. She licked her swollen, cracked lips at the thought of such a delectable treat. She chewed slowly and savoured each imaginary morsel of food.

Suddenly, she became aware of footsteps nearing her at the riverbank. Her eyes popped open, and she instantly jumped to attention.

"I didn't mean to startle you," Dimitri said in a quiet voice. "I just came to check and see if you are alright. I would hate to find you dying here on the riverbank!"

Shocked and embarrassed, Lilyana blurted out without thinking, "How is it that you always manage to sneak up on me? Where do you come from, and how do you know where I am?"

"That is for me to know, and for you not to find out," he replied with a silly smirk on his face.

Lilyana glared at him as he watched her closely.

"Oh. I seem to have angered you now," he said with a chuckle. "That was not my intent. What are you doing here, stretched out in the river?"

"What do you think I am doing here?" Lilyana said with a hint of annoyance in her tone. "Trying to find some relief from this stifling humidity! What are you doing spying on me?"

"*Spying* is it?" Dimitri remarked. "I thought I was watching out for you to make sure you were okay."

"Hmm! I would thank you to stop surprising me like this!" Lilyana exclaimed.

"Well then, how would you prefer me to announce my approach from now on?" Dimitri asked. He imitated the sound of a trumpet heralding, "Toot-ta-ta-toot… Warning! Warning! Dimitri is coming, Miss Prawoslaw! Dimitri is coming! Toot-ta-ta-toot. Ta-toot-ta-ta-toot!"

Amused by the soldier's nonsense, Lilyana failed to stifle a hysterical laugh. She hadn't been that humoured in a long time.

"I am glad that I have finally managed to put a smile on your face!" Dimitri said.

He leaned up against the tree where Lilyana had been sitting. "Nice night to enjoy the outdoors," he commented.

"Yes, if you like being eaten alive by mosquitoes," Lilyana tried to say as she inhaled and choked on one of the nasty insects buzzing around her face.

"…and if you enjoy eating them too!" Dimitri joked.

Lilyana couldn't help wondering where this Russian soldier had acquired his sense of humour. The Soviets were not known for joviality or wit. Sombre seriousness was more their style. She doubted this quality had been passed down to him from his Russian father. Most likely, Dimitri had inherited his sense of humour from his Polish mother, but she dared not ask him about it.

The soldier switched gears, and a serious expression came across his face. Lilyana waited for what was to come next.

"There is something I need to tell you," Dimitri started to say. "It is something I feel you have a right to know."

He hesitated, and just as he was about to continue, Lilyana saw Marta starting down the slope toward the river. Seeing the soldier standing next to her friend, Marta stopped dead in her tracks. Dimitri and Lilyana looked up to where she stood.

Reverting to the Russian language, Dimitri said, "I will leave you with your friend. We will continue our conversation some other time."

He turned and worked his way back up the ravine, nodding respectfully to Marta as he passed by. "Good morning to you, Miss Dobrowolski."

Then he was gone, leaving Lilyana desperate to know what he had wanted to tell her.

Marta remained frozen in place, not knowing what to do. It wasn't until the soldier was completely out of sight that her legs were able to move, and she joined Lilyana down by the river.

"I was so worried about you!" Marta gasped. "I saw you were gone from the shelter, and then I heard voices and laughing. I came to see who was here. Are you alright? What were you doing out here with that Russian soldier?"

"Everything is fine, Marta!" Lilyana explained. "Now that you and I are alone, I can tell you this Russian soldier is friendly. He means no harm. He just comes to converse with me sometimes... and that is all!"

"Converse!" Marta shouted wildly. "You know what chatting and friendliness can lead to!"

"Shhh!" Lilyana hissed. "Be quiet or you will have everyone else in the shack coming out here! The soldier and I chat whenever he comes by. He is actually very nice."

Marta couldn't believe what she was hearing.

"But he is *Russian*, Lilyana! What do you and this soldier have to talk about? And you are not very articulate in the Russian language. Why is he befriending you? He must want something more from you!"

"All I can tell you is that he will not bring any harm to us as long as you do not tell anyone about my meetings with him!" Lilyana protested. "Promise me you will not tell a single soul about this, Marta... not even your own mother!"

Marta let out a reluctant sigh and agreed to keep Lilyana's secret safe. As they climbed back up the ravine together, Marta sang softly, "Lily has a boyfriend... Lily has a boyfriend!"

"No, *I* don't! ... No, *I* don't!" Lilyana quietly responded in the same tune.

The girls looked at each other and smiled all the way back up to their living quarters.

The remainder of the night was a wash for Lilyana as far as sleep was concerned. She lay awake next to Aunt Janina on the sleeping platform until it was time to go to work in the forest. Dimitri's last words kept turning over and over in her mind.

"… *something I need to tell you…* I *feel you have a right to know.*"

What could that mean? Did he have some dire warning to pass on to her? Was she, or any of the people in her dwelling, in impending danger? Was there a nasty eventuality coming their way? Why hadn't Dimitri just blurted out what he had to say?! Now he had left her hanging with all sorts of worried thoughts and fears. She wanted to share this quandary with Marta, but she knew Marta would become as perplexed and panicked as she was, so she kept her worries to herself.

***

Later in the summer, Mrs Dobrowolski, Marta and Lilyana were sent into the forest to pick mushrooms and berries. They would be paid one-and-a-half rubles for every kilogram of berries and five for every kilogram of mushrooms they brought in. All three women were very quick at picking berries and rooting out mushrooms. They picked every day, so they could save up as many rubles as possible.

Aunt Janina managed to harvest a small crop of carrots, beets and potatoes from her garden plot, but unfortunately, the turnips and cabbages failed to grow. Perhaps the soil was not suitable for them, or maybe Mrs Leski's turnip and cabbage seeds had been too old? The women bought more potatoes and some salt at the state-run store with the rubles they had earned in the forest. They rationed out all the root vegetables and boiled them down until they became very soft.

Everyone in their dwelling suffered with tender gums. Their teeth had become very sensitive as well, and they could no longer bite on anything hard. It would cause their gums to bleed, and they would feel excruciating pain. However, they considered themselves lucky; deportees in other dwellings had developed scurvy. They cooked their vegetables together in a soup and mashed them down so they would be more palatable.

Every evening, Aunt Janina returned from work, exhausted and coughing. The smoke from the branches she was ordered to burn was affecting her lungs. At times, she had difficulty catching her breath, and at night Lilyana could hear wheezing sounds in her aunt's lungs while she lay next to her on their sleeping platform. They sounded very much like the noises that little Helena Dobrowolski had made before she sadly died of pneumonia. Sabina Albinski said there was little that could be done for Janina without removing her from the source of her ailment, and providing proper medical attention.

Lilyana was desperate to help her aunt survive. She decided to appeal to the authorities for her aunt to receive medical care, and she begged them to have Janina's job assignment changed. Lilyana made her request when the NKVD officers attended their dwelling during a daily inspection. The officer in charge said he would consider what could be done, but nothing ever resulted from her request, and Aunt Janina's condition continued to get worse.

Lilyana felt she had to do something. At the risk of getting arrested for acting without permission from the commandant, she dragged her aunt to the forest to work with her picking berries and mushrooms instead of burning branches as she had been assigned to do. Her aunt blended in very well with the other women picking berries and mushrooms. Lilyana and Janina hoped the guards in their work zone would assume she had been transferred to a new work brigade, but on the second day, they caught up with Janina's unauthorised disappearance from her assigned work.

As they busied themselves picking berries, an NKVD officer came and arrested Aunt Janina. She was being carted off to Headquarters for interrogation. Lilyana saw what was happening and became terror-stricken. How could she save her aunt now? She knew Janina was so beaten down she would admit to anything the authorities accused her of, and she would surrender to any punishment the officials doled out. There was simply no fight left in her. Lilyana knew she had no choice but to go with Aunt Janina to Headquarters and try to rescue her from whatever impending fate was about to unfold. The only way she could do that was to get arrested alongside her aunt.

As the officer led Janina away, Lilyana ran after them, shouting, "Wait! Where are you taking my aunt? She has done nothing wrong!"

The officer spun around and yelled at Lilyana to get back to work with the other women.

"*No!*" Lilyana hollered. "She is innocent! She has not committed any crime! I won't continue working until you release my aunt!"

Another camp guard quickly restrained Lilyana, preventing her from chasing after her aunt and the arresting officer. Mrs Dobrowolski and Marta stood by in horror, watching the scene unfold. Marta crossed herself and asked God to have mercy on her courageous friend.

The NKVD officer motioned for the guard to bring Lilyana over to him. She noticed Aunt Janina was silently pleading for her to go back to work and not create any more fuss, but Lilyana did not.

With an angry expression, the officer looked at Lilyana and spat in her face.

"Stupid Polak," he cursed. "Guard… bring this rebel into Headquarters with the old woman!"

Lilyana and her aunt were escorted back to the village together, handcuffed in the back of an old army vehicle.

Once inside Headquarters, they were turned over to another guard, who directed them past many Soviet officers and soldiers working at desks in various departments. When they went by the commandant's large office, Lilyana observed a smaller office area adjacent to it, where she was surprised to see Dimitri and another young soldier seated at a desk. It then occurred to her how Dimitri had known she'd been summoned to the commandant's office last autumn on that rainy, muddy day. Her eyes scanned the brass plate inscribed on the door of Dimitri's department door. She was shocked. It read "*Administrative Assistant of Interrogation*". Surely, her pleasant soldier friend didn't have anything to do with the cruel and unrelenting interrogations of innocent Poles? Dimitri appeared to be busy working over a stack of papers piled up on his desk. Lilyana thought he had not noticed her being escorted down the lengthy hallway, but indeed, he had. He was just as stunned to see Lilyana and her aunt being brought in for questioning as Lilyana was to discover his position at NKVD Headquarters.

A tall, balding officer sat at a desk in the room where Lilyana and Aunt Janina were taken. He looked up from his work as the escorting guard motioned for the women to be seated and briefly explained why they had been brought in. They were speaking in Russian as the guard pointed at Lilyana, but she didn't bother trying to decipher what was being said. She was still reeling from her discovery of Dimitri's position.

The guard left the room, closing the door behind him. The officer at the desk continued writing something on the paper he was working on. He said nothing to them. The room remained very quiet and still. The only noise to be heard was the sound of grinding gears coming from the clock positioned on the wall above the officer's desk. A faint braying of horses was perceived in the distance through an opened window located behind the man.

It felt oppressively hot. It didn't help when the officer lit up a foul-smelling cigarette and puffed away on it. Occasionally, he coughed and snorted as he inhaled the pungent smoke. Janina was sitting so close to Lilyana she could feel her aunt's body shaking as the silent minutes slowly ticked past. Lilyana began to wonder whether this was one of the psychological methods she had heard other deportees saying the Russians used to break you down. Had Elzbieta, Mrs Bablak and Mrs Cieslak been brought here to undergo the same treatment before they mysteriously disappeared?

After twenty minutes had ticked by, the officer finally looked up from his paperwork. He eyed Lilyana and her aunt with a threatening gaze.

"So… you women would choose to disobey orders and do as you please!" he bellowed. Following a spasm of coughing that interrupted his words, he continued, "We have a certain protocol for rebellious people. If you find it too difficult to do as you are told here, there are other places where we can put you… places where there is no room for disobedience!"

A wave of horror swept over Lilyana then. Could this man be hinting at sending them to one of the forced labour camps further north? Was that what had happened to the women who had disappeared from their living quarters? Lilyana needed to put a stop to this immediately.

"Please sir. We do not wish to disobey orders. My aunt's health is failing, and she needed to—" she began.

"Shut up!" the officer shouted as he erupted into more convulsive hacking. "You both have violated the ordinances set out for you in this colony. We will not tolerate such insubordination!"

He stood up very quickly, appearing even more menacing once he reached his full height, lording his authority over them.

"Disobedience is dealt with very stringently here. We will see how you feel about contravening the rules after you have spent some time in a holding cell. We have ways of dealing with disruptive rebels. You will see!"

The officer then stomped over to the door of the interrogation room and flung it open. He peered out into the hallway and snapped his fingers to get the attention of a guard standing nearby.

Looking back at Lilyana and her aunt, he shouted, "I don't have time to deal with you Polish whores right now. I will see what punishment is fitting for your crimes later!"

Lilyana and her aunt feared what retribution they would be dealt. Would they be stripped naked and beaten? Would they be forced into a small, intolerable space and be deprived of food and water for days? Would they die as a result of whatever chastisement the officer inflicted on them… or would they be shipped off to one of the corrective labour camps, where further suffering and death were inevitable?

They were hastily marched along the hallway and down a series of stairways into a smelly holding cell. As they were led away, the interrogation officer could be heard violently hacking as another coughing spell took hold of him. After they were locked up, their documents from Headquarters' files were ordered to be brought to the interrogation room.

Lilyana was angry with herself for putting her aunt in this position, and she was furious that the Russian officer hadn't allowed her to explain why her aunt needed to be removed from her previous work assignment. She had tried to bring this matter to the attention of the authorities beforehand, but her request had been ignored.

If Dimitri were to sneak up and surprise her again, Lilyana wished it would be now while she and Aunt Janina were in the grimy holding cell. She had seen him working diligently at his desk when they were directed past his office and thought he had not noticed them. Despite the job title posted on his department door, Lilyana found it difficult to believe he would have anything to do with the abusive interrogations of deportees. She had heard so many horrific stories about callous methods the Soviets used to force false confessions from innocent Poles and the duplicitous ways they manipulated people into signing inaccurate documents and statements. She couldn't see Dimitri doing any of those terrible things. It did not fit the kind-hearted soldier she was slowly getting to know.

She could not appeal for Dimitri to come and see her in the holding cell, because the authorities would question why she was asking for him. It would cast suspicion, and he would come under their scrutiny as well.

Even if he had any leverage at Headquarters, she could hardly expect preferential treatment. Dimitri himself would be investigated if he were to show favour toward her. She didn't know what to do. She wanted him to know she was being held at Headquarters, but she believed it may be better if he had no knowledge of the fact.

Lilyana and Aunt Janina tried to sleep on the hard benches inside the holding cell. Between their apprehension over what fate awaited them and the discomfort inside the damp, smelly hole, sleep did not come. In the middle of the night, a guard came and escorted them back upstairs to the interrogation room. The Russians always seemed to bring people in for questioning in the middle of the night. Some said it was because their Imperial Leader, Stalin, did not sleep at night, and his officers needed to be ready to respond to his orders at a moment's notice; they worked through the night to keep the same hours as Soviet Head Office.

Deportees needed not do much to be charged with frivolous crimes. Lilyana knew Poles from their settlement had been taken to Headquarters and interrogated for things as trivial as singing religious songs or stealing a loaf of bread or a cabbage for their starving children. She assumed Mrs Cieslak had been sent away for praying her Christian prayers in atheistic Russia. Many people had disappeared without explanation. Some returned months later having served sentences in jail or one of the many forced labour camps throughout Siberia, but most were never seen again.

Outside the interrogation room, a familiar voice instructed Lilyana to sit down on a chair in the hallway where she was to wait. Lilyana immediately looked up and held back a smile when she saw Dimitri standing there with a pad of paper tucked under her arm and a pen in his other hand. Had it not been for the guards stationed nearby, she may have acknowledged him in some way.

He ushered Aunt Janina into the interrogation room and closed the door behind him so the investigation could begin. Lilyana felt a little relieved, hoping Dimitri would listen to what she had to say about the circumstances of her and Aunt Janina's arrest, and that he would dole out a fair penalty to both of them, rather than any form of harsh punishment. Nevertheless, her hopes for an easy judgement were dashed when she heard the ghastly hacking sounds of the older, balding officer coming from inside the room, and realised the senior officer was heading up the investigation. Dimitri was merely his assistant, and he had to comply with whatever judgement the senior officer handed out.

A couple of hours later, her aunt emerged from the room looking nervous and spent. Before she had a chance to say anything to Lilyana, one of the guards grabbed Janina's arm and led her back down the stairs to the holding cell to await her fate.

Dimitri appeared in the doorway, motioning for Lilyana to come into the interrogation room. As she entered, she observed the disgruntled officer who had threatened her and her aunt the previous afternoon. He sat at his desk puffing away on another cigarette, choking and gagging on the smoke. Dimitri had Lilyana sit across the desk from the officer, while he sat to the side and slightly behind the older man. The paper pad was opened in front of Dimitri, and taking his pen in hand, he prepared to write down whatever statements she would offer.

Lilyana felt foolish for having thought Dimitri would be the one to interrogate and allot punishment, when he was only an assistant to the interrogations officer. Here in the investigation room, Dimitri's countenance was as stern and distant as the Russian officer sitting across the desk from her. Despite the circumstances, he looked handsome in his soldier's uniform, and Lilyana hoped he was merely playing the role he had to perform here.

Lilyana wished it were possible to speak with her young soldier friend in private. She needed to know what her aunt had told the interrogator. Had her aunt stuck to the story she insisted Lilyana corroborate, blaming herself entirely for her unauthorised abandonment of her work brigade, or had the officer broken her down and discovered that it had been Lilyana's idea to change Janina's job detail? It angered Lilyana, how the Soviets were always trying to find fault with the deportees and bring further hardships on them. Obviously, the Russians were attempting to eliminate as many Poles as possible by whatever means they could.

"Surname?" the interrogating officer began. "Given name? Place of birth? Date of birth? Age? Occupation? Father's name? Father's nationality? Father's occupation? Mother's maiden name? Mother's nationality?"

The interrogator methodically ran through a list of initial questions listed in the document lying open in front of him. It was little more than a robotic exercise until it came time for the more dangerous questions relating to certain times and events. Lilyana was grilled in reference to her outburst defending her aunt at their worksite in the forest on the previous day.

The questions became complex when she was interrogated regarding what the authorities deemed to be her attack on the arresting officer. Dimitri quickly scribbled down Lilyana's words as she carefully answered each question in turn. Intermittently, the older officer held his hand up in the air, requesting that Lilyana wait until he had looked over Dimitri's record of her account.

Sometimes, the bald officer erupted into fits of coughing as he puffed on his noxious black cigarettes. Lilyana would have to wait until he stopped hacking before she could continue with her defence. If anyone understood Aunt Janina's need to get away from the effects of the smoke given off from burning branches in the forest, surely it was this old officer. His breath was raspy, and he choked and sputtered every time he lit up another cigarette. The man was suffocating from his habitual inhalation of smoke, and the interrogation room reeked of his foul habit. Lilyana hoped he empathised with her aunt's suffering.

She had difficulty understanding the interrogator's questions, and she struggled when trying to explain the details to him in Russian. She feared he would take her fumbled words and transpose her statements into something other than what she was reporting, thereby laying grounds to charge her and her aunt with fabricated crimes. At one point, she worded something incorrectly or mispronounced some of her limited Russian vocabulary, and the interrogator looked shocked and angered by what she had said. She didn't know where she had gone wrong, but she noticed Dimitri was looking stunned as well. Then Dimitri playfully jabbed at the older officer's arm and made a joke of what Lilyana had just uttered in Russian. Both men burst into exuberant laughing until the officer became swept up in another fit of coughing. Lilyana failed to interpret what Dimitri had said, but he appeared to have appeased the interrogator, and her investigation continued.

Intermittently, the officer would tap his pen impatiently on top of the document open on his desk and eye Lilyana suspiciously. Frequently, he picked up his diminishing black cigarettes and took in quick puffs of the obnoxious smoke. More coughing and gagging ensued. Lilyana found the man to be exceptionally ill-mannered and vile.

"Let us try this again!" he shouted. "This time, tell us the truth, Miss Prawoslaw! Why did you insist on chasing after Janina Prawoslaw and her arresting officer in the forest? Tell me why you challenged the guards and the officers when you were supposed to be working in the forest."

"I was worried for my aunt," Lilyana stated for the tenth time. "As I told you, she has not been well in recent weeks."

"Watch your attitude!" the bullish officer shouted with disdain. "Answer the questions I am asking you! No more condescending remarks!"

Dimitri remained unmoved. He waited with pen in hand, ready to continue writing when Lilyana resumed her explanation. The interrogating officer had Lilyana repeat details many times over. Occasionally, he poked holes in her comments and her reasoning. He came from many different angles in questioning certain aspects of her account, obviously attempting to trip her up and manipulate her into stating something other than what she intended... and eventually, he managed to twist her facts, creating an entirely different scenario from what Lilyana had presented.

Every time the officer had Lilyana repeat certain details, she stuck to the story the way her aunt told her to tell it: *It was her aunt's desire to get away from burning branches and brush in the forest because she was suffocating from the smoke. Her aunt had chosen to join Lilyana's work brigade picking berries and mushrooms because she would be healthier and more productive doing that work. Therefore, she would be a more profitable worker for the Russians. She was ailing from the brush-burning smoke and did not want to become a burden to the collaborative effort of the colony. Neither she nor Lilyana had meant to cause any trouble, and for that, they apologised. She had only tried to work to the best of her capabilities.*

In due course, the interrogations officer pulled out a lengthy document from Lilyana's file. Looking over it, he growled, "Tell me, Miss Prawoslaw, was it not *you* who asked the inspections officer at your living quarters to have your aunt's work designation changed? Was it not *you* who requested medical attention for Janina Prawoslaw? Can your aunt not speak for herself? You are a *liar*! Your aunt did *not* determine to abandon her work brigade in the forest. She is a frightened mouse! It was *you* who instructed Janina Prawoslaw to join your work crew picking in the forest without authorisation!"

The officer stared threateningly at Lilyana for a long time, but she refused to flinch. His face contorted into a fierce look of wrath, and his anger grew as he continued staring her down. Lilyana managed to maintain her composure. It was obvious the interrogator was infuriated by his inability to unnerve her.

The enraged man finally shouted, "*You are an instigator*! *You* blatantly chose to disobey rules and order! *You*, Miss Prawoslaw, will pay for your defiant disobedience! *You* are a rebellious influence! *You* are a destructive and undisciplined element! *You* have demonstrated contempt and hostility toward the Russian people. *You* harbour individualistic tendencies and dare to oppose the Communist establishment! *You* are subversive to the Soviet Union and its interests! I charge you with being an unworthy citizen towards the Soviet government. *You* will report to court in Arkhangelsk, where *you will be sentenced for your crimes*!"

The officer's final words became muffled as he attempted to speak through another fit of convulsive coughing. Some of his words were not part of Lilyana's Russian vocabulary, and with his hacking, she could not decipher all that he had stated. It wasn't until she noticed the shocked look on Dimitri's face at the officer's garbled charges that she realised her situation must be dire.

Mulling over the interrogator's words, she misinterpreted what had been said and believed she was being sent further into the interior of the Soviet Union to a corrective labour camp. She felt a sudden tightening in her throat, and a wave of nausea took hold as the room began to spin. Her head throbbed, and she broke into a sweat as panic consumed every fibre of her being. Unable to control her fear, she was paralysed. Her hands clung tightly to the sides of the chair where her diminutive form was perched. Momentarily, she swayed from side to side as she fought hard to remain conscious. She absolutely would not allow this callous Soviet officer to see her collapse.

A smug look of satisfaction slowly crept across the interrogator's face. He felt he had finally unhinged the brave young rebel, and it brought him joy to think he had beaten her down.

Lilyana drew in a breath and reached deep inside herself for that inner fortitude she had been relying on for many months now. Her dizziness subsided, and she managed to steady herself just in time to hear the old man ordering Dimitri to summon a guard to escort her back to the holding cell.

"I hope you enjoy Arkhangelsk, Miss Prawoslaw!" the officer scoffed.

He let loose with a boisterous laugh, which quickly developed into another fit of coughing. Dimitri took Lilyana by the arm and led her toward the doorway where another guard was waiting for her.

With the interrogator hacking and fighting for breath, Dimitri quickly whispered to Lilyana in Polish, "Stay calm. I will see if I can do something to rectify this situation."

Before Lilyana had a chance to digest Dimitri's words, the guard was poking at her back and pushing her along the hallway down the stairs to the holding cell area. Janina was curled up in a ball weeping in the corner of the cell.

"Oh, Lilyana!" she wailed between her sobs. "I'm not sure what happened! I did not understand what the brute was asking me. He had me very confused answering his questions. You know I cannot speak or write Russian. Your name was mentioned repeatedly during my interrogation."

Lilyana embraced her aunt and replied calmly, "It will be alright, Auntie. Don't fret so. Everything will be fine. Just wait and see."

"But you don't understand, Lily! I think the officer fabricated accusations against you. I did not comprehend what he was suggesting. I think he fooled me into signing something that produced charges against you! What have I done? Why did I let him do that to me? The more I think about it, the more I fear for your safety and wellbeing. It is unforgivable! Why couldn't I just die before I was taken in for questioning? I have put your life in jeopardy now!"

Lilyana should have cringed with fear and dread upon hearing her aunt's confession, but instead, she remained inexplicably serene. She recalled a passage from the Bible that spoke about God's peace that surpasses all understanding. That would define how she felt at that moment. Was this divine intervention, or had Dimitri's words when exiting the interrogation room settled her nerves? Lilyana believed that despite the circumstances, everything would turn out well in the end.

Aunt Janina's tears continued regardless of Lilyana's optimistic outlook. Lilyana couldn't do anything to extinguish her aunt's sorrow and fear. The two women remained in the holding cell for two days and nights before an NKVD officer came to remove them and transport them to a Soviet prison far away. Once there, they would wait for a mock trial to begin. They would be transported in a covered army vehicle loaded with many other prisoners. All were prevented from escape, a view of the outside world or contact with civilians.

Lilyana wondered where Dimitri was. Would he follow through on his promise to try and resolve her and her aunt's dilemma? She also pondered what it was that Dimitri had intended to tell her down by the river a short time ago. Why was this man always leaving her tangled up with loose ends that needed to be resolved? Even though her situation looked bleak, Lilyana did not lose faith in believing that Dimitri would come to her rescue, as he had been doing ever since she arrived on Russian soil... but where was he now? She was being transported far away. Had the window of opportunity to save her from this situation closed?

***

Aunt Janina wore an expression of death on her face as they journeyed in the army transport. She had given up hope of ever seeing her surviving children or her husband again. At that point, she believed she would never be free. She prayed she would fall into a deep sleep and never wake up again.

Lilyana did everything in her power to try and keep her aunt's hope alive... all to no avail. A familiar grey pallor washed over Janina's impassive face, and the glazed look peering from her stony eyes revealed that Auntie's prayers had been answered here on the road, halfway to the prison. Lilyana sat next to Janina's lifeless body, swaying with the motion of the vehicle as it plodded along the rough terrain. She embraced her aunt and said a prayer over her for one whose life had been prematurely snuffed out in the merciless conditions. She sobbed as she clung to Janina, knowing that nobody else in the prisoners' transport would care about her aunt's demise. All the prisoners had lost loved ones in this place of abominations, and as heartless as it seemed, they had become immune to reaction and sentiment.

Upon reaching their destination, several Red Army soldiers appeared when the vehicle moved beyond the iron gates of the prison yard. The tailgate on the transport was lowered, and the captives were pushed and hurried down from the vehicle. Lilyana hung back, trying to protect her aunt. She wanted all the prisoners to disembark before she got out. Having witnessed how the ruthless soldiers would pick up dead bodies and toss them aside like sacks of grain, Lilyana did not want her aunt to be callously thrown from the vehicle like that. A Soviet guard started to jab at her with his rifle, ordering her to get down, and a commotion erupted inside the back of the vehicle when she refused to let go of her aunt's body. The other prisoners who remained in the lorry scattered like ants, wanting nothing to do with any developing conflict.

Two more soldiers poked their heads inside the vehicle to see what was happening. With a burst of fury, they jumped up into the transport and grabbed Lilyana by the arms, wrenching her away from Janina's corpse. One of them pushed Lilyana so forcefully that she fell out of the vehicle onto the ground by the prison gates. Harsh words and curses were flung her way, not only from the Russians. Some of her fellow captives were also exasperated by her apparent lack of compliance. She was riling up the Russian soldiers, and that would make the guards harder on all of them.

Suddenly, the soldiers surrounding her went rigid and stood at attention. An approaching officer ordered them to back off. When he reached Lilyana, she could see that this man must be a commander or somebody of great authority here at the prison.

"What is going on?" he demanded to know.

The soldier in charge of the prisoners' escort quickly replied, "This prisoner refused to cooperate, sir. We had to use force to remove her from the transport."

The commander was now towering over Lilyana. His hands were neatly tucked behind his back, and his imposing form emitted a sense of power and authority. When she finally managed to find her feet, Lilyana looked up at him. He looked familiar to her. She felt that she had seen this officer somewhere before.

"Name!" the commander yelled.

"Lilyana Prawoslaw," she replied meekly.

"...and tell me, Miss Prawoslaw, why did you resist orders to get out of the vehicle? You are only making circumstances more difficult for yourself... no?"

The man seemed even more familiar once he had spoken. There was something about his mannerisms that was vaguely recognisable. However, she could not place where she had encountered this man before. She quickly explained about her aunt's passing en route to the prison, and how she'd wanted her aunt's corpse to be removed from the transport in a dignified manner. She told the commander that she'd been waiting for all the other prisoners to get down from the transport ahead of her so she could take her aunt's body out of the vehicle with care and respect.

A couple of the surrounding soldiers grunted and expressed dissent with what Lilyana had to say.

Seeming unimpressed, the commander approached the back of the transport and peered inside. His hands remained neatly placed behind his back as his eyes came to rest on Aunt Janina's rumpled corpse on the floor of the vehicle, where she'd come to rest when Lilyana was yanked outside.

He looked at her longer than necessary, and then, turning to Lilyana, said, "Then we shall remove your aunt's body carefully for burial... no?"

Several of the soldiers standing at attention raised their eyebrows and flinched a little. Obviously, this was not the usual protocol for deceased captives arriving at the prison. Lilyana could only imagine what usually happened to the bodies of those unfortunate souls.

The commander ordered the soldier in charge of the transport to have his men remove Aunt Janina's body and bring it to the prison morgue.

"A fitting burial should be awarded to one whose niece would dare to resist a contingent of soldiers for her, no?" the commander announced.

The soldiers looked one at another, appearing confused and disoriented now, but they were bound to obey the commander's orders.

"We will bury this woman with the other prisoners in the morgue awaiting burial," the commander stated. "You, Miss Prawoslaw, will not attend any funeral, because none will be forthcoming. However, this woman, your aunt, will be buried with dignity."

Lilyana attempted to thank the commander as she was led away to a prison cell with the other prisoners. They were processed and ushered into smaller groups sent off in different directions, the men separated from the women. Lilyana was thankful she had prayed for her aunt in the transport before they arrived at the prison. Sadly, that would be the only prayer offered up for Aunt Janina.

***

"No time for pity... no time for grieving!"

It was an older woman prisoner who spoke those words to Lilyana inside the prison cell.

"If you give in to emotion, you will become weak! You will not survive!" the old woman scolded. "I saw what happened in the transport. You are strong. You are brave. You can survive all of this. Go forward and prove to our oppressors that the Polish will outlive all the atrocities the Bolsheviks inflict on us. They *will not* wipe us off the map! We will be made stronger by the evil deeds done to us, and we will go back to our homes one day and live our lives in a *free* Poland again!"

Lilyana looked at the old woman and felt an affinity with her. The woman did not speak idle words. There was a fiery strength, faith and a vision of hope in this woman's eyes. The woman managed to give Lilyana the boost she needed to overcome all that lay ahead.

Strangely, Lilyana never saw the old woman again. Where had she gone? Did Lilyana only dream her words, or had the encounter ever really happened? Whatever the case, it had recharged Lilyana with the fortitude she needed to carry on.

She needed to be tenacious now. Being in a Soviet prison brought a whole new list of hardships. The cell was damp, windowless, and overcrowded. It was made of concrete... the floor, the walls and the ceiling. A bare lightbulb hung high up and cast very little light. Many of the women inside the cell were tough characters who could curse and fistfight as viciously as any man. Some were insane and posed a danger to themselves and the people around them. Some sat gazing off into space all day. Others cradled their arms and rocked and cooed at invisible babies who no longer existed. Some screamed and howled continually, while others hallucinated and thrashed out at whoever happened to be positioned nearby. Lilyana had to sleep with one eye open.

Like Dimitri had told her earlier on, she needed to be aware of things around her all the time. Manifestations of lice and bedbugs remained unchecked. The outbreak of insects in the prison was even worse than that in the living quarters at the settlement. Mice and rats scurried everywhere. For amusement, some of the tougher women would corner the biggest rats and anger them enough to make them stand up and hiss. The same women stabbed and mutilated the rodents. It was disgusting.

Food and water were severely rationed, and often the violent women would steal food from the less aggressive inmates. The smell inside the cell was unbearable. The stench of so many festering bodies crammed so close together was only outdone by the smell given off by the two large buckets positioned in a corner of the cell where all the women had to relieve themselves. Eventually, urine and faeces would overflow from the buckets and create huge puddles of messy excrement the more violent women took pleasure in pushing docile women into. Sometimes, gangs of women would force the passive ones to lie down in the excrement and use their tattered clothing as rags to clean up the vile spillage. If a prisoner refused to do so, the gangs would violently beat the victim into unconsciousness. A few ladies were beaten to death inside the cell.

These gangs of women had come from insane asylums, and from the Soviet penal system. Political prisoners like Lilyana were thrown together with them after prisons throughout Russia became overcrowded as a result of the Soviets' massive arrests of innocent people during their occupation of Poland. Many different languages were spoken, and the prisoners tended to group together according to their nationalities. Sometimes ethnic battles spilled over into the prisons. The weak would not survive. It was not a safe place for anyone.

Lilyana was fortunate to be taken under the wing of a gang of Polish peasant women in her prison cell. Gossip spread fast, and these women had heard about Lilyana's brave opposition to the Russian guards. That cemented her place as a tough member among their group. If anyone in their cell tried to mess with Lilyana, the women in her gang were quick to defend her. The only price she had to pay for their shielding was to share her limited rations of food and water with the woman who was regarded as their leader. Lilyana did so willingly when she discovered how difficult it would be to survive in the prison cell without their protection.

The environment was worse than anything she could have imagined. She concluded that conditions in Hell could not be any more depraved than conditions inside a Soviet prison. She was thankful that her aunt had not lived long enough to become an inmate here. Aunt Janina would have been an easy target.

Every night, women were taken away by the guards for interrogation, or to their trials. Lilyana prayed that her turn would come soon. She worried how her little cousin Larissa was doing back at the settlement. She knew Marta and Mrs Dobrowolski would take care of Larissa in her mother's absence, but she also knew the little girl would be scared and upset with her and Janina gone.

Three guards came to fetch Lilyana one week after she had been jailed. She was escorted to the showers, ordered to remove her clothing and to take a hot shower using the harsh soap provided. It was a painful experience as she scrubbed down her body and her hair, but it relieved her from the infestation of lice. She was humiliated and embarrassed as the guards stood and watched. She worried what might happen to her, recalling the sordid details Olga's sister had described in her letter about rapes in her camp.

One of the guards threw prison clothes at Lilyana and demanded she follow them. With dripping hair and bare feet, she quickly pulled on the prison trousers and shirt as she was forced through a maze of corridors and up some stairs to where the prison administrative offices were located. She was ushered into a very ostentatious office and told to sit down in a chair across from a massive desk. The escorting guards seemed to disappear into the luxurious space surrounding them. Lilyana looked around the office and concluded that it belonged to a very meticulous person. Judging by the neat and orderly placement of things, she assumed this person was obsessive about cleaning and tidiness. How contrary the room was to the repulsive conditions that lay beneath in the bowels of the same building.

Lilyana's thoughts wandered until the office door opened, and in walked the authoritative commander whom she had encountered upon arriving at the prison a week earlier. The man did not look at her. He unbuttoned the jacket of his uniform and slipped around the meticulous desk, taking his seat. He dismissed the accompanying guards, motioning for them to leave the room. This seemed to take the guards by surprise, but they left without question.

With hands folded neatly on of top his desk, the commander finally looked intently at Lilyana from across the huge expanse. He spoke not a word, but just stared. Lilyana felt awkward and embarrassed. It appeared that the commander was going to say something, but his words remained stuck in his mouth. It was most bizarre. An uncomfortable silence hung heavily in the air between the two of them.

Thankfully, a knock at the door broke the unpleasant silence. The man stood up to re-button his jacket, casually assumed his official stance with his hands tucked behind his back, and told the person at the door to come in.

When the door opened behind her, Lilyana could not see who was there. A man entered and formally greeted the commander in Russian. The voice sounded familiar, and when the man said, "You look like a drowned rat, but I see you have managed to survive," in her native Polish, she realised it was Dimitri.

This was the biggest surprise and relief Lilyana could ever have asked for! She wanted to acknowledge him but decided not to as it would rouse suspicion from the prison commander. She sat quietly in shock, trying to process the fact that Dimitri had shown up for her trial and spoken to her in Polish in front of the prison authority. Even more stunning was the fact that he behaved so informally around the prison commander. All the other soldiers and the guards would stiffen up, jump to attention and salute in the officer's presence.

The commander gave Dimitri a stern look and ordered him to sit down. Dimitri pulled up a chair and sat next to Lilyana. The two men then commenced a dialogue in Russian. Although her understanding of the language was somewhat limited, Lilyana was able to determine that they were discussing something about a transport vehicle being loaded and ready to move. She hoped they would turn their attention to her pending trial soon, as she was becoming increasingly more anxious.

Words continued to be exchanged very quickly between Dimitri and the commander. She had difficulty deciphering what else was being said. It almost seemed as though the men were speaking to each other in secret code, and then their intense conversation ended just as abruptly as it had commenced.

Lilyana's expectation for her case being heard in a mock trial instantly dissolved when the commander turned to her and announced, "I exonerate you from all wrongdoing, Lilyana Prawoslaw. You must return to your work brigade at your assigned settlement and never put yourself on the wrong side of the authorities again! I only give you a pardon once. If you are ever brought here again, you will face certain death. Do you understand?"

Lilyana questioned whether she had translated the man's words correctly. Was he freeing her without a trial? What had Dimitri said to the man to make that possible? Confusion cluttered her mind. She realised Dimitri must have much more influence than she could have ever imagined to be able to get her out of a bad situation this easily. There were no words to express the extent of relief and gratitude she was feeling. Thankful tears threatened to fall from her eyes, but she was still guarded against showing any sign of weakness in this horrible place. She gulped at the back of her throat to prevent the tears from flowing.

The commander repeated one more time, "Do you understand?"

Lilyana managed to nod her head and say, "Yes, sir. I understand."

The man folded his hands on the desk and looked down at the pens and stacks of paper neatly piled in the corner. He made a futile attempt to reposition the papers and straighten them again, only to return the pile to the spot where he had removed it from.

Strangely, Dimitri asked Lilyana, "Have you no words of gratitude to offer your uncle for his generous gift in releasing you today?"

Lilyana wanted to thank the prison official, but she was afraid she would choke with tears if she dared to speak... wait! Had Dimitri just called the commander her *uncle*? What?!

Her heart began to race. She observed the man sitting across the desk from her and said nothing. Did the Russians have another meaning for the use of the word uncle? She must have misunderstood what Dimitri was saying. She was too confused to make sense of anything anymore.

Looking at the commander, Dimitri said, "I think we have some explaining to do."

The older man nodded his head in agreement. Motioning with his hand, he invited Dimitri to take the lead. Lilyana noticed that all sense of decorum had evaporated now. Dimitri was taking liberties, and the commander seemed to have relinquished his authority over the entire proceedings.

Dimitri spoke in Polish now. "Lilyana, you know that my name is Dimitri Yatskaya." Then, pointing across the desk to the older man, he said, "This is Viktor Yatskaya. He is my father."

Lilyana let out a sudden gasp. Her hand immediately went to her chest, and her heartrate increased. She shook her head to clear her thoughts. Then she realised why Dimitri was being so informal and had so much pull with the commander. *Dimitri is the son of the prison commander. This officer is his father*! A look of astonishment crossed her face as she processed the revelation. Everything came crashing together like pieces of a fractured puzzle being reassembled. She now understood why she felt she had seen the prison commander before. The man bore many similarities to Dimitri. The resemblance in their mannerisms was evident, and now that the two of them were in the same room, Lilyana could see that they even looked a little bit alike.

"Lilyana. Did you hear what I said? Viktor Yatskaya is your uncle. Perhaps the terminology was confusing you when I spoke it in Russian?"

She was very confused by Dimitri's words. She thought that the term *uncle* must have a different meaning to the Russians. What was Dimitri trying to say?

Lilyana looked across the desk to the commander again. He peered back at her awkwardly, and with some degree of ineptness, he attempted to speak in Polish. His words were quiet and clumsy, and a thick Russian accent overshadowed his Polish pronunciation, but he managed to say, "We have a family secret you know nothing about, Miss Prawoslaw. It is time for the truth to be revealed."

At first, Lilyana wondered what the Yatskaya family secrets had to do with her... unless Dimitri's father really was her... *uncle*?

"How can that be?" she whispered. "No! All my relatives are Polish... and now there are only a few of us who have survived here in this formidable land!"

Dimitri and his father looked down at the floor as if in shame. Lilyana's innocent statement had revealed the extent of human destruction resulting from the Soviets' war crimes against the Polish people.

Dimitri got up and walked over to a large window that faced out into the prison yard. Looking outside, he paused briefly while he collected his thoughts. He wanted his words to be unclouded and precise.

"Not all Russians are evil, Lilyana," he said. "We are human too. Many of our own people suffer the same persecution and hardship that deportees endure inside forced labour camps and colonies in Northern Russia and Siberia."

He turned and looked at Lilyana now.

"Although there are many Russian soldiers and guards who do take liberties in their abusive treatment of exiles and prisoners, don't overlook those among us who care about the plight of deportees, and who do try to help in subtle ways. We do not choose to persecute others. There are some among us who are disgusted at the brutality of our own people. Nevertheless, orders are orders, and we are obliged to obey the commands of our superiors. If we do not comply with the directives of the Communist regime, we will be charged with criminal offenses against the Soviet Union and sent to prisons or camps ourselves. Then, we will not be here to do anything to help those of you who fall victim to the circumstances you are living now. Have I not shielded you from certain death in recent months? There are many Russian soldiers who feel empathy toward deportees. These are the guards who will joke with you and be lenient when you fail to follow protocol."

Dimitri came back and sat down next to Lilyana again. "You must have encountered a few kind soldiers here in the Soviet Union, Lilyana? We are the ones who calm the rage of more aggressive guards in dealings with the exiles, or when no one is looking, drop a piece of vegetable or fish into the ration bowl of a suffering child in the settlement. We overlook it when a work brigade piles up a stack of logs with hollow spaces in the middle, thinking the soldiers will not notice they have not completed the daily quota. We see it, but we issue the ration card for a full day's work anyway. Please don't paint all of us with the same evil brush."

Lilyana listened intently to what Dimitri was saying and felt a twinge of guilt herself. She and Marta had encountered a few considerate soldiers at the settlement and in the forest working zones. Marta certainly had a way of rooting out the kinder ones, and if Lilyana had anyone to thank for a show of compassion and helpful consideration, it would be Dimitri himself.

"I must thank you for your kindness shown me, Dimitri," Lilyana acknowledged. "It is true that there are a few soldiers and guards who are more thoughtful and kinder than the many heartless, brutal ones. Your unexpected food packages have saved those in my living quarters at the settlement more than once, and the Christmas tree you left for us brought great joy and delight to the children in my shelter at Christmastime."

The commander had had no idea his son had performed these good deeds. Dimitri glanced over at his father, who remained stalwart in his official chair—nonetheless, appearing slightly amused.

"I know you have never heard the details I am about to tell you," Dimitri said, looking back to Lilyana. "It is what I was about to tell you down by the river at the settlement. You have a right to know the truth."

Dimitri got up then and walked back to the large window. He put one arm out and leaned against the wooden frame.

Looking over at Lilyana, he continued, "I know you must find it difficult to believe that Viktor Yatskaya could be your uncle, but it is true."

He waited for Lilyana to react in some way. She felt shocked and numb inside. Common sense told her not to believe what must be a fallacy that Dimitri was presenting to her. Was this another one of the psychological tricks the Soviets used to confuse the deportees?

"No! That can't be so! Why are you saying this to me?" she demanded to know.

"Ah… but it *is* true, my dear," the commander interrupted. "There was one Prawoslaw family member who came to Russia and married here years ago. Her name was Anna. She was your father and Jerzy Prawoslaw's older sister."

Lilyana knew that her father had had an older sister named Anna, but that the sister had died a long time ago when her father was a little boy.

She looked squarely in the prison commander's eyes and said, "There is obviously some mistake, sir. My father's sister died in Poland when my father was eight years old."

"Yes… yes. I realise that is what you were told," the commander replied.

Lilyana looked over at Dimitri standing by the window and stated, "My father would never lie to me about such a thing."

"But he did not know the truth, Lilyana," Dimitri hastened to add. "Please allow us to explain the circumstances to you."

"Alright. I am listening," Lilyana declared. "But that does not mean I have to believe whatever you are going to tell me."

She sat scowling with her arms tightly folded across her chest. A quiet laugh erupted from the older Yatskaya man.

"Stubborn," he exclaimed. "This one truly is a Prawoslaw!"

Dimitri looked over at his father and smiled. Then he proceeded to speak in Polish, telling Lilyana all that he knew about Anna. Lilyana had never been told any of the details that Dimitri revealed to her.

"Did you know your grandfather Prawoslaw had been married before he met your grandmother?" he began. "He and his first wife, Maria, had a daughter they named Anna."

This detail took Lilyana by surprise. She had always assumed that Anna was the daughter of Grandma Lena and her Grandfather Prawoslaw.

Dimitri continued. "Unfortunately, Maria died of pneumonia when Anna was only five years old. A few years later, your grandfather married your grandmother, Lena. Together they had two sons, your father and your Uncle Jerzy. Anna was a few years older than her brothers, and she helped to raise them when they were young. When Anna was eighteen, she met a Russian officer and fell deeply in love with him. The officer was just as enamoured with Anna, and he asked her to marry him. However, your grandfather would not give the Russian officer permission to marry his daughter and have her move to Leningrad with him. Grandfather Prawoslaw was a counter-revolutionary, and the thought of his daughter becoming a Communist did not sit well with him. Anna was so in love with the officer though, and she wanted to become his wife, so against her father's wishes she stole off to Russia and married him. They lived happily together in Leningrad for many years.

"The only thing was, Anna's father never forgave her for marrying the Russian. He disowned her and cast her out of the Prawoslaw family forever. He informed everyone that Anna had died. That is why your father believed his sister was dead. Anna wrote many letters to her family in Poland, but they were all returned unopened. Your grandfather never saw what Anna had to say to him… all her heartfelt apologies, her begging for forgiveness and the news about the birth of her son. Eventually, Anna gave up trying to contact her family in Poland. The pain of rejection became too much for her to bear, and it would follow her to her grave."

Dimitri had painted a very clear picture with his words. His narrative seemed to come from a place of sincerity. Lilyana knew about her grandfather Prawoslaw's political views, which made the story about his shunning of Anna for running off and marrying a Communist very plausible.

Lilyana looked across the huge desk to the older Yatskaya man, who was sitting there quiet and deep in thought. His expression was one of pained memory, and in that moment, Lilyana realised Dimitri was telling her the truth.

"You are the Russian officer my aunt Anna ran off to marry, aren't you?" Lilyana blurted out, pointing to the prison commander. "And you, Dimitri, are the son that Anna gave birth to in Leningrad! You are the grandson that my grandfather never knew he had… and that makes you…"

"Yes, Lilyana. I am your cousin." Dimitri grinned.

The room went silent for a few minutes while Lilyana digested everything she had just learned.

"I wanted to tell you sooner," Dimitri said. "Only, there is a great risk for all of us sharing these facts. Nobody outside this room must ever hear any of the details I have just divulged to you. It will put all of us in grave danger. We can never speak of this again, and we must continue to play our roles that life has allotted us… you the Polish deportee, me the Soviet soldier, and my father the prison administrator. I hope a time will come when peace exists between our two nations, and then we can sit down together and break bread as families are meant to do. Until that time comes, try to keep yourself out of trouble with the guards at the settlement, and I will continue watching out for you as best as I am able to in my position there, without raising suspicion."

"How very sad," Lilyana lamented.

"What?" Dimitri asked.

"Anna's life story… your mother. Why did she not attempt to contact her brothers later, after they had grown up? My father would have embraced her with opened arms if he'd known that his sister was still alive. He was a very kind and loving man. He would not have harboured any grudges or judgements against her. She could have reconnected with her brothers… and not have died with a broken heart."

It was Viktor Yatskaya who answered Lilyana this time.

"Anna was afraid that your father and Jerzy would not believe she was their long-lost sister. By that point in time, the brothers had believed she'd been dead for many years. How could they possibly fathom that some stranger in Russia was now claiming to be their dead sister? They had been bringing flowers to her mock grave in Poland for years, where your grandfather falsely claimed she was buried. Anna learned this from a friend in Stolpce whom she remained in contact with. For her brothers, it would have seemed like a cruel joke for Anna to suddenly emerge from the grave somewhere in the Soviet Union."

Lilyana shuddered. She had memories of her father taking her to Anna's gravesite to pay tribute to his dead sister when she was a little girl. Anna must have still been alive at that time.

Looking crestfallen, Viktor Yatskaya added, "Besides, if the brothers were to learn the truth, Anna feared they may have rejected her for marrying a Russian. She was afraid that your grandfather would have turned them into anti-Soviets like himself. Anna would not have been able to handle being cast out of the family a second time, so she just let it go."

"My mother had many regrets about losing her family, Lilyana," Dimitri added. "She often told me stories about growing up in Poland on the family farm. She described the sights, the sounds and the smells so precisely that I believed I had visited there! She talked a lot about your father and Jerzy. She missed them terribly. She became sad whenever she spoke of her family in Poland. She bore the brunt of many wasted years resulting from the circumstances. The heartache she felt caused her health to deteriorate in later years. She always wondered what had become of her younger brothers. She would have been pleased to know Jerzy continued managing the family farm."

Dimitri became silent when he realised the gaffe he had just made. He wanted to kick himself for that last remark. The Prawoslaws' farm had now been confiscated by the Soviet occupiers.

Viktor Yatskaya changed the subject quickly by saying to Dimitri, "We must not waste too much time if our secret operation is to remain on schedule."

Lilyana extended a look of confusion and curiosity Dimitri's way.

**

The return journey from Arkhangelsk was a very revealing one. Dimitri provided Lilyana with an old peasant dress and some boots. She learned that after she had been charged with her crimes and sent away from the settlement, Dimitri had informed his father of the development. The commander had then arranged for his son to escort a new group of prisoners to the prison where Lilyana was jailed. Two soldiers had been assigned to assist the young officer in collecting and transporting more prisoners from various settlements along the way. Dimitri had driven the army vehicle to the prison compound where the detainees were unloaded, and he was ordered to pick up a full load of supplies that needed to be transported back to the settlement on his return journey. Uncle Viktor saw to it that the legal papers were prepared for Lilyana to re-enter the colony free and clear of all charges. Normally, she'd have to wait until a separate transport arrived to return her and a few other freed detainees to the settlements they had come from, but Uncle Viktor made secret plans for Dimitri to return her safely without having to wait days or weeks for another transport. Viktor immediately sent orders for the two soldiers who'd accompanied Dimitri to the prison to be transferred, so they remained in Arkhangelsk serving as prison guards. Against usual procedures, Dimitri was the only officer in the transport driving back to the settlement. He hid Lilyana in the back of the vehicle amongst provisions of food and other supplies he'd been ordered to deliver to the colony.

Lilyana did not mind being bounced around surrounded by barrels of smelly fish, sacks of flour and Soviet work coats and boots designated for forest workers. When any soldiers or lorries were spotted along the road, or whenever the vehicle was ordered to stop, she was instructed to crawl under the government consignment of coats and remain very quiet and still.

The transport was ordered to halt at an official checkpoint on the outskirts of a large town. The guards had vicious dogs leashed beside them at the gate. When Dimitri brought the vehicle to a stop, the dogs jumped up and started sniffing around. Lilyana feared those mean dogs the Soviets used for searching. She worried she would not be able to control her shaking if any of them were to search inside the vehicle. Surely they would sniff her out.

Dimitri started chatting with the guard at the checkpoint gate, offered him a cigarette and distracted him with idle chat. He was very good at side-tracking the guard, and the transport passed through the gate without being searched. Lilyana remained undetected. Dimitri teased her, saying that she would have been safe because she had taken on the smell of the rotting fish next to her in the back of the vehicle, which would throw the dogs off her scent.

In more remote areas, Lilyana was permitted to sit up against the back of the cab in the transport's rear, and

Dimitri opened the little window behind him so he and Lilyana could talk while he drove. Lilyana didn't mind having to yell above the din of the vehicle's engine. She asked many questions. She was puzzled and wanted to know how the Yatskayas had managed to trace her family among the multitude of Polish deportees being shipped off to Siberia.

Dimitri grinned in the rearview mirror and said, "Ah... that was a fortunate twist of fate for you. I was assigned to be one of the officers escorting convoys of Poles overland to their colonies. I always looked at the names listed in the transport schedules. When I came upon the names of Prawoslaws from Stolpce, I made a mental note of the information written next to the names. I contacted my father with the information, and he did some investigating. He got back to me saying that you Prawoslaws were indeed Anna's relatives. He told me to keep an eye on all of you. He said my mother would want us to watch out for you, and that she would not rest peacefully in her grave if we let anything happen to any of you."

There was a brief pause before Dimitri continued.

"Unfortunately, we cannot turn back the tide of time. So many of your family members had already disappeared or perished before you even arrived in Russia... your father and Uncle Jerzy, Wasyl, baby Danuta and your own mother as well. I am truly sorry for your losses, Lilyana!"

Another heavy pause lingered before Dimitri added reflectively, "... and now the loss of Michal and Aunt Janina have added to your sorrows in Russia. I know life is very difficult for those of you who remain here."

"Yes." Lilyana nodded. "Circumstances have altered our lives drastically. It is exhausting and punishing trying to survive in such inhumane conditions."

"I am sorry for all of that, Lilyana. When my father and I discovered that my mother's family was being sent to a colony here in Siberia, Father had me assigned to supervise your convoy overland. When your settlement designation was determined, he had me transferred from my previous post to my current position at Headquarters in the village where you are located. He has a lot of discrete friends in high places who owe him a favour or two.

"He told me to keep an eye out and remain vigilant for all of you. I have done my best to assist you without raising any suspicion from the authorities and the other soldiers in the settlement. It is not always easy for me to know what is happening in your living quarters or at your work locations in the forest. I have struggled to keep appraised of things, and I have done my best to keep you safe."

"I know you have been doing so, Dimitri, and once again I thank you for all that you have done for me and my family."

"When I saw you and your... *our* aunt being brought into Headquarters for questioning, Lilyana, I was beside myself with worry. You know I was assigned to assist with interrogations there. I contacted my father and told him about your situation. He told me to ensure that you and Aunt Janina be sent to Arkhangelsk where he could intercede.

"I must maintain my position at the settlement without drawing suspicion from my superiors and fellow officers. It is a difficult act to juggle. I must be extremely careful in assisting you. Eyes are watching everywhere, and ears are always listening. Nobody trusts anybody in these difficult times we are living now. Some do not hesitate to turn in their best friend on false pretences if it will mean saving their own backside. We must ensure that nobody will ever discover our secret kinship. It puts a large target on both of us, Lilyana. I am sure you realise that I must maintain an air of indifference toward you at the settlement, and you must remain oblivious to me. Some of my fellow officers have fallen victim to sentencings and been exiled to forced labour camps for demonstrating compassion and friendship toward deportees. Russian officers are not exempt from the harsh punishments dealt to those who are suspected of the slightest infraction in rules and conduct. Everyone is paranoid. I will continue to watch out for you and Larissa from a distance as best as I can. It is more difficult for me to keep a watch over Aleksander, with him working so far away from the settlement… but all of you must cooperate with the authorities, even when it goes against the very fibre of your soul."

"I understand what you are saying, dear cousin," Lilyana said, "and I am aware of the difficult situation my family has put you in. Please be careful in all you do for us. Do not jeopardise your position. I understand that it is not in your nature to treat us harshly, but it is the attitude you must feign to avoid suspicion from the authorities. I am fortunate to have you as my cousin here in Russia. Please tell your father I am grateful for all he has done for me and my family as well. Both of you have gone to great measures to keep us safe… even at the risk of your own welfare and security."

"As I've said before, Lilyana, my mother would not rest peacefully if we did anything less for you."

"Just tell me one thing, Dimitri. Your father, my uncle Viktor, did he love my father's sister through all the years they were married? Did he treat Anna well?"

A broad grin spread across Dimitri's face. Years of happy memories were reflected in that smile.

"Oh yes, yes, yes!" he answered hastily. "My father adored my mother. He treated her very well. He grieved with her over the loss of her Polish roots throughout all the years they were married. It almost seemed as though he blamed himself, and he tried to make amends for causing that loss, which pained my mother until her dying day. He bought her many fine things… a wonderful house on the outskirts of Leningrad, beautiful jewellery, splendid clothes and anything her heart desired. She was his life. When she passed away, she was only thirty-five years old. My father mourned like nothing I had seen before. He had always been a pillar of composure and strength, but at her gravesite I saw him weep openly without shame in front of everyone who attended my mother's funeral. He will always blame himself for her death, and a large part of him went to the grave with her. He still laments that she is gone. He loved my mother with all his heart and soul!"

"Oh!" Lilyana moaned. "How incredible to be loved so passionately without reservation! I am happy that you told me this, Dimitri. My father would have been pleased to know his sister was so adored and well taken care of during her life in Russia."

The journey back to the settlement provided an opportunity for Lilyana and Dimitri to become acquainted, and to catch up on all the years they had missed as cousins living in very different places. Lilyana asked a lot of questions about Dimitri and his family in Leningrad, especially about his mother, Anna, her newly discovered aunt. In turn, Dimitri asked about his Polish relatives from Stolpce. He deliberately tried to avoid inquiring about Lilyana's father and Uncle Jerzy, but Lilyana outlined in graphic detail the vicious nature of her uncle's arrest... the harsh treatment from the NKVD officers, the brutal way they attacked him, the pain and horror of their younger cousins witnessing all of it, and the heartbreak for Aunt Janina.

Dimitri cringed. "I am so sorry for everything that has happened to you and your... *our* family," he said regretfully.

He asked about Aunt Janina's children... the cousins he had never met. Concern washed over his face when Lilyana told him about cousin Wasyl, the oldest of Janina and Jerzy's sons.

"If he is arrested," Dimitri said, "there will be nothing anyone can do to help him. Acting out in anti-Soviet activities such as you describe will bring certain death upon our cousin. This one, Wasyl... he carries too much of our Grandfather Prawoslaw's rebellious spirit inside him!"

Then, hearing the details about baby Danuta's perishing on the train journey into Siberia, Dimitri let out a sorrowful sigh.

"The little ones never have a chance," he said. "Epidemics of typhus, whooping cough and measles wipe out endless numbers of infants and children. I see far too many small ones and older people suffering and dying. We dig mass graves and throw their bodies into the earth like cords of wood, one on top of the other. We push the dirt over the top to cover them up. No prayers are offered, and no grieving relatives are present to honour them. No markers are planted to signify that precious souls are resting in those spots. One life after another... wasted... and for what?!"

Dimitri shuddered and shook his head as if he were trying to dodge the mental images these harsh realities conjured up. Lilyana remained quiet as she soaked in all that Dimitri had just said. He stuck his head out of the side window in the cab and pretended to be looking for ruts and potholes in the road to guide the vehicle around. However, Lilyana noticed tears brimmed at the edge of his eyes. He was different from the other Russians she had encountered in Siberia. Anna must have introduced Dimitri to Christian values while he was growing up. Atheistic Russians never uttered words like he had just spoken. It was obvious he had been close to his mother, and Polish blood ran deep through his veins.

He'd been Anna's only child, at home alone with his Polish mother while his father was away doing military service in the Russian forces. Dimitri had a deep understanding of where his mother came from, her family and the Polish language and customs. Lilyana recognised it must be difficult for her Russian cousin to be a part of two worlds, with one of them destroying the other. What a complicated truth! She sensed that Dimitri was torn between the two, and her heart went out to him.

"Our cousin, Larissa... she is doing well in your living quarters, no?" Dimitri asked after he had recomposed himself.

"As well as can be expected, considering the conditions," Lilyana replied.

Dimitri looked up into the rearview mirror to catch sight of Lilyana's face.

"Larissa looks very much like my mother," he said.

He reached into the inside pocket of his uniform jacket and pulled out a folder that fell open. With one hand remaining on the steering wheel, guiding the transport over the bumpy terrain, he removed a photograph from the folder.

He passed it to Lilyana through the small, opened space in the cab's back window for her to see.

"Take a look," he said. "Tell me you can see the family resemblance."

Lilyana had never seen a photo of Anna before. She studied it carefully. The image of a young woman smiled back at her. The woman was not beautiful, but there was an air of sophistication and class about her. Her dark hair was neatly combed into a tidy bun, and in front, a wave of loose hair swept up and over into a stylish roll. She wore a knitted sweater with a plunging neckline. There was a lovely rose-shaped brooch on one side of the sweater. She was sitting at a small table with one hand neatly placed on top of it. The other rested in her lap on her tailored, tweed-knit skirt. Her legs were crossed, and she appeared to be tall and slim in build. Although she was smiling in the photograph, a definite sadness framed her large, dark eyes and diminished the happiness she was trying to express. Her nose, narrow and long, reached up into a pair of arched eyebrows that followed the contour of her forehead.

Dimitri broke into Lilyana's thoughts, saying, "Our little cousin looks very much like my mother, no?"

"Yes. There is a certain resemblance," Lilyana decided. "It is in the facial expression around the nose and eyes. I think Larissa will look more like Anna when she matures."

Neither Lilyana nor Dimitri ventured to say it, but they both were thinking, *if Larissa lives long enough to grow into a woman.*

The long journey back took Lilyana and Dimitri through scattered villages and open fields, and across wild terrain where no other vehicles or soldiers were seen for miles. Dimitri said he wanted to stop at an old, abandoned barn he had observed on his way to Arkhangelsk. Now, passing by on his return journey, he brought the vehicle to a stop in the field where the dilapidated structure stood. He told Lilyana she could come out of the transport to stretch her legs. When she stepped down, Lilyana found herself surrounded by overgrown stalks of wheat. The plants had grown so high they formed long tunnels when they bent down in unison with the summer winds blowing through them. Dimitri retrieved his rifle and a knapsack from the front of the vehicle and started walking across the field, motioning for Lilyana to follow him. She was happy to do so, even though the tall plants kept getting caught up in the skirt of her dress as she and Dimitri trekked toward the barn.

Eventually, the field opened out into a flat area where the old barn was positioned. Dimitri instructed Lilyana to stay where she was while he went in to see what condition the barn was in. Lilyana heard some squawking and a lot of flapping noises as Dimitri unsettled a flock of birds that had taken up residence inside the old structure. A number of pigeons came fluttering out of the barn with a cloud of dust and debris surrounding them. Lilyana had to chuckle as she heard her cousin cursing at the birds, mice, rats and dust that had accumulated inside the barn.

"What did you expect to find in there?" she called out to Dimitri when she heard him coughing and sputtering.

Loud noises ensued as Dimitri started moving larger objects around. Clouds of dust and dirt occasionally billowed from the doorway and swirled around Lilyana outside. She swatted at the rolling mass, stifling a few sneezes in the process.

"Come in here," Dimitri managed to call. "You've got to see this!"

Lilyana hesitated at first, but then she heard the muffled sound of a few notes being played on what sounded like a tinny piano. Inside, she found Dimitri leaning over a dusty piano, half-covered beneath a dirty tarp.

"Do you play?" Dimitri asked.

"No," Lilyana said, waving her hands in the air to disperse the clouds of dust that surrounded her.

Then, to her surprise, Dimitri began playing an old Polish folk song on the damaged piano. Some of the notes sounded off because of the piano's battered condition. Nevertheless,

Dimitri's fingers slid easily along the dirty keys as he played and belted out the song, clunking notes and all. Lilyana couldn't help but join in singing alongside Dimitri—the song was one of her favourites.

Together, they sang long and loud. Lilyana had not felt so free and alive in a very long time. A huge weight had been lifted. Their voices blended harmoniously and echoed across the barren land as they sang all the old Polish songs Dimitri's mother had taught him as a child.

When the singing and piano playing finally stopped, Lilyana said, "You are full of surprises, Dimitri Yatskaya! Where did you learn to play the piano so well?"

"That was terrible!" Dimitri responded. "I've never heard a piano make such a horrible din!"

"But you played it well!" Lilyana repeated.

Dimitri smiled. "My mother had me take piano lessons at the conservatory in Leningrad when I was a little boy. I guess I can play well enough, but my fiancée is really the one who mastered the instrument with proficiency."

"Oh, Dimitri! You must tell me more!" Lilyana begged. "I feel that I have only skimmed the surface of who you are!"

"There is not much to tell," he replied. "What is it that you would like me to tell you?"

"Well, you can start with your fiancée. This is the first I have heard about her!" Lilyana teased.

"Let's explore this farm a little more," Dimitri suggested. "You can ask me whatever you want while we walk."

They ventured further away from the wheat field and discovered a large stream that eventually made its way down into the briny sea. They sat by the edge of the rolling tributary, and Dimitri pulled out some bread and water from his knapsack. They ate and chatted as the afternoon hours passed into evening.

Through further conversation, Lilyana learned that Dimitri was twenty-four, making him a few years older than she was. His fiancée, Valentina, was back in Leningrad. Dimitri said she was a wonderful lady who came from a well-to-do family in the city. She was an accomplished pianist who loved art and the theatre. He missed her very much, and he looked forward to the time when they could be married.

Later, when Dimitri started up the transport and their journey back to the settlement resumed, Lilyana asked, "Why did you want to stop and look at that old barn?"

"I have a confession to make," Dimitri said. "That barn used to belong to Valentina's grandfather many years ago. She has told me about it many times. She said she was brought there every summer to stay with her grandparents while her parents remained in Leningrad, working. She enjoyed running through the fields, sailing toy boats in the stream, and she would practise her piano lessons on that very piano I was playing. The farmhouse has long since collapsed, and a local farmer has taken over growing wheat in the field... but I wanted to see where my sweetheart's happy childhood memories lay. Valentina will be happy to know that I have seen it now."

"It is a shame that she was not here with you as you explored it, Dimitri."

"Yes. That would have been nice!" he said. "...and what about you, Lilyana? Is there a special young man who has stolen my Polish cousin's heart?"

Something about the way Dimitri said that made Lilyana laugh. Not to be outdone by him, she responded, "Yes... of course! I have a wonderful young man. He is hardworking and intelligent. Even my father approves of him... and believe me, Dimitri, your Uncle Prawoslaw is a difficult man to please!"

"Does your beau have a name?" Dimitri asked.

"Jozef. Jozef Nowakowski from Stolpce!" Lilyana stated with pride... but thoughts of Jozef quickly brought renewed sadness to her heart. Quietly, she added in a dejected voice, "Jozef was arrested and sent to a forced labour camp somewhere. I no longer know where he is or how he is doing."

"Oh. I am sorry," is all that Dimitri could think to say.

He wanted to kick himself again for dredging up memories that upset Lilyana. Chatting with his Polish cousin was a little like walking through a minefield. He hated being a Russian in these oppressive times.

He did not let Lilyana know he had learned about her father's fate. Commander Yatskaya had called in to Central Office and spoken with one of his friends in authority there. Through a series of records, the official had traced a paper trail back to the names of detainees who were rounded up and brought in for interrogation in Stolpce. Lilyana's father's name had appeared prominently on several lists of *people of interest*, and beside Mr Prawoslaw's name, the word *deceased* had been scribbled in. Nobody needed to clarify what kind of tragedy had terminated his life. Dimitri and his father instinctively knew that Lilyana's father, Anna's brother, being a prominent capitalist, had been shot to death early on when the Soviet occupation of Poland began.

Dimitri attempted to block this knowledge from his mind, and he went on to tell Lilyana that he knew where their cousin Aleksander was working. He told her the lad was part of the large work brigade that was sent many kilometres downstream from their settlement to roll logs up from the water onto the riverbank for cutting and stacking deep in the forest. Dimitri said that recent paperwork going through his office at the colony described Aleksander Prawoslaw as one who had established a reputation for being tough. The boy had got himself into trouble for fighting with a local peasant at the worksite and ended up being sent into the punishment hole for two days. Dimitri seemed impressed that Aleksander had survived the experience and emerged unscathed.

"Punishment hole! What is that?" Lilyana asked with trepidation in her voice.

Dimitri didn't realise that Lilyana knew nothing about the punishment hole. He knew she would not be happy with the truth of the matter, so he glossed over the details by telling her that it was like a small prison cell where workers were sent into isolation for a couple of days with almost no food or water. He said the intent was to make the offender contemplate his wrongdoings and determine not to repeat his defiant misconduct.

"No food or water for two days!" Lilyana exclaimed. "I'm shocked that he did not die of hunger and thirst! He is already all skin and bones!"

"Yes… but he is tough, Lilyana! Men like him manage to hold on and come back stronger than they were before they went into the hole. It is surprising how much resilience the human body can muster when a young one like Aleksander is determined to live. He is a survivor!"

Although Dimitri was trying to present the best scenario so Lilyana would not be upset, he hoped that Aleksander's rebellious defiance would not go too far. He knew guards who would beat a worker to death for brawling. He could not be there to do anything about it with Aleksander working so far away.

"Aleksander is a smart young man," Lilyana said. "I am sure he walks a fine balance between standing up for himself and going too far. He is still young, and he can be foolish at times, but I know his will to live is strong."

Dimitri prayed that Lilyana's assessment of Aleksander was correct. He had witnessed too many violent altercations resulting in severe punishment being inflicted on the younger, more spirited deportees.

They drove through the night and drew close to the settlement by early morning on the following day. Dimitri told Lilyana she needed to get out of the transport and walk the remaining distance along the road to the settlement. It was imperative to keep a safe distance between them to avoid any suspicion. They could not be seen together. Eyes and ears were always looking for something dubious to report to the authorities. He said her Uncle Viktor had arranged for the interrogations officer with the vile cough to be transferred to another location, so she needn't worry about encountering him in the village. Lilyana was starting to realise how deep her Russian uncle's authority was in the Siberian wasteland.

She was to report to Headquarters with her prison release papers in hand when she arrived back at the colony. From there, she would be returned to her dwelling, and assigned to a new work brigade in the forest where the guards would know nothing about her recent clash with the authorities.

With his characteristic smirk, Dimitri added, "The Russian soldiers there will just see you as another scraggly Polish girl working in the forest."

Lilyana laughed alongside her cousin. "You are just as horrible as Wasyl and Aleksander," she said. "They love to tease me too!"

Dimitri seemed pleased when she said that.

"The family connection is strong, no?" he remarked.

Dimitri helped Lilyana down from the transport. He reminded her once again to not disclose their family secret to anyone, warning her of the consequences that would follow if others were to discover their secret.

"…especially the chatty one who resides with you," Dimitri said. "She will surely slip up and blab the details to everyone!"

Lilyana assured him their secret would be safe with her. She hoped for a day when life would return to some semblance of normality and Aleksander and Larissa could learn about Dimitri and their uncle in Russia. In the meantime, it was a confidence shared only between Dimitri, Uncle Viktor and herself.

***

It was a warm, sunny day. Lilyana held onto Larissa's hand as they walked along the dusty road leading toward the village. The two cousins had been reunited one week earlier with Lilyana's return to the settlement. Her roommates were surprised but pleased when she came back. None of the other women who'd disappeared from their dwelling had managed to return, and they had believed they would never see Lilyana again. Marta suspected her friend's good fortune had something to do with the Russian soldier who had befriended her, but she never asked about it because she knew Lilyana would not answer any of her questions in that regard. Marta decided to be content that her good friend was back.

Larissa was deeply saddened when she learned about the death of her mother. However, loss had become a fact of life for everyone in the colony, and news of Janina's passing was not unexpected. Larissa had bounced back quickly, and she clung more closely to her older cousin. She was happy to have Lilyana back in their living quarters.

Walking with Larissa to the village shop, Lilyana felt as though a burden had been lifted. Knowing that Cousin Dimitri was covertly watching out for her and Larissa's wellbeing, she felt more secure and settled, even though living conditions remained abhorrent. Sickness, bug infestations and starvation persisted, and most of the guards continued to make life miserable for all the deportees. Lilyana knew that if she did what she was told to do without creating any trouble, she could get through each day with renewed hope and perseverance.

She had no way of knowing that her life was about to be dramatically altered once again. People in the northern settlements were cut off from news of current world events, and unbeknownst to them, German forces had been building up along the Soviet border for some time. Outside of the colony, rumours were surfacing about the Nazis preparing to invade. The Soviets were in denial about any approaching war with Germany, and thus, Russia was unprepared when the German invasion commenced in June 1941.

The situation went badly for the Russians on all fronts as the Nazi forces pushed forward quickly and took out many Red Army units. The course of the war was changing, and along with it, the trajectory of all deportees in the settlements and forced labour camps.

EIGHT
FORCED LABOUR CAMP
NOVEMBER 1941

In recent months, a few new arrivals had been added to Jozef's barracks. One newcomer was a gruff man who went by the name Vladik. He had been a soldier in the Polish Army when the Russians invaded and occupied Eastern Poland at the start of the war. He escaped to the forest when the Polish Army fell, joining the guerrilla fighters in the woodlands. An unofficial army was formed with Polish soldiers who had evaded capture and retreated to the timberlands. Several farmers who had managed to avoid being rounded up by the NKVD for deportation also took refuge in the forest and were absorbed into the guerrilla army to join the continuing fight for freedom against the Red Army soldiers. The guerrilla fighters managed to hold out for several months despite harsh conditions in the woodlands, but eventually, many of them were captured and sent to prison.

Vladik had been interrogated and tortured by the NKVD for weeks. Finally, in a weakened state and barely clinging to life, he was tricked into signing a false confession stating that he had been spying on the Soviet Union. Rather than sending him to a forced labour camp, the authorities dropped him off in the frozen wilderness in the middle of nowhere with an unfortunate group of prisoners, to endure the harshest punishment the Soviets could dole out. It was only his deep hatred of the Russians, and his strong desire to retaliate against them, that sustained him.

The job detail was referred to by the camp authorities as resettlement. When existing camps became overcrowded, or when the Russians wanted to open a new area for development of natural resources, they moved out a group of prisoners to develop a new camp. The area was surrounded by barbed wire so none of them could escape. The prisoners began the building process with the camp walls, then the commandant's quarters, guard watchtowers and living quarters, administrative buildings, kitchen, storage sheds and outbuildings.

They started by surveying the area and using stakes to mark out the plots for each one of the buildings. Other men dug through the snow and chipped away at the frozen ground to make holes for the main posts of the structures. Some men worked in the nearby forest felling trees and lopping off branches and treetops. More labourers were used to haul the huge logs to the campsite. At the camp, other workers shaped the logs with axes and erected the buildings from the logs they had squared.

Prisoner barracks were the last structures built. This meant that the prisoners were forced to live outside in the inclement elements until the officials were satisfied with the other camp buildings. Only then would the authorities permit them to build barracks for themselves. Few men survived resettlement during the winter months in the northern regions. More and more prisoners were sent to replace those who died during the inhumane camp-building process, carried out with primitive, blunt tools and their bare hands. The prisoners' frozen extremities blistered, and their bodies ached. Vladik lost two fingers on one hand due to severe frostbite, but he was one of the few men to miraculously defy death in the frozen nightmare.

Eventually, Vladik was transferred to Jozef's labour camp, and assigned to the barracks where Jozef and his allies slept. Radoslaw befriended Vladik, and once he had proven himself worthy of their trust, Jozef's group absorbed Vladik into their alliance. He exhibited a crafty military mind, and his sheer physical size and brawn were useful to intimidate others. Any antagonists had to answer to Vladik's iron fists.

In November 1941, winter already had a firm grip on the frozen Siberian wasteland. Bread rations had slowly been reduced, and due to starvation, all the men had lost extensive muscle tissue. Wrinkles had developed on their scruffy, bearded faces. They had not bathed, shaved or had haircuts since they'd arrived at the camp. Scurvy was becoming widespread. All the men developed festering ulcers on their bodies. Many suffered with swollen limbs.

Night blindness was common. Following sunset, many prisoners had to be led around by those who still had some remaining vision while they continued working in the darkness. Entire brigades of labourers were frequently seen robotically marching home from the work zone with their hands on the shoulders of those in front of them to find their way back to the camp.

Jozef tended to the open sores on his legs and arms as best he could. He knew that a brew made from pine needles would help with the scurvy. No brew was offered here, so Jozef chewed on pine needles while working in the forest, which held the scurvy at bay. His gums only bled a little, and his teeth didn't come loose like many others' did. He encouraged the men in his work brigade to chew on pine needles as well.

Vladik was always scheming to get more food, and to find logical ways of escaping from the labour camp. Icy winds continued to numb the prisoners, and constant hunger gripped their bellies. With all they were going through, Vladik's ambitious thoughts of escape somehow managed to keep them going.

All the Soviet Union was starving, including the Red Army soldiers fighting on the frontlines, and the guards and administrative officials in the camps. Jozef and his friends started observing a few changes. Breaks in the work zone had become more frequent, and all the Polish prisoners had been put together in the same work brigades. The guard escorts seemed less formal as well.

On a bitterly cold and windy November morning, a member of the camp's administrative office came to the work zone and told the guards to escort the ex-Poles back to camp right away. A high-ranking NKVD official had arrived and wanted to talk to them.

All Polish work brigades were marched back immediately. When they arrived, the NKVD officer was seen clad in a heavy winter overcoat with thick fur trim. He carried a shiny leather briefcase up to the speaking platform. The commandant called all the prisoners to attention as the officer reached into his briefcase and pulled out a paper. Holding it high in the air with his gloved hand for everyone to see, he declared that there was an important announcement for all ex-Poles to hear. Fear and a cautious interest surged through the entire group of prisoners as the official began reading a statement from the document in his hand.

He informed the prisoners that the German fascists had attacked their so-called peace-loving Soviet Union. With all the drama and theatrics of a devout Russian Communist, he babbled on for a few minutes about their workers' paradise, beloved leader Stalin and the invincible Soviet Red Army, before finally getting to the news that the prisoners were anxious to hear. The Soviet Government had signed a treaty with the Polish Government-in-Exile in London (where the Polish prime minister and government had transferred to following the fall of France). Germany had invaded Russia, and a Soviet-Polish agreement had been made so that a Polish Army could be formed in Soviet territories in defence of Russia. The Soviets had declared a general amnesty for all ex-Polish citizens held in prisons and labour camps, and for those forcefully resettled, including all former Polish military personnel. Recruitment for a new Polish Army had begun, and those who wanted to could join. All prisoners included in the amnesty were encouraged to fight alongside the Red Army and annihilate the German fascists. The decree had been ordered by the head of the Supreme Soviet Union of Soviet Socialist Republics. All Poles were to be given deportation papers and could apply for permanent residency in the Soviet Union.

Once the NKVD official had made this surprising announcement, he returned the document to his briefcase and abruptly said, "That is all!"

He was hastily ushered away by the camp commandant and disappeared amongst the administrative buildings where the camp authorities worked and resided.

A murmur slowly rippled across the crowd of Polish prisoners. All the men looked around in disbelief. Those who better understood Russian were now explaining to others what had just been declared.

The prisoners found it difficult to believe the news. Some worried it may be a trick encouraging them to leave so the camp guards could use them for target practice, claiming they were trying to escape. Oddly enough, some of the guards in the camp appeared to be just as perplexed. Some of them had left their posts, and gathered in groups to discuss the situation among themselves. It appeared that many of them had not been prepared for what was announced in the prison yard that morning. Some of the guards nervously kept their rifles trained on the large gathering of prisoners, fearing the men would suddenly turn on them and attack.

Mixed emotions engulfed the prisoners as they stood around the camp in bewilderment. Many of them surrounded Ivan, with his fluent understanding of the Russian language, and demanded that he clarify details the NKVD officer had just stated. Some of the other men were whooping and hollering like crazed banshees as the details began to sink in. They chose to accept the facts at face-value, not wanting to test fate by questioning the amnesty granted by the Russians. While some revelled in cheers of delight and tearful joy, others stood silent and stunned. Some had worried expressions on their faces and wandered around aimlessly questioning each other about what was happening. Suspicion and distrust of Russians fuelled their scepticism. Could the decree be believed… and what was to become of the prisoners from other ethnic backgrounds, including the Ukrainians, Czechoslovakians, Romanians and Lithuanians? Jozef tried to remain calm and logically assess all that was transpiring around him.

Ivan was surrounded by fellow prisoners who needed reassuring that the decree had really stated they were now free within the Soviet Union. During his time in the labour camp, Ivan had curried favour with one of the guards who worked closely with the camp commandant in the administrative office. He saw the guard smoking with a few others in a group a short distance away and approached the cluster of guards; they became silent and eyed him with suspicion. Cautiously, Ivan asked the commandant's guard if he could speak with him privately, wanting to know whether he had any further information to offer regarding this strange turn of events. At first the guard didn't respond, puffing away on his cigarette until there was nothing left of it. Then he sauntered toward one of the tall watchtowers inside the main gate, motioning for Ivan to follow.

"I must ask you what you know about this new development," Ivan said. "With this amnesty being given to ex-Polish citizens immediately, does it mean the Poles are free to leave the confines of this labour camp now?

The guard looked around the spot where he and Ivan stood. It appeared that Ivan was the only one to be made privy to any information the guard would offer up.

"I only know a few details about this," the guard stated, "but I will tell you the little that I know."

He pulled a half-smoked cigarette from the pocket inside his heavy winter overcoat, lit it and inhaled deeply. Then he offered a drag to Ivan, who complied so he wouldn't offend the Russian. Ivan choked as the thick, foul-tasting smoke filled his weakened lungs.

"Ach! The Poles have no appreciation for the fine tobacco of a Russian cigarette!" the guard scoffed.

He took it back from between Ivan's fingers and started puffing liberally on the cigarette himself.

"I was preparing some documents a few months ago that required the commandant's signature," he said. "When I went into his office to ask him to sign the papers, he was sitting at his desk reading a copy of the Communist newspaper. He was so deeply engrossed in the article that he didn't notice me standing there at first. As soon as he saw me, he folded the newspaper quickly and put it aside. I was curious, but the man said nothing about what he was reading."

The guard stopped talking and looked around to see whether anyone else was within hearing range. Satisfied that nobody could hear them, he resumed speaking. "Later, when I knew the commandant had retired to his living quarters, I returned to his office and found the newspaper hidden inside the bottom drawer of his desk. I took it out to see what he had been so intrigued with."

Ivan moved in closer, hanging on every word the guard uttered. The guard continued puffing on his cigarette stub, and when he was not forthcoming with more information, Ivan asked, "And what did you find?"

"Patience… patience, dear man!" the guard teased. "I will get to the details in good time."

Ivan leaned back and waited for him to finish smoking. Then the guard launched into an eloquent soliloquy about the patriotic and wisdom-filled articles one could read and learn from in the Communist newspaper. He insisted that nothing but the truth was ever printed in the Communist paper.

"An educated man like yourself would do well to read it," he added.

Eventually, the guard came around to telling Ivan about the article he had seen the commandant reading. It substantiated the German invasion of Russia, the amnesty of ex-Polish citizens and the call to arms of ex-Polish prisoners. The guard confirmed the formal decree as a legitimate pronouncement, because he had seen it printed in the commandant's paper.

Ivan asked the guard if he knew anything about the Polish Army that was to be formed. All he knew was that the new army was to be established in the south. To enlist, the prisoners had to make it to Southern Russia on their own. Apparently, the Germans already had a stronghold on the Eastern Front, so the new army had to be formed further east, where the men were to be trained. The guard did not know the exact location where the new army was to assemble, but he told Ivan the men had to head south.

Ivan was angered when he realised this news had taken so long to reach the Polish men in their northern labour camp. He wondered whether the officials had deliberately kept the details secret for so long, delaying the news so that they could continue using the prisoners to fulfil their work quotas for as long as possible. If the Poles had learned the details earlier in August when the news was first released, it would have been easier to leave the camp and find their way to the recruitment location for the new army. It was November now, and winter already had its icy grip on all the land. Ivan realised many men would perish in the harsh Siberian conditions when they left the camp to go in search of the army.

Ivan's peers were anxious to learn what he had gleaned from the commandant's guard. Radoslaw danced around in circles with his hands waving in the air, whooping and hollering in celebration when he learned the amnesty was real.

"Free! Freedom! We are freed!" he repeated as others looked on.

Vladik's military mind was immediately set in motion. He knew the Soviet Union was facing a difficult situation because of the war. It was obvious that food was in short supply, and it appeared that there was a shortage of almost everything else as well. From all indications, transportation was inadequate for getting people and supplies to where they needed to be. Even the administration seemed overworked and troubled. He realised that Russia was in a terrible mess. With the Soviet's sudden desire to have the former Poles fighting alongside them against the Nazis, the war must not be going well for the Russians. Vladik was aware that the Soviets were now exploiting the Poles by using them as reinforcements and fodder in their battle against their long-standing enemy, the Germans… or were the Soviets thinking it would be an easy way to eliminate their anti-Communist problem by sending the Polish prisoners to the front and letting the Germans kill them off?

It felt strange meandering around the camp unaccompanied by guards and doing things without permission from the authorities. Most of the men remained close together in their separate work brigades. Gradually, prisoners wandered back to the barracks they had been assigned to. Some strolled cautiously in and out of their barracks, checking to see what was going on outside.

When Jozef's group had reassembled inside their quarters, Vladik initiated the conversation.

"Now the Soviets want us to fight the Germans," he said. "They appease us by telling us that the army to be formed will be a Polish Army. The Russians will undoubtedly have some control over the new army, but this is a means for all of us to get out of here!"

A reticent "*whoopee*" went up among the men in the barracks.

Vladik continued, "Ivan has told us we must find our own way south to the new army. Have you noticed that the guards are already standing watch over the storehouses and the shed? I doubt we will be given any provisions to take with us to help in any way. If the camp authorities do not allow us to take any supplies, we must try to barter with the guards before we leave to get what we need."

Tomasz broke in, saying, "We won't be able to haggle with them! Even if we had anything to offer in trade, the guards will never barter with us. The commandant considers bartering a bribe, and the penalty for that is serious. The guards are too afraid to bend the rules. Recently, I offered my full bread ration to a guard in exchange for his gloves. He shook his head and hurried away. No amount of bread or tobacco will bribe them!"

"Yes, but that was before the amnesty," Jozef said. "Now we are free to leave. Maybe they will be willing to work with us, as they are asking us to fight alongside them for a common cause."

Another man in the barracks spoke up, saying, "Things will be different now. If we manage to establish a good rapport with the guards, they may help us. After all, we will be joining them in their battle against the Nazis. That should count for something. If they want us to join their fight, they should be willing to see that we are adequately supplied so we can arrive in the south healthy and prepared to do battle against the Germans."

A disgruntled murmur spread throughout the barracks. Many of the men let it be known that they would prefer to head out and return home to Poland.

"What chance do you have of arriving there safely?" Vladik jeered. "The roads will be blocked by Russian and German fighting units in the east. Even the forests and the fields will be full of armed battalions. You will be killed for sure. It would be wise to join this new army. Going south is the only safe way out of here."

Nobody said anything for a while. All the men were in deep thought as they mulled over their options.

Finally, Ivan broke into the silence, saying, "The commandant's guard told me they are already drawing up the deportation papers. We may be able to leave the camp by tomorrow if our papers are ready."

"Winter is already here in full fury," Vladik pointed out. "Remember the harrowing march to the camp through the deep snow and the deadly winds? We must learn from that experience and plan our walk out of here very carefully.

No detail can be overlooked. We cannot afford any fatal errors!"

"But Southern Russia is thousands of miles away! We will never make it across the frozen wasteland without any transportation or supplies!" whined Nikolai.

Jozef patted the lad's bony shoulder and said reassuringly, "We made it across the ice-bound land once, my friend, and we will do it again!"

"Yes, we will!" Tomasz chimed in. "I will carry you on my back if I have to! We will not stop walking until we arrive at this undisclosed place where the new army is to assemble!"

Despite Jozef and Tomasz's attempts to encourage their comrades, many of the men were questioning whether they would be able to walk out of frozen Siberia and then across the vast mountains into Southern Russia. Even in the best of health, that would be a daunting challenge. With their ailing and weakened bodies, it seemed an impossible feat. Many of them were already destroyed physically and mentally. Nikolai had been slipping further and further into the downward spiral. His mind and body had already started giving up.

Vladik and Ivan were discussing how best to tackle the formidable journey that lay ahead. Together they decided the men should follow the route markers south that the guards had used getting them to the camp, until they reached the Trans-Siberian Railway. Then they would begin their search for the assembly spot of the new army.

The men quickly set about trying to find ways of acquiring food and other provisions to ensure their journey would be successful. All the Polish men in the camp seemed to have the same idea as they started frantically bartering with the guards and among themselves. To the guards' astonishment, men were pulling out items they had made and hidden inside nooks and crannies the guards had overlooked. Small trinkets made from bits of wood, pieces of rag, hardened bread, and even spoon handles and knives suddenly appeared and were offered up in trade. Chaos ensued as men scurried between barracks and other buildings, exchanging things to get what they needed for the long journey ahead.

Vladik encouraged Nikolai to help him dig deep into the ground underneath their barracks. It was a taxing and painful endeavour as they tried to open the frozen earth that was tightly bound by frost. However, Vladik would not be deterred. He wanted to pull up clumps of dried roots from the grasses and weeds that had grown along the side of the barracks during the brief Siberian summer. He was also searching for bits of flint. Young Nikolai struggled with the task, so Vladik sent him to collect dried moss and wood shavings from around the camp. Those necessities would help keep them alive during their long trek across the frozen tundra.

It was difficult collecting the fire-starting materials from their frigid domain, but Vladik put all that he and Nikolai managed to gather into a large sack he had obtained. Nikolai followed Vladik into their barracks and stood in amazement when Vladik extracted a small metal file he had secretly hidden inside a narrow crack in the side post of his bunk. The boy beamed with self-importance when Vladik gave him a quick wink and said that only the two of them needed to know about the file. Nikolai knew Vladik had pulled through in the frozen forest for months in Poland with no provisions at all, until he had been captured by the Red Army, and so he held Vladik in reverent respect, knowing that the ex-soldier was a survivalist. Nikolai would do whatever Vladik told him to do.

It took longer than expected for the deportation papers and the certificates of release to be typed up for all the men. No photos were attached to these papers, but they required an official stamp. A few lines of words were typed on the documents, followed by the commandant's signature.

Every day, various groups of Polish prisoners were released. Within a few days, the Poles from Jozef's barracks were set free. Some of the prisoners in his barracks were not Polish citizens. Coming from other ethnicities, they were ordered to stay behind. There were some Polish men who were too ill to get up and travel. They were left behind as well.

The departing Polish men were given their deportation papers and taken in a large group by two guards to the camp's main gate. They lined up in single file as their papers were checked against the lists, and then they exited through the gate, one by one.

A large group of ex-prisoners gathered outside the main gate in the early morning darkness. One guard pointed towards the snowy treeline in the distance and instructed them to head off in that direction. Had it not been for the dim moonlight, the treeline would not have been distinguishable at all. The second guard told them to cross over the icy river beyond the forest and to search for the route markers that would lead them southward. The two guards then returned to the inside of the camp compound, slamming the huge iron gate shut behind them.

This was the end to the Polish prisoners' life of horrors in the Siberian forced labour camp, but it was the start of further hardship and suffering.

NINE
IN SEARCH OF AN ARMY

Many ex-prisoners from Jozef's and a few neighbouring barracks left the camp that morning. As they set out on their long walk, various groups of men gathered with friends and allies they had formed inside their own dwellings. It was not long before the clusters dispersed through the woodlands; some wanted to camp and rest, while others chose to keep walking. Vladik insisted his group remain close together as he, Jozef, Ivan, Radoslaw, Tomasz and Nikolai continued moving. He warned them to never lose sight of each other. If one should become lost, they would never make it out of Siberia on their own.

The men were in control of their own destiny now. There was no one to answer to but themselves. They could talk freely and make their own decisions. They were to ration what little food supply they had managed to gather in the camp, search for rabbits and birds to eat along the way, and fish. There was always some wild game in the forest, and most of the men in Jozef's group were familiar with trapping and hunting techniques. However, without the proper equipment, they needed to hunt with the precision of skilled woodsmen to survive the journey.

It would take some time before the men arrived at the river the guard had directed them toward. While they plunged on through deep snow in the icy forest, they discussed what they would do to ice fish on the river when they got there. Radoslaw would use the axe he had stolen from a sleeping guard in the camp to break open a hole in the ice. Vladik had a long piece of string and some wire he would use to fashion a fishing line and a crude hook. Jozef would take a small piece of his bread ration and chew it up into a heavy, doughy consistency, then attach it to the end of the wire hook, ensuring it stuck solidly so it wouldn't fall off in the frigid water below the surface of the ice.

"Surely you are joking, my friends!" Tomasz said. "Even the fish will find the Russian bread repulsive! I doubt any will bite on it!"

Then he made a grimacing face, and all the men laughed hysterically. Their voices rose high above the tops of the snow-laden trees. The desolate forest had not heard such a joyful sound in a very long time.

When they finally reached the river, they cleared off a patch of snow on the frozen surface with their bare hands. Radoslaw, Tomasz and Jozef took turns chipping away at the thick, dark ice with the dull axe until they managed to break open a hole large enough to fish through. A gush of water suddenly splashed up through the hole, and a few fish were washed up in the surge. They lay helplessly flapping at the men's feet on top of the ice. Tomasz and Radoslaw quickly grabbed at them before they had a chance to wiggle back down the hole into the icy water. Tomasz looked amazed as he clung tightly onto a fat trout flapping in his hands. Nikolai looked dumbfounded. Jozef explained that the fish had been attracted to the sound of the axe banging on the ice, and because of the change in air pressure when the ice broke open, the water spurted up out of the hole, bringing the fish with it.

The fish must have been as hungry as the men were, because they quickly went for the bait when Jozef dropped the line down into the water. He snagged a large catch. The men had not seen that much food in ages.

While Jozef continued to fish, Tomasz and Ivan built up a snowy enclosure where the men could rest away from the harsh wind. Vladik established a large fire inside the fort. He took bits of the dried roots and moss from his sack, and together with some kindling wood gathered from the nearby forest, he showed Nikolai how to create fire. He demonstrated how the flint made sparks when struck against his metal file in the correct manner. The sparks eventually set fire to the tinder placed around it, and once the dried materials caught into flames, the kindling wood was added slowly. Dead branches and small logs from the woodlands were added carefully until a roaring fire came alive.

Inside their snow fort, they cooked the fish over the open fire. They did not bother to gut them or remove the heads and tails, they simply speared them through the mouth with sticks and held them over the flames, turning them slowly to roast them on all sides. The men ravenously tore into the meat that lined the inside of the fish skins. This meal was a treat they'd never have dared to dream about just a few days earlier. They ate until some of them began vomiting. Despite how famished they had felt, their stomachs were no longer accustomed to accepting such a large amount of food all at once. It would be some time before they would be able to digest food properly again.

The men were growing increasingly concerned for Nikolai. With his weak, asthmatic lungs, he coughed and heaved against the bitter winds, fighting to breathe. His chest rattled and wheezed with each struggling breath he took. His frail body convulsed with chills and fever, and he became weaker with every passing day. As promised, his good friend Tomasz carried the lad through the woodlands on his back. The strain while trudging through deep snow across gullies and up hills started to take a toll on Tomasz, so Vladik stepped in and helped share the burden. Like faithful big brothers, the two men continued watching out for the boy. They encouraged him to drink hot water that they boiled down from melted snow in Ivan's open pot over the fire. At first, the lad took in bits of food and water, but eventually he could not even hold that down. The coughing erupting from deep inside his lungs caused him to heave whatever they tried to feed him. All the men took turns sharing their body heat with Nikolai while sleeping by the fire at night, but no amount of warming seemed to help the poor boy.

On the sixth morning after they had left the camp, young Nikolai's journey ended. His comrades awoke to find the lad lying quiet and stiff beside the fire. All the compassionate efforts in the world could not have saved Nikolai without hospitalisation and proper medication.

Tomasz took the boy's passing very hard. He had kept the lad alive while struggling to get to the labour camp, and he had managed to help the boy survive inside. He'd known Nikolai was weak and vulnerable and had kept the boy close to the men in their work brigade. All of them had watched out for the lad, but Tomasz had adopted him like a younger brother. He felt as though he had failed Nikolai because he could not save the boy from Siberia's icy winds of death.

Arctic gusts continued to swirl around their sheltered snow fort, and large snowflakes began to fall. All the men assured Tomasz there was nothing more he could have done to save Nikolai in the cruel winter elements. They dug a deep hole in the snow beside a tall pine tree with their bare hands, and there they laid poor Nikolai to rest. They packed the snow down hard on top of the winter grave so wild wolves and bears would not uncover him. They took their tattered hats off and held them close against their chests as they sang an old lamenting Polish hymn that seemed appropriate for the sad occasion. Ivan offered up a Christian prayer over Nikolai's grave while the others bowed their heads. Jozef was sure he saw tears falling from Tomasz's eyes, but the gruff man would blame it on the incessantly cold winds. Quietly, the men gathered up their meagre possessions and continued their long, frozen walk out of Siberia.

Traces of scattered footprints appeared in the snow on the other side of the river. It was evident that another group of ex-prisoners had crossed over just ahead of them. Vladik picked up their trail as his group of men started to enter the forested area. Radoslaw followed the embedded prints, but Vladik called him back, pointing out that the men who made those prints were veering off in the wrong direction. He speculated that the course of the riverbank had thrown their bearings off.

"How can you be so sure of that?" Radoslaw demanded.

Vladik quickly pointed out that the mossy growth on the trees indicated the other men had made a critical error. Instead of continuing to move southward, they had turned slightly south-east. He worried that those men would drive themselves deeper into the Siberian interior if they continued that way.

"We all know moss grows on the north-facing side of trees, out of reach from the sun's rays!" Radoslaw shouted. "Why did those fools stray away from nature's compass and wander off in any direction other than what the trees are telling us?"

Radoslaw and Tomasz had both become increasingly ill-tempered toward Vladik as the journey continued. Jozef worried that either one of them might come to blows with Vladik before long. Pangs of hunger continued to plague them, and all of them were exhausted. The perpetual cold and darkness played havoc with their health, but they struggled on in the deep snow, blinding winds and through more thick forest growth.

After crossing the frozen river, they had difficulty following the route markers that the guard said would be there. Visibility was hampered by extended periods of darkness and incessant gales that blew the snow around. Posts were hard to find in the drifting snow, and large gaps between the markers made it difficult to keep on the designated route. Several times they lost their way, but Vladik used his military skills, keeping the men moving southward. He navigated by the positioning of the moon, and the stars when they could be seen. On clear nights, the moon offered light and direction. In the darkness, the men often tried using fiery log torches to light their way, but the wind continually snuffed out the flames. They often rotated positions, taking turns breaking a trail in the snow ahead of the others so that no man would become overly exhausted.

The further south they travelled, the more the wooded terrain began to alternate with open fields. On a calm day, having come upon a large clearing, the route markers reappeared for some distance until the winds and snow picked up again. Then the markers virtually disappeared. With thick snow falling, strong winds reduced visibility to nothing in open areas. Blinding snow blocked the moon and the stars, and their progress was severely impaired. They questioned where they were headed. They could stop and camp until the snowfall subsided, but sometimes these snowstorms would last for two or three days at a time. Fires were difficult to start in the strong, icy winds and blowing snow. If they camped for too long, they would freeze to death. They had to keep moving to stay warm and protect themselves. It was the deadly Siberian winds that killed many men.

The snow was equally lethal. In the blinding snowstorm, the men could no longer see where they were going. Each had to place his hands on the shoulders of the man struggling in front of him so that they would not lose sight of each other and become separated. Covered in a layer of white from head to foot, they protected their faces from the cruel elements with heads bent downwards. They resembled snowmen marching along in a single line.

During the blizzard, snow piled up waist deep and seriously hampered their progress. Drifts were even higher in the open fields. They knew they had to keep going to stay alive, but eventually their bodies could struggle no further. Their energy was drained. Vladik knew they had no choice but to rest when all the men were ready to drop in the snow from exhaustion.

Radoslaw and Tomasz complained they were wasting time and energy wandering in circles. Vladik managed to persuade them to follow him as he broke open a snowy pathway toward the edge of a field. They set up camp there in a sheltered spot among a cluster of trees. The men had carefully continued their southward march across a field beside a sparsely treed-in area. With what little reserves they could muster, they piled up a snowy wall around themselves as a barricade against the wind and snow, and they stomped down on the snow with their frostbitten feet until there was a flattened space in the snowy thicket. They gathered pine branches and long pieces of bark stripped from surrounding birch trees, and lay on top of them. After battling for a long time against vicious winds and heavy snow, Vladik finally coaxed a tiny flame onto some tinder and kept it going long enough to ignite a pile of kindling inside their fort. This was achieved when all the men got together and formed a human barrier against the pernicious conditions. Once the fire was lit and built up with branches they had gathered, they huddled near the flames, trying to warm their frozen bodies. Vladik advised them not to put their feet or hands too close to the flames because their frozen extremities would not feel when they were burning until it was too late. He suggested they remove their boots and rub their feet to get the circulation going, and then tuck their feet under their thighs in a crossed-leg position by the fire. Their frozen hands were to be folded under their armpits. They endured excruciating pain as their feet and hands began to thaw, and painful blisters plagued their extremities.

Ivan pulled out his metal pot and filled it with clean snow, then placed it close to the fire. The melted snow warmed very quickly and was passed around carefully from one man to the next. Each one drank some of the warm liquid. They shared the last of the bread they had brought with them from the labour camp. Each man was given one small ration of the foul staple. It was the only thing they had to provide them with much-needed sustenance that night.

The men slept in shifts for two or three hours at a time. If they slept longer than that, they could fall into a death sleep and freeze to death. They preserved their body heat by sleeping close together. Two of them would stand guard while the others slept, and then the sleeping men would be woken up and their roles would be reversed. The fire had to be watched so the flames would not go out. If it wasn't stoked on a regular basis, the fire would fade away and the men would freeze to death very quickly.

Wolves were heard howling in the distance. The animals had posed a problem at one of their previous camps. The men on watch that night had held onto small logs set ablaze to defend their position when a pack of wild wolves started circling, threatening them. Vladik had set several more logs ablaze by the edge of the fire. All the men had woken up to collectively jab the fiery logs at the animals when they got too close. Wild animals needed to be scared off, but it was doubtful any wolves would appear this night in the middle of a Siberian blizzard.

The men had no idea how long they lingered in the wooded area. They'd lost track of time. Jozef was wakened from a few hours of sleep and found snow piled up high against the trees and along their icy fort. He had to shake off a thick coating of snow from his clothing as he raised himself from the wintry floor. The air remained frigidly cold, but the fierce winds and heavy snow had ceased. Visibility was markedly improved. He saw Vladik brushing off snow from tree trunks nearby and knew Vladik was feeling for the mossy growth to give him some bearing on directions. It was time to forge ahead.

The men circled around the treeline until a route marker became visible, and then they followed the course of the markers along the rim of a steep decline into a valley. They were trudging along in waist-deep snow across a massive snow-covered field, with Tomasz leading the way under Vladik's direction, when Tomasz fell over face-first into a large drift. He struggled to regain his footing and cursed about being unable to see hidden rocks beneath the thick snow. Radoslaw, Vladik and Jozef advanced and veered away from the spot where Tomasz had floundered. Ivan was in the rear. When Ivan passed by the spot, he kicked at the snowy area where Tomasz had stumbled.

Suddenly, he yelled out in a loud voice, "Stop!"

To their horror, a few frostbitten fingers from a dead man's hand emerged through the surface of the snow. Within seconds, all the men were digging around the gruesome discovery. Eventually, the body of a frozen man was revealed.

"Stupid fool!" Radoslaw shouted. "That's what he gets for wandering off on his own!"

Ivan was quick to point out, "Maybe he wasn't on his own. He may have fallen away from his group in the blinding snow and lost his way in the storm if he was at the back of the line."

Vladik was examining the way the man was lying in the snow.

"Ivan is correct," he said. "It appears this man dropped forward into the snow when he could go no further. It may be that he was walking at the end of the line with his group and fell away. His comrades would not have realised he was gone until it was too late. If he had been at the front of the line or in the middle, they would have noticed him fall."

Jozef and Vladik struggled to haul the corpse up out of the snow and turn it over. The man's face was so frozen that a thick crust of crystalised ice enveloped his frostbite-blackened features. It was difficult to tell if he was someone they'd known, but they assumed the man was a Polish ex-prisoner who had been trying to make his way south to join the new army.

"Poor bugger!" Tomasz exclaimed. "He never had a chance! He probably passed out from hunger and exhaustion walking in the blizzard gales. He fell into his death sleep without anyone noticing!"

There was nothing any of them could do for the unfortunate man now, so they dug down into the spot where he had fallen and replaced his stiff body there. With numbed fingers, Vladik worked hard at prying open the rigid pocket on the man's frozen jacket. After several minutes, he managed to crack the crust of ice that sealed the pocket, then forced his fingers deep into its brittle contours, searching for the man's papers to see if he could be identified. Vladik felt a round object, and grappled with it to break it free from its frozen confines. In the process, a sharp, icy edge around the top of the pocket pierced Vladik's skin. He felt no pain, but his wound started to bleed profusely as he continued to probe and pull until he managed to extract the item from the man's icy pocket. A broad grin spread across his face as he held up a metal compass for all his companions to see. It was covered in Vladik's blood, but the needle inside the instrument was frozen in position pointing south.

Vladik immediately pressed the compass deep into his own pocket where he hoped it would thaw. The men could rejoice in this find later. For the moment, they wanted to show respect to a fallen comrade and offer him a Christian burial. They entombed the body beneath a thick layer of snow and forced a hard, trampled down layer on top of the burial mound. Ivan traced a Christian cross on the snowy heap and offered up a prayer. Then the men picked up the march where they had left off, across the snowbound field.

Jozef and his companions lost all perception of distance and time as they struggled on. Days merged into night, and nights blurred into a continuum. They fought on endlessly against the coldness, hunger, darkness and fatigue. They constantly battled the wind and snow to build their camps and fires. Wild game could only be found in the forested areas, and the rabbits and birds were adept at avoiding capture. The men did not have the luxury of setting traps or snares and waiting around to catch game; they had to keep moving forward on their quest. Vladik did manage to capture a few rabbits with some assistance from Jozef, whose boyhood experience hunting in the Polish woodlands was put to the test. The rabbits were very lean, and the meat did not stretch far among the hungry men. Nevertheless, all of them were grateful to have what little food they provided.

The route markers had long since vanished. They had lost the course, but Vladik continued leading them southward. The burden of that objective had eased now he had a compass to refer to. He continued using indicators provided by the sun, the stars and the moon when they were visible, and he always checked the trunks of trees for mossy growth to verify their direction. He did not trust the compass entirely.

They tracked back over the same snowy terrain that had directed them to the labour camp two years earlier, and they recalled how they'd been forced to march with the convoy of lorries after reaching the end of the railway line. They remembered going past a huge frozen river shortly after their march had begun. They had followed it for some distance, until the Russian soldiers cunningly guided them further away from the shoreline to keep the prisoners out of sight of people living in the small villages that dotted the area. Now, the men were passing through the same lush forestlands, hills, ridges, deep valleys and expansive fields, in the opposite direction.

Ivan informed them that the waterway they were recalling was not a river but a very old and very deep lake. Having studied the topographical map of Siberia hanging on the wall in the commandant's office before they left, he'd noticed that the body of water was Lake Baikal, a crescent-shaped lake stretching north to south for hundreds of kilometres.

None of the men questioned Ivan's information. The man harboured as much knowledge pertaining to Soviet history and geography as any Russian scholar. He had memorised the names of towns, villages, rivers, lakes and even estuaries from the signs that were posted all the way from Eastern Poland to Northern Siberia, and he was able to cite historical significance connected to any given area throughout that massive territory. He never ceased to amaze his comrades with his knack for reciting miniscule details, and his fluent mastery of the Russian language was something to be admired.

Using a stick, Ivan drew a rough sketch of the lake in the snow. He pointed out that they would be lucky if they reached the western shore of the lake when they arrived further south. He put a dot a short distance west of the lake and said this was where the town of Irkutsk was located. The Trans-Siberian Railway terminated in that area. If they could find the town, the railway tracks should be nearby. Arriving on the eastern shoreline of the massive lake would take them much longer to get where they needed to go, because they would have to walk around to the western side.

"It would be quicker to walk across the frozen lake to get to the other side," Tomasz proposed.

Ivan advised him that a swift underwater current prevented Lake Baikal from freezing over completely in the middle. Because the lake was so vast and deep, and because it was fed by many rapid rivers, the ice in the centre remained very thin and probably would not support a man's weight.

"Hmm," Vladik murmured as he took in the information, viewing the crude map Ivan had drawn in the snow. "We must be sure of our bearings when we arrive at this lake then," he said. "Hopefully, we will reach the lake at its northern end, then we can work our way southward along the western shoreline to this town, Irkutsk, as Ivan says. Such a massive lake!"

"It will be a strenuous march," Ivan proceeded to say. "According to the topographical map back at the camp, the surrounding terrain is very challenging. The landscape is riddled with thick forests, steep hills and many mountains. It will require vertical climbs, and descents into deep valleys below. The area is intersected by numerous small rivers and streams that run down into the lake. This walk would prove difficult at any time in the year, but it will be particularly onerous traversing this terrain now, with the fierce winds and blowing snow we must contend with. We will follow the shoreline through the forest and the mountains. It will be a long walk. However, we have come this far already, and we will continue until we find the railway tracks near the point where the lake ends in the south."

"How far is this town, Irkutsk, from the southern point of the lake?" Jozef wanted to know.

"Judging from what I saw on the commandant's map, I estimate it to be sixty to eighty kilometres from the southwest tip of Lake Baikal. We should be able to walk there in a few days after we reach the end of the lake."

"And the railway tracks are there?" Vladik questioned.

"Yes… somewhere around Irkutsk," Ivan reiterated.

***

The men knew they had covered endless kilometres of snow-packed ground when they arrived at an area where the white carpet suddenly fell away into a steep decline. They stopped and surveyed the landscape from high above. A windswept pattern lay on the flat surface far below.

Tomasz turned to Ivan, who gave him a knowing nod. Then Tomasz burst into a hearty laugh and lunged forward toward the embankment. He scrambled down, half-running and half-rolling to the flat level below. A cloud of swirling snow surrounded him as he tumbled down the snowy slope. Small branches cracked as he lumbered into them on his descent.

The others watched as Tomasz came to a stop at the bottom. He immediately started digging into the snow with his bare hands, throwing piles into the air like a frolicking child in the first snowfall at the start of a new winter season. He motioned for the other men to join him.

"This is the lake, comrades!" he was yelling. "We have found the lake! We are on the road back to civilisation!"

Jozef and Radoslaw quickly descended to where Tomasz was digging. They hoped to discover a layer of ice not too deeply hidden beneath the thick blanket of snow.

Ivan and Vladik remained high above, determining their exact location. They scrutinised the surrounding terrain. With so many connecting rivers criss-crossing the region, this could be any one of many tributaries that they had stumbled upon. However, they observed how high the banks rose to meet the shoreline, and they evaluated the breadth of the body of water. Both of them determined it had to be the mighty Lake Baikal. It was simply too large to be a river tributary. The question was, had they arrived on the eastern or the western side of the lake, and since it appeared to stretch on endlessly in every direction from where they stood, how far were they from the southern tip? The brief sun was already beginning to set, and Ivan and Vladik were anxious to establish their bearings before darkness fell. All angles of direction were tested against the position of the setting sun and mossy growth on the tree trunks lining the shoreline. The compass indicated they were moving in a southwesterly direction.

The other men worked together to hack open a patch of ice with Radoslaw's axe and prepared to do some ice fishing on the lake. Tomasz leaned in very close to the hole as it was being cracked open. He wanted to be ready to catch any fish in the sudden spurt of water he expected would spew when the surface was breached. He and Radoslaw laughed hysterically when several small fish leaped into his arms. Tomasz fought to keep the slimy, flapping creatures from sliding back into the icy hole.

The men fished through the ice for a short time with Vladik's line of string. Bits of dried roots taken from Vladik's sack were all they had for bait. Jozef disguised the roots to look like worms on the end of their fabricated wire hook, and a small catch of fish was snagged up through the hole. The men feasted gluttonously around the campfire they built on the shore of the lake that night. The much-needed nourishment invigorated them, and the next morning they set out with renewed energy and enthusiasm.

"I can't say for certain where we are situated, but because it does appear as though we are on the western side of the lake, we will proceed in a southerly direction keeping as close to the lake as possible. If my calculations are correct, the lake will direct us southwest toward Irkutsk."

As Ivan spoke those words, he had a clear mental picture of the long, crescent-shaped lake stretching southward.

The image was etched in his memory from the map he had seen in the commandant's office. He knew the lake would eventually direct them toward the railway lines near Irkutsk if they kept close to the shoreline.

"Then what?" Radoslaw asked.

"We will locate the Trans-Siberian Line and follow the tracks to the Ural Mountains. If we are lucky, we will find a train to take us west… but for now, we will focus on finding Irkutsk. It will be a terrible disappointment if we arrive there expecting to find transportation and there are no trains. We have to move south-west to find the area where the new Polish Army is to assemble."

***

Jozef noticed that the air felt slightly warmer near the lake. The sky was mostly clear, and sunshine lasted a little longer. The height of the snowdrifts had dropped to knee-deep as the warmer temperature, sun and winds evaporated the top layer of snow. Conditions would have been pleasant had it not been for the incessant winds that blew along the shore of the lake.

When Jozef mentioned his observations, Ivan told him that a microclimate regulated the temperature here. He said that the climate around Lake Baikal was unique because of the massive surface size of the water, and the mountains that surrounded it. In winter, the air temperature would be about ten degrees warmer than the air further away from the lake, and in summertime, the temperature would be slightly cooler than it was inland. Ivan said the forestlands encompassing the lake also contributed to this effect. These unusual conditions were also the cause of the perpetual mountain winds that blew along the coast.

Before long, various species of birds and small animals were seen inhabiting the forested area by the lake. A bounty of wildlife flourished. Jozef and his comrades were able to capture rabbits and large hares. They also snagged wild birds and squirrels hiding in the wooded areas and observed many other varieties of wild game.

From their campsites high atop the lofty mountains around the lake, they sometimes spotted campfires of other groups making their way south in the distance. It gave Jozef and his allies confidence to know they were not the only ones travelling this route in search of the gathering spot for the Polish Army.

Despite the challenging terrain, the journey seemed to become a little easier the further south they ventured. Perhaps it was because they now managed to find nourishment along the route to improve their stamina, or maybe psychologically they realised they were getting closer to where they needed to go with every passing day. In some areas, the forest thinned out and diminished to sparse clusters of trees along the mountain passes. A thicker mossy growth appeared on the trees. Clumps of grasses were observed between the evergreens as the sun broke through. Brownish-yellow blades started peeking out from the snow around the base of some trees.

Fierce icy winds continued to challenge them, but the men managed to climb the snowy slopes through the mountains at an even stride. They planted their frozen feet firmly on the ridges above. They traversed many frozen rivers and streams that flowed down into the lake, and they scrambled down precipitous bluffs that dropped into deep valleys. They tried to stick close to the lower hills as much as they could, avoiding higher peaks wherever possible. They frequently trudged across the icy surface along the shoreline of the massive lake but had to turn back into the hills and the wooded areas whenever the icy winds threatened to turn them in the wrong direction.

From on top of the hilly precipices, they could look down into the valleys along the lake, where small clusters of wooden houses sporadically appeared. Upturned boats were pulled onto the shoreline, and wooden poles could be seen set out in arrangements typically used by fishermen to dry their nets. Ivan had predicted there might be scattered fishing villages in the northern regions of the lake, and he reckoned they would encounter larger towns dotting the southern area where industries existed within reach of the Trans-Siberian Railway.

They steadily advanced southward, always keeping the shoreline of Lake Baikal in view. It was almost three weeks before they arrived at the bend where the crescent-shaped lake made a gradual turn toward the west. Ivan said they were reaching the bottom end of the lake, and he suggested they start moving westward away from the shoreline. If they continued following the lake, it would direct them around the southern tip and loop them back up northward along its eastern shore, back into the heart of Siberia.

The men had hoped to discover an access pass to follow westward once they reached the southern end of the lake. People residing in nearby Irkutsk must have established a route to get to and from the water. Nevertheless, they found themselves continuing to trek through the wilderness. They were anxious to reach Irkutsk and find where the railway tracks were located.

It was a day after they had turned westward away from the lake when they came upon a trail. Radoslaw was the first one to spot the primitive route running east to west through the forest. From a mountain cliff, he noticed it cutting its way through the trees down below, little more than a well-worn path. He called his comrades over to the edge of the ridge. Together they peered down at the narrow track slicing through the surrounding woodlands. They carefully descended the sloping crest and found themselves standing in the middle of the crude trail. Snow was firmly packed underneath their feet, and their boots made loud crunching sounds when they walked on it.

They wondered how far they were from the town, and they hoped they would arrive there within the next day or two. They walked for a long time along the trail, seeing and hearing no one. They began to question if this was indeed the route to Irkutsk, but they would continue following the trail as long as it kept directing them in a westerly direction. When darkness fell, the men agreed they would rest for the night and made camp in the forest next to the trail.

Early in the morning, while they were busy packing up their camp and getting ready to set off again, Jozef hushed all of them into silence. He was sure he had heard a noise in the distance. He whispered for all of them to listen. At first the other men didn't hear anything, and they wondered whether Jozef was losing his mind. Then, very faintly, the sound of approaching sleigh bells could be heard. All the men turned towards the sound.

A minute or two later, a winter sled could be seen coming toward them. The scrawny horse pulling the decrepit sleigh was being driven along the snowy trail by an elderly man. Jozef and his comrades moved closer together, not knowing what to expect as the old man drew near. The man slowed the horse down and a distinct fishy smell suddenly filled the air as he brought the sleigh to a stop not far from where they stood. Only then did they notice a small boy was seated in the sled next to the man.

The old fellow asked if they were Poles. Ivan responded, and quickly became engaged in Russian dialogue with the man. He and the boy seemed to be harmless enough. Jozef realised Ivan was speaking very basic Russian and purposely mispronouncing some words. Soviets were suspicious of foreigners who spoke Russian too well, and Ivan didn't want to raise any mistrust with the man. Jozef was able to follow most of the conversation.

The old man pointed in the direction he had come from and told Ivan that Irkutsk was about fifty kilometres further west through the woodlands. He and the boy, who turned out to be the man's grandson, had come from a small hamlet located nearby. They were fishermen on their way to the lake to bring in a catch of fish to sell at the local market near their village. Ivan remarked that it was a fair distance to the lake from where they were. It had taken most of the previous day for him and his comrades to reach this location. The old man smirked and cussed in Russian. He informed Ivan that the lake was a mere ten-minute ride in the sleigh from the hamlet where he lived. If the Poles had followed the trail from where it began, closer to the lake, their walk would have brought them to this location quickly. Regretfully, Ivan had to admit that he and his comrades hadn't found the passage in the forest until they happened upon it during their movement westward through the mountains and the trees. The old man laughed until he sputtered and began coughing. He spat out a gob of bloody spit into the snow near Ivan's feet. There were large gaps in his mouth where teeth had once existed, and his remaining teeth were blackened from years of wear and lack of proper care. He and the boy were clad in tattered coats that had been stitched over in threads of many colours, and they smelled of rotting fish and dirt. The boy's nose was running, and his eyes appeared red and swollen. Jozef felt for the small lad, and he wished he had something to offer him to eat. The hollows in the boy's cheeks and his emaciated form made it evident that he was terribly malnourished. He sat pale and silent next to his grandfather as Ivan and the man continued talking. Ivan asked the old man if he knew where the railway tracks were located near Irkutsk. The man didn't say, but he told Ivan that the local people had seen a lot of Polish ex-prisoners coming down from the northern prisons and labour camps in search of the place where they could enlist for the new army. When Ivan began pressuring him for answers pertaining to the railway line and about conditions in Irkutsk, the old fellow grew nervous. He insisted he did not know those details. All he would say was that he could direct them in the direction of the town, and that many Poles had already passed by this way. Then he clucked for the horse to start moving again. Giving the reins a sharp jerk, he and the boy hurried away in the sleigh.

Watching the back of the sled disappear into the distance, Ivan said, "Well, at least we know we are heading in the right direction. We should hurry. We have another fifty kilometres to cover before we get to Irkutsk!"

Jozef was relieved that Radoslaw, Tomasz and Vladik did not understand the Russian language well enough to grasp what the old man had told Ivan regarding their needless push through the forest on the previous day. His comrades would have been angry and discouraged if they had known, and they would have blamed Ivan for misdirecting them. Neither Ivan nor Jozef mentioned anything about it in order to keep peace between the men.

With the snow and ice packed down hard on the trail through the forest, they were able to move at a quicker pace. Their tired legs trudged on for several kilometres up and down the hilly terrain until they arrived at a fork in the path. A second route split off and turned in a different direction. They stopped at the fork while Ivan and Vladik tested compass directions and checked for mossy growth on nearby trees to determine which path to take. The men noticed there were tracks made by a single horse and sled along one trail, appearing fresh and undisturbed. It probably served as a trail leading to the old man's settlement somewhere in the forest. The other fork appeared to be more widely used, with a multitude of horse hooves and sleigh imprints along its course. The ruts were flatter and frozen over on the larger trail. Although it appeared to be a high-traffic route, there was no evidence of recent travel.

The Poles followed the more-travelled route along a frozen stream through the forest. It wasn't long before they found themselves entering a large clearing where a small village had been established. Everything in the hamlet seemed old and run down. The buildings looked dark, damp and dreary. As they walked into the small village, a scattering of people milling around outside eyed them suspiciously. A woman opened the door of her house and yanked two little children inside who were playing in the snow. The door quickly slammed shut with an audible thud. An older woman pulling a sled full of firewood hurried away and disappeared between two dilapidated buildings. Several young boys who were working over an open fire in the centre of the village stopped what they were doing and stared at the bedraggled group of Polish men entering their domain. Jozef and his comrades stood still and looked around cautiously.

"Hello," Ivan called out to the boys in Russian.

The men were still a fair distance away from where the boys were working. The lads failed to reply but continued staring.

Ivan called across to where they gaped. "We are Polish men looking for Irkutsk. Can you point us in the right direction? We are not sure which way to go."

Still the boys hesitated to respond. It was an awkward moment. Jozef and his comrades didn't know what they should do. The old man they had encountered along the trail had said the local peasants saw many Polish ex-prisoners travelling this way in search of the Polish Army... so why were these villagers so dumbfounded by their presence?

Faces could be seen peering out from windows in run-down dwellings. Jozef observed a girl pulling a tiny child away from the dirty windowpane of one home situated close to the trail. An eerie silence enveloped the village as all activity ground to a halt.

A grey-bearded man suddenly emerged from the tallest building and started walking toward them. He was dressed in typical Cossack style, like the pictures of old Russian cavalry men Jozef had seen in history books. A long sword resting in its sheath hung from the Cossack's waist. He eyed Jozef, Ivan, Vladik, Radoslaw and Tomasz with a look of disdain. They couldn't help feeling intimidated.

"Who are you? Why are you here?" the Cossack demanded.

Purposely speaking in broken Russian, Ivan replied that they were Polish men looking to find the town of Irkutsk.

"We need to find our way south so we can locate the assembly place for the new Polish Army," he said. "We want to enlist, and help the Red Army fight the Nazis."

Jozef realised Ivan's words were well-planned. The sentiment he evoked should appeal to the Cossack's sense of nationalism.

"Do you have any rubles?" the Cossack wanted to know. "Do you have any food with you... anything worthy of trade for the information I can provide you? Our children are hungry, and they cry for food."

Radoslaw and Tomasz had smoked a few fish overnight on a tree branch hanging above the fire at their campsite. Although the conditions hadn't allowed them to smoke the fish properly, nor for long enough, their effort had helped to preserve the fish, which were wrapped in a piece of sackcloth inside Radoslaw's coat pocket.

Ivan mentioned this, and the Cossack man moved in closer. He demanded to see the smoked fish. Radoslaw looked as though he might protest, but Ivan insisted Radoslaw remain quiet and do what the Cossack asked. Radoslaw slowly relented and pulled the package of fish out from his pocket. He handed the bundle to Ivan, who opened it up and held it out for the Cossack to inspect.

The man approached and quickly snapped up one smoked fish from Ivan's hand. He took a bite from it, then threw the remainder back into the wrapping. He turned and nodded in the direction of the large building he had come out from. An elderly woman emerged from the door, and the Cossack ordered her to take the fish from Ivan. She did so, then hastily retreated into the structure, slamming the door behind her. Radoslaw could be heard grumbling under his breath about the last of their food being taken away.

The Cossack then slowly worked his way along the line that the Poles had formed. He looked sternly into each one of their faces, and Jozef silently prayed that Vladik and Tomasz would not react to the Cossack's scrutiny. Both were blatantly staring back into the Cossack's eyes.

"Ah!" the Cossack said, pointing to Tomasz and Vladik. "They are ready to take up arms and join the fight!

Already their blood boils with the vexation of a warrior's might and spirit! These will be good soldiers!"

The ex-prisoners were met with the Cossack's approval, and he let them know they travelled the correct route. He said there was another branch in the trail, located approximately ten kilometres to the west. At that point, they needed to take the fork on the left, which would direct them onto a more developed roadway leading directly into Irkutsk. The Cossack said it was a large, busy city. The railway station there moved trains westward to the Ural Mountains. He knew nothing about availability of trains or any other details, but he knew the Polish men needed to get to the train station in Irkutsk as soon as possible.

Back on the trail, Radoslaw complained that the Cossack had given them few details beyond what the old man in the sleigh had already offered them… and he had taken what little food they had left.

Vladik nudged Radoslaw and said, "He told us we are following the correct path, and he warned us about a fork in the trail ahead so we can continue on the correct route. He also let us know about the railway station in Irkutsk. I believe this information was worth the price of a few stale fish, my friend!"

Tomasz let out a voracious laugh and slapped Radoslaw across the back of the head. A playful fight ensued between the two comrades. The others chuckled as they watched Tomasz and Radoslaw tussling like two boys in a schoolyard brawl. Knowing that the Trans-Siberian Line was within reach, the men continued along the trail feeling the happiest they had been since they left the labour camp.

More Russian peasants began to appear along the route as they grew closer to the city. All of them looked worn-down and ragged. They passed by men on emaciated horses, and families in dilapidated sleighs. Some galloped by without so much as a nod or any sign of acknowledgement. A few stopped to chat, but all were cautious of the dirty, bearded, scruffy ex-prisoners and offered little information when Ivan attempted to converse with them. All they really would say was that other Poles had been seen travelling west in search of the new army. Jozef realised their reluctance to talk was due to their fear of the NKVD. Soviets would imprison or shoot their own people on the slightest charge if they were deemed to be sympathetic toward foreigners.

When they reached the main road leading into Irkutsk, they came across another group of ex-prisoners heading toward the city. Those men had come from a labour camp located west of where Jozef and his comrades' camp was situated. They had laboured clearing the forest of trees and brush to create a wide, open roadbed. They said it was tough work as they had been forced to use primitive tools and inept wheelbarrows made from heavy planks of wood. The wheelbarrows had solid wooden wheels that shook back and forth, and were impossible to push along. The prisoners' strength had been tested trying to get the wheelbarrows to move. They'd had to dig through the earth to make a smooth, level pathway. In difficult places, they had to cut through small hills. The dirt was heavy and clay-like. Whenever they'd pushed their dull shovels into the ground, the clay would stick to them, and they'd had to scrape off their shovels with every push. Temporary pathways had to be created to move heavy clay in the useless wheelbarrows from the bottom of trenches up to the top of hills, where the earth was emptied into a nearby swamp. Wheelbarrows refused to co-operate and would not budge, so the prisoners had to force them, loaded full of heavy dirt, along to the marshy area. The awkward things had to be moved across narrow planks laid over the top of the swamp, which if they slipped off, would settle themselves deep into the muddy bog. It would take several struggling men to free the wheelbarrows from the swamp, only to repeat the same arduous task time and time again. The Soviets never told the prisoners what the road was for, but they assumed it was going to be a new railway line.

The two groups of ex-prisoners compared their abhorrent experiences, and all agreed that despite everything, they should not complain. They had survived! According to the horrific accounts that had filtered down into their camps, working in the mines was even worse. That was a certain death sentence. No one ever survived working in the mines.

Jozef's group joined the new cluster of men and they headed toward Irkutsk together. It remained windy and cold. The streams were solidly frozen over, and snow continued to fall. They travelled through the night.

Lights could be seen in the distance as they drew closer to the city. By dawn, they were walking along a major roadway. Telephone poles lined the route, with large insulators supporting the heavy wires. Weathered signs along the thoroughfare hailed Stalin and the glorious Russian state. The men cursed in Polish at the Communist propaganda. Outlines of tall buildings and rows of smoking chimneys began to appear as their destination gradually came into view. Distant factory horns and sounds of civilisation started to blend with the sights and pungent smells of city life as they drew closer to the metropolis. Lorries began to pass by them on the road as the citizens of Irkutsk started waking up to a new day.

They felt many eyes on them as they entered the city, but no one seemed surprised to see them there. The inhabitants had grown accustomed to the sight of scruffy Polish ex-prisoners wandering the city streets in their tattered prison-issued rags as they searched for the railway station. City-dwellers would point them in the right direction, but all were wary of appearing friendly, as NKVD officers patrolled the roads. The residents were fearful of being reported, sent to prison or put to death for aligning themselves with any of the anti-Communist ex-prisoners.

Jozef and his comrades had never seen the station at Irkutsk before. They had been dispersed into the open fields from an isolated siding nearby when they came to the end of the railway line on their journey to the labour camp. Arriving at the railway junction now, they found an immense building of brick and wood. Despite the fact that it was decaying and run-down, Jozef was able to look beyond the deteriorating exterior and envision the station's grandeur in better times. He couldn't help feeling impressed by its stateliness. The architecture was magnificent in all its finer details. The vision was only spoiled by the huge statue of Stalin standing out in front of the station with a painted sign declaring him to be Russia's Beloved Leader.

The station was a very busy place. People filled the entranceway and lined the walls along the building. Jozef was amazed to see how many ex-prisoners were there. Many more would arrive in the days to come.

It was discouraging to learn there had been no trains coming to the station for days. Some people had been waiting for more than a week already. A Russian railway worker at the station could only tell people that a train was due to arrive soon. They quickly realised the worker had no idea if or when any trains were coming. Some men at the station were saying that tickets would not be required.

Ivan advised his group to stick close together as they eased their way through the crowd and into the station building. It was damp and poorly lit inside. The floor was covered with sleeping people. It stank of dirty bodies and stale, mouldy air. The men staked out a small claim in the main lobby. They stretched out and fell asleep quickly, clinging to their meagre possessions. All of them were totally exhausted.

Jozef was awakened by the sound of Ivan's voice some time later. He overheard Ivan speaking to somebody in Russian. Several local militiamen had come to check on circumstances at the station. It appeared they wanted the ex-prisoners removed as desperately as the Poles themselves wanted to leave.

"Do you know whether any trains are on their way here?" Ivan asked the militiamen. "Is it true we do not need tickets to ride on the train? Is there anywhere to find food or water nearby while we wait for a train to come?"

One of the militiamen laughed hysterically.

"Food indeed!" he remarked. "Russian people are starving to death, and you ask for food! Polish prisoners... you ask for too much!"

The man's face morphed into a miserable scowl, and he pushed Ivan aside as he made his way through the crowd. The other militiamen followed him, but one of them did stop long enough to tell Ivan that no tickets would be required when a train did come to transport them west. He advised Ivan that water could be retrieved from a pump in the kitchen area of the station, but no food was available. The Poles were on their own now. He also mentioned that the new Polish Army was to gather east of the Volga River, in the south.

As the militiaman walked away, he suddenly turned around to look at Ivan again, and said, "Go to your new army and fight for Russia. Destroy the fascists who continually invade our land. Show no mercy toward them! Have no remorse!"

The man's impassioned words reminded Jozef of how intense and deeply rooted Russian patriotism was. The Russian people had a strong nationalistic spirit. Not even their terrible living conditions, fear of being imprisoned or shot for crimes they did not commit, the injustices of the Communist regime or Stalin's terror campaign could destroy their devotion to their Sacred Motherland.

Jozef and his comrades had not eaten anything in two days. Thoughts of food plagued them, and their bellies ached with hunger. They did not have anything to use for bartering, but they suspected none of the other Poles at the station had spare food for trade anyway. They would have to find a creative way to get some food before long, or they would perish from starvation before any trains arrived.

Something of interest caught Jozef's eye as he scanned the sea of scruffy, bearded faces surrounding him. He pressed his way through the crowd and approached a huge, painted board displaying an image of the Trans-Siberian Railway Line. Studying the map of Siberia, and using the printed reference chart below, he gauged the distance to the Ural Mountains from Irkutsk to be thousands of kilometres. He knew he and his comrades would require a train to carry them across that huge expanse. All the men were weak and exhausted. Many ex-prisoners in a deteriorating state were already dropping dead.

Ivan and Vladik joined Jozef, studying the Trans-Siberian route map. They agreed they should take the train west to Sverdlovsk, where the railway line started slicing through the Ural Mountains. They needed to remain east of the Urals. Once they reached the mountains, they would head south, keeping east of the Volga River, where the militiaman had said the army was forming. According to the large map, it appeared the final leg on their trek would take them several hundred more kilometres to the south. When the others were informed of their plan, Radoslaw complained it would be a crowded train ride followed by another long walk. Nevertheless, all of them realised they had no choice but to reach the Urals by rail.

The next day, there were many more Polish ex-prisoners waiting for transportation at the station. A massive crowd spilled out onto the grounds surrounding the building. Local militiamen nervously patrolled the area, trying to prevent the Poles from fraternising with civilians in the street. They did not want the local inhabitants to hear about the maltreatment and horrific experiences the ex-prisoners had endured in the forced labour camps further north.

It proved to be extremely cold while the men waited for a train to come. Some started to make fires on the property next to the station to warm themselves. Initially, the railway workers and local militia tried putting a stop to the fires, but in the end so many were lit that they ignored them.

All the men suffered from hunger and thirst. A group of old women approached the station, while the militiamen tried to hold them back. The women tossed stale rolls and loaves of bread out to the starving men, who fell upon the offerings like hungry wolves. Several fights broke out as men fought over chunks of bread that had fallen to the ground. Jozef managed to snag a loaf that was thrown his way. He rationed it out between himself and his comrades. Ivan had secured some pieces of raw turnip from another ex-prisoner by serving as translator between the Pole and one of the local officials. The man had wanted to question the officer regarding finding his family members. He told Ivan he had taken a couple of turnips from a woman's wagon as he and his comrades followed her through the city streets when they were searching for the railway station. Ivan, Jozef, Vladik, Radoslaw and Tomasz gnawed on small pieces of the turnip, but it did little to stave off their hunger pains.

It was another full week before a locomotive finally arrived. Snowstorms in the west had delayed the engine. A massive crowd formed by the tracks as it rumbled into the station, coming to a screeching halt. Black smoke spewed from the smokestack and rained down on the anxious throng. Railway workers busied themselves connecting additional cattle cars to the steaming engine. Some time later, the boxcar doors were opened and the ex-prisoners started climbing into the cars in the groups they had arrived with. Despite the volume of passengers scrambling in, the cars were not as crowded as they had been on the long journey coming into Siberia. There was room in Jozef's car for all the men to sit down. The railway workers made a point of reminding the Poles that they were on their own now. There would be no food or water offered to them along the way. It would be another long and difficult journey.

The men debated how long they thought it would take them to reach Sverdlovsk. More than two weeks would pass before they arrived. The train was delayed when heavy snowstorms stopped it dead in its tracks in the middle of nowhere. The men waited, shivering inside the boxcars, for three days before the snow and winds abated so their rail journey could resume. Starvation and freezing cold conditions were reminiscent of their horrific passage into

Siberia, but this time they were free men, and the soldiers and railway workers were not as harsh with them.

The train stopped at all the railway stations the men had observed on the large map in Irkutsk. Each time the boxcar doors were opened, they were permitted to roam freely around the station in search of food and water while the locomotive was loaded with more coal. Some men gathered loose bits of coal along the tracks and filled their pockets with the black rocks so they could burn them in the primitive stove set up in the middle of the railway car. There was never enough coal collected to burn for any extended length of time, and the men remained frozen for much of the journey.

Jozef and his comrades scooped up large amounts of fresh, clean snow into a metal pail that Tomasz had taken from the station in Irkutsk. They put the pail on the stove inside the boxcar when it was lit, and they passed the bucket of melted snow around for all the men in their car to drink from. Other times they would simply take handfuls of clean snow and allow it to melt inside their mouths. It helped to quench their thirst.

At each station along the route, more Polish ex-prisoners were picked up and loaded into the cars. Large groups had gathered at Krasnovarsk, Novosibirsk and Omsk. All were seeking passage to Sverdlovsk. In Novosibirsk, an influx of men stepped up into Jozef's boxcar, and it became quite crowded. Complaints were squelched when three of the newcomers opened their winter jackets and doled out delicious fresh rolls to all the men inside the car. The crafty rogues had pilfered the treats from a bakery a short distance away from the station in Novosibirsk. Their eyes twinkled with devious delight when they spoke of their silent entrance into the back of the bakery shop. While the baker and his wife argued in the front of the shop, the men had loaded their coats with the tasty little breads and slipped away undetected into the early morning darkness. 'A fortunate moment of opportunity,' was how the tallest of the thieves described the dastardly deed.

When the train was being serviced in Omsk, Ivan managed to talk a couple of reluctant, older peasant women at the side of the station into giving him some sausage and a loaf of bread to ration out with his comrades. He had helped the women free their cart from the ice after it froze in place while they were inside the station purchasing food for the local hospital. He begged for a small portion of the food the women had purchased. With no rubles, nor any items to barter with, such inventive means were the only way to acquire much-needed food. By begging, borrowing and stealing, most of the men managed to survive the journey into Sverdlovsk.

They were met with utter confusion when they arrived at their destination. Endless numbers of Polish deportees coming from labour camps and collective farms were arriving at the station in Sverdlovsk. Thousands waited inside the crowded building. Women and children lay sick, sleeping or dying on the floor. The dead bodies of many severely malnourished and diseased individuals were stacked in the snow outside. Many had died upon arrival. Typhoid fever, dysentery, and respiratory illnesses were widespread throughout the crowd. Weak and crying children clung to tired, half-conscious adults. Mothers showed no emotion, their faces gaunt and hollow. Rags hung from their emaciated bodies, and blood and pus oozed from the open sores that covered them. They remained blank and impassive. It was as though life had departed them a long time ago. The women's actions appeared mechanical as they sorted out who the new arrivals were; they swarmed the newcomers, begging for money and scraps of food to feed their ailing children.

Viewing this sad reality, Jozef worried about his own family. Had they been deported to some godforsaken settlement following his arrest? Had his mother, brothers and sisters suffered and died in the Siberian wasteland like so many others, or were they clinging to what remained of their former selves like the sorrowful mothers and children assembled here?

Feelings of hatred toward the Russians bubbled to the surface once again. Radoslaw and Tomasz cursed under their breath about the deplorable state the suffering Polish people had been reduced to. Ivan fought back tears as he pondered the fate of his young wife and their infant whom he had not yet met. Vladik swore he would cut the heads off as many Soviets as he could once the new Polish Army was done helping obliterate the Nazis.

Ex-prisoners who left the train at Sverdlovsk congregated near the front of the station. Jozef and his comrades instinctively migrated toward the group. Many were planning to transfer to another train heading south. There were some men who had arrived at the station on foot several days earlier from a camp further north. They informed the newcomers that tickets were required to ride the train from Sverdlovsk. Railway workers in the station told them they could work at some of the local farms to earn enough rubles to purchase tickets. Without tickets, they would not be allowed to board any of the trains that might turn up.

One man said several ex-prisoners in the station had left on a train two days earlier. Apparently, they had received fifty rubles and a train ticket to a destination of their choosing when they were released from their labour camp. According to the official decree, all Polish ex-prisoners were supposed to have received money, train tickets and a small ration of food to help with their travels when they were released. Most had not received any provisions. Having been denied those prescribed essentials, the journey was more difficult for the majority.

A man in the back of the crowd told the newcomers that two days earlier another man had stowed away on the train. The stowaway had dared all the ex-prisoners at the station to join him in his quest. The others had tried to reason with him, saying it would be impossible to get on a train without a ticket. Railway workers and militiamen were guarding the trains, and all the cars were locked. The man hid himself beneath the undercarriage of a car and clung tightly to the train as it pulled away from the station. He had planned to come out from under the train and blend into the crowd milling about at the next station, then climb into one of the cars and ride the remaining distance to his destination. Later that day, a railway worker told the remaining ex-prisoners in Sverdlovsk Station that a stowaway had frozen to death beneath one of the boxcars. The man's stiff body had been found lying on the tracks several kilometres outside of Sverdlovsk.

"Fool!" Radoslaw blurted out.

The others nodded in agreement. They knew they would have to find a legitimate means to acquire a ticket to ride the train.

Jozef's group collectively believed their best option would be to accept an offer of work nearby to earn the price of a ticket, and they knew they should do so as quickly as possible. Due to the delay in receiving news about the amnesty at their camp, and because of the lengthy time it had taken them to travel on foot and then by train to Sverdlovsk, they were already months behind in finding the Polish Army. They had lost track of time along their journey, and it worried them to learn that a new year had already rolled around. According to the calendar posted inside the station, it was now January 1942!

Ivan managed to work out a deal with an old farmer several kilometres away from the train station. He and his comrades would do a variety of jobs by day to earn money at the old man's farm, and at night they would sleep in a draughty barn that reeked of moulding hay and horse manure.

The man's farmhouse suffered from years of decay and neglect. It was a typical wooden structure crafted from squared logs, with small windows framed by decorative, hand-carved patterns. The low-peaked roof was covered in a mossy growth, and a dilapidated wooden fence encompassed the farmyard. All the outbuildings showed similar signs of disrepair. Two bony horses stood motionless in the paddock, their heads hanging low. Steam rising from their nostrils in the cold winter air was the only indicator that they were still alive. The land surrounding the house and barn was caked thick with frozen mud, and deep wagon ruts made the ground difficult to walk on. Signs of poverty were everywhere.

The men were left in the hands of the old farmer's son, who was more interested in finding his next bottle of vodka than doing the much-needed work around the farm. While he drank himself into a stupor inside the barn, Jozef, Radoslaw and Tomasz set about doing repairs to the structure, mucking out the horse stalls, cleaning and filling the feeding troughs with fresh hay and water, sweeping out the barn and doing all the other menial barnyard tasks that had obviously been neglected for some time. Once they had the barn back in tidy, functioning order, they joined Ivan and Vladik in the nearby forest felling trees. They lopped off the top branches and cut the tree trunks into sizable logs suited to burning inside the farmer's fireplace. The men made some repairs to the battered farmhouse and repaired the surrounding fence. They worked non-stop for a full week and prayed that the old man would have enough rubles to pay all of them for their labour.

He was a stern Russian man who had inherited the farm from his father many years before. He was now old himself, and ailing, but he still enjoyed sitting by a roaring fire inside the house while looking out into the farmyard from the window beside his chair. He had watched as the Polish ex-prisoners toiled all week getting his house and barn back in order. At the end of the week, the old farmer went out into the yard and called for Ivan and Jozef to come into the house.

Inside, there was further evidence of how this family's livelihood had suffered. A large adobe stove made from clay stood in the centre of the kitchen. It was tall, rising to the height of the ceiling. A ledge for pots was attached to the stove, and at the back of the ledge was a scooped-out hearth for cooking in. Rows of dusty dried onions, garlic and bunches of herbs hung upside down from the rafters.

A small table with four chairs was wedged tightly into a corner of the room. A dim lamp cast eerie shadows across the kitchen. A wooden bed and wardrobe were barely visible in the next room. On the other side of the kitchen, there was a tiny sitting room area with a chesterfield, and the old man's chair prominently situated by the fireplace. A well-worn braided rug covered the aging slats of wood on the sitting room floor.

This humble farmhouse must have been a cosy residence at one time. Now it was damp and moulding. Plaster was cracking and peeling on the ceiling and walls.

Three framed photographs stood on a tiny table in the corner of the sitting room. One was a wedding photo of a young man and woman. Beside it was a photo of two small children sitting with the young couple, and the final photograph was of the old man and an elderly woman whom Jozef assumed was his wife. A tiny vase of dusty dried flowers stood on top of a lacy cloth in front of the three photographs.

Some wooden skis and snowshoes were neatly tucked into the corner of the sitting room. In the early evening shadows, the old farmer's slumped form was outlined on the wall as he stood leaning on his cane beside the blazing fire.

The farmer spoke in Russian, asking Ivan and Jozef where they and their comrades had come from. How had they gotten to Sverdlovsk? What did they do in the labour camp? Did they intend to enlist in the new Polish Army and fight the Nazi fascists in defence of Russia? The elderly man's questions were endless, and it was not until his curiosity had been adequately satisfied that he finally stopped interrogating them.

The old farmer then turned the conversation around to matters concerning his own circumstances. He complained that life in Russia was not much better than it was for those on the collective farms in Siberia. He said that people across Russia were starving, ill or freezing to death. They feared the oppressive NKVD, and they were paranoid of everyone and everything.

Jozef and Ivan were surprised to hear a Russian speaking out about the obvious hardships existing in the beloved Motherland... the so-called glorious workers' paradise. They knew he would instantly be shot if the Russians heard his subversive, anti-Soviet speech, but they assumed he was a dying old man who felt he had nothing left to lose, so he would speak the truth. They listened intently as the old fellow went on to say that because of the war, there were severe shortages of food and supplies of every kind across the Soviet Union. His farm suffered because of it. At one time he had reaped the benefits of a lucrative operation, producing and selling his wheat crop. Now, there was no way to get his crop to market due to a lack of transportation. All the train routes had been taken over moving troops and prisoners across the Soviet Union. While the Russian people and soldiers on the front lines were starving to death, he had stacks of grain piled up and rotting away with no way to move it. His crop now lay decaying under a blanket of snow in his fields. The rail system was strained, as were government resources.

He blamed the Soviet difficulties on the Germans. He said the Nazis had invaded their peace-loving country in a cowardly attack, and he applauded the Poles for choosing to join the army to fight the fascists. He had heard rumours that a Polish general was to take command in forming the new Polish Army at Buzuluk, where the Polish Army Headquarters was established.

Ivan quickly replied, "We hope a train will come to take us south. My companions and I are exhausted and weak from our long walk across Siberia, and we are not adequately equipped to undertake another long journey on foot through winter's inclement conditions. We want to reach the new army quickly. We will be no good for the cause if we arrive there on death's doorstep, following another long and difficult walk."

"You will have to go to Buzuluk to enlist," the old man said. "Buzuluk is south in the Orenberg Province. Go by way of Christopol. Thousands of Polish ex-prisoners coming from the labour camps have already marched through Sverdlovsk to Christopol. From there, you can take a train to Buzuluk."

"How far is Christopol from here?" Jozef asked.

"Several hundred kilometers away," the old man replied.

He then began to talk more about his own hardships. He said his wife had died the previous winter during the height of the typhoid epidemic. His son's two children had contracted the illness, and they had died within days of becoming ill. Finally, his daughter-in-law also succumbed to the deadly sickness, turning his son into a crazy, bitter man.

As for himself, he said he was now old and sick. Soon he would be dead as well. His son would be left holding the entire future of the family farm in his hands, and because his son had taken to vodka as his solitary companion in the days following the deaths of his wife and children, the old man reckoned he would not be able to hold on to the farm for very long. The Red Army had expelled his son due to the man's drunken and disorderly behaviour. He guessed that his son was presently in the barn drowning his sorrows in vodka.

The old man seemed pleased with the work the Poles had done in catching up with the menial tasks around his farm. He leaned over and pulled out a tin box from underneath his chair beside the fireplace. He opened it and carefully counted out the exact number of rubles required for each one of the Poles who had worked on his farm to purchase train tickets. Pressing the money into Ivan and Jozef's hands, he made them promise to go and fight the Germans, and to kill off all the Nazis. With a crafty wink of his eye, he told the ex-prisoners his spirit was going with them into battle.

***

When Jozef and his comrades arrived back at the station in Sverdlovsk, conditions inside the building were even more appalling than they had been a week earlier. Many more ex-prisoners, as well as women and children coming from the settlements, had arrived while the men were working at the nearby farm. Ailing and starving people cluttered the floor, the doorways and any place else where they could lay their emaciated bodies down. The stacks of dead bodies piling up in the snow outside had grown to astonishing heights. Small clusters of orphaned children grouped together and wandered the station begging for money and food. Some of their parents had died from illness and starvation while waiting for assistance at the station. Others had been abandoned there by their mothers, in the hope that they would be taken to an orphanage where they believed the children stood a better chance of surviving.

The next afternoon, a train arrived. All deportees with money for tickets were permitted to board the train destined for Christopol. Railway workers and militiamen had a difficult time controlling the crowds as everyone who could still get up and walk tried to get on the train. Many people were driven back as the officials sorted out who had tickets and who did not. Amidst the fighting and the chaos, Jozef and his comrades were allowed to board the train when they produced the tickets they had purchased.

The train pulled away from the station while those left behind cried out in despair. Some fell to the ground, as though their last bit of energy had been spent trying to get on board. Jozef observed hundreds of blank faces outside staring at the train as it slowly crept away from the station. Those remaining without tickets would have to face the continuing torment, horrors and hopelessness that permeated the station. Jozef knew many more of those unfortunate souls would be dead before the sun rose again the following morning.

The train crawled at a slow speed most of the way to Christopol. It was held up for various reasons during the journey. The temperature was warmer than it had been in the subarctic conditions they endured in Northern Siberia, yet the train stood still on the tracks for two days in the middle of nowhere while a Russian blizzard blew by. Hunger and cold continued to gnaw at all those on board.

Poverty was evident in every rundown village they travelled through. In some of the more populated areas, train tracks ran next to dirt roads that were reduced to large tracks of mud as continual human traffic passed over them. Masses of deportees walked toward Christopol. Sickly-looking groups of emaciated Poles dressed in rags, many without shoes or boots on their feet, continued trudging on.

As the train drew closer to the town, army vehicles and military personnel were spotted here and there. It was difficult to determine whether they were Russian or Polish units, but Vladik insisted they were Polish. Jozef felt a surge of excitement and national pride welling up inside at the thought of becoming a Polish soldier. He and his comrades were becoming increasingly frustrated by the length of time it was taking to get to the recruitment location.

As expected, the station was overcrowded with deportees when they finally arrived in Christopol. An endless sea of Polish ex-prisoners waited at the station, and there were almost as many women, children and orphaned refugees arriving there, searching for the army. The refugees hoped to find food, shelter and medical attention for their families and themselves under the umbrella of the Polish Army. Unfortunately, many of them would die from typhus shortly after they arrived, and the number who perished from malnutrition was so extreme, it would never be estimated.

Trains were running on a more regular schedule from Christopol. Jozef and his comrades only had to wait one day for a train to come and transport them to Buzuluk. When they arrived there, many Polish soldiers and army vehicles were standing by to take the incoming men to Polish Army Headquarters. As they neared the large building in an open army transport, a Polish flag could be seen flying atop the red brick structure. It had been over two years since the ex-prisoners had seen that flag freely flapping in the wind. A surge of nostalgia and national pride engulfed the transport. Emotions were difficult to keep in check.

The vehicle did not stop at the headquarters building, but slowly crept past it along the muddy streets of Buzuluk. Eventually, the men arrived in a large forested area where the new army was camped. They were told this was the site where new recruits were to enlist. Jozef and his comrades were euphoric. They had finally reached the assembly area where the new Polish Army was being formed. Now they could get on with the business of becoming soldiers.

TEN
FAREWELL TO RUSSIA
SEVERAL MONTHS EARLIER...

Viktor Yatskaya was listening to Stalin's radio address to the nation concerning Germany's betrayal. Earlier on, Molotov had made a speech condemning the German bombing over Russian territory in June. Now, Stalin was encouraging all Soviet citizens to fight the fascists with everything they could muster.

Viktor had seen this eventuality coming, even though both Soviet and German politicians had been denying it. A build-up of German forces along the Soviet border and sightings of Hitler's Luftwaffe reconnaissance planes frequently flying over Russian territory had indicated something was afoot. Viktor had recognised that signs of approaching war were mounting, and as indications began to increase, rumours of war emerged.

He had already spoken to his son, Dimitri, about the inevitable outcome of war with Germany. The older Yatskaya realised this development would prove detrimental to all the ex-Polish citizens being held captive in the labour camps and settlements of Northern Russia and Siberia. He worried about his departed wife, Anna's, surviving Polish family members in the Soviet Union. Anna's nieces, Lilyana and Larissa, remained in a settlement along the Dvina River area, while her nephew, Aleksander, was working deep in the forest further east. What would happen to them now that Germany had declared war on Russia? Viktor called his son to return to his office at the prison in Arkhangelsk under the guise of transporting supplies, so they could discuss the situation.

"Conditions will be very difficult for the Poles," Viktor said. "What limited resources there are will be spent on the war effort. There will be nothing left to help support Polish deportees in the Soviet Union. They will have to fend for themselves or die. We must honour your mother and protect those who remain in her family lineage. We have to find a way to relocate your cousins to a better place."

Dimitri listened intently to his father's words. He knew Viktor spoke the truth. The gravity of what his father was saying weighed heavily on Dimitri's heart. Dimitri nervously tugged at the stubbly growth of whiskers that framed his bony jawline.

"What can we do to help them?" he asked.

Viktor sat back in his chair and peered across the desk at his son.

"Didn't Lilyana mention she had a relative living in England?" he asked.

"Yes. She told me several times that her father has a cousin… Tadeusz Prawoslaw, I think she said his name is… a cousin to my mother as well. Lilyana's father was trying to get all the Prawoslaws in Poland over to England, but his efforts were too late. Just as his arrangements were in order, our army moved in and occupied Eastern Poland. The Prawoslaws did not have a chance to escape."

"Hmm…" Viktor sighed. "Do you know if her father had already made arrangements for them to go to Tadeusz Prawoslaw in Britain?"

"I'm not sure about that," Dimitri said. "Lilyana never told me what the family was going to do if they had made it into England."

Dimitri stood up and wandered to the large window next to his father's desk. The Soviet guards were performing practice exercises in the prison yard below his father's office. The young lads were teenagers trying hard to hang tough and execute the manoeuvres to impress the senior officers drilling them. Dimitri knew that his Polish cousin, Aleksander, was the same age as these young soldiers, and he believed Aleksander was no different in his determination to join the fight and serve in the army... but it would not be right to force Aleksander to become a Red Army soldier. Dimitri was aware that young Poles who were conscripted to join the Red Army were doomed. They were forced onto the frontlines and used as fodder in the fight against the Germans. Aleksander wouldn't stand a chance.

Dimitri realised his father's thinking was right. Lilyana, Aleksander and Larissa needed to get out of the Soviet Union in order to survive.

***

Lilyana and Marta had recently stopped working in the forest when they were ordered to report for work at a kolkhoz. They were assigned to a brigade of women cutting grass with scythes to clear extensive pasturelands; they walked a lengthy distance to the collective farm every day. The job was not hard, but it was dirty and tedious. Thankfully, it was safer than working in the forest. On sunny days, it became extremely hot as they laboured in the fields. The pay was poor, and their wages did not reflect the extent of the toil they put forth through long hours on the farm.

Kolkhozy were organised so that peasant co-operatives worked together for joint agricultural production. District authorities consolidated individual land, resources and labour into collective farms. The kolkhozy were controlled by local officials, and collective labour was enforced under Stalin's rule. Soviet authorities viewed collective farming as the answer to their problem of agricultural distribution. As the Soviets pushed ahead with their ambitious industrialisation programme, almost all agricultural land was collectivised. Rural farmers were forced to become part of the co-operative, with their land, their livestock and all their assets coming under the control of district authorities.

Farmers were forced to sell their harvest to the state for low prices set by the Soviets. The state would then turn around and charge high prices to consumers for those same crops. It was a lucrative means of income for the government.

Farmers and labourers were arrested and sent to jail, or to a forced labour camp, if they were suspected of stealing any crops or seeds. Farmers were not allowed to leave the kolkhozy without special permission. If they opted to pull out of collective farming, the government would strip them of everything they had ever worked for and owned. The Soviets reduced food rations when harvests were poor, while the peasant farmers slaved away to deliver the compulsory quota of produce. It was a harsh farming life that took away the farmers' livelihood. Many peasant farmers died from starvation, disease and exhaustion alongside the deportees who had been relocated and forced to labour on their collective farms.

Lilyana and Marta worked at the kolkhoz for most of the summer in 1941. They dragged their weary bodies off to the farm early every morning with several other women from the settlement in tattered dresses, their dishevelled hair bound in kerchiefs. They walked seven kilometres along a muddy road to reach the farm, and again back to their living quarters late in the evenings following a hard day's work. Their clothes were worn threadbare and dirty. Their shoes had disintegrated to nothing, forcing them to walk barefooted. The mud oozed between their toes, and they had to be careful not to slip and fall in the mire. Mud covered their legs and the hems of their ragged garments. They would return exhausted, weak and starving.

Disease and starvation persisted throughout the settlement, and the number of deportees continued to diminish. Eugenia and Melka Cieslak both perished from malnourishment that summer. A pestilence of gnats, mosquitoes and midges added to their grief during the summer months, while plagues of bedbugs and lice seemed to continually increase.

Early in September, they were informed that Polish deportees were to have a day off work and attend an important meeting in the village. The women worried this might mean the Soviets were planning to relocate them to another area. Lilyana could not sleep the night before the meeting. Fear and worry gripped her. Where would they go? How would they get there? It was a bad time of year to be moving people again. Winter weather was to begin very soon, and they did not have proper winter attire, nor any food, money or provisions to take with them. Even worse, if the Soviets were planning to move them out to another area, Dimitri wouldn't be able to watch out for her and Larissa's wellbeing. Conditions were worsening, and Larissa was so frail now. Another upheaval might do her in. Lilyana needed to get in touch with Dimitri to see if he knew anything about what was to happen. Could Dimitri rescue her and Larissa from one more fate?

Lilyana slipped outside from the shelter. If any of the others lay awake anticipating what the meeting the next morning was to bring, they said nothing. She carefully made her way down to the river beside their living quarters. This was the designated spot where she and Dimitri had agreed to meet in emergency situations. Small pebbles and sharp grasses tore at her feet in the darkness, but the soles of her feet were already so raw and callused she hardly noticed. She sat down on her favourite rock beside the river and prayed that her Russian cousin would come and tell her what impending doom was about to transpire. Dimitri had promised to keep her apprised of any new developments within the settlement.

An hour later, Lilyana heard a motor running on the hill in the distance, but the engine noise vanished as quickly as she detected it. She remained seated on the rock with her feet dipped in the cool water while the river ran by, swatting at the annoying insects that were making a feast of her emaciated bones.

"Psst! Lilyana! It's me," a voice whispered in the blackness.

Surprised, Lilyana spun around quickly to look in the direction the whisper had come from. A vague silhouette began to emerge from between the trees next to the river.

Before she could stop herself, the words tumbled from her mouth, "Is that you, Dimitri?"

"Who else are you expecting?" Dimitri teased. "Were you planning an encounter with a secret admirer?"

"Oh you!" Lilyana scolded. "There you go, teasing me again!"

Dimitri let out a stifled laugh. He did not want to alert any of the others in Lilyana's dwelling to his presence down at the riverbank.

"...but really, Lily! We've got to stop meeting like this. People will start to talk!"

"Ha, ha!" Lilyana replied in an awkward tone. "But perhaps you have come with news about this meeting for the Polish people, Dimitri? Tell me, what do you know about this development?"

Dimitri did not answer right away. The moon had emerged from behind a bank of clouds, and an outline of the trees next to Lilyana's rock could be seen in the semi-darkness.

"Would you look at that! The beetles have stripped all the bark from this tree. It will never survive winter without its outer bark. You may as well chop this tree down and use it for firewood, Lily!"

She did not know whether to laugh or become annoyed. Was her cousin always this inattentive, or was he toying with her again? When he turned his head to look at her, she stared him down.

"Ah... the grim Prawoslaw stare," Dimitri scoffed. "I recognise that look! That is how my mother would look when I did not do what I was told to do. Must be a family trait."

"Ahem!" came Lilyana's response.

Dimitri's mouth turned up into his good-natured grin. "Alright! Alright!" he stammered. "I do have news, and I will tell you all that I know… but you must not breathe a word of this to anyone!"

"You have my promise on that," Lilyana responded. "I will not say anything to anyone, but please, tell me what this meeting is about! I am afraid something bad is coming."

"Bad? No… not exactly," Dimitri answered. "In fact, some may think that it is good news."

***

Lilyana shuffled from one foot to the other as she waited impatiently for the announcement to be made at the village square the next morning. A large crowd of Poles had gathered now. She held on tightly to Larissa's hand so the little girl would not become lost. They were accompanied by Marta and Mrs Dobrowolski, Frederyk Cieslak, and Sabina and Karina Albinski from their living quarters. Everybody in the assemblage appeared grim. Many Soviet officials were attending this special meeting. Worry was etched on all the adult faces. Although her Russian cousin had informed her about what was to come, Lilyana needed to hear the news from the mouths of the authorities.

Finally, a senior NKVD officer stepped forward, raising his hand in the air to silence the crowd. In the following minutes, the deportees were informed that Stalin had signed an agreement with the Polish General Sikorski, Commander-in-Chief and Prime Minister of the Polish Government-in-Exile, in July. It was an amnesty pact that allowed all Polish people who had been deported to the Soviet Union to leave their settlements and enforced labour camps. The Poles were now free people.

News of the amnesty created a lot of excitement in the crowd. People were clapping and cheering. Some even began to sing the Polish national anthem. The Soviet officials could only look on with disdain.

Everybody quickly began to apply to the Polish Consulate in Arkhangelsk for passports. The women in

Lilyana's living quarters applied while waiting for further developments to emerge. They were anxious to get out of the Soviet Union.

News of the war between Russia and Germany had taken them by surprise, as they had been cut off from all outside news since arriving in the settlement. There was much debate about the formation of the new Polish Army in Southern Russia. Up until the amnesty, the Polish Government-in-Exile in London could do little about the predicament of Polish people enslaved by the Soviet Union. However, when Germany attacked Russia, the Polish government had taken the opportunity to help its citizens. It made Stalin agree to the forming of a Polish Army in Russia to help the Soviets fight the Germans, the release of the deportees, and the handing over of Polish children to the International Red Cross.

Stalin had delayed releasing the Polish labourers. He knew it would be difficult to replace the thousands of young men who toiled in the Soviet Union for free. He realised those men wanted to free themselves by enlisting in the Polish Armed Forces, thereby leaving a huge void in the Soviet workforce. The Russians tried pressuring the Poles to enlist in the Soviet Red Army, but the Poles wanted to enlist in their own new army. Unfortunately, some of the deportees who had been exiled to the labour camps furthest away from the staging area of the new army, were not able to get there, and they were ordered to serve in the Russian Army. If they refused to do so, they were sent to jail. Their fate was sealed.

The Polish government wanted to get as many Polish children as possible out of the Soviet Union before they all died of starvation or disease. They did not trust the Russians, and true to form, Stalin would put a stop to allowing any Poles to leave the Soviet Union several months after the amnesty was signed.

News of the amnesty reached the Prawoslaws' settlement in September. The Poles were now permitted to leave, but they had no idea where they would go or how they would get there. They could not return to their homeland, because Poland was embroiled in chaos and war.

Any able-bodied young Polish men aged sixteen or older could join the new army. The women in Lilyana's dwelling wondered whether Aleksander Prawoslaw and Edward Leski were still alive, and if they had left their work at the forest substation to join the army. The lads had not returned to the settlement, and they both were of age to enlist. The older boys in the colony had already departed to join the new Polish Army.

Many women, children and elderly people remained behind as they contemplated what to do. The long Russian winter was about to begin. Endless snow and winds were to beat down on them soon, and the inclement conditions never subsided until late into the following spring. Officials made it clear that the deportees were not to be provided with any food, provisions or transportation; they were on their own to find their way out from the settlement.

Lilyana and Marta watched as some people began to construct primitive rafts from willow branches and logs. They fashioned thinner pieces of logs into crude paddles. Those people planned to guide themselves down the river in search of a village or a town where they hoped to find a train station or other mode of transportation to get out of Russia. They covered themselves in hay to keep warm as they did not have any blankets or proper attire to protect themselves from hypothermia. They shoved off from the riverbank, praying that their rafts would hold up, and that they would reach civilisation before the water had a chance to freeze over in the oncoming winter. Every morning when Lilyana and Marta set out for work at the kolkhoz, they watched as more and more rafts floated past them along the river.

The days moved slowly, but time was quickly running out for leaving. Dimitri had advised Lilyana to stay behind with Larissa at the settlement until he could find a safe way to relocate them. On the night when she'd met with him at the river before news of the amnesty was announced, Dimitri had told her that his father wanted him to go and speak with him in Arkhangelsk. Dimitri had left the following day. It was now late September, and Lilyana had not seen nor heard from him since that night. She and Marta were able to transfer their work assignment over to a brigade of women working in the forest once again, but their wages were so low they could not earn enough rubles to purchase food for all the people living in their dwelling. Those who remained would probably starve or freeze to death. Lilyana prayed for Dimitri to come through with an effective plan to get all of them out before that happened.

Some of those remaining at the settlement had decided to wait until the heavier snows came. They planned to build winter sleighs and walk to the nearest town pulling their meagre possessions behind them. Marching up the hilly terrain would be difficult, but they anticipated gliding down the other side of the slopes in their sleighs, reaching civilisation quickly.

Mrs Dobrowolski and Marta debated what they should do now that they were free. It confused them when Lilyana did not contribute much to their discussions, but Lilyana was secretly waiting to hear what plan Dimitri would come up with. She trusted that he would return soon and let her know what arrangements he had made to safely extricate the people in her living quarters. After a lot of prodding from Marta and her mother, and because her Russian cousin had not yet come forward with any plan, Lilyana told Marta and Mrs Dobrowolski she thought they all should remain at the settlement through the winter months. Conditions would be much more treacherous going out onto the river now or marching across the frozen land in wintertime. Lilyana suggested that she, Marta, and Mrs Dobrowolski should take on whatever work they could get in the forest to bring in as much money as possible for purchasing food through the winter months. Sabina Albinski could remain in their dwelling caring for her daughter, Karina, and for Fryderyk

Cieslak. Larissa could continue attending the village school. In spring, the river current would be strong, and it would pose added dangers if they tried to travel by raft. Lilyana felt they should wait until next summer when the river became more tranquil and the air warmer, then they could leave the settlement in search of civilisation. This plan was similar to the strategy that Marta and her mother had been formulating, so they all agreed to it.

On a snowy morning in mid-October, a young officer arrived at the new worksite in the forest where Lilyana, Marta and Mrs Dobrowolski had started working. Lilyana was told to accompany the official back to the village because one of the NKVD authorities wanted to speak with her at Headquarters. Marta and her mother looked on with worried faces as Lilyana was led away.

Little did Lilyana know, this would be the last time she ever saw Marta and Mrs Dobrowolski.

***

A bright light burned in the office Lilyana was taken to. It reflected off the shaven head of a gaunt deportee who sat in a chair with his back to the door as she entered the room. Dimitri sat across from the man, facing the door. Her Russian cousin always looked so official in his crisp, clean uniform, but today, one of his legs was raised on top of his desk, and she couldn't help but notice that the lace on his boot had come loose and was hanging down, half-untied. He seemed to be chatting freely with the subject sitting across from him. It amused her to think what her prim and proper Uncle Viktor would think to see his son being so casual and informal while on duty. Dimitri thanked the accompanying officer for bringing Lilyana to his office and told him to close the door on his way out. She stood in the room feeling rather lost.

"Ah yes... here she is," Dimitri said to the bald deportee.

Dimitri quickly got up from his desk and walked around to the other side. Patting the bald man on the shoulder, he told him to turn around.

"I have been getting acquainted with our young cousin here," he said. "Aren't you going to welcome him back?"

"Alek!" Lilyana squealed. "You have returned! How good it is to see you are still alive!"

She rushed forward and gave Aleksander a huge hug, which he returned in grand fashion.

Dimitri returned to his chair with a broad smirk spreading across his face. "My father had me pick him up on my way back to the settlement," he explained. "News of the amnesty has not yet reached the substation, so we knew I would find him still working in the forest."

Lilyana could see that Aleksander's time spent at the forest station had taken a toll on him. The lad appeared even thinner than she remembered him being when he was sent away several months ago. His face was hollow, and his head was totally scabbed over with insect bites and open sores. His tattered shirt revealed arms of skin and bone. Huge, dark circles framed his sunken eyes, and wrinkles around his mouth and neck made him look much older than his sixteen years.

"It is good to be back," Aleksander said. Then, giving Lilyana's arm a gentle squeeze, he added, "Who knew we had a cousin in Russia? What kind of surprise is this?"

Lilyana looked over to Dimitri, who nodded and acknowledged that he had told the lad the story about his mother, Anna… their long-lost aunt.

"… and we are all sworn to secrecy on this!" Dimitri added, giving both of his Polish cousins a stern look. "Even though the amnesty has freed the Polish people in the Soviet Union, we must be careful what we say, and not let anyone else discover our kinship. It could still put all of us in jeopardy!"

"He speaks Polish with a foreign accent!" Aleksander joked.

"Ah!" Dimitri shouted, waving his hands in the air at Aleksander. "This boy can be a handful! How many times did they put you in the punishment hole... yet you still berate Russian authority! It is a good thing we are cousins, or else I would have to—"

"Have to what?" Aleksander butted in as he made a playful jab at Dimitri.

It was obvious that Lilyana's two cousins, the Russian and the Pole, had bonded during their travel back to the settlement from the substation where Aleksander had been working. She watched in amusement as the two of them light-heartedly poked fun and nudged each other.

Then it was time to get serious. Dimitri had an important matter to discuss with his cousins. He quickly resumed a solemn tone and told Aleksander and Lilyana to sit down.

"Is there anything of value you have in your possession at your living quarters?" he asked Lilyana.

When she told him she had nothing except for a special book that her mother, Olisia, had left her, Dimitri said he would see that the book was brought to his office.

Lilyana looked puzzled, and Dimitri went on to say, "I am having Larissa brought here this afternoon. An officer will be sent to fetch her from school, and I will also instruct him to pick up your mother's book from your dwelling."

He was about to say more when Lilyana interrupted him. "Larissa will be petrified when an officer comes for her. Why must she be brought here... and why do you want my mother's book to be delivered here? The other women in my living quarters will wonder what is going on when an officer comes to search through my things."

"Please, Lilyana... let me explain. You will understand when I have told you all that I need to say."

"But I should be there for Larissa," Lilyana insisted. "She has been through so much in her short lifetime, and she is very frail. Ever since Aunt Janina died, I have taken over mothering her. She..."

Lilyana's voice trailed off immediately when she noticed Aleksander's sudden shocked reaction to the mention of his mother's passing. Only then did she realise that he must not have been told about Janina's demise. She turned to him with a sad, sympathetic look.

"I am so sorry about your mother, Alek," she said, gently touching his arm. "I really tried hard to keep her going, but it just seemed like she gave up living. There was nothing anyone could have done for her in the end. Her spirit died long before her body gave out. I am so, so sorry!"

Aleksander looked down at the floor, sadly shaking his head. "It is not your fault, Lily," he replied. "I knew when I left for the forest substation, I might not see her again. She was dead inside even then. She was no longer the mother I remembered. I should thank you for all you did for her, and for taking care of my little sister after my mother passed."

Tears brimmed at the edge of Lilyana's eyes, and she gave Aleksander an affectionate hug.

"Larissa will be so happy to see you. She has been asking if you would be coming back to the settlement. It will do her a world of good to see you are still among the living."

Dimitri had wandered over to the window while his Polish cousins talked privately between themselves. He stood there with his hands firmly placed behind his back, peering out at the world beyond the windowpane. Lilyana turned to look at him, and she could not help noticing how much he resembled his father, Viktor, in that official pose. He was a nice-looking young man, and if Viktor had looked anything like him in his younger years, Lilyana could understand why Anna had been so taken by the Russian officer years ago.

"I am sorry I interrupted you, Dimitri. What is it that you wanted to say?"

Her Russian cousin returned to his desk and leaned over to tie up his undone boot lace.

"My father has contacted the Polish Consulate in Arkhangelsk on your behalf," he began. "At his request, the Consulate got in touch with an official at the Polish

Army Headquarters in London. Your father's and my mother's cousin, Tadeusz Prawoslaw, has been located. The Consulate's office in Britain has been in touch with him. Tadeusz was delighted to know that some of you remain alive. He had feared that all the Prawoslaws were killed at the start of the war when he lost contact with your father, Lilyana."

She and Aleksander said nothing as they tried to digest this news. Following a brief pause, Dimitri went on to say, "Through the British military attaché in Moscow, Tadeusz has telegraphed some funds to you. The money is to be used for purchasing provisions, and to buy the two of you and Larissa safe passage out of Russia. The window of opportunity is small. The war is encroaching upon us, and we must act quickly before winter sets in."

While his cousins remained silent, Dimitri took a cigarette from his top pocket and lit it. He offered a putrid Russian cigarette to Aleksander and Lilyana, and when they declined, he continued speaking where he had left off. "We have to be careful that the Soviet authorities do not discover these details, or they may prevent you from leaving Russia. Tadeusz knows nothing about my mother's life in Russia, nor about my father and me. He must never know that it was my father who took this action on your behalf. It will bring my father and me into questioning by the Soviets. They will view us as sympathisers toward subversive anti-Communist foreigners. I hope you both understand how sensitive this matter is for all of us."

Lilyana and Aleksander were dumbfounded by Dimitri's news. It was a lot of information to take in all at once, and it left a lot of unanswered questions in Lilyana's mind.

"England is very far away," she said. "How can we get there safely now, with this war going on? And we do not know the language or the customs there. We have never even met my father's cousin, Tadeusz. What if he is not a nice man? Maybe he just wants us to come to be servants for him and his family. So many uncertainties! This is all very sudden and worrying. Poor Larissa! She has had so much turmoil and sadness in her young life. Can she withstand a treacherous journey to a faraway land, and will she be able to adjust to life in another country?"

Dimitri squashed the stubby end of his cigarette into the ashtray that sat on the corner of his desk. He folded his arms and looked Lilyana square in the eye. He needed to reassure her as best he could, because there was no other alternative to get his Polish cousins safely out of the Soviet Union.

"If you do not follow through with the arrangements my father has made for you, I doubt any of you will survive here much longer. It is true that Britain is also at war with Germany, but with my father's help, you will be able to reach England safely. He has a solid plan to put in action. I will tell you more about that later. In Viktor Yatskaya's position as a senior officer with the Red Army, he is privy to certain information and perks. Our intelligence officers are sharing war details coming out of Britain. While the Soviet Union struggles with a shortage of supplies, a lack of transportation, inclement weather conditions, starvation and illness, circumstances in the United Kingdom are better. The war effort is much more organised there, and the British Red Cross provides food and healthcare for those in need. The Red Cross will help you reach Uncle Tadeusz. You will be much better off there than you will be anywhere in the Soviet Union… and as for Larissa, she is still a child. She will learn the language and adjust to life in England faster than you or Aleksander will!"

Dimitri's last statement was intended to encourage Lilyana, but neither she nor Aleksander felt inspired.

"You make a very good case," Aleksander said. "Nevertheless, I intend to go south and enlist with the new Polish Army like so many of my friends will undoubtedly do."

"A very noble gesture," Dimitri remarked. "I will also be heading to the front in a few weeks' time… but first I must help to get all of you safely on your way to Tadeusz in Great Britain."

Aleksander insisted that it was his wish to fight for freedom. He was determined to find the assembly area for the Polish Army and fight alongside his fellow Poles.

Dimitri could see it might be difficult to sway Aleksander into wanting to leave Russia, so he explained that the lad would be able to fight with the Polish Army if he went to Britain. His health would be restored in England, and then he would be able to join the Polish Armed Forces that were established in London.

Aleksander was exhilarated by this revelation. He took on a whole new attitude once he was made aware of this fact.

"Besides," Dimitri continued, "it will be best for you to accompany Lilyana and Larissa on this journey to the United Kingdom. A male presence may help to keep them safe. If you follow through with my father's plan, all of you will probably find yourselves safely in Britain by this time next month."

Aleksander was feeling important now, but Lilyana still had a few qualms. She wondered what the other women in her living quarters would think when she and Larissa suddenly disappeared. They would be worried to think that the Soviets still had control over the deportees' comings and goings. The Poles were supposed to be free to make their own choices with the amnesty now in place. Marta would be especially distraught, thinking that something terrible may have happened to Lilyana and Larissa.

Lilyana stared blankly at the huge framed portrait of Joseph Stalin positioned on the wall behind Dimitri's desk as she mulled over her thoughts.

"It is a good thing you didn't rush ahead and try to leave in one of those crude rafts that some of the Poles were building," Dimitri said. "I was afraid you and your friend Marta might already be gone by the time I got back from Arkhangelsk. Some of those who left the settlement that way have met with accidents in the river current, and many died of exposure. Their bodies are washing up on the shoreline further downstream."

This was the first that Lilyana had heard about deportees dying on the river. She thought about all those she knew who had taken to the river in rafts they'd quickly scraped together in their rush to leave before winter arrived. However, she had no time to lament the loss of those unfortunate souls; Aleksander and Dimitri started to discuss how the Yatskayas proposed to get the Prawoslaws safely to England. She listened carefully to what was being said.

"I will have both of you remain in a holding cell downstairs for a few hours," Dimitri said. "The guards will find nothing suspicious when I send you there. Don't worry; no punishment will be dealt to either of you. I will personally bring Larissa there when she arrives at Headquarters. When things quiet down at night, and all the labourers have returned to their living quarters for sleep, I will escort the three of you outside to a waiting lorry. There will be fewer people milling about and less chance of anyone noticing us leaving then. If any officials question why I am transporting you, I will say that I have been given orders to deliver you to the jail in Arkhangelsk. My father has prepared phony documents for me to present to the authorities."

Lilyana cringed when Dimitri mentioned the jail in Arkhangelsk. It brought back frightening and dreadful memories of her brief time spent there. She did not want to ever see that building again!

Having observed Lilyana's adverse reaction, Dimitri quickly added, "Don't worry, Lilyana. My father and I are not going to put you in jail. We are to meet with your Uncle Viktor there to move forward with our plan."

Dimitri pulled out a piece of paper that was secretly adhered to the underside of his desk drawer. He quickly folded it and put it into the upper pocket of his uniform. Patting his chest where the paper was, he advised Lilyana and Aleksander that the forged orders would get them safely past Headquarter gates and out onto the road in the army transport.

"Once we arrive in Arkhangelsk, we will meet with my father, and he will explain the rest of the plan. Some smaller details are still being worked out."

"What about the others in my living quarters?" Lilyana asked. "They will wonder what has happened to Larissa and me. When I do not return, Marta will be particularly worried. I cannot leave without first saying goodbye to them and letting them know we are alright."

Before Lilyana had a chance to express more of her concerns, Dimitri put his hand in the air to stop her. "My father explicitly told me to ensure that once you have been brought here to my office, you, Aleksander and Larissa are not to have contact with any other individuals in the colony. We cannot afford to let anyone know about my father's arrangements regarding this plan. He has been exceptionally careful to cover our tracks. If the three of you are to leave the Soviet Union safely, the details of your departure *must* be kept secret. The future for all of us would be in peril if the facts were to reach the wrong ears. I cannot emphasise this enough! Do you understand, Lilyana?"

"Yes… I suppose you are right," Lilyana replied, looking downcast. "Nevertheless, Marta will suspect something odd has happened. She knows Larissa and I have done nothing to warrant punishment, and she will be suspicious when we suddenly disappear after being summoned to Headquarters without any goodbyes or words of explanation."

"It is for that reason that I cannot allow you to return to your dwelling. It is also why I had you removed from your work brigade without any advanced warning, and why I am having Larissa pulled from school this afternoon. The others in your living quarters would demand answers if you were to pack up your belongings and announce that you are leaving… and I know you well enough to predict that you are not capable of lying to them, Lily. They would see right through you if you were to attempt deceiving them in any way. They would insist on hearing the truth, and because you are an honest person, you might divulge our secret plan to them."

Lilyana knew her Russian cousin was right. The others in her dwelling would demand to know why she and Larissa had suddenly changed their minds about staying until next summer. They would beg her and Larissa to remain at the settlement. Without being able to provide any explanation for the unexpected change in plans, Lilyana would find herself in an awkward position. She could not divulge the truth to them, because the details of Uncle Viktor's plan had to remain securely under wraps to go forward without any negative repercussions.

It saddened her, knowing that she and Larissa were leaving without a proper farewell for the people who had become family to them during the past eighteen months. They had endured so much heartache and hardship together. What affected one affected them all. They had shared a special bond through life's most difficult times. The others would mourn the loss when she and Larissa were gone.

Worse yet, conditions would become even harder for those left behind. Lilyana would no longer be there to add her wages to the dwelling's coffers, and the long, difficult winter months lay ahead. She felt a piercing thread of guilt. She prayed that those remaining in her living quarters would be able to survive through the coming winter and forgive her unforeseen departure.

Lilyana grieved the loss of her dear friend Marta most of all. The two of them had become like sisters. Lilyana felt that Marta was the best friend she had ever known. Back in Poland, Lilyana's mother had made her associate with the aristocratic girls. The ones she'd befriended were not always nice. They valued their possessions more than anything, and they prided themselves on their physical appearance. At times they were condescending and rude, and they were so self-absorbed. Marta on the other hand, although well brought up and educated, was unpolished, genuine and kind. She cared about her family and her friends, and instinctively knew how to encourage others to find joy in the most despicable of circumstances. Polite and thoughtful, Marta would never offend anyone. Her bubbly spirit and generous heart were bigger than anything Lilyana had believed possible, given their dire circumstances in Russia.

Tears began to trickle down Lilyana's sunken cheeks. She was deeply upset. Not knowing how to console her, Dimitri shifted awkwardly in his chair.

"I am truly sorry, Lilyana," he muttered. "But this is how it must be!"

Aleksander leaned over and gave his cousin a hug. "Edward and my other friends at the forest substation will be wondering what has happened to me, too," he said. "Dimitri came and whisked me away so quickly I don't think they even noticed me leaving the forest... but I know they will want to join the new Polish Army when news of the amnesty reaches them. I hope they survive now that the Nazis are at war with Russia."

Lilyana suddenly felt very selfish. She had not even asked Aleksander if Edward Leski was still alive.

Dimitri reached into his pocket and pulled out another cigarette. He started puffing on it nervously.

"The three of you will have to remain in the back of the transport like prisoners until we reach Arkhangelsk," he said.

This was the first time Lilyana had ever noticed Dimitri appearing less than confident. His uneasiness reinforced how very delicate it was for him and Uncle Viktor to be helping Aleksander, Larissa and her get out of Russia. While the rest of the Soviet Union deemed them to be nothing more than three worthless Polish deportees, her Russian cousin and uncle were putting their own careers and lives on the line for them. Lilyana intended to do everything that Dimitri and his father told her to do for their plan to go smoothly and, for their protection, she intended to encourage Aleksander and Larissa to do the same.

***

It was a cold and windy night as the lorry bumped along the rough road leading toward Arkhangelsk. Snow was already beginning to fly, and their Russian cousin wanted to move quickly before it piled up into deep drifts along the roadway. They passed by many open fields where snow blew, accumulating into tall mounds. Lilyana, Aleksander and Larissa were each given a government-issued blanket to wrap around themselves to help stave off the cold in the back of the transport. Dimitri also fitted them with government-issued boots to cover their feet. They managed to slip away from the settlement in the early morning hours without anyone stopping to question them.

Little Larissa had not spoken many words since an officer had brought her to Headquarters the afternoon before. As Lilyana had suspected, her nerves had been shattered when an officer fetched her from the village school. She had soiled herself, and now she lay pale and weak against Lilyana's side, wrapped in her blanket. It was obvious she was not feeling well. Aleksander was not surprised that his younger sister had failed to recognise him when she'd arrived where he and Lilyana were being held. Illness, starvation and hard labour had altered the way all of them appeared.

Lilyana clutched tightly to the book her mother had left her. It was all that remained of her family's former life in Poland. Whenever she held onto the book, she felt her mother's presence was close by. She would treasure it for the rest of her life. She wondered what the others in her living quarters had thought when the NKVD officer came and feigned a routine search of the dwelling in order to confiscate the book.

Somehow, Aleksander had managed to hang onto a few scant possessions of his own. A dirty stain was evident on the small sack he carried with him... remnants of the soil he had scooped up from his family's farm and into a handkerchief when the Russians came to take them away all those months ago.

"I have been forced to march through pouring rain and blizzard snows so many times in this inhospitable land," he said. "Every time the sack was soaked through, more of the soil was flushed away. Now all that remains from my Poland farm is a muddy stain."

Lilyana smiled and told Aleksander the stain would remain as a permanent reminder of the Prawoslaws' proud heritage back in Poland.

Aleksander looked rather serious and said, "I will always remember that, Lilyana. It was the wonderful memories of times spent with my family on the farm that helped me get through my darkest hours here in Russia. Without those positive images to reinforce good things in my mind, I never would have been able to overcome the harsh realities, nor had hope for finding happiness again. Reminiscing about my family's life in Poland is all that kept me sane during those long, cold, dark hours spent inside the punishment hole. If I did not have those memories to cling to, I surely would have gone mad."

Lilyana leaned over and hugged her brave, young cousin.

"I am so happy that you remained strong," she said. "We only have each other now, and together we will move on. We will always have memories of our happy days in Poland to carry us forward into another place. As difficult as it will be, we must try to bury the sadness and suffering we have experienced here. We must not allow our trauma to define our future lives. We are most fortunate to have been given this opportunity to secure a better life elsewhere, while so many other Poles are left behind to fend for themselves. Many will never leave the Soviet Union. We must honour this gift that our long-lost Aunt Anna has given us by way of the Yatskayas, and move on with a positive attitude, creating good lives for ourselves in Britain. Maybe one day we will be able to thank our Russian uncle and cousin properly for all they are doing for us, when peace returns to this fractured world."

Dimitri had been listening to his Polish cousins' conversation in the back of the lorry as he drove on toward Arkhangelsk. Lilyana was taken aback when she learned that he had heard them above the din of the motor. She became aware he'd been eavesdropping when Dimitri quoted a Bible passage:

"But they that wait upon the Lord shall renew their strength; they shall mount up with wings as eagles; they shall run, and not grow weary; and they shall walk, and not faint."

How odd it was to hear a Communist quoting a biblical passage. It occurred to Lilyana that even though her Russian cousin may have been raised as an atheistic Communist, his mother had been a Polish Orthodox Christian. Obviously, Anna had acquainted Dimitri with the Bible. What a strong woman she must have been… teaching her son about God's word in the middle of a strict Communist environment. On some levels, Lilyana felt connected to the aunt she had never known. She wished she had been given the opportunity to meet Anna.

***

The two-day journey into Arkhangelsk was relatively uneventful. A few times, the lorry had been slowed by drifts of snow that blocked the road. With nobody in sight for miles around, Dimitri had Aleksander and Lilyana climb down from the vehicle to help him open up a passageway wide enough for the lorry to pass through.

Dimitri had often stopped the vehicle to chat with other NKVD officers who were traveling in the opposite direction. Larissa would sob quietly in the back of the lorry, shaking with fear, even though Lilyana tried to assure her that Dimitri would not let anything bad happen to her. She clung tightly to Lilyana as Dimitri chatted with the officials, plying them with cigarettes and idle chat. Much to their relief, the vehicle was never searched.

It was very apparent how traumatised Larissa had become as a result of their ordeal in Russia. Lilyana knew she would have to help her young cousin overcome the deep scars that would haunt the child for years to come. Her concerns regarding Larissa increased when the little girl refused to eat any of the bread Dimitri passed back to them in the lorry, and that she had trouble swallowing the water Lilyana encouraged her to sip. Even though it remained frigidly cold in the back of the vehicle, Larissa's head was warm to the touch. She was spiking a fever.

Closer to the city of Arkhangelsk, the transport merged onto a better-maintained road, and signs of civilisation appeared. Before long, Dimitri guided the lorry toward a darkened tunnel that seemed to slice through the middle of a broad hill. Halfway through the tunnel, Dimitri pulled the lorry over to the side of the road and shut the engine off. He opened the small window separating the cab from the back of the vehicle and poked his head through.

"We must wait here in the darkness for my father to come," he said. "My father decided it would not be wise to go to his office at the prison, because the three of you would draw a lot of attention. He instructed me to meet with him here in the tunnel instead, away from prying eyes and ears. You must remain in the back of the lorry, and if any officials stop to talk to me here in the tunnel, all of you will have to hide beneath the tarp that Aleksander is resting on. Stay very still and quiet. I will do my best to prevent any search of the vehicle."

"You are good at doing that!" Aleksander sniped.

"… and that is a fortunate thing for all of you!" Dimitri responded.

"They must teach diversionary tactics and the art of deception in Russian Army School," Aleksander mused.

"Ack!" Dimitri scoffed as he slammed the cab window shut.

They all sat quietly in pitch blackness inside the tunnel. The outline of Dimitri's face became visible in the subtle light he created each time he lit up a cigarette and reclined back in the driver's seat. He crossed his arms and seemed to assume a more relaxed position as he waited for Uncle

Viktor to appear. Whenever any lights were detected in the distance as other vehicles approached, Dimitri would snuff out his cigarette, trying to avoid drawing attention to the transport sitting idle in the tunnel.

He was no longer the carefree, jovial young man Lilyana remembered him being when she and Dimitri had returned to the settlement from the jail in Arkhangelsk several months earlier. The secret mission to get his Polish cousins safely on their way to England was a very serious matter.

She must have drifted off for a while, because the next thing Lilyana knew, a military vehicle was pulling up behind the lorry. Its lights momentarily filled the inside of the transport until they were switched off. Uncle Viktor quickly shut down his vehicle's engine and climbed out into the darkness. He surreptitiously slipped into the passenger's seat next to Dimitri.

Uncle Viktor and Dimitri began a quick conversation in Russian. Lilyana could only understand a few words of what they were saying. She was able to grasp that they were discussing something about a house somewhere, and she heard something mentioned about the water. Uncle Viktor accepted a cigarette from his son. Lilyana could see the two of them sitting inside the cab together as the glowing ends of their lit cigarettes cast a vague glow around them.

Dimitri took a large envelope from his father. Uncle Viktor warned him to guard it with his life, stressing the importance of whatever the contents were.

"Is that our Uncle Viktor?" Aleksander whispered as he poked Lilyana's side. "Kind of looks like an older version of Dimitri, doesn't he?"

"Yes," Lilyana whispered back. "They look a lot alike, and some of their mannerisms are the same too. I met Uncle Viktor when I was taken to prison last summer. Conditions were abominable, and violent women ruled that wretched place. It was Dimitri and our uncle who saved me from certain death in the prison!"

"Dimitri told me about that on our way back to the settlement," Aleksander said quietly. "I can't imagine you in a place like that, Lilyana! I have heard from others how horrific conditions are in Russian prisons."

"It was the most vile thing I have ever experienced!" Lilyana moaned.

Just then, Dimitri pulled open the small window of the cab, and Uncle Viktor poked his head into the back of the transport. Cigarette smoke quickly wafted in, filling their space as Dimitri translated into Polish what his father was saying to them in Russian.

"It is difficult to see you in the darkness. I am happy that you remain alive. Although we will never be able to get to know each other, my wife, Anna, would be pleased to know that a few of her Polish relatives will make it out of Russia. On her behalf, I wish all three of you the best of luck in reaching England safely. I hope the future holds better things for you."

He stopped talking for a moment, and then with a forlorn sigh, Uncle Viktor added, "Dimitri tells me that Larissa is unwell. I will send a doctor to see to her tomorrow. Dimitri will pass along the rest of the details to you. I must leave before anyone comes by and questions what I am doing here. Be careful and do as my son and I instruct you to do. Our plan will ensure that all of you reach England very soon."

When Uncle Viktor turned back toward Dimitri in the cab of the vehicle, Lilyana made a sudden attempt to thank him. She intended to show him her gratitude for everything he had done for Aleksander, Larissa and her, and to say she would always remember the kindness he had shown them.

As she spoke her words in broken Russian, Dimitri stifled an amused chuckle.

Uncle Viktor looked at Dimitri with a serious expression on his face.

Later, Lilyana would ask Dimitri about the blunder she had made in her attempt to speak Russian to his father. He would tell her that her pronunciation of some words had been terrible, and what she'd said could be misconstrued to mean she was thanking her uncle for services rendered, while she would always love him. When she heard that, Lilyana's cheeks turned red with embarrassment, and Dimitri and Aleksander had a good laugh.

A brief discussion was had between Dimitri and Viktor when her uncle exited the lorry. Lilyana overheard them mentioning Leningrad. Judging by his reaction to his father's words, whatever Uncle Viktor said evidently upset Dimitri. Uncle Viktor quickly stepped down from the transport and disappeared into the darkness of the tunnel. Following his father's exit, Dimitri seemed to be on edge.

Without saying a word, Dimitri waited until the lights on his father's vehicle faded into the distance. Then he started up the lorry and continued driving through the underpass. When they came out the other side, it was difficult to determine what time of day it was. The sun and moon could play tricks for hours on end.

A short distance later, Dimitri pulled over and asked Aleksander to hand the last huge can of diesel fuel down to him from the back of the lorry. They had already stopped several times along their journey to refuel. Aleksander told Lilyana he hoped they were nearing their destination, because it seemed like the last fuel can was almost empty.

"We have enough fuel to get to where we are going!" Dimitri snapped.

Lilyana wondered what Uncle Viktor had told Dimitri to cause him to become so irate. This was so out-of-character for her Russian cousin.

They drove for some distance more before they finally arrived at the place where Uncle Viktor had instructed Dimitri to go. When she poked her head out of the back of the covered transport, Lilyana was surprised to see a wooden chalet prominent against a beautiful background of snow-covered trees. Dimitri told them to remain quiet and wait inside the vehicle until he came back; he had a few details to take care of. The air was even more frigid than it was when they'd left the settlement two days earlier. Shivering beneath her government-issued blanket, Larissa coughed and wheezed, moaning in pain with each coughing episode.

Lilyana and Aleksander looked at each other with worried expressions.

"She is very weak," Lilyana said. "I hope she has not contracted pneumonia. Many of the school children at the colony had been falling ill with it."

"She is tough," Aleksander insisted. "She survived the typhus outbreak when so many others did not. She will recover from whatever ails her now! Uncle Viktor told us he will send a doctor to see to her. No need to worry!"

Lilyana wondered whether Aleksander was trying to convince himself, or her, of his optimistic prognosis for Larissa. Recollections of how little Helena Dobrowolski had died with pneumonia in their living quarters last winter were painfully fresh in Lilyana's mind. Without the proper medications, nutrition and decent living conditions, there was nothing anybody could do to save people at the settlement who suffered a slow and painful death from pneumonia. As Marta used to say, death is never a smooth ride into eternity in Russia. Lilyana could only pray that Larissa would hang on, and that the doctor would come to see her as Uncle Viktor had promised.

As he leaned over the top of the transport's tailgate to look outside, Aleksander wondered, "Where are we now? Is Dimitri planning for us to spend the night here, or is he just picking up more supplies? How does he know about this place? Who does that chalet belong to? What a grand-looking place!"

"It appears we are far away from any other houses or roads. Perhaps Dimitri will let us rest here before we continue our journey," Lilyana hoped out loud.

Aleksander pondered, "I wonder if there is any food inside the chalet?"

"Don't get too far ahead of yourself, Alek!" Lilyana warned. "We have to wait here quietly like Dimitri told us to do, and then he will tell us what is to happen next."

***

Lilyana, Aleksander and Larissa waited in the lorry for a long time before Dimitri came back. Looking more relaxed, he had changed out of his uniform into some ragged old work clothes. He told them they could climb down from the vehicle, as they were to spend a day or two at the chalet… much to their delight.

He escorted them around the back of the chalet to a small sauna shed. A fire was blazing outside, and he already had several metal buckets of steaming water lined up along the inside of the sauna room walls. He told them they needed to go inside one at a time and remove all their clothing. They were to put their clothing outside the sauna room door, and their rags would be burned in the fire pit by the frozen brook. He instructed them to scrub themselves down with the brush and lye soap they would find inside the sauna. Afterwards, they were to rinse themselves very thoroughly with the hot water he had prepared in the buckets. He warned them that the soap would sting terribly because of the numerous open sores on their bodies, but it was a necessary step to rid themselves of all the lice they were carrying before entering the chalet. He warned the two girls that their hair would have to be shaved off once they had scrubbed themselves down, because the lice had eggs and larvae hatching in their lovely, long locks. Aleksander's head had already been shaved. Dimitri said he would need to burn their government-issued blankets also. Undoubtedly, the lice had taken up residence in those. He was to douse himself in the sauna when they were finished; the parasites had probably hitched a ride on him as well.

"How are we supposed to dry off and cover up when we are done? We have no other clothes to put on," Lilyana asked in a worried voice. "And how are we going to manage with Larissa? She is so gravely ill and weak, she can hardly stand up!"

Avoiding the last part of Lilyana's question, Dimitri indicated that his father had left some clothing and boots in the carriage house for them to put on. He would bring the garments and some towels to the sauna and leave them outside the door for them to use. He motioned with his head to where the carriage house was located. Lilyana had not even noticed it.

"Take Larissa inside with you now, Lilyana. Help her do as I have said. Throw all your clothing outside, and I will have Aleksander burn it in the fire. When you use up the hot water in the buckets, toss those outside too, and I will fetch more water to put on the fire for Aleksander and me. I am going to the carriage house to get the clothing for you now."

Lilyana's heart broke as she scrubbed Larissa with the harsh soap and brush. The child had to lie down on the wooden bench inside the sauna room because she was too weak to sit or stand. Too indisposed to even scream or cry, she could only utter feeble, hoarse whimpers as the soap seared into her tender skin. Blood and pus oozed from her open wounds as Lilyana carefully scrubbed. The child coughed and heaved in painful spasms, crying for her mother. Tears ran down Lilyana's cheeks. She hated seeing how much Larissa was suffering. She prayed her little cousin would survive the ordeal.

Once Lilyana had endured the painful ritual of purging herself of parasites, she found the pile of fresh, clean clothing that Dimitri had left outside by the door of the sauna house. She bundled Larissa in a loose cotton dress with a warm winter coat over top. The boots proved much too large for the child, but they would have to do for now. She found a pretty peasant dress to wear herself, and there was a bulky winter cardigan that she put over it.

Scrubbed down, dried off and dressed, Lilyana came out of the sauna feeling cleaner than she had in her entire life.

Aleksander and Dimitri were much quicker when they took their turns scrubbing down inside the sauna, and both emerged wearing plain trousers and heavy pullovers. Dimitri apologetically cut off all Lilyana's long hair and threw it into the fire. Then Aleksander and Lilyana helped prop up Larissa so Dimitri could do the same to her. Dimitri gave both girls a kerchief to wrap around their bald heads, and then he stood back to look at the results.

"Not bad for scrawny Polish girls!" he teased. "You could fill out the clothes a little more, Lilyana, but this will have to do for now."

Lilyana said nothing in return. She felt awkward standing there, with her emaciated form, bloodshot eyes and all the scabs and oozing sores covering her body. Now with her head shaven as well, she knew she must look a sorry sight.

Larissa had to be carried into the chalet by Aleksander. Dimitri told him to put her on the chesterfield by the open hearth as he quickly set about building a roaring fire to warm the dwelling. He fetched some blankets, and Lilyana made a cosy bed for her little cousin where she lay.

Uncle Viktor had instructed Dimitri to bring his Polish cousins to the Yatskayas' vacation house located along the Northern Dvina River in the northern outskirts of Arkhangelsk. It was a luxurious cottage by Russian standards, in a picturesque spot with a beautiful view stretching beyond the trees, hills and the stream. Dimitri had spent a lot of time there when he was a child and he had many fond memories of childhood days spent there.

Anna's presence was felt in her magnificent artwork, which was displayed throughout the chalet. Numerous oil paintings of majestic landscapes filled the walls in every room. Lilyana compared her aunt's paintings to those she had seen hanging at the art gallery in Warsaw when her father took her there as a little girl.

"How beautiful!" she whispered.

She sensed how special her Aunt Anna had been. In some of the paintings, there were several small children playing together. One painting portrayed a little dark-haired boy and three blonde girls floating bits of bark and tiny twigs down a babbling brook. In another, the little boy was flying a kite while the girls fawned over a baby in a pram nearby. Then there was another, in which Lilyana immediately identified her Uncle Viktor sitting outside on a wooden log. It must have been painted many years before, because her uncle looked much younger. The small boy who appeared in a few other paintings was leaning into her uncle in that depiction, and Uncle's arm was wrapped around the youngster.

Dimitri when he was a little boy, Lilyana realised … but who were the other children that Anna had included in many of her paintings?

Dimitri explained that the chalet was shared by his father and his father's older brother's family as a year-round retreat. The other children in the paintings were his cousins, Viktor's brother's children. They had spent many summers together when Anna was still alive. After his mother passed away, Uncle Viktor did not enjoy coming to the chalet anymore. So much of Anna remained in the place as a reminder of their loss.

Dimitri mentioned that his oldest cousin, Irina, one of the blonde girls in his mother's paintings, was a doctor. She worked in the hospital at Arkhangelsk, and she was the doctor who was to come to see Larissa. His father had contacted Irina and asked her to look in on the child. Irina had been told about Dimitri's three Polish cousins and their circumstances, and Uncle Viktor had sworn her to secrecy.

Lilyana prayed that Doctor Irina Yatskaya would come soon.

***

Early the next morning, Lilyana was awakened to the sound of sleigh bells outside. She had stayed up half the night with Larissa, who was now beginning to have difficulty breathing. She heard a man and woman talking in Russian by the door of the chalet. Looking out the window, she saw a tan-coloured horse standing in the snow. A well-worn sleigh was hitched to the horse beside a large tree in the yard where the driver had left it.

The doctor, Lilyana thought. She quickly tried to straighten her dress and rearrange the kerchief on her newly bald head. As she did so, a pretty blonde woman entered the room, closely followed by Dimitri.

The young lady spoke to Lilyana in broken Polish, saying, "Hello Lilyana. I am Irina. Uncle Viktor has told me about you… and oh, that cardigan looks better on you than it did on me!"

Now Lilyana was self-conscious.

"I am sorry," she replied. "I did not know it was yours."

"I have not worn it in years. Please wear it and stay warm," Irina told her.

"Thank you," Lilyana said shyly.

"Now… to see to the little one," Irina said. "I will examine her, and then I must continue on my way to the hospital… so much sickness everywhere these days!"

Lilyana helped Larissa sit up so the doctor could listen to her heart and lungs. Irina looked in the child's throat and ears, registered her temperature and checked for responses in her muscles. She asked Lilyana many questions relating to Larissa's past health and her current illness. In the end, Lilyana's worst fears were realised. Larissa was seriously ill with pneumonia.

"She should be in the hospital," Irina stated. "Dimitri has informed me that it would be impossible to hospitalise her if you are to follow through with the special arrangements Uncle Viktor has made for all of you to leave Russia. Uncle Viktor has already said that the plan must go ahead as arranged, but the child is gravely ill. I will be frank with you; I do not know whether she will pull through. Her lungs are very congested. She should be admitted to the hospital where her condition can be monitored, and where she can be given oxygen."

Dimitri then asked Irina something in Russian. Lilyana realised he was asking if she could give them some medication to help Larissa recover. Irina shook her head, pointing to the ailing child.

"I can leave you some medicine, and she will need to stay here and rest, but she is so terribly malnourished! If she pulls through, it will be some time before she is well again! Keep her warm by the fire. She needs to have lots of rest, and she needs to be fed a thin soup made from vegetables, as much as she can hold down to build up her strength."

Fighting back her tears, Lilyana sat down on the chesterfield next to Larissa. She hugged the unresponsive child, praying for God to grant Larissa one more miracle.

Before she departed, Irina gave Lilyana instructions on how to care for Larissa. She left the medicine for the child, and she even gave Lilyana a special ointment to help heal the open sores that plagued the three Polish cousins. Then Irina set off in her horse-drawn sleigh, the bells fading away into the distance.

After she was gone, Dimitri handed Lilyana a sack of vegetables that Irina had brought for all of them to share.

Lilyana gasped, "Where did she get them? I have not seen fresh vegetables in such a long time! Now we will be able to make a nice broth for Larissa! Oh… what a blessing Irina has been for all of us!"

Dimitri smiled. "Irina gathered some things from her root cellar before she drove here. She and her husband have a large greenhouse on their property, not too far away. Their cellar is full of summer's bounty."

Lilyana immediately went into the kitchen and began preparing the soup. After Dimitri had stoked the fire in the main room with more wood, he asked Aleksander to join Lilyana and him in the kitchen where she was working. He had some serious matters to discuss with them concerning their journey to Britain.

While Lilyana peeled turnips, carrots, potatoes and onions and chopped a cabbage into chunks to throw into a large pot, Dimitri attempted to reveal details about their forthcoming travels. However, it was apparent that Lilyana was too preoccupied to listen to what he had to say. She was simply overwhelmed by the *luxury* of the vegetables. Once the soup started to boil and the aroma began penetrating the room, that was all Lilyana and Aleksander could talk about. Seeing how distracted his starving cousins were by the pot of thin soup, Dimitri decided to wait until after they had eaten. Maybe then they would be more receptive to the important details he needed to tell them.

***

"This is the best thing I have ever tasted!" Aleksander sputtered as he swallowed down his second bowl of vegetable soup.

Lilyana expressed her hope that the medicine Doctor Irina had left for Larissa would help the child breathe easier so she could take in some of the soup she so desperately needed.

"You worry too much," Aleksander snorted. "I told you before, Larissa is tough. She will get through this illness like she did all the other sicknesses here in Russia."

"I wish I could be as confident as you are," Lilyana said.

She looked over at Dimitri, who was now indulging in his second bowlful of the soup. She could see he did not share Aleksander's optimism.

Attempting to change the subject, Dimitri began telling his cousins more details about their exit plan from Northern Russia. He said his father had seen to it that the necessary passports, travel papers and other documents required for travelling were prepared, and he had secured the funds that Tadeusz Prawoslaw forwarded for them. Those were the items contained in the envelope Uncle Viktor had passed on to Dimitri in the lorry the previous afternoon. Some of the rubles had been used to pay Uncle Viktor's associates to forge the official papers, but a large portion remained. The three Poles were to be transported to the port at the estuary of the Northern Dvina River. Dimitri explained that because the Soviet Union was in desperate need of supplies, Russia's allies were coming to their aid now that Germany was opposing them. Arctic convoys were starting to sail from the United Kingdom, Iceland and North America to the Northern Russian ports at Murmansk and Arkhangelsk. These were oceangoing convoys of merchant ships escorted by Allied navy ships and military aircraft. Convoys were to cross simultaneously back and forth every month. The merchant ships were to deliver necessary supplies to the Soviet Union. Dimitri explained that it had something to do with an international plan known as the Lend-Lease programme. Uncle Viktor would call Dimitri on the telephone at the chalet to advise him when the sailing date from Arkhangelsk to the United Kingdom was confirmed. It was expected within the next few days.

"We are to sail across the Arctic Ocean to reach England?" Aleksander asked.

"You will leave the Russian estuary and enter into the White Sea, travel into the North Sea and on to the United Kingdom," Dimitri replied. "Let's hope Larissa is well enough by the time my father calls to tell us when all of you must be moved to the port for transport in the convoy."

Aleksander wondered how safe it would be crossing the northern waters at this time of the year with winter setting in and a war going on. He questioned Dimitri about the convoy that was to take them to Great Britain. Was it wise to be crossing the frozen waters in November, and wouldn't the Nazis be trying to destroy ships involved in assisting the Soviet Union with the war effort now that Russia was fighting on the side of the Allies?

Dimitri attempted to skirt around Aleksander's concerns by giving him simplistic answers devoid of extensive details and explanations. However, Aleksander pressed him for specific facts, and Dimitri could no longer avoid telling him and Lilyana the truth. He admitted there were many dangers that would threaten the Arctic convoy. The ships had to pass by Norway for a great distance, and Norway was now occupied by the Nazis. This left the convoy open to attacks by German U-boats, surface vessels and German aircraft. However, Dimitri tried to reassure his cousins that the merchant ships were closely guarded by air support and a large escort of ocean minesweepers, destroyers, anti-submarine trawlers, fleet oilers and freighters of the British Royal Navy, the Royal Canadian Navy, and the US Navy. He hastened to ease their concerns by advising them that a few Arctic convoys had already successfully run the gauntlet and returned safely to the United Kingdom's naval base in Scotland.

Aleksander seemed cautiously excited about the possibility of being thrust into war activity while crossing the northern waters, but Lilyana was terrified by this revelation. Dimitri tried to convince her that although danger was there, it would be a safe crossing, given the heavy military presence escorting the merchant ships. Seeing how fearful Lilyana truly was, he refrained from telling his Polish cousins about further complications putting the ships and all on board in danger. The merchant convoy was large, and it had a great distance of open sea to traverse. The Germans were aware that convoys were sailing the northern waters bringing vital supplies to the Soviet Union, and they were relentless in their attempts to destroy ships carrying armoured tanks, fighter aircraft, army vehicles, food and other supplies for the Russian war effort. Many merchant ships were torpedoed and sunk by German attacks while crossing in open waters. Some of the ships would founder in heavy seas, and some would ram into each other in heavy fog. Some ships would become top heavy from ice build-up and turn over when ferocious waves washed over their decks and froze. Also, drifting pack ice interfered with the convoy ships' ability to stick together in darkness. To make matters worse, the mingling of cold and warm seas produced strong currents that made it difficult to navigate.

***

That night proved to be a pivotal point for Larissa. The child's temperature spiked even higher, and her breathing became far too shallow. Lilyana sat by Larissa's side all night long, placing rags drenched in ice-cold water around Larissa's head and feet in an attempt to bring the child's fever down as Doctor Irina had instructed her to do. She forced the medicine down Larissa's throat as the girl coughed, sputtered and gagged. Lilyana held the girl's mouth firmly closed for the medicine to be swallowed down. It was a battle between life and death, and Lilyana was determined to save her little cousin.

She knelt beside Larissa and prayed fervently, asking God to spare the life of this sweet child. Too many of her family members' lives had already been taken in this place of suffering and misery. Halfway through the night, Dimitri suddenly appeared, asking Lilyana how the child was doing. He got down on his knees next to Lilyana and prayed alongside her. Without a single misstep, Dimitri prayed all the familiar prayers in unison with Lilyana, and then he petitioned God to bring healing to Larissa. He pulled something out from his shirt pocket and pressed it into Larissa's tiny hand, cupping his large hands around hers. Then he stood up and silently retreated into the night. Shortly afterwards, Larissa's little fingers came unclenched, and a rosary fell to the floor from her hand.

Lilyana picked it up and examined it closely. She realised it must have belonged to Dimitri's mother. Now she was certain that Aunt Anna had ensured her son would become a Christian, despite being raised in a Communist milieu. On one hand, Lilyana felt comforted in that knowledge, but on the other, her heart went out to her Russian cousin who must have felt trapped between two different worlds.

In the early morning hours, Larissa's fever finally broke. The combination of prayer and potent medicine was starting to take effect. By noontime that day, the child was holding down small amounts of vegetable soup when Lilyana mashed the vegetables into the broth. Larissa was breathing a little easier, and it was no longer such a struggle to get the medicine into her. She was still very weak and ill, but Lilyana now believed her little cousin would recover.

Lilyana thanked God for granting Larissa another miracle, and she prayed that the child would be well enough to travel when the time came for them to leave Russia. She also asked God to give all of them safe passage to England. It seemed that she was constantly in prayer for one thing or another through all the hardships they had to endure. God was faithfully answering her pleas.

***

The day before the Polish cousins were to depart for Great Britain, Dimitri and Aleksander went out into the snow and frolicked like a couple of schoolboys. They built snow forts and bombarded each other with crusty snowballs. Then they chased each other around in the snow outside of the chalet until they wore themselves out. Lilyana watched from a large window that overlooked the yard, and she giggled at her cousins' antics. It had been such a long time since any of them had felt so free and alive. However, Lilyana sensed an undertone of melancholy that had been weighing heavily on Dimitri ever since they arrived at the chalet. His demeanour had changed following his conversation with his father in the tunnel.

If not for worrying about the perilous voyage that lay ahead, Lilyana would have been bathed in bliss. She considered pleading her case to stay at the chalet in Northern Russia where she felt happy and safe. The war had not yet reached this area, and there was nobody around for miles. Who would know she and her cousins were there? Nevertheless, she knew that Aleksander, Larissa and she would be much better off in Britain.

The journey to Uncle Tadeusz's home in England would begin the following day. Uncle Viktor telephoned Dimitri and informed him that his three cousins needed to be at the port in the estuary of the Northern Dvina River early the next morning. The Arctic convoy would be fitted and set to sail through the gauntlet of peril across the northern waters of Russia, heading toward its destination in the United Kingdom.

***

Early the next morning, a strange man stood outside the chalet, smoking and talking in Russian with Dimitri. The man was tall and lean, and his dark, bushy hair blended well with the thick moustache lining his upper lip. Upon closer observation, Lilyana saw he wore a Russian Navy uniform. His jacket was decorated with several medals glorifying a long, successful naval career, and service in the Great War. He was obviously a man of prominent stature. His powerful presence commanded the respect afforded a senior ranking officer.

Curiosity got the better of Aleksander.

"Why is that officer here, and why is he in full dress uniform?" he queried as he opened the door to step outside.

Lilyana watched through the opened doorway as Dimitri introduced Aleksander to the imposing stranger. The man grasped the boy's hand and greeted him in a formal manner.

Lilyana helped Larissa pull on a furry coat and hat that Dimitri had taken out from a closet in the chalet. Their Russian cousin had presented each of them with their travel clothes earlier that morning. He had provided Aleksander with a pair of woollen trousers and a flannel shirt from his own personal wardrobe and topped it off with a heavy winter overcoat, hat, gloves and boots. Larissa was given a woollen dress Dimitri said was one that Irina's daughter had outgrown, in addition to her winter coat and hat and some smaller winter boots. Dimitri explained that his father's brother's family had spent a lot of time at the chalet prior to the war, so clothing and other things were always left in closets and drawers, which they could use.

A small closet was filled with the clothing her Aunt Anna used to wear when she spent time at the chalet. Dimitri offered Lilyana a stylish green dress made from fine linen, which once had belonged to his mother. Lilyana felt she could not accept such a sentimental gift, but Dimitri insisted she take it. He maintained that his mother would be honoured to have her niece wear the dress.

"We have to clothe you nicely. What will Tadeusz Prawoslaw and his family think if you arrive in England looking like a scraggly Polish girl?" Dimitri joked.

When Lilyana donned the beautiful dress and appeared in the main room that morning, Dimitri stared at her. Then he winked to indicate that she met with his approval.

The dress was a little large on her gaunt form, and it proved to be a little bit too long as well. Lilyana reckoned her Aunt Anna must have been a tall woman. She relished the fine texture of the material as she smoothed it out over her body. She felt it was the most exquisite thing she had ever worn. Her own mother, Olisia, had owned some elegant dresses that she'd worn to sophisticated socials back in Poland, and Lilyana believed this dress was of the same exceptional quality. Dimitri also offered Lilyana his mother's fur coat, sheepskin gloves and ankle-high winter boots with fur trim along the top edge. However, it was the fuzzy woollen hat with attached jewel-encrusted band Lilyana placed on her bald head that made her feel the part of a well-dressed woman. The luxurious apparel helped to hide the ugly scars and sores covering her body.

Lilyana asked Dimitri if Uncle Viktor would be upset with her taking Anna's clothing, and Dimitri told her that it was his father's suggestion for her to do so. Tears sprang to Lilyana's eyes when Dimitri told her that. She gave him an affectionate hug to show him her appreciation. His cheeks turned red, and he reciprocated with an awkward pat on Lilyana's back.

Now, Lilyana was observing Dimitri standing outside the chalet in an intense conversation with the Russian naval officer while Aleksander looked on. Dimitri had changed into his Red Army uniform.

Lilyana carefully helped Larissa walk out the door. The child was still exceptionally pale and weak, not steady on her feet, and prone to nasty coughing spasms that would end in gagging and tears.

"You girls look wonderful!" Dimitri remarked.

It was then that Lilyana first noticed a Soviet military vehicle parked a short distance away from the chalet. She realised the tall stranger must have driven it there.

Dimitri introduced her to the officer, telling her the man was Doctor Irina's husband. Lilyana would not remember what the officer's name was, but she noticed he appeared to be a few years older than Irina. He had retired from the Russian Navy, and he was the one who would be escorting the three Poles to the Arkhangelsk seaport that morning.

Lilyana was taken aback. She had assumed Dimitri would take them. However, Dimitri explained that he was on his way to meet up with a military transport heading south. He was going to join an army unit being sent to the front very soon. He had to return to Arkhangelsk quickly so he could see his father before being deployed. He was to join the army unit there, and then head to the front.

Aleksander was excited about his Russian cousin moving onto the battlefield in conflict with the Nazis.

"Before long I will be joining the fight too," he insisted. "As soon as I can, I will enlist with the Polish Army in London!"

Lilyana tried to hide her dismay. They had to part ways and say their final farewells to Dimitri now. She had anticipated this difficult moment would not happen until they were boarding the ship at the port. She was not prepared to do it just yet, and to make matters worse, the old naval officer seemed to be watching her every move, making her feel unsettled.

There were so many things Lilyana would have liked to have said to her Russian cousin before she departed.

Dimitri had been a guardian angel to her and Larissa. They never would have survived the harsh conditions back in the settlement had it not been for his assistance and intervention, oftentimes risking his own position and wellbeing to come to their aid... and she surely would have perished in the Arkhangelsk prison if Uncle Viktor had not arranged for Dimitri to come to her rescue. Thanks to her Russian uncle and cousin, she had also learned the truth about her father's long-lost sister. What a legacy Aunt Anna had left behind in Russia... especially in her son, Dimitri. Lilyana would miss having him around. She would hang on to the fond memories of times they had shared in the land of the white bears for the rest of her life.

"Would it not be safer for you to remain at the settlement and work in NKVD Headquarters?" she found herself asking Dimitri.

She worried that the cousin she had just come to know would be killed in active duty fighting the Germans.

With eyes downcast, Dimitri replied, "I am a trained soldier, Lily. There is a war raging not far from here. It is my duty to defend Russia from the German fascists who have betrayed us. I must do my part to help push back the Nazis. As we speak, German troops have encircled my hometown. Leningrad is now under siege. Hitler is trying to force the city into submission. The situation is grave. The Germans are relentlessly bombarding the city with air and ground attacks. They have cut off supplies of food, fuel and medical necessities to the city. With winter upon us now, many thousands of people will suffer and die if the siege is not broken soon. People will begin to starve and freeze to death or die from illnesses and injuries. I must fight to help liberate my city. We need to annihilate the Nazis to free Leningrad!"

Mixed emotions swirled around inside Lilyana. Of course Dimitri would choose to fight. Dimitri's father's family, the Yatskayas, and his fiancée, Valentina, all lived in Leningrad. She wondered how they were doing with their city under siege. Was this the news Uncle Viktor had given Dimitri in the underground tunnel that afternoon when his mood had suddenly changed? No wonder he had seemed despondent these past few days.

While she mulled over her concerns, Dimitri went on to say, "I have not heard from Valentina or her family since the Germans laid siege to Leningrad. My father has not been able to contact any of the Yatskayas there for many days. We do not know whether they are alive or dead. Nobody is able to get in or out of the city, and thousands have been slaughtered by Nazi forces."

"Oh! I am so sorry, Dimitri!" Lilyana lamented. "How utterly dreadful! I truly hope that Valentina and the Yatskayas are alive and well! I will pray for them, and I will pray that Leningrad is liberated quickly."

"Yes," Dimitri responded. "I will feel so much better when I join the fight. I need to do something to help bring an end to this dire situation."

"Of course," Lilyana managed to say.

She realised she would never be able to repay Dimitri for the risks he had taken protecting her, Larissa and Aleksander in his attempt to preserve what remained of his Polish mother's family. Now he would have to fight to help sustain the lives of his Russian family as well. When had the world become so deranged?

With tear-filled eyes, Lilyana hugged her Russian cousin. She thanked him once again for all that he and Uncle Viktor had done. She told him to go and fight for Russia, and to return to his beloved Valentina, healthy and well.

There was more she wanted to say, but she could not get the words out. She choked back her tears as Dimitri and Aleksander shook hands and gave each other a manly hug. When Dimitri leaned down to hug Larissa, kissing her on the forehead and wishing her well, tears flowed freely down Lilyana's cheeks.

The Russian naval officer was waiting impatiently. He motioned for the three Prawoslaws to head toward the car.

As he started to nudge Lilyana along, she pulled away from the old officer and, turning to Dimitri, she said, "I pray that God will be with you and keep you safe."

A thin smile spread across Dimitri's lips as he replied, "And you as well, Lilyana. May the Lord direct and guide you toward a safe and happy life!"

Before Lilyana climbed inside the large military vehicle awaiting them, she looked back at Dimitri one final time. She would always remember him standing by the door of the chalet in his crisp, military uniform with his hands behind his back in the familiar Yatskaya pose, looking handsome and self-assured. He gave Lilyana a salute as she clambered into the car. Her heart was filled with a new sadness. She had a strong feeling this would be the last time she ever laid eyes on her Russian cousin. Silently, she prayed that he would survive the war, but years later she learned he did not. Dimitri became one among thousands of Russian soldiers who perished during the fight to liberate his beloved city, Leningrad.

***

As much as Lilyana wanted to leave Russia, she dreaded the journey ahead. The dismal ride to the Arkhangelsk port only heightened her anxiety. The naval officer did not speak to the Prawoslaws. Aleksander attempted to initiate a conversation with him, but the officer insisted he be quiet. Unlike Dimitri and Irina, the man did not speak Polish. He seemed to prefer smoking copious cigarettes in silence as he drove the car, giving off smoke that aggravated Larissa's fragile lungs. She coughed in spasms and cried. It was obvious the officer was not happy having to transport the Poles to the seaport, and Larissa's condition only exacerbated the situation. Lilyana concluded that the Russian officer must have been coerced into driving them against his will as a favour to his wife, Irina Yatskaya. She sensed he did not approve of ethnic Poles, and she felt uncomfortable around the antagonistic man.

Military personnel, transports and weaponry were everywhere as they drew closer to the seaport. Dimitri had told them that Arkhangelsk was a major port of entry for Allied aid as Russia's normal supply line had been cut off by the Nazis. The port was heavily guarded. Although German forces had not captured the city, they wanted to take control of the area and had plans for military attacks. The intense presence of army, navy and air force detachments made Lilyana more petrified of the ocean voyage they were about to embark on.

They passed by the major railway line that connected Arkhangelsk with Moscow, and Lilyana wished that an ocean did not separate the European continent from Great Britain. If there were a solid land mass joining Russia to the United Kingdom, it would have been possible for a rail line to exist overland all the way. Lilyana preferred to travel via train, believing it safer than crossing the dangerous northern waters of Russia as a floating target for German U-boats, submarines and overhead aircraft. However, Aleksander was certain that trains travelling the rails were prime targets for the German Luftwaffe to bomb... and as he pointed out, there was no military escort to help protect them travelling along the railway lines. Whether by land or by sea, their lives were in jeopardy as they endeavoured to escape to England.

The Northern Dvina River emptied into the White Sea, and the Arkhangelsk port lay on both sides of the river. When they arrived at the estuary where the seaport was located, everything looked grey and depressing. Ships were veiled in a shroud of fog and could only be seen as they drew closer to the quay. A series of low-lying mountains and numerous islands off the delta were barely visible in the distance.

The old naval officer had to bring the car to a halt several times at various checkpoints when they approached the harbour. At every gate, port authorities straightened up and saluted the officer. It was obvious he held a position of power as he drove through all the security checkpoints without any questions asked. His Polish passengers' documentation was never in question. Lilyana realised now why Uncle Viktor had requested that this officer bring them to the port. He knew his way around the port very well, and Dimitri wouldn't have been able to breeze through the security gates the way this naval officer's position entitled him to do.

When they reached a large wooden structure perched on the wharf, the car journey came to an end. The officer parked beside the building and motioned for the Prawoslaws to get out. He directed them into a sparsely furnished office. The staff members inside immediately stood at attention and saluted him. He returned their salutes while hurrying Lilyana, Aleksander and Larissa to a room at the end of the building. Once inside, he closed the door and instructed them to sit down in chairs set out along a lengthy table. He sat across from them and pulled out a brown envelope from inside his jacket. Lilyana recognised it as the one Uncle Viktor had handed over to Dimitri inside the dark tunnel a few days earlier. The officer opened the envelope and took out three phony passports, and three sets of stamped travel documents in each one of the Prawoslaws' names. He placed them on the table in a tidy pile, then pulled out a wad of cash and counted it. He shuffled the money back into a neat stack and took several bills off the top for himself.

Lighting up another cigarette, he sat back and stared across the table at Lilyana in defiance as he puffed away, quickly filling the room with his infernal smoke.

Lilyana opened her bag and pulled out the medicine Doctor Irina had prepared for Larissa. She poured a small amount of the mixture into the spoon she had brought along and encouraged the child to swallow it, hoping it would alleviate Larissa's coughing spasms. The anxiety level in the room began mounting. Lilyana found it difficult to believe that Dimitri's cousin had married such an ignorant man. Irina had been so pleasant, yet her husband appeared to be an arrogant fool.

They sat in agonising silence for some time before a door at the back of the room suddenly burst open and a feeble-looking, young sailor entered. Lilyana couldn't help noticing that his regalia was not of the Russian Navy. He saluted the senior officer and quickly began ranting in a foreign language. Lilyana assumed the sailor and the stern Russian were speaking in English. The sailor appeared nervous, as beads of sweat started to line his upper brow.

The officer rose from his chair, picked up the Prawoslaws' forged passports, the money and their important papers, and went out the back door with the sailor. He motioned for the three Polish cousins to remain seated. Another deep voice joined in the conversation by the door on the wharf.

Moments later, the young sailor suddenly popped his head back inside the room where the Poles waited and indicated they should come outside. Lilyana was shocked to see a British officer speaking to the Russian a short distance away. The newcomer's uniform indicated he may have been a captain with the British Navy. He spoke English with the Russian, who was discretely handing over a generous amount of the Prawoslaws' cash to the man. Both officers casually looked around while chatting, as if to ward off any interference from the guards stationed all along the wharf. The Russian wanted Aleksander to be responsible for carrying the Prawoslaws' official documents, so he passed them to the young sailor, who was instructed to hand them over to Aleksander.

The Russian said something in a gruff voice to the British captain, they shook hands, and then he made his way toward the other side of the building. Without so much as a farewell, he returned to the military vehicle parked out in front. They watched him go as he drove off in the direction from which they had come.

The British sailor herded Lilyana, Aleksander and Larissa along the wharf. He encouraged them to follow the captain, who was heading toward a merchant ship docked nearby. They were briskly moved up a gangway onto the ship. The officer waved to the soldiers guarding the vessel, indicating that the three strangers had clearance to board the ship with him. They were marched past several seamen who looked on with curious stares.

The captain said something in English to the sailor, who stood at attention and saluted the officer before ushering the Poles below deck and placing them in some tight living quarters away from the sailors' cabins. He disappeared, not having said a word.

This would be Lilyana's, Aleksander's and Larissa's temporary home until they arrived in the United Kingdom. Lilyana would soon learn how strong her faith really was, having to walk into her greatest fear and trusting God to see her through.

ELEVEN
THE POLISH ARMY-IN-EXILE

Jozef carefully observed his new surroundings. The army base was strewn with tents throughout the woodlands near Buzuluk in Southern Russia. It had been a crowded ride to the camp in a transport, bringing him and many others from the train station at Christopol. All the men were in search of the new Polish Army being formed.

He queued up in a lengthy line outside the enlistment tent with his comrades, Ivan, Tomasz, Radoslaw and Vladik. Everyone in the huge column was searching the faces of those around them in hope of finding others they might recognise. Every one of them had arrived starving and cold, dressed in rags and tattered shoes. Some even had rags wrapped around their feet in place of shoes. Most of the men were infested with lice. Large, open sores could be seen all over their bodies. Many were losing teeth from beatings and malnutrition. They were weakened and exhausted by their intense physical exertion in the labour camps, inclement weather conditions, illnesses and starvation, followed by their long and difficult treks across a frozen continent in search of the army. All of them looked like withered old men. So many had died while crossing through forests and stark, demanding terrain, on trains, and while waiting in stations for trains to come as they tried to get to the Polish Army camp. Some died shortly after arriving at the base to enlist. Others dropped dead right there in the queue. Many were hospitalised for treatment and care following their preliminary exam by the Polish medical officers stationed in the camp. None would be turned away, but every month numerous newly recruited soldiers continued to die.

Soviet officials who were posted around the camp attempted to recruit Poles to join the Russian Red Army, but the ex-prisoners coming from so-called corrective labour camps and prisons shared a mutual hatred toward Russians. They resented the persecution and abusive treatment the Soviets had inflicted on them. Even their release by the amnesty was offensive. The Poles had done nothing wrong. All of them had been arrested and imprisoned or deported on fabricated charges. Polish recruits only trusted the Polish officials at the camp.

As the army began to take shape, numerous women and children also arrived daily from across Russia. They came exhausted, in tatters, ailing and telling stories about the horrible atrocities they had suffered at the hands of the Soviets, and of the fate of family members and friends. Limited food rations and provisions were shared with the starving Polish civilian deportees. An overwhelming number of Polish prisoners and deportees who had been sent to Russia at the beginning of the war perished before they ever reached the new army.

Jozef and his comrades signed up without hesitation when they finally got to the designated enlistment area. The Polish Prime Minister and Commander-in-Chief, General Wladyslaw Sikorski, operating in exile from London, had nominated General Anders as commander of the new army. General Anders had been commander of a cavalry brigade in Poland when Germany attacked at the beginning of the war. A few weeks later, he was seriously injured and captured by Soviet troops when Russia invaded Eastern Poland. Anders was hospitalised and interrogated mercilessly by the NKVD. He was sent to prison on trumped up charges, refusing to accept their offer to join the Soviet Red Army. While in prison, he was tortured and terribly mistreated. Later, he was transferred to the Lubyanka prison that was reserved for people of special interest to the Central Office of the NKVD. Endless threats and interrogations continued.

After the Polish-Soviet agreement was signed, Anders was suddenly given special treatment by the prison guards and authorities. He was informed that the Russians and Poles would now work together to defeat the Germans, and he learned he had been appointed by the Polish authorities to be commander of a new Polish Army. The army would become part of the Polish Armed Forces and participate in battles alongside the armies of the Soviet Union and Allied powers against the German Reich. In exchange for his freedom, he was to take on the responsibility of organising this army as quickly as possible.

More Polish officers were released from prisons and began to report for duty at Buzuluk. Their physical condition was appalling, but they wanted to get the new army organised. General Anders was shocked to discover the small number of officers remaining from the multitude that had been in command at the start of the war. Equally shocking was the depleted number of rank prisoners who were left in the camps. So many of them had disappeared without a trace. Soviet officials insisted they did not know where the rest were or what had happened to them. They tried to convince Anders that the missing officers and other ranks would be found eventually. However, the horrific truth would be revealed in the months to come.

General Anders was authorised to begin the enlistment of recruits once his Headquarters were quickly established at Buzuluk. He carefully observed the men who were finding their way from the labour camps and prisons to enlist. All arrived in terrible physical condition, sick and injured. He wondered if he could form an army with them. Would they be able to tolerate the rigorous military operations required of them?

Anders watched his new, emaciated recruits parading past him in formation for his review. Despite their open sores, ragged clothes and malnourished bodies, he was moved by the fact that all his men were clean shaven now and displaying a soldierly pride. He sensed the strong will and hope that each one of them possessed. Anders saluted the ailing, ill-equipped troops as they marched by in their columns.

Upon arrival in Buzuluk, Jozef and his comrades were housed in the Soviet-made summer tents that were set up in the forest around the army base. At night, the temperature plummeted, and often the men would wake up to a fresh covering of snow on the ground. Many men huddled together inside the freezing cold tents during the night, and in the daytime, they had slush and mud to contend with all around the camp.

The Soviets were astounded by the number of Poles who were making it to the army recruitment area and signing up for military service. They had assumed that fewer of them would arrive, and they'd presumed the young men would not be well enough for active duty. The number of recruits to Anders' Army did not include the masses of women and children to be cared for at the army base. From the very beginning, it was apparent the Russians were not prepared to feed and care for the Polish people properly. Uniforms, armament, vehicles and other equipment were supposed to be supplied as much as possible by the Soviet government, and by the government of the Polish Republic from supplies secured under the Lend-Lease Act. However, the Soviets failed to carry out their terms of the agreement. Provisions were slow in coming, and General Anders had to continually put pressure on the Soviets to get anything. There was little food, no arms or munitions, and few resources of any kind. Without any weaponry or ammunition, they practised army drills using sticks as wooden rifles, with make-believe ammo.

Soviet officials were difficult to deal with, but as numbers of volunteers arriving to join the Polish Forces increased daily, Anders managed to convince the Russians that a few more divisions would be necessary. The army headquarters would remain at Buzuluk, with added divisions and a reserve regiment posted elsewhere. The following spring, the organising centre was relocated to Uzbekistan.

Anders believed it was essential for all Polish citizens to do their part by offering their services to regain freedom and independence for Poland. He managed to gain permission from the Russians to organise a chaplains' service, going against Soviet beliefs, and to establish a women's auxiliary service. He knew there were many women and girls from Russian prisons, concentration camps and settlements who were willing to offer their service for the Polish cause. Like the men, the surviving females believed there was a reason God had saved them from dying a horrible death in the Soviet Union. Anders appealed to the Polish people's national pride, which helped them find new strength and purpose. Many young, single Polish men and women joined the army as new divisions started taking shape. The new camps were just as ill-prepared, without adequate food rations, proper supplies or support, as the garrison in Buzuluk, but General Anders saw the same spirit of courage and determination in every division he visited as they were being set up.

Anders would come to be recognised as a born leader. The Polish Forces under his command would become known as Anders' Army. Having survived his ordeal as a political prisoner, he shared the same hardships and suffering that the new recruits from the labour camps and prisons had endured. Like others who had been released by the amnesty, Anders would continue to fight for his homeland, believing that Poland would be liberated at the end of the war. Anders took inspiration from his troops, and he took on every difficult duty his army was faced with.

With the Soviets' reluctance and inability to provide food and needed supplies, and continued friction and lack of cooperation, Anders' Army was eventually granted permission to leave the Soviet Union, following lengthy political arguments and a direct appeal from the British Prime Minister, Winston Churchill, in a letter to the Soviet Premier, Josef Stalin. Stalin finally agreed to the evacuation of Poles through the Persian Corridor to Persia, as part of the Allied Occupation Force in British controlled territories.

Anders would lead a mass departure of men, women and children under the British Mandate Administration.

In the spring of 1942, the first group of Polish evacuees travelled by goods trains to the port of Krasnovodsk on the Caspian Sea. They boarded an old, rusty Soviet coal-loader ship and left the Soviet Union. The ship was so tightly packed that the evacuees had to remain in the same sitting or standing position throughout the voyage across the sea, but none of them minded the cramped conditions because they were sailing to freedom. They were overjoyed to finally be released from the suffering and hardships they had experienced in Russia under Stalin's tyrannical control.

Jozef and his comrades were fortunate to be included in that initial group of evacuees. When they arrived across the sea at the harbour of Pahlevi in Persia, Radoslaw and Vladik ran down to the sandy beach and jumped into the sea with many of the others, who bathed and splashed about in jubilation. Many emaciated men, women and children took part in the revelry. Unable to suppress their relief and happiness, Jozef, Ivan and Tomasz dived into the sea as well. Pahlevi was in the Soviet Zone, and Russian soldiers could be seen roaming about, but the Poles were now outside the boundaries of the Soviet Union and they could freely convey their exuberance.

The Polish troops camped on the sand along the Caspian Sea. The new army was properly fed and equipped by Britain now. General Anders was invited to march past the Polish soldiers on the beach. It was a happy scene that he would always remember fondly.

The Polish women and children under the protection of the new army were placed in Persian transit camps in and around Tehran, not far from Pahlevi, and later transferred to Palestine, India and British East Africa.

There would be a second huge evacuation across the Caspian Sea that summer. Smaller evacuations were conducted overland both from Russia to the railhead at Mashhad in Persia, and from Uzbekistan to Mashhad.

Those who were lucky enough to depart from the Soviet Union were saved by the evacuations.

In the spring of 1943, the Germans pushed further into Russian territory, and mass graves were discovered in the Katyn Forest. Evidence proved that the Soviets had murdered the thousands of Polish officers found buried in the graves. Polish authorities arranged for an independent and international Red Cross investigation into the massacre, but the Russians hampered their attempt. The Soviets claimed that the Germans who had come upon the mass graves were the ones responsible for the murders, and they accused the Poles of conspiring with German propaganda. Eventually, an international commission determined that the Katyn killings had taken place shortly after the war began, when the Soviet Union controlled Poland.

Angered by this, Stalin quickly severed ties with the Polish Government-in-Exile. The evacuation of General Anders' army was abruptly halted, the Polish-Soviet Amnesty was withdrawn, and once again Soviet citizenship was forced on all Polish people living in Russia, and on those living in Polish territories that had been taken over by the Soviets at the start of the war. Anders campaigned for the continued release of Polish citizens remaining in the Soviet Union, but his pleas fell on deaf ears. Most Poles who were condemned to remain in Russia, living in uncertain conditions, were never heard from again. General Anders ordered his troops to refrain from activities directed against the Russians, and not to talk about their horrible experiences in the Soviet Union. He did not want anything to make the deteriorating relationship between Poland and Russia worse, or to cause more serious repercussions for the Polish people left behind in Russia.

Polish authorities estimated that a large number of Polish children and orphans had been gathered together in Russia. Britain, Canada and the American Red Cross had planned to evacuate most of them, but the Russians would not agree to it. Pleas for the children's release continued.

The Soviets claimed that transportation problems were the issue, and that the Polish children were not in any danger. They did not want the outside world to learn the terrible truth, which would earn them worldwide condemnation.

There was a huge number of Polish citizens still in the Soviet Union. However, the Russians informed the Polish embassy that the number was much smaller and claimed there was no longer any need for Polish welfare agencies to remain on Soviet soil. Many Polish hospitals and orphanages were immediately shut down across Russia and taken over by Soviet authorities, along with all internationally donated supplies.

The evacuated Polish troops and refugees were met with compassion from the Persian people. British officers did all they could to welcome and to help the Polish people despite numerous difficulties. General Anders was especially taken by the way they cared for the Polish children. The fortunate Poles who made it into Persia felt as though they had woken up from a long nightmare. Their living conditions were greatly improved with the relief assistance from British, American, Polish and Persian authorities. Diseases acquired in the Soviet Union, which continued to kill a large number of refugees after they arrived in the Middle East, were gradually brought under control. Field hospitals tackled the typhus, dysentery and malnutrition that the troops and refugees brought with them.

When the Polish women and children were sent to different countries from their camps in Persia, they always experienced kindness from the governments that welcomed them, and from native populations in those areas. They were greeted with empathy and encouraging words. Government officials visited them to check on their wellbeing. The refugees were debriefed and urged not to speak with outsiders about their ordeals in Russia. The delicate balance between the Soviet Union and its Western allies had to be maintained.

The Allies never officially contradicted the Soviets' insistence that the Germans were to be blamed for the cold-blooded execution of the Polish officers in the Katyn Forest. Their silence helped to preserve the good name of Stalin's evil empire, while the Red Army fought alongside its Western allies against the German Reich.

Having survived starvation and epidemics in Russia, Jozef and his comrades were overwhelmed by the abundance of food available in Persia. They were fed well now. With proper medications and a sunny, hot climate, the young soldiers started to recover quickly.

Persia welcomed the Polish troops. The locals showed the Polish soldiers how to make life in the desert more bearable by spraying the inside of their tent walls and mosquito netting with water. They demonstrated how to deal effectively with the sandstorms and the heat.

Anders' Army would be designated as the Polish Army in the East. Their stay in Persia ended shortly afterwards, when the Soviets occupying the northern area became antagonistic and German armies started closing in, posing a threat. The Polish troops were then transported across the Persian desert to Iraq.

Along the way, an orphaned bear cub was adopted by the soldiers. They named him Wojtek and he became a prominent mascot for the Polish Corps. The young bear was fed milk from an empty vodka bottle and progressed to eating fresh fruits and honey. Wojtek moved with the soldiers to Iraq, living in their tents with them. A wooden crate was made to transport him in a lorry, and he travelled with them throughout the war. He eventually enjoyed drinking beer and smoking or eating cigarettes.

Anders' Army arrived in Iraq with his troops on the mend. Army Headquarters was comprised of crude huts, and the soldiers' tents stretched across a large expanse of desert sand. Where once the Poles had to endure the frigid cold tundra of Siberia, they now had to tolerate extreme desert heat and invasions of mosquitos. It was not long before many of the troops came down with malaria. It took the British medical officers several months to bring the outbreak under control. Two of Jozef's new tentmates were infected with the illness, and after they had recovered, both remarked that the Soviet experience had been far worse than a nasty case of malaria.

The Polish soldiers did not complain about the epidemic, the blowing sand, the dangerous snakes and spiders or the scorching heat. They were more concerned about how long it was taking to receive equipment and arms, causing a delay in their training. The troops were becoming restless. They wanted to get to the war in the hope of liberating Poland.

Despite having to cope with the extreme desert conditions and insufficient weaponry, morale remained high. Special education programmes and theatrical productions promoted rehabilitation and relieved boredom. Further training and equipping now came under operational contract with the British Middle East Command.

By the end of the summer, additional troops had joined them. Most were ethnic Poles, but some Belarussians, Ukrainians and Jews had also enlisted. Intensive training began when guns and munitions were issued in Iraq. General Anders believed in a high standard of drill and discipline. The appearance of his soldiers was important to him, and he paid close attention to details, keeping well informed about the ongoing war in Europe. Attacks would be studied closely and elaborate training methods for each type of assault would be practised.

The new army was rearming and reorganising. It needed to be mechanised. Troops had to learn new methods of assault and how to handle new weapons. Soldiers were specially trained in many different divisions, broken up into different locations because of their size and need for specialised training.

New sections were added to Anders' Army, and the Polish Auxiliary Services were set up. Jozef and his comrades were all assigned to different areas once the reorganising began.

Anders' soldiers marched with pride in their new military uniforms and leather boots issued by British Command. The troops boldly displayed the Polish white eagle in a prominent spot on their helmets. However, frustration continued to grow as the soldiers became increasingly anxious to get to the front and fight to win Poland's freedom back.

The army moved to another area in Iraq, where conditions for large-scale exercises were better. Polish soldiers helped guard oil wells in the vicinity. Oil was crucial in the war strategy as it was a major requirement to fuel an army's war tanks, vehicles, and other machinery. The training of the troops was now fully under way, and the army was becoming an effective fighting force.

Polish Prime Minister-in-Exile and Commander-in-Chief, General Sikorski, arrived in Iraq to inspect the troops. He promised to involve them in active service soon. Unfortunately, Sikorski died in a plane crash at Gibraltar several weeks later.

The Polish Army in the East was re-designated as the 2nd Polish Corps in June 1943. The 1st Polish Corps had been formed in Britain with Polish men who had successfully escaped across the Romanian border when the Soviets marched in and occupied their territory at the start of the war.

Jozef's division was moved across the Iraqi desert to Palestine, where it settled into a large camp at Gaza. His unit then became a new Carpathian Division, integrated with the former Polish Carpathian Infantry Brigade, which had just moved to Palestine following their successful defence of Libya and Tobruk in North Africa. Jozef's unit reinforced the infantry brigade and became part of the 3rd Carpathian Rifle Division. The troops progressed quickly in their training, and other reconnaissance regiments soon joined them in Palestine. Vladik was assigned to the Heavy Machine Gun Battalion, while Tomasz and Radoslaw were trained on Sherman tanks. The 2nd Polish Corps went out on manoeuvres at various locations in the desert, as all divisions improved their field and battle skills.

General Anders reluctantly gave up many of his prime soldiers to reinforce the Polish Air Force in Britain. A struggle had developed between the Polish government and the army over control and command powers of the armed services, resulting in further reorganisation of the 2nd Polish Corps. Anders opposed the decision as a lot of his young men were prioritised for training and sent to Britain. Other soldiers volunteered to supplement the Polish Navy, Armed Corps and paratroops in England. They were sent to Britain for special training.

Volunteers were sought to parachute into occupied Poland to join the underground resistance movement, serving as Morse code operators for the secret radio stations passing intelligence on to Britain. They would begin training in Palestine, and then the best of them would be sent to England to be trained for underground activities before parachuting into captured Poland. Jozef's comrade Ivan signed up with the special Independent Unit under the command of an electrical engineer from the Tobruk campaign. Ivan had previous experience with Morse code and the workings of shortwave radio transmissions and receivers. Being a perfect fit for this risky mission, he was selected as one of the elite men to become an intelligence radio operator with the underground resistance. He was sent off to a smaller camp where his special unit was to begin its training. His long-time comrades, Jozef, Tomasz, Radoslaw and Vladik were spread out in different areas. Ivan sent a letter to each one of them, wishing them God's speed in their fight alongside the Allies, and he promised to meet up with them for a celebratory drink in a liberated Poland at war's end.

A unit from the Women's Auxiliary Services of the Polish Army was often seen marching in formation around the Palestine Camp. The women looked smart in their neatly pressed British uniforms and Australian army hats. Receiving formal training, the women's unit contributed a great deal to the war effort. If the men were not out practising manoeuvres, they enjoyed watching the women marching past in formation. Being youthful fellows, it was only natural they would be attracted to the young ladies. However, Jozef had an ulterior motive for watching the women's unit on parade; he always had a watchful eye out in search for his beloved, Lily.

For recreation, Jozef attended the camp cinema with his comrades from the Carpathian Division. Feature films were shown nightly. Two or three good movies from pre-war Poland were viewed in Polish. During brief visits to Tel Aviv, the soldiers could purchase Polish newspapers and listen to the radio in Polish, as many Jewish people living in the area had come from Poland. They had set up schools and printed Polish newspapers.

The British military, under command of General Montgomery, began to make plans for Anders' Army. In late 1943, the 2nd Polish Corps was moved to a small mountain village in Lebanon, where the soldiers were trained to fight on the mountain slopes. The manoeuvres in the mountainous region were part of their final training intended to adapt the soldiers to the type of terrain they would be battling in when they arrived at their destination. Polish units were equipped, organised and trained to British standards and guidelines. The Brits and the Poles would be grouped together in a single theatre of war.

After the death of Polish Prime Minister Sikorski, British Prime Minister Churchill met with General Anders. The time had come for Anders' soldiers to fight. It was decided that the 2nd Corps would be sent into operation as reinforcements for the Mediterranean campaign in Italy, where they were desperately needed.

At the end of 1943, Anders' troops were relocated to Egypt as a staging post for deployment in Italy. They spent almost two months exercising in the Egyptian desert while waiting to be sent. Orders finally came in February 1944.

Two Polish ships arrived at Egyptian ports for embarkment of the troops and equipment. Escorted by destroyers from the Polish fleet, they crossed the Mediterranean Sea, disembarking at Taranto in southern Italy. General Anders reported to Lieutenant-General Sir Oliver Leese at British Army Headquarters and the 2nd Polish Corps officially became an independent part of the British 8th Army. They were transported to Tora, which was a small village near Monte Cassino, where they were given lodgings in private homes. The 2nd Corps' base, including hospitals, other supporting and servicing units, and the 7th Infantry Division as its training reserve, followed them.

The transfer of Polish troops from Egypt to Italy continued until the middle of April, with Polish forces landing at a few different locations to ease pressure on the ports. It would take six transports to move the entire 2nd Corps to Italy. Units were set up in five camps running along the main road in the San Teresa area. Roads were in good shape there, and olive groves offered some protection from aircraft activity overhead.

Jozef and his comrades were finally back in Europe, and they were anxious to join the war.

TWELVE
THEATRE OF OPERATIONS
ITALY, FEBRUARY 1944 - MAY 1945

In early 1944, things had reached a stalemate on the Italian front. Germans were positioned in the mountains south of Rome, and Allied forces had not been able to break through. In the west, the Nazis held the Rapido, Liri and Garigliano valleys, as well as the surrounding mountain peaks and ridges. Atop the largest hill, Monte Cassino, the town of Cassino and an ancient abbey blocked the entrance to the Liri and Rapido Valleys. The Liri River Valley was the only pass through the mountain range, but the valley was blocked by many smaller hills. The Germans built and reinforced lines across Italy known as the Gustav Line and the Hitler Line. Geography in the area provided the Nazis with a perfect defence that was thought to be invincible.

The Germans had fortified themselves all around Monte Cassino with mines, barbed wire, concrete bunkers and machine gun nests. They had taken up defensive positions deep in the slopes below the abbey walls. The historic monastery offered the German Army advantageous views of the Liri Valley on all sides. Hitler's troops surrounded the abbey and controlled Allied air and ground fire as any movement on the hills could be seen and thwarted from their vantage point. Attacks from any direction were inundated with crossfire from German artillery and firearms.

The Americans had bombed the monastery, believing that the German defenders were using it as a lookout post.

However, after the bombing, German paratroops established positions in the ruins. The bombing had created ample rubble for the Nazis to protect themselves from air and artillery attacks, thereby making it an even stronger defensive position.

Every Allied attempt to take Cassino had failed. Progress had been slowed by difficult terrain, wet weather and the strategically placed German defences. With the arrival of winter blizzards, air support and the troops' ability to advance on the rough mountain slopes had been made impossible. Allied forces took heavy losses and were forced to withdraw from battle.

Germany's Gustav Line across Italy had effectively stopped the Allies' advance north to Rome. The line stretched east to west, extending two miles east of Monte Cassino then traveling south through the Liri River Valley and southwest to reach the coast. South of Monte Cassino, the Gustav Line followed the River Garigliano, making it an ideal German defence.

It was the Allies' goal to break through the Gustav line, seize Rome and link up with Allied forces that had landed at Anzio. However, the town and the monastery blocked their route north. There had been a few major assaults by the Allies to take the heavily guarded abbey at Monte Cassino in early 1944. The forces of the USA, the UK, France, India, Canada, South Africa and New Zealand had attempted to capture the town and the abbey overlooking the Rapido River Valley. Thousands of men had been lost in those battles, and still the German defensive lines remained intact despite heavy bombings and artillery shelling of the monastery.

Jozef entered battle with the 3rd Carpathian Division along the front on the Sangro and Rapido Rivers in the Southern Apennines in February 1944. During those early weeks, the 2nd Polish Corps played a laid-back defensive role in a large area on the Sangro River. This was a high-priority zone positioned between the British 5th and 8th Armies, where the Poles protected the Brits' flanks while holding the front along the river. The 2nd Corps stayed with the 5th and 8th Armies on patrol, with localised actions taking place.

The Polish 5th Kresowa Infantry Division soon joined them on the front. Preparations for a spring offensive were getting under way. The troops were given orders to relieve the 2nd Morocco Division and take over their sector. Poor weather conditions caused problems with their mission. In some places, the soldiers marched through ankle-deep mud. Reserves were used in rotation of units to help carry out operational activities and keep up the troops' strength while moving munitions and food forward to jump-off points. That included manually handling weaponry that weighed many tons. Mules were brought in to carry the army's requirements on their backs. During the Italian campaign, mule trains became indispensable in the hills.

General Anders needed to recruit more soldiers for his army to replace losses that would be incurred during battle. With the Soviets refusing to release any more Eastern Poles from the Soviet Union, Anders had to look elsewhere. He managed to enlist an additional number of men by screening Poles from Western Poland who had been forced into the German Army and subsequently taken as POWs by the Allies. Having been released, these men were sent to the 7th Reserve Division in Palestine for training to make up for unit losses, reinforcing the 2nd Polish Corps.

In March, Anders' Army was given the battle order to capture Monte Cassino. It would be a combined offensive involving many Allied divisions along a lengthy stretch from Cassino to the Gulf of Gaeta. Preparing for action, Anders and his staff interviewed commanders who had participated in the previous attacks on Cassino. He carefully examined the details of their experiences. Anders scrutinised the terrain by land and air in preparation for the major assault. A large-scale relief model of Monte Cassino's position and topography was fabricated.

This massive attack was intended to break through the Gustav Line and open the road to Rome. It was strategically planned, going by the code name Operation Diadem. The US was to begin the assault on the left, moving up the coastal route towards Rome. On the right, the French Expeditionary Corps was to attack from the bridgehead across the River Garigliano into the Arunci Mountains, which created a barrier between the Liri Valley and the coastal plain. In the centre, the British 8th Army was to cross the Garigliano and attack north up the Liri Valley.

Commanded by General Anders, the 2nd Polish Corps was given the most difficult task of the operation, to capture the town of Cassino and Monastery Hill. The 2nd Corps needed to cross the Rapido River, attack Monte Cassino and isolate the abbey. Then they were to advance around behind the monastery into the Liri Valley and link up with the British 8th Corps, pushing forward and squeezing out the Germans from the Gustav Line.

Anders hoped the Polish Forces would be large enough to overwhelm the German defences and render them incapable of giving fire support to each other's positions. The Canadian Corps would be held in reserve, ready to take advantage of the breakthrough. The US would advance from the Anzio beachhead to cut off the retreating Germans in the Alban Hills. Success of the mission would depend on the ability of the Polish and British corps to render the Nazi defences ineffective.

Prior to the Monte Cassino assault, an intense bombing campaign against German supply lines began. It was hoped this would cut off supplies from reaching German forces at Monte Cassino. In addition to that, the Allies set a plan in motion to trick German Field Marshal Kesselring at Cassino into thinking they had given up on further attacks on the Gustav Line and that their new objective was to land at Civitavecchia, north of Rome. Allied troops were sent to the coastal region to practise amphibious landings and assault training, and phony signposts were created along roads to make the Germans believe a seaborne landing was being planned. Radio signal traffic with coded messages was deliberately sent with false information to be intercepted by German intelligence, indicating an Allied landing by US and Canadian forces was imminent. Allied air forces made reconnaissance flights over Civitavecchia's beaches. The elaborate deception was intended to keep German reserves held back from the Gustav Line, and the plan worked. Kesselring sent armoured divisions to Civitavecchia with additional reserves on standby. There were only a few German divisions remaining on the Cassino front when the Allies attacked.

While the bombings of supply lines and the Allied deception were taking place, preparatory measures for Operation Diadem were secretly moving forward. The preparations took a couple of months to complete. The procedure had to be carried out in small stages to maintain secrecy and the element of surprise. Allied positions at Monte Cassino and Rapido were heavily reinforced under camouflage. Troop movements in forward areas were performed under the cover of darkness. Movement of armoured units from the Adriatic front left dummy tanks and vehicles behind so the evacuated areas appeared unchanged to German aerial reconnaissance. With spring weather imminent, it was hoped that ground conditions would improve and make it possible to deploy armour and large formations of troops successfully. Crossing the rivers was dangerous, but it had to be done so the Allies could attack the Germans atop Monte Cassino from all sides. The riverbanks were mined, and German snipers and machine guns were placed in tactical positions, preventing mine clearing from being done during daylight hours. Engineers precariously cleared mines during the night and placed markers to help the troops advance. During the day, German mortar bombs obliterated the markers. When the infantry arrived at the rivers to cross in darkness, it was difficult to find the route. It was an arduous process. Nevertheless, the troops continued to advance.

Later in April, the 2nd Polish Corps started moving units into forward positions as they prepared for the jump off. They dug small protective shelters in the rocky terrain to keep themselves safe from flying shrapnel, rocks and splintered trees. They had to make do with dry rations, as fires for cooking meals were not allowed. Water had to be rationed. Flamethrowers, special tools for digging trenches and camouflage suits for special commandos and snipers were delivered to their positions. Troop movements remained secret.

Jozef and his fellow soldiers climbed the steep, jagged mountain terrain in the night to remain undetected by German forces, while carrying hundreds of pounds of weaponry and ammunition on their backs. Thousands of tons of ammunition were manually carried up a gorge that gave them cover from the Nazis above.

Having moved with the 2nd Corps through Iraq, Syria, Palestine and Egypt, the Poles' adopted bear, Wojtek, was officially drafted into the unit as a private with the British 8th Army in the Italian campaign to get him onto a British Transport ship. During the Cassino operations, the bear helped his comrades move ammunition up the mountain, and he would later be promoted to corporal.

In daytime, troops had to be silent and hunker down inside craggy rock formations or caves to remain unseen. In some places along the slopes, miles of special camouflage material concealed their location and allowed for the construction of bridges. The 2nd Polish Corps moved in and relieved the British 78th Division in the mountains behind Cassino.

General Anders deemed the task of taking Monte Cassino significant for the future of the Home Army in Poland. When the time for battle arrived, he addressed his soldiers saying that the thoughts and hearts of the Polish people were with the troops. He talked about this long-anticipated time having come, to take revenge and punish their enemy, Germany, for all the suffering in Poland and for what they had suffered in Russia, including separation and loss of their families. He implored his men to be brave and to keep God, honour and Poland in their hearts.

Anders' troops felt invincible. They went to battle believing their effort and sacrifice would free Poland from the hands of their oppressors. The soldiers did not go to fight because they had been ordered to do so, but rather because of their patriotic love for homeland and hate for their tyrannical subjugators.

British soldiers would be quick to acknowledge the Poles' fighting spirit. Polish soldiers wanted to kill Nazis and regain their honour. When taking over posts from the British, the Polish troops would simply move in with their weapons, ask where the Germans were and start firing. The Brits would say that the Poles showed no fear and fired on the enemy with no restraint.

The strategy of the German defence relied on their ability to shift from sector to sector and counterattack any offense. General Anders believed that the plan to capture numerous hills all at once and prevent the Germans from organising their attack would succeed in forcing them to split up their reserves and weaken their defence. He knew the Germans and the Allies would be forced to fight to exhaustion. The 2nd Corps would be battling against Kesselring's entrenched, mountain-trained troops, but Anders' soldiers were hardened by the Soviet experience and determined to regain their homeland. There was no doubt in Anders' mind that his soldiers would fight for Poland with everything they had.

The 5th Kresowa Polish Division attempted to capture one hill, clearing it bunker to bunker to secure the heights in early May. They took a high percentage of casualties, and Anders ordered them to withdraw because of the large number of dead and injured.

The massive Allied assault on Cassino began the following week. Polish troops waited anxiously in position until the code word to begin battle was given late into the evening. Fighting started with intense artillery bombing from guns on the 8th and 5th Army fronts by British, American, French, New Zealanders and South Africans aimed at German positions all along the lengthy Rapido Valley coastline. The Germans were completely taken by surprise. They had been starting relief operations, unaware of the size and strength of the Allied forces opposing them.

Shortly after the artillery firing began, the 2nd Polish Corps shifted from their infantry positions. With blackened faces and equipment, they put on their camouflage wraps and began the assault on Monte Cassino. The attack was fully under way in all four sectors following the opening bombardment. Fighting was intense. German units had dug deep into the terrain, and the Allied divisions met with stiff resistance. Hills were heavily mined. The Germans had a network of well-concentrated bunkers built into rocky ground and bushy growth that could not be penetrated, allowing them to continue firing from strategic positions, slowing down the action. Even with the Allies' armoured backing, and many units in defensive locations providing support and protection on their flanks, most divisions continued to be under constant mortar and small arms fire, including their rear positions coming under artillery fire. In the first hours of fighting, Allied battalions lost an incredible number of men.

The same scene was played out simultaneously on many hills around Cassino. All were under attack by multiple divisions of Allied forces. Horrific battles took place against a backdrop of magnificent scenery. At the junction of the two river valleys, Monte Cassino rose high into the clouds, being the tallest of the hills. The wide Rapido Valley crossed over into Cassino, surrounded by extensive olive groves, wooded areas and streams. Monte Cassino was a huge mountain etched with large ravines, rocky ledges, steep slopes and rugged crests. The mountainside was covered with evergreen, oak and acacia trees. Red poppies and spring wildflowers dotted the hillside.

Sounds of war continued to blast across the valley. Shelling was deafening. The mountain shook with constant exploding artillery. Machine-gun fire and detonating mortars filled the air and rained down like a firestorm, lighting up the night sky. The impact of torpedo attacks loosened the earth and created huge craters on the mountain landscape. The smell of damp earth and shattered trees blended with the stench of burning wood as fires erupted along the front. Explosions sent shrapnel, dirt, rocks and vegetation in all directions. Mines were detonated as more troops advanced into the cataclysm from their positions below, adding to the scattered rubble and smoking ruins. It made their advance even more dangerous and difficult. The ground became littered with dead soldiers and dying mules. Bits of helmets, uniforms, weaponry and body parts lay like pieces from a fractured puzzle tossed randomly along the slopes.

Jozef suddenly became aware of blood running down the side of his face. He feared he had been hit by enemy fire, but then the body of the soldier beside him slumped forward and fell out of position from their location on the mountainside. The man tumbled a short distance down the slope and came to rest in a small crevice filled with loosened rocks. A pair of blank eyes stared up at Jozef from where the body lay. It was a horrible, haunting sight. The soldier's blood and flesh covered one side of Jozef's camouflage wrap. Moments before, the man had stood beside him as they loaded and fired a field artillery piece together. Now, the soldier lay dead. The cruel reality of combat and death filled Jozef's senses as blasts of shrapnel and rock continued to pelt him from above.

Artillery shelling continued through the long night and into the following day. At dawn, a major air attack began. Anti-aircraft fire added to the noise and chaos. By morning, the Americans and the French Corps had succeeded in their goal and were spreading out in the mountains toward the 8th Army front, shutting down German positions between the two armies. Many Allied corps had managed two crossings over the heavily fired upon Rapido River. Engineers had been able to bridge the river, allowing the Canadian Armoured Brigade to cross and fend off counterattacks from German tanks. The Polish infantry, supported by tanks, finally managed to cross the start lines in the early afternoon. All divisions were coming under a constant barrage, and some had to ward off repeated counterattacks on several hills as the Germans managed to regroup. German fire, coming from concealed bunkers filled with artillery and mortars, was powerful, and the Allies found it difficult to take control. This was especially true on the sheltered side of the mountain slopes. More bridgeheads were placed along the Rapido River by mid-afternoon, despite fierce German counterattacks.

By the next day, the Allies had started to make steady advances around Monte Cassino. German reserves were pushed further up the front line, but they continued to defend the abbey with ferocious intensity on top of the mountain. Polish units suffered major casualties. The French Expeditionary Corps, Moroccan Mountain Division and special forces from the North African mountains were adept at handling the difficult terrain and successfully captured key areas around Monte Cassino. The French Corps achieved its goal and was positioned to assist the British 8th Army. Kesselring had every available reserve firing on the 8th Army while working toward switching to the German's second defensive position, the Hitler Line, several miles to the rear.

Signs indicated that the German troops on the coast and in the hills were starting to wear down. Air support fired on hidden German artillery located in crucial sections along the front. The 8th Army continued to encounter powerful opposition, but finally achieved its second objective when it captured the main road.

In the mountains above Cassino, the ridge was captured by the Poles, but then taken back by German paratroops. A fierce battle raged for three days, resulting in heavy losses to both Poles and Germans. The Polish divisions charged with capturing Monte Cassino Hill suffered extraordinary casualties. Their assault was driven back, and the infantry division met with devastation. Mortars, small-arms fire and artillery shelling completely wiped out the two leading Polish battalions. General Anders and General Leese agreed to stop further action until the Polish forces regrouped.

It had only taken several hundred German soldiers to drive back entire Allied divisions. Nevertheless, General Leese was satisfied that the Poles' attack had successfully drawn artillery fire and reserves away from the British, thereby enabling them to force the German Army away from part of the hill, and from the town of Cassino.

Armoured regiment tanks opened fire in the ravine as a distraction so engineers could clear a pathway through the minefield in preparation for the next assault on Monte Cassino. The ground through the mountain beside the Liri Valley was undefended because it was deemed impossible to cross, but the Moroccan Gourmiers, specialising in mountain warfare, travelled through the mountainous ground and assisted the 8th Corps in the valley, outflanking the Nazi defence. The southern contingent of German defences was annihilated. Another British division arrived at the 8th Corps' line fresh from reserve, having passed through the bridgehead division to carry out the turning move, and isolating the town of Cassino from the Liri Valley.

The 2nd Polish Corps regrouped and re-entered battle in mid-May for their second assault on Monte Cassino. Blasting crucial sections along the front, the 3rd Carpathian Division captured two important hills, while the 5th Kresowa Infantry Division took the main ridge and moved on to attack two more slopes. With little natural cover to protect them, the 2nd Corps came under constant mortar and artillery fire from fortified German positions. Fighting was fierce, casualties were high, and thousands of men were lost. Tanks came down the southern ridge in defence of Polish forces.

Despite strong opposition from Polish artillery, the Nazis attempted to counterattack. Other Allied battalions continued in conflict against heavy fire. The Germans managed to recapture a major southern slope, but more

Allied units were called into action, and the southerly peak fell that evening. Troops from parallel divisions were drafted into battle along with artillery and anti-tank regiments. By day's end, the 3rd Carpathian Division held the northern, southern and eastern slopes. The 5th Carpathian Battalion was called in for additional support from reserve. Hidden mortar positions were bombed by hundreds of aircraft, and finally the German defences started to collapse.

The troops dug in for the night. Large patrols continued in most sectors because the Poles knew Germans would try to escape. Night patrols gathered intelligence by scrutinising enemy positions.

The next day, the 3rd Carpathian Rifle Brigade and 5th Kresowa Infantry resumed their assault. The Poles had to take out isolated positions one at a time because the Germans tried to counterattack, stubbornly holding on until the very end. Before the battle ended along the front line, thousands of tons of Polish ammunition had been spent. On the heights of Monte Cassino, confusion and disarray ensued. There were no longer any formal formations. Platoons and sections of Germans and Allies were scrambled together. Every man had to use their own initiative, and fighting was reduced to hand-to-hand combat. The weakest soldiers could no longer keep up.

The 2nd Polish Corps linked up with a British division in the Liri Valley a couple of miles west from the town of Cassino. With the German's supply line threatened by the Allied advance in the valley, the Gustav Line could no longer hold. The French broke through the Line, and the German Army was ordered to withdraw. Germans reluctantly pulled back from the top of Monte Cassino to their new defensive positions on the Hitler Line. The 2nd Polish Corps had achieved its objective. The German defence on top of Monte Cassino was finally cleared.

On top of Monte Cassino, Jozef and other survivors of the 2nd Polish Corps' offensive action were drained, physically and mentally. The Poles had intercepted the radio message sent to the German troops when they were ordered to withdraw, but were too pummelled to pursue them. They were within a few hundred yards of the summit and did not have enough strength left to climb to the peak. It would take them a long time to reach the crest and occupy the abbey ruins.

Polish Headquarters sent a message to the 3rd Carpathian Division to send a patrol from the Polish Lancers Reconnaissance Regiment to scout the monastery. The Lancers found the defences at the monastery abandoned, with only wounded Germans remaining. The abbey atop Monte Cassino had fallen. It had taken one week to capture. The Polish flag was planted and flew above the ruins. A Polish soldier played the Polish signal on his bugle amid the rubble of the monastery to announce the victory to the Allies.

By late afternoon, most Polish divisions were holding defensive positions. Some bunkers had still not been cleared or captured. The Carpathian and Poznan Lancers engaged in a two-day campaign, and eventually, Germans holding on to the last bits of hills surrendered.

The Battle for Monte Cassino would be declared one of the major, most strategic and historic campaigns of World War II. It proved to be a difficult and costly military operation with repeated assaults waged by Allied forces, resulting in terrible losses for all Allied nations involved, and for the civilians caught up in the war zones. Thousands of Poland's 2nd Corps soldiers were killed, wounded or declared missing in action. Damage to the ancient monastery on top of Monte Cassino was irreparable, and there was unimaginable devastation to the infrastructure of the town of Cassino and the surrounding hills.

Jozef and other surviving infantry men were completely drained and bereft of emotion. When the barrage of shelling and mortar fire finally stopped, they stood silent and in shock. Their ears rang with the residual effects. Overwhelming sights of destruction stretched across miles of mountain terrain in all directions. Everywhere Jozef looked, the land was scarred by the ugliness of war. Corpses lay in distorted human shapes all over the slopes, German and Allies alike. Bloodied bits of bodies and shattered limbs lay on the ground and hung from fragmented trees. Everything appeared charred. Where healthy groves of trees and other vegetation once stood, eerie black remnants of barren trees now poked out of the ground like spent matchsticks scattered across a scarred landscape. Shattered bits of guns and weaponry littered the mountainsides. Here and there, a helmet or two lay devoid of soldiers. Upturned tanks with broken caterpillar tracks poked up from the ground in an array of awkward positions. The smell of gunfire, damp earth and the miasma of blood and death hung heavily in the air.

A bone-chilling quiet pervaded the scene once the shelling and explosions had ended. It wasn't until the bugle sounded that officers and soldiers unashamedly let their tears fall freely. No one remained unaffected by all that had happened in those hills.

***

The 2nd Polish Corps was immediately given orders to continue fighting despite their battle fatigue and decreasing numbers. They needed to attack east to infiltrate the Hitler Line before the Nazis could command it. Their objective was to capture Piedimonte, a heavily fortified town absorbed into the Hitler Line. The Germans had turned it into a fortress with an elaborate minefield. Attacking ground units would have to be extremely careful crossing the terrain. Spare Allied units were brought in to support the exhausted 2nd Corps.

An assault was launched by armoured divisions, taking the Germans by surprise. The attack temporarily broke through the Hitler Line, and a second attack a few hours later infiltrated the centre of Piedimonte. However, the Allies remained open to fire from heavily defended buildings and had to retreat.

Two days later, a new attack followed, with self-propelled tank guns firing on specific bunkers. This provided needed cover for the infantry, but progress was slow due to continuing strong artillery and mortar fire from the Germans. By late afternoon, the Allies were inside the town, clearing it building by building, but again they were forced to withdraw to the outskirts of the town walls for protection at day's end.

The next day, another assault resulted in the Allies breaking through the defences. Unfortunately, tank support was lost when the streets became too narrow to pass through, and the Germans had the advantage once more. The Allies were forced to retreat to the positions they had assumed the night before.

One day later, the Polish Corps hammered the town of Piedimonte into ruins with artillery. The Canadian infantry broke through the Hitler Line, and the Canadian Armoured Division streamed through the breach. The Poles had to push back a counterattack a few days later.

At the end of May, a Polish battalion captured the hill. An armoured division with tanks moved in and took Piedimonte early in the morning. When the Poles captured the town, the Hitler Line collapsed. The German Army was in full retreat. Units from the 5th Kresowa Infantry were sent to defensive positions, while other Polish divisions began to clear landmines and repair damaged bridges. With the defeat of the German stronghold around Cassino, the road north to Rome was finally opened. American and British divisions advanced on to Rome and captured the city in early June. This victory prevented the Nazis from moving more troops away from Italy to Northern France, allowing the Normandy Invasion to begin two days later.

***

The 2nd Polish Corps was ordered to withdraw to the Adriatic Coast. The Allies were now too far north to use the southern Italian ports. They would need to capture Ancona, a key harbour on the eastern coast of Italy, to carry out further operations. Gaining possession of this seaport would bring them closer to the fighting and shorten their lines of communication.

In mid-June, the 3rd Carpathian Rifle Division replaced the Indian Division. Supplemental British regiments and Italian units reinforced the Corps' strength and became part of the 2nd Polish Corps under General Anders, who was given command of the Adriatic sector in the Italian theatre.

The 5th Kresowa Infantry Division, the Armoured Brigade and the 2nd Corps' artillery arrived shortly afterwards. Anders ordered his units to pursue the Germans as quickly as possible and capture the Ancona harbour. Speed was necessary in moving forward to prevent the Germans from blowing up bridges along the way.

The Battle of Ancona began in mid-June with an attack executed by the 3rd Carpathian Rifle Battalion, Italian and British infantry, armoured divisions and Polish commandos. Anders tricked the Germans into believing that the 3rd Carpathian Division would attack along the coast road by sending a series of false radio messages, while masterfully manoeuvring his Kresowa and Hussar divisions into a surrounding movement inland. The German division fell apart, and the Poles were able to move up the Adriatic Coast quickly.

Supported for the first time by the air squadron from the Polish city of Gdansk, the Poles crossed the Aso River. They captured towns along their advance with help from the Italians and met stubborn resistance around the Chieti River against the German Mountain Corps, stalling the Polish onslaught. The Germans had dug in deep and were prepared for a major counterattack.

Heavy fighting continued in the region until the end of June. Italian partisan units helped the Poles in action along the rivers. Teams of engineers cleared mined roads, and forward units cleared German rearguard action as the Poles crossed the Chienti, hastening their advance. The final obstacle on the way to Ancona was the River Musone, but the Germans had no time to reinforce their defences there. The heights of the Musone's northern bank were taken at the beginning of July.

The advance to Ancona was seriously interrupted at the village of Loreto, where a critical battle ensued for eight days. Night bombings by the German Luftwaffe allowed the Nazis to re-supply troops and munitions. The 2nd Polish Corps had to take out airfields in several locations. The Poles gained air superiority when the Gdansk Reconnaissance Squadron, equipped with cameras, gave them accurate intelligence from sweeps over the Adriatic Coast.

A major assault on Ancona began in mid-July. Following fierce fighting under a barrage of heavy Nazi artillery, German lines were broken. Polish armoured troops outnumbered the German troops defending Ancona. The 3rd Carpathian Rifle Battalion and Armoured Regiment reinforced the Infantry Brigade with artillery fire to weaken German defences as they captured a strategic ridge. The Poles crossed over the river, taking more towns and another ridge along the way. The units continued to advance, capturing towns all the way to Ancona. They reached the Adriatic shores later in July, cutting off German defenders of Ancona from the northwest.

With the Germans quickly withdrawing units from the area, falling back towards the sea, Polish troops faced little resistance entering Ancona. Numerous German prisoners were captured, in addition to many German deserters dressed in civilian clothes. The Poles secured Ancona in two days. The Germans suffered a high number of casualties, and a lot of equipment and supplies were captured.

Germany's last major line of defence in the Italian Campaign was along the northern summits of the Apennine Mountains. It was known as the Gothic Line and had been expertly created as a result of mistakes made by the Allies. Following the breakthroughs at Cassino, the Allied forces in Italy should have trapped the Germans in a pincer movement and carried out the original plan for the Anzio landing. The US was supposed to send most of its army east to surround the German Army, cutting off their northern line of retreat from Cassino. Instead, the US general redirected a large part of his intended Anzio forces toward Rome in an attempt to take honour for liberating the city. This gave the Germans time to strengthen the Gothic Line.

Kesselring's troops escaped and fell back to the Arno River, where they built a lengthy zone of fortifications stretching south from Ancona on the east coast all the way across to the Arno River and into the Apennine Mountains. This formed an unbroken, natural defensive wall stretching for miles into the high mountain peaks. Along the Gothic Line, the Germans created enough machine-gun nests, bunkers, observation posts and concrete-reinforced gun-pits, trenches and artillery-fighting positions to repel any assault.

The 2nd Polish Corps was assigned to push the Germans over the Metauro River and prepare positions for a strong assault with Canadian and British corps on the Gothic Line. The Germans were already prepared for a stiff defence in the mountains. General Anders' plan of action was to outflank them and throw their communications into disarray. As they had retreated, the Nazis had blown up bridges and mined roads and river crossings to slow down the 2nd Polish Corps' advance. The Poles encountered strong opposition battling the German parachute and infantry divisions. It took the 2nd Corps more than a week to reach the Misa River. They slowly captured a few towns and managed to advance.

The Germans were determined to hold the Gothic Line. They retreated behind their main defensive lines on the Metauro River. The Polish Armoured Brigade crossed the Cesano River and continued the outflanking operation. German lines had been reinforced with a battalion of mechanised infantry using powerful anti-tank guns. As the Polish Armoured Corps approached the Metauro in August, a major battle began, with heavy artillery and tank fighting. Due to good field intelligence and air superiority, accurate artillery fire prevented German reinforcements from entering the action. The Nazis suffered high casualties and losses in the battle. Depletion of anti-tank guns seriously impeded the German defence on the Gothic Line. The Poles crossed the Metauro River and reached the Gothic Line later in August.

The Allies reorganised their forces before the assault began on the Line. The 2nd Polish Corps was on the furthest right flank at the Adriatic Coast, with the 1st Carpathian troops on the left. Going by the code name Operation Olive, the battle in the Adriatic sector began toward the end of August. Infantrymen waded into the olive groves in waist-deep water on the far side with guns raised above their heads, dodging defences, moving into the bridgehead for the attack. Without artillery support, they were underpowered, and they lacked replacements.

The troops moved ahead slowly during the night while shells poured down a short distance in front of them. A division of Nazi paratroopers were caught withdrawing out into the open. The Poles fired heavily on them. When the Polish, Canadian and British corps attacked, the eastern flank along the Gothic Line was broken. Allied divisions were well across the river and into the hills before dawn. The Poles began the assault and captured high ground. Battle lines reached several miles inland from the coast with the two Polish divisions advancing side by side.

The Kresowa Infantry Division fought for a few days before finally taking a strategic position. On the right flank, mechanised cavalry units continued to advance. The Canadian Corps quickly pushed deep into German lines. With the Polish Carpathian Rifle Brigade causing immeasurable damage, the German Paratroop Division was rendered useless. Despite the German Panzer Division being brought into action, the Germans had no time to prepare a counteroffensive. The Allies captured two hills by mid-September, and after an aggressive battle, the Gothic Line was broken.

Thousands of Allied soldiers had taken part in Operation Olive. The heaviest combat in the Adriatic sector was the fight for Metauro. It took the Poles a few months to break through the Gothic Line. General Anders would say it was the courage and skill of the Polish and British tanks that made capturing Metauro possible.

***

Having completed their order of battle, the 2nd Polish Corps was withdrawn from the frontline for three weeks to recover. Following this brief period of rest, the 2nd Corps returned to the battlefield.

Operating on the Adriatic shores, the British 8th Army reached the Rubicon River by the end of September. Autumn rains soaked the ground and caused the rivers to swell, delaying operations. Jozef's rifle brigade was put into action as rearguard on the Brits' western flank, threatening the Germans with an outflanking movement in the mountains and securing success in the Adriatic arena.

The 2nd Polish Corps was reassigned to action in the Northern Apennines. There were few roads in this mountainous region. Mule tracks had to be used to travel through the territory, and mules would become the only means of mobility and supply. The region was not suitable for mechanised operations, and heavy rains seriously hampered military activity. It was a miserable ordeal. Mud slides caused by the torrential rain made it difficult to keep roads and tracks open. Soldiers had to plod on through endless rain and deep mud as they attacked and battled in the hills, pushing back the Germans. Persistent fighting required great effort by the troops. Proceeding beyond the hills, the plains were saturated by a series of swollen rivers that ran across their line of advance, preventing the 8th Army's armour from moving forward.

A larger assault was launched on the hills in mid-October. The Germans responded with a ferocious counterattack, but territory was seized, and Allied divisions came together in a bridgehead on the River Rabbi. Later in the month, more heights were captured.

By the end of October, the Allies faced several German divisions. The British 8th Army attacked up the coastal Adriatic plain, while the US Army attacked through the central Apennine Mountains. The Polish 3rd Carpathian Infantry Division captured a few strategic heights at the beginning of November. The Poles crossed the River Lamone on their way to the River Senio. More rain, mud, and snow arrived in November while the 2nd Polish Corps made its way through the Apennine foothills, taking further strategic points through to December.

The fighting was tenacious in the drenched mountains and the flooded plains. Exhaustion and combat losses weakened the army's capabilities. They had managed to break the daunting Gothic Line defences. However, they did not manage to advance into the Po Valley before winter weather arrived, making further progress impossible. By the end of December, operations in the region ended. The 2nd Corps listed many officers and other ranks as losses in those fierce battles.

A new commander, Richard McCreery, took over command of the British 8th Army from General Leese. McCreery recognised the effort the Poles had put forth in successful operations throughout demanding terrain and in terrible weather conditions in the Apennines. He congratulated General Leese and the 3rd Carpathian Division, saying it was a fine achievement with the lack of roads in the area. He gave credit to the gunners and the engineers.

In January, the Italian front was quiet. Following the hard-fought river crossings, the 8th British Army was situated on the banks of the River Senio. Any attempt to cross was out of the question, with snow falling and winter well-established. Armoured operations were not possible due to soaked ground. The winter offensive was on hold due to a shortage of troops and munitions, reducing major actions to artillery duels and foot patrols in the brutal weather. Most Allied forces used the winter conditions to withdraw and rotate frontline soldiers to regain combat strength. Forward formations spent the rest of the winter in extremely harsh conditions while preparations were made to resume military operations in the spring when better conditions returned.

***

Between October and January, the 2nd Polish Corps was reorganised and reinforced. During this same period, the Italian campaign was affected by foreign policy and international events. Earlier on, General Anders had met with British Prime Minister Churchill when the prime minister had visited Polish Headquarters. Anders had advised Churchill that Stalin was lying about wanting Poland to be free and secure. He talked about the Katyn Forest massacre, and he mentioned that the Soviet Red Army was acting aggressively toward Poland. Anders stated that the Poles would rather die than live under Soviet authority. Churchill assured Anders that he was sympathetic toward Poland's plight and that Britain would not cast Poland aside.

Prime Minister Churchill of Great Britain, the United States President Roosevelt and the Supreme Soviet Stalin met at a Russian resort on the Black Sea at Yalta for a week in February. Stalin had insisted they meet in the Soviet Union. By the time this conference took place, the Western Allies had liberated all of France and Belgium and were advancing into Germany. In the east, the Soviet Red Army was approaching Berlin, having pushed back the Germans from Poland, Romania, Bulgaria, and most of Yugoslavia. Germany was only left with shaky control over the Netherlands, Denmark, Norway, Austria, Northern Italy and Northern Yugoslavia.

The meeting, known as the Yalta Conference, was convened so that the post-war reorganisation of Europe could be discussed. The aim was to form a post-war peace, shared security, to plan for re-establishment of Europe's war-torn nations, and to determine the fate of Germany after the war.

Each of the three leaders had their own ideas about what should happen to post-war Nazi Germany and a liberated Europe. Roosevelt wanted Soviet support in the US Pacific War with Japan, and Soviet participation in the United Nations that was being formed. Churchill advocated for democratic governments and free elections in Poland and Eastern and Central Europe. Stalin demanded that Russian political influence remain in Eastern and Central Europe as a necessary part of the Soviet's national security plan. He argued that Poland had always been used as a passageway for foreign forces attempting to invade Russia, posing a security threat. Stalin admitted to the Soviet Union's wrongdoing against Poland, and he claimed the Soviet government was trying to make amends for it. He maintained that the Soviet Union wanted to see Poland strong, free and independent, but insisted that the Polish Government-in-Exile's demand to liberate Eastern Poland from Russia was not negotiable. The Soviet Union would keep the territory it had annexed at the start of the war, and it would repay Poland by extending Poland's western border into Germany. Stalin promised free elections in Poland despite a Soviet-sponsored interim government already being installed in the Polish regions occupied by the Red Army. At the time, Russia's army occupied Poland and held Eastern Europe with great military power.

The Yalta negotiations were totally dominated by Stalin. Roosevelt and Churchill consented to a series of agreements set out in the conference. Stipulations included the demand for Germany's unconditional surrender, a promise from the Soviet Union to enter the US war with Japan, the repatriation of Soviet citizens and a temporary government to be established in Poland. Stalin promised free and unrestricted elections in Poland, based on the universal right to vote, as soon as possible. He also vowed that the Polish government would be reorganised to expand its base and include members of Poland's Government-in Exile. However, he never honoured any of his promises.

All three leaders agreed that the Curzon Line would be the new accepted Polish/Soviet border, giving the centre of Europe to the Soviets. Stalin was adamant that all Soviet citizens be repatriated to the Soviet Union whether they wanted to be or not, including those displaced people from other nations that the Soviets had taken over. Roosevelt and Churchill bent to Stalin's post-war territorial demands and, without knowing it, they condemned thousands of exiles, refugees, displaced people and objectors to death as those nations became confined behind the Communist curtain.

As a result of Roosevelt and Churchill giving Eastern Poland to Stalin, Poland's new borders made it impossible for Anders' soldiers to return. The *Yalta Betrayal* condemned Eastern Poland to Soviet authority. The return to their families and the land they loved and fought for was now an impossible dream. If they were to return, the Russians would deem them tainted citizens. They would face persecution and possible deportation back to labour camps, or death. The changes to Poland's borders rendered Anders' troops without a country.

When General Anders heard about the terms agreed to by Stalin, Roosevelt and Churchill in the Yalta Agreement, he was infuriated. He wrote a letter to General McCreery letting him know how this would impact his soldiers negatively once they learned the horrible truth. He reminded the British general that the 2nd Corps' troops had come from the torture of Russian labour camps, marched thousands of frozen miles to form an army, suffered thousands of casualties together and fought battle after battle on demanding frontlines to secure their right to go home to their families in a liberated Poland, as had been promised them. Now, all that his men had suffered through was for nothing. He was appalled; without ever being consulted, the 2nd Polish Corps' homeland had simply been handed over to Soviet jurisdiction.

In March, Anders met with General McCreery, British Field Marshal Alexander and American General Clark. He advised them that, given the fact that his men had nothing left to fight for, he could not ask them to continue risking their lives in battle for nought. He wanted to withdraw his soldiers from the line.

General McCreery cautioned Anders that if his troops were pulled away, there were no soldiers to replace them, and a lengthy breach would open along the line. General Clark expressed his opinion that the Polish soldiers had every confidence in Anders' command and would accept any decision that Anders would make.

Anders considered McCreery's words and realised that the removal of his Polish troops would be detrimental to the Allied victory in Italy, and Western Poland's claim to be an independent nation. He knew Hitler had to be defeated. He told the other commanders they could count on the 2nd Polish Corps' participation in the next battle.

Anders' troops learned the devastating news when Churchill spoke to them by radio. Bitterness filled the room. Many soldiers wanted to lay their arms down immediately. Churchill complained that he had to give their part of Poland to the Soviets because of the Curzon Line. He ended by assuring the troops they could go home to Poland after the war if they wished to, but if not, Britain would welcome them with employment and homes. The majority of the soldiers would wisely choose not to return to Russian authority.

Despite many soldiers having considered throwing down their weapons, the Polish Corps continued to fight. After the war, it would be said that the Polish soldiers showed a great deal of dignity in their unfortunate situation. They may have lost their country, but they managed to keep their honour.

***

At the end of 1944, Harold Alexander was named Allied Supreme Commander of the Mediterranean Theatre. The problem of troop depletion continued as Allied infantry divisions and corps were sent to other areas of operation. In January, there were only a handful of divisions remaining in General McCreery's British 8th Army.

A lot of reorganisation and redistribution of armies took place across the European theatre. Reinforced with fresh troops specially trained and equipped, the Allied armies in Italy were re-designated as the 15th Allied Army Group, with troops now outnumbering the German divisions who opposed them. General Clark became their new commander.

The final Allied attack during the Italian campaign took place early in April, with an assault into the Lombardy Plain. The Allies needed to contain the Germans to finally defeat them. Their goal was to destroy the maximum number of enemy forces south of the Po Valley, force crossings over rivers and capture towns along the way. To lure German reserves away from the main assaults that were to come, diversionary tactics were set in motion on the furthest right and left flanks of the Allied front before the main attacks were under way.

The 8th Army was given battle orders to break through the Po Valley and take Bologna and Florence. A major assault began with heavy artillery bombardment on the Senio defences. Jozef's 3rd Carpathian Rifle Division led the ground attack across the Senio River north toward Bologna with the 5th Kresowa Infantry Division in reserve. The soldiers had an arduous job crossing the river with its artificially raised banks rising to unbelievable heights and embedded with defensive tunnels and bunkers at the front and rear. Hundreds of Allied aircraft dropped fragmentation bombs on German defences for several hours, interspersed by fighter bombers. One aircraft released its bombs too soon, hitting the Carpathian Division caught outside the bridgehead. Numerous Polish officers and soldiers were killed, and many more were wounded. General Anders arrived at the site where the accident had happened, and he managed to calm his troops and persuade them to continue fighting. That same day, the Poles achieved their first objective by capturing the heights above the Senio River.

Having crossed the Senio, the assault divisions had to push forward and cross over the Santerno. The 2nd Polish

Corps would widen the front further with their attack across the river, moving toward Bologna. They arrived at the boundary between ferocious German Panzer divisions. The 3rd Carpathian Division began a courageous assault, supported by New Zealand and Indian divisions. Using flamethrowers on tanks, they managed to break through a gap between German units, opening ground between the Senio and Santerno rivers. The Germans posed a powerful resistance trying to hold their positions, launching fierce counterattacks, but the Allied forces managed to restrain them. The New Zealanders, Indian Division and 2nd Polish Corps arrived at the Santerno in mid-April.

The Poles broke through the river and encountered an aggressive German rifle division. Once again, fierce fighting began. During the next few days, the Polish divisions pushed the Germans back through nearby canals with infantry and tanks. They were confronted by a German parachute regiment and the German Parachute Rifle Division while attempting to cross the heavily defended Gaiano River. Again, the Poles fought with reckless abandon, and the assault was successful. German divisions were annihilated.

Polish units captured the Germans' battle flag and advanced into the Po Valley alongside Bologna. Caught in the open countryside, the Poles were again fired upon by US artillery who thought they were retreating German divisions. Despite that, the Poles continued to advance. They destroyed a few German divisions in their fight for Bologna, pushing them further back toward the lakes and mountains.

In the third week of April, Jozef and his comrades from the 3rd Carpathian Rifle Division entered the town of Bologna. The German flag was presented to General Anders as a trophy, and two days later the 2nd Polish Corps stood down. The liberation of Bologna ended the Polish Corps' lengthy operation in the gruelling Italian campaign. They would not fight again. The Germans agreed to surrender at the end of April, but hostilities did not end until early in May.

Congratulatory letters arrived from General McCreery, who said that the 2nd Polish Corps had demonstrated skill and endurance in great battles. He sent his admiration to all ranks. In a tribute to them, McCreery pointed out that the Poles had faced Germany's best divisions and pushed them back. Churchill said that the British government owed a debt of gratitude to the Polish troops who had served valiantly under their command. Field Marshal Alexander honoured the Polish soldiers by stating he would choose them if he were to choose any soldiers to command. Other British officials stated that they had underestimated the dignity and devotion of Anders and his men. They admitted that the Poles had fought with distinction on the frontlines of fierce battles. British Field Marshal Montgomery felt that Anders' soldiers' service had caused the enemy to fear them and earned the Allies' respect. He believed only the best troops could have captured the long-defended Monte Cassino fortress as the Poles had done in one of the greatest conflicts of the Second World War. Major General Wladislaw Anders had been an inspiration to his fellow Poles, and he was seen by the Allies as a military leader who commanded great respect. He had led the 2nd Polish Corps from training in the Middle East through the formidable fighting during the Italian campaign and became a national hero in Poland.

Aside from the accolades, the soldiers of the 2nd Polish Corps who served in the Italian theatre earned several medals for their courage and sacrifice. Following Polish military operations in and around Monte Cassino, the Polish Government-in-Exile created the Monte Cassino Cross as a battle honour to commemorate the tough conflict. All members of Polish units who fought at Cassino received the Commemorative Cross. Capturing the strategic point at Cassino had proven very costly, but the battle exemplified the heroism of the Polish troops.

Those Poles who had served under British command also qualified for the British Defence Medal, British War Medal, Italy Star and the 39-45 Star. Some of the soldiers also received the Cross of Merit, and some were presented with the Polish Army Medal. All of them proudly wore the 2nd Polish Corps Badge on their dress uniforms above the left pocket, midway between the breast and collar.

In the aftermath of the courageous fight at Monte Cassino, a Polish song writer, Feliks Konarski, who had taken part in the battle, wrote a song he titled, "Red Poppies on Monte Cassino". It was published in Poland and became a famous anthem among the Polish troops. However, it was banned by Stalin when the Russians attempted to curtail the memory of the Polish Armed Forces fighting in the west. In the song, Konarski declared that the Polish soldiers went to war angry and vengeful, fighting for their honour. He described how the soldiers walked on the poppies along the mountainsides at Monte Cassino and fell in battle. He stated that the years would pass, and few sights of the fighting would remain, but the poppies of Monte Cassino would always bloom red from Polish blood.

Later, an amphitheatre-style Polish cemetery was established at Monte Cassino for the Polish soldiers who fought and died there. Many graves in the burial ground were marked 'unknown'. A dedication ceremony took place at the opening of the cemetery where thousands of soldiers from the 2nd Polish Corps were laid to rest. At the main entrance to the cemetery, a large obelisk was erected, bearing the inscription: *Passerby, tell Poland that we fell faithfully in her service, for our freedom and yours, we Polish soldiers gave our souls to God, our bodies to the soil of Italy, and our hearts to Poland.*

Many other Polish soldiers who died in subsequent battles were put to rest in a Polish war cemetery at Bologna.

***

Polish patriots who returned to their towns in former Poland were persecuted. Turmoil continued as the Soviet Communist Party pretended a Polish People's Republic existed. Anders' Army was not allowed to exist in Communist Poland. Returning soldiers were quickly arrested, and many disappeared.

The NKVD began a new wave of arrests and deportations to Siberia. Under Soviet rule, many repatriates were tried as war criminals, or were executed for fighting against the Russians when the Soviets first invaded Poland at the start of the war. Members of the Polish Underground Army who had resisted German occupation were also targeted along with their families because they had been in contact with the Free Polish Government in London, representing a free and democratic Poland.

The repatriation of former Polish citizens was a planned means to ethnically cleanse the occupied territory, to implement total control and to communise post-war Poland. The Polish population was trapped inside the country under a Communist dictatorship claiming to represent the worker and peasant classes. Non-Russians were deemed to be enemies of the people. The Communists ruled by deception and crime as the Soviet government controlled all aspects of life. Militia and party bureaucrats and the NKVD collaborated with them. They controlled the masses with lies, fear and hunger.

Repatriates' lands in former Eastern Poland were officially annexed to the United Soviet Socialist Republic as a result of the Soviet-Nazi pact at the beginning of the war, and later by the Yalta Agreement between Russia and the Allies at the close. Some repatriates were sent to the west of Poland in regained territory.

Deportations of thousands to forced labour camps in the Soviet Union continued for many years after the war had ended. Few of those people survived. Later, stories would emerge about children being deported to Siberia as convicts and slave labourers because the Communists viewed them as the children of class enemies who had served the Polish capitalist society. Anyone found to have family abroad in a capitalist country, who had served in the Polish Army and not returned to Poland after the war, was blacklisted. Jozef's family members would become victims of this opprobrious stigma as a result of his choice to never return. They would have difficulty accessing education and advancement in employment, because Jozef was deemed to be a class enemy abroad in a capitalist country.

THIRTEEN
A NEW START... A NEW LIFE

A bright moon shone outside Lilyana's bedroom window, causing the trees in the garden to cast shadows across the bedspread she had curled up under. As music from the big band continued to echo in her thoughts, Lilyana quietly hummed the tunes that had become so familiar to her now. Sleep continued to elude her.

It had been a nice evening shared with her beau, Stefan, at the Polish/English dance in town. Lilyana loved to dance. Having twirled and boogied to the rhythmic sounds, she was too fired up to sleep. Following the dance, she and Stefan had embraced the cold evening air outside and gone to watch fireworks lighting up the night sky. The dancing and fireworks made it a wonderful evening spent with their closest friends. How different her life had become since she came to live with her father's cousin Tadeusz and his wife Paulina's family in England.

It was now three weeks since her cousin Gita had married, leaving Lilyana with the bedroom they had shared all to herself. Dear, dear Gita! What would Lilyana have done without Gita when she had first arrived in Britain? It was Gita who had helped her learn the English language so perfunctorily and adapt to wartime life in England. Without her support and friendship, things would have been much more difficult for Lilyana.

The journey across the frozen waters from Russia in early winter had been a dangerous one fraught with terror and hardships. The convoy of merchant ships had been escorted by Allied navy ships, yet that had not hindered the Germans from firing on their fleet. While leaving the port at Arkhangelsk, military aircraft around the harbour had supported the convoy. Further out into the sea, they were more vulnerable to attacks from German U-boats, surface vessels and aircraft.

The Arctic convoy had run the treacherous gauntlet with the merchant ships guarded by a large contingent of destroyers, anti-submarine trawlers, minesweepers, fleet oilers and freighters. Severe Arctic weather had created vicious storms, thick fog, massive waves, strong currents and drifting pack ice. A thick layer of ice had formed over the entire exteriors of the ships while crossing the sea, resulting in navigational problems due to interference with instruments and other equipment. Lilyana had sensed peril throughout the entire crossing. The ships had been fired upon, and a few merchant ships from the fleet were sunk.

Lilyana's fervent prayers were answered as she, Aleksander and Larissa eventually arrived safely on British soil, having survived on the scant rations a sailor on board the ship brought to them in their hiding place each day.

Arriving in a feeble state, they were immediately taken by the Red Cross care workers to hospital at the naval base in Scotland. Lilyana and Aleksander were treated for malnutrition and dehydration. Little Larissa required more intensive care as her lungs were full of pneumonia, and her heart was extremely weak. The doctors could not believe she was still drawing breath. The medical team in charge of their recovery was shocked at the terrible state they found the young, Polish refugees in. Lilyana was relieved that her Russian cousin had seen to it that they were deloused before being shipped off. It softened the shame and humiliation she felt about her condition upon arriving there. Even so, scars remained on her body from festering bites. The nurses checked the refugees very carefully for signs of lingering parasitic insects and infection.

Through his naval contacts, Uncle Viktor in Russia had been kept informed of the convoy's progress and arrival at the naval base in Scotland. He sent word through private associates to Tadeusz Prawoslaw regarding the entry of his young Polish cousins into Britain, so Tadeusz would be there to greet them.

Tadeusz and Paulina arrived while the three remained under hospital care. They were shocked to see how pale, thin and sickly their new charges were. Arriving with only the clothes on their backs and Lilyana's special book of poems from her mother, it was a sad sight for Tadeusz and Paulina to behold. Immediately, Paulina began planning how she would feed and nurture the three young ones back to good health.

Lilyana and Aleksander were released into Tadeusz and Paulina's care within a few weeks, but Larissa would remain hospitalised for three months. Throughout her first month in hospital, the little one remained so medically fragile that the doctors could not guarantee she would survive. Although her condition did gradually improve with proper medications and nutrition, Larissa would never fully recover. Her lungs were seriously damaged. She suffered with breathing difficulties and a frail heart for the remainder of her life.

Once they had adapted to Tadeusz and Paulina's home in England, life quickly became better for the three refugees. Although the war was ongoing when they first arrived, conditions in Britain were an improvement over what they had suffered through while struggling to survive in Russia. The house on Bramford Lane in Ipswich became smaller with the new additions, but it was clean and tidy. Here, traces of life in Poland remained on shelves and walls with things Tadeusz and Paulina had brought with them from the home country when they emigrated to England. Even though it was not as grand, their home reminded Lilyana of the house she had grown up in with her parents in Poland. The smells of familiar foods and the sight of customary things brought back comforting feelings of home. Lilyana cautiously allowed contentment and joy to creep back into her heart.

Tadeusz and Paulina's children, the cousins that Lilyana, Aleksander and Larissa had never met, welcomed the Polish survivors into their home with open arms. Gita was close in age to Lilyana, and the bond between the two young ladies was instantaneous. Brothers Yuri and Fredek were equally as amicable, and only slightly older than Aleksander and Larissa respectively. The family fell in love with sweet Larissa. They coddled and protected her in every way they could. Tadeusz and Paulina initially spoke to their new family members in Polish until they became more proficient in the English language, but Gita and her brothers spoke only in English with their new cousins, making it more imperative for Lilyana, Aleksander and Larissa to learn the King's English quickly.

During her early years in Britain, Gita taught Lilyana ongoing wartime practices of civilian life in England. Dangers were always close at hand, and when England sank to its lowest point in the final year of World War II, it seemed as though the Germans were right on Britain's doorstep.

By law, everyone of appropriate age was expected to pitch in and do some type of war effort work if they were not in the armed forces. At the beginning of the war, volunteers were recruited for local defence, and the Home Guard was established to help resist German invasion of home and family. Tadeusz had joined the Home Guard and attended regular meetings to prepare in case the Nazis attacked in their local community. He and fellow members marched and practised defence measures on local sports grounds. As a precautionary measure, Tadeusz kept a loaded rifle ready in the front room of the house. Home defence was an honourable deed.

A local Territorial Army had also been formed to defend the community, and Tadeusz's oldest son, Yuri, was a proud member. The Territorial Army worked in co-operation with the Royal Air Force against enemy barrage and air raid attacks. The group would often parade and practise manoeuvres in open fields and parks. Yuri was trained in machine gunning, and he operated searchlights in coastal defence drills where heavy-calibre weapons were used.

Aleksander envied his cousin's experience in the Territorial Army, and he anticipated participating in some type of military contribution to the war effort himself.

Gita was a volunteer in the First Aid Brigade, where emergency preparedness and triage procedures were learned and practised. On the nights when she was to be on alert, she would ride her bicycle to the fire station in darkness. A light on the front of her bike had to be covered with a cap that had narrow slits in it, allowing only a minimum amount of light through. It was essential that cities and towns remain black at night. Any illumination would draw attention and serve as a guide for Germans to chart strategic targets to bomb during their nightly air raids. There could be no light emanating from homes or buildings, nor along the streets and roadways. Black drapes hung in every window of their home to prevent any luminosity from shining through.

The battle for Britain was fought entirely in the air. The German Luftwaffe was relentless in its ambition to bring Britain to her knees. Every night, the low-droning sounds of Nazi planes rumbled overhead, and early every morning the high-pitched sounds of British spitfire planes could be heard as they came limping home across the English Channel from battles over Europe. Ipswich lay close to the flight path from Germany to London, and the Luftwaffe flew overhead on bombing raids almost every night. Tadeusz had constructed a small underground bomb shelter at the end of his garden. It was unsettling when the air raid sirens sounded in the night and the family had to get up out of bed and hurry outside to the shelter. Larissa was especially terrified by this reality following her traumatic experience in Russia.

Towards the end of the war, the family no longer bothered going into the garden bomb shelter every night. Bombs were dropped on Ipswich, but the town's saving grace was the trees surrounding it in a valley, thereby reducing its vulnerability and preventing it from being as ravished as London and some of the surrounding towns.

Tadeusz and Paulina's oldest daughter, Celina, was away serving as a Land Army girl in the north of England. Like many other young women in Britain, she had volunteered to do farm work to keep Britain going during that turbulent time. Lilyana did not meet her cousin Celina until she returned home after the war had ended.

Paulina did not contribute to the war effort in any volunteer capacity. It was a very worrying and depressing time for her. She had many family members in England to be concerned for, and back home in Poland also. Once Lilyana, Aleksander and Larissa arrived, Paulina learned firsthand about the extent of devastation in Eastern Poland and became increasingly concerned for her family members who remained there. She could only hope and pray that her relatives would survive the atrocities being inflicted on the Poles under Soviet control. Morbid details released over radio broadcasts and in the papers concerning the situation in Europe further added to her anguish. Oftentimes, she would retreat into a state of quiet reserve. The world had become a very uncertain place, and Paulina prayed for its future.

Lilyana listened with astute interest to the details Gita imparted regarding her volunteer duties. She was required to attend weekly meetings at the fire station and practise first aid skills. Gita would stay at the station on alert all night long when she was on duty, waiting in preparation for fire bombings or poison gas attacks. She worked with the mobile first aid posts, always prepared for action.

The Germans had large stockpiles of poisonous gases in their possession, and it was feared they would drop those over Britain during air raid assaults. Mustard gas was the one most feared because it was a liquid gas spray that could be spread over large areas. It would burn and blister skin on contact, then burn down into the bloodstream, killing quickly. Gita's training prepared her for this possibility. She would be responsible for distributing gas masks and applying first aid if gas attacks occurred. Donning thick rubber boots, heavy oil-skinned clothing, and a special helmet and gas mask, Gita had to protect herself. She would also assist the nurses in the mobile first aid posts. Fortunately, the gas attacks never came.

When Lilyana first arrived at Tadeusz and Paulina's home, Gita was working in an aircraft factory during the day. Women had to step up and occupy positions traditionally held by men while the men were away serving in the armed forces. Once Lilyana had settled into civilian life in England, she joined her cousin and became a welder at the factory also. This was considered an essential service. Gita introduced her to many of their coworkers at the plant, new friendships were formed, and despite the hard work, a new life began for Lilyana. Away from work at the factory, she enjoyed the company of her new friends attending dances and other social events. The young ladies were often given opportunities to meet off-duty airmen at a nearby air base in Ipswich. Lilyana was invited on dates by the young servicemen, but due to her self-consciousness in speaking English, she held back from growing too close to any prospective suitors.

Britain suffered shortages of most things during the war years. Food rations were monitored, and times were tough. Fortunately, Tadeusz was a resourceful man and he had turned over Paulina's flower gardens into areas where fresh vegetables were grown for his family. He also had set aside an area at the back of the garden where chickens and rabbits were raised. The family would always have a bit of meat to throw into a stewing pot. Fresh-laid eggs were a special luxury during the war years. Tadeusz was adamant that the girls not make pets of the baby rabbits and chickens in the garden, stressing that those animals would be what filled their bellies in coming weeks. He discouraged the family members from having contact with the critters, other than to feed and water them and to clean their cages. However, when Tadeusz was away from home, Gita, Lilyana and Larissa would go into the garden and cuddle the baby bunnies. Larissa even named a few little rabbits and chicks before they were butchered, and Lilyana soon realised why Tadeusz had been so insistent that they not treat them like pets. Even though she was hungry, she always felt bad about eating little Isabela, Zyta or Monika when Sunday dinners rolled around.

Although they managed well according to wartime standards, Paulina was disheartened by the few food rations civilians were allotted. She masterfully created tasty dishes with what little she had to work with, but she missed the butter, sugar, fresh fruits and other whole ingredients she enjoyed cooking with. All the best staples were going to the men serving in the armed forces. The grey flour, powdered eggs, meagre sugar rations and other substandard fare issued by the government didn't allow Paulina's meals to measure up to the quality she was used to achieving with her cooking skills.

The world was ecstatic in May 1945 when it was announced that the German Reich had fallen. After six long years of turmoil and sacrifice, World War II had finally come to an end. Conditions in Britain and Europe would be slow to recover from the unprecedented devastation caused by the largest and most costly war in human history. Military personnel and civilians alike suffered from modern methods of warfare, famine, epidemics and the attempt to exterminate entire ethnic groups. The suffering and degradation of the war's victims was unlike anything the world had ever seen. Warfare had been revolutionised by nuclear weapons, many were left homeless, and the world had become a very different place. Geographical boundaries were altered, and society remained politically unstable. The USSR and USA emerged as main powers, and world peace remained questionable as a new conflict between Western powers and the Communist Bloc developed.

Lilyana was twenty-five years old when the war ended. She felt as though her life had been robbed from her by the war. She had lost so much. However, she was determined to turn a new page and start a new life with the opportunity her Uncle Viktor and Dimitri had generously afforded by helping her, Aleksander and Larissa flee from the Soviet Union. She realised how blessed they were to be among the minority of Eastern Poles who had been liberated from Stalin's evil empire. The circumstances of the Prawoslaws' escape would never be discussed with their relatives in England. Instinctively, they all knew that even the slightest hint of details overheard by the wrong ears could rain calamity down on Viktor and Dimitri back in Russia. The gift of freedom was something Lilyana never took for granted. Knowing the terrible circumstances that the Poles who were left behind in the Soviet Union faced, she believed she owed a lifetime of gratitude to her Russian relatives for the extraordinary blessing of liberty.

Post-war life began to improve slowly. Cousin Gita helped Lilyana secure a job as a store clerk at one of the shops in Ipswich. Her small wages allowed her to pay rent to Tadeusz and Paulina, with a little left over to purchase new clothes and other necessities.

During the first few years following the war, Lilyana felt a sense of relief and renewed spirit. Together with her and Gita's mutual friends, she enjoyed going to the cinema to watch the latest films coming from America. Sometimes the ladies would wait in long queues for hours to get in. She also took pleasure in bicycling with friends to the Felixstowe seaside several miles away. They spent those days swimming in the North Sea and revelling in the entertainment along the promenade. Often on Saturday evenings she and Gita would attend the English/Polish dances at the Legion Hall in Ipswich. They would dance the night away with many displaced Polish soldiers who had survived the war and were now making their home in Britain.

Lilyana became a popular choice for the soldiers to dance with. She was a compassionate, gentle soul who appreciated all that the men had been through in their effort to liberate Poland. The Poles appreciated the fact that she hailed from their homeland. It was easy to have long conversations with her in their native language, and her familiarity with their cultural background made Lilyana very appealing to them.

Gita met her husband, Patryk Orlowski at one of those dances. He was a retired officer from Anders' Army. Patryk and Gita had fallen in love quickly. Gita would confide in Lilyana that she'd known after the first dance she shared with him that she and Patryk would be married one day. Theirs was a love story that could have been scripted into one of the Hollywood films Lilyana loved watching. Patryk was quick-witted, kind, generous, and caring... and as Gita liked to point out, he was not hard on the eyes either. Lilyana was happy for her cousin, who was more like a sister now. Gita was a wonderful young lady who deserved the joy and contentment Patryk brought into her life following the war.

It was at Gita and Patryk's wedding that Stefan had been introduced to Lilyana. Patryk chose Stefan, a fellow officer from the Polish Army, as his best man. Gita selected Lilyana, along with her sister, Celina, as bridesmaids. Stefan and Lilyana got along well, and immediately following the wedding, Stefan was accompanying Lilyana to the cinema and the dances.

Gita had always encouraged Lilyana to get more serious with the Poles who frequently asked her out on dates. Lilyana tended to lose interest in the young men when they started becoming serious with her. With Gita's perpetual insistence that Lilyana should not give up so easily, Lilyana finally told Gita about her friend Jozef back home in Poland. She spoke fondly about the memories she carried in her heart of that beautiful summer day in 1939 when she and Jozef had walked together along the shores of the Neman River in Stolpce. They had spent the afternoon happily meandering along the shoreline, and just before they returned to her family's mercantile in town, Jozef had gently taken Lilyana's face in his hands, leaned in and tenderly kissed her on the lips under the large tree by the bridge. Then he had brushed back her long, auburn locks, and whispered in her ear, "*I love you.*" Lilyana spoke of the memory as though it had happened yesterday. She told Gita that she could still feel the warmth of his breath in her ear. In that moment, Jozef had captured her heart forever, and filled her with feelings of love that she had never felt before. He had never left her heart since that day. Lilyana sensed that her feelings for him would remain in her heart forever, and no matter how wonderful the young Polish men she met at the dances were, she would never find another love like she felt for Jozef.

Gita dared to remind Lilyana that there was no way of knowing what had happened to Jozef in the subsequent years. So many young Polish men had been lost to the forced labour camps in Siberia and to battles fought in Italy. He may not have survived. She encouraged Lilyana not to pine over what was lost, but to settle down with a nice Polish husband there in England.

"Have a few Polish babies and carry on," Gita insisted.

It did seem as though Lilyana was becoming more invested in her beau, Stefan, and Gita could only hope Lilyana was following her suggestion. Stefan was a delightful man, and Lilyana enjoyed his company… but she did not tell Gita that she couldn't see herself ever marrying him.

FOURTEEN
AFTER THE WAR

It had been a long road fraught with difficulties getting to the fight in Italy, and in the end, thousands of young Poles were killed in action, wounded or listed as missing. They had fought with distinction. At the end of the war, the men and the women in the auxiliary service making up the remainder of the 2nd Polish Corps were mostly former Soviet prisoners and exiles, and nearly all were former citizens of Eastern Poland.

Jozef remained in Italy doing service with the Polish Forces and continued to train under British command. There was a feeling that a war between the Western Allies and the Soviet Union was brewing.

Since Poland had been allocated to Soviet jurisdiction, the Polish soldiers were opposed to the Yalta accords. Most of them refused to return to Poland under Communist rule. Consequently, many of their lives were saved, but they were left homeless by the betrayal.

The Poles who chose not to return to their homeland stayed near Ancona performing occupation duties and providing care for displaced Polish refugees. Following the war, many released Polish prisoners-of-war and refugees wound up in Austria and Southern Germany and made their way into Italy.

Jozef was billeted with an Italian family that was exceedingly grateful to the Polish soldiers for liberating Italy from the Nazis. The family provided board and lodge for Jozef in their home on the Italian coast. Although food remained scarce, the matriarch of the family, Rosa, managed to prepare exceptionally tasty meals. Jozef relished the culinary skills of the old woman who took him under her wing, calling him her little son. Indeed, she reminded Jozef of his own mother back in Poland. Rosa pampered him and his comrades, whom she could not thank enough for eliminating the Germans.

The Italian family residing next door had a daughter named Maria, who was close in age to Jozef. In time, the young lady and Jozef became acquainted and began courting. The language barrier between Polish and Italian was sometimes comical to observe, but it was obvious that Jozef and Maria were fond of each other. They dated, together with a few of Jozef's comrades who had also found Italian girlfriends in the villages where they were billeted. Quite often, the Polish/Italian group would spend a pleasant evening by the seaside, swimming, eating and teaching each other words and phrases in their native languages, or going to the cinema to watch films in Italian, or to a dance. Newfound freedom, the beauty of the Italian countryside, and the pleasure of Maria's company made Jozef feel alive. He enjoyed working and relaxing in the Italian sunshine with the young lady by his side.

However, during the night, he would experience horrific nightmares and flashbacks common among veteran soldiers who had experienced war trauma. It would take a long time of adjustment before the men could settle back into civilian life away from the frontlines. Due to prolonged, irregular eating and sleeping patterns while constantly on battlegrounds, it took a while for the men to calm down sufficiently to reconcile themselves to a post-war schedule of consistent stability. Adrenaline had surged through their veins for so long while they kept up their guard fighting German defences. They remained alert and on edge for some time after the battles had ended, with many of them reacting to any sudden noise or unexpected movement nearby.

Some soldiers were still recovering from their battle wounds. Jozef was left with scars where scattered shrapnel had penetrated his body. The shrapnel remained inside him, and he would live with it for the rest of his life, but he felt lucky to have dodged major injury and death.

Regular sleep was always interrupted by the horrific night terrors. Men would wake up screaming, dripping in sweat, trembling and lashing out against invisible enemies they imagined were surrounding them. They did not like talking about the heinous things they had seen and heard along the battlefront, although they were always conscious of the terrible images, sounds and smells they had experienced. Sleep came intermittently and restlessly, with visions of exploding bombs, friends moaning in pain, missing limbs, and shrapnel piercing their bodies. Battle fatigue, or shell shock, was a normal aftermath for veteran soldiers who had experienced the prolonged terrors on the front lines of battlefields. Years later, the condition would be better understood, and come to be known as post-traumatic stress disorder.

Everybody was looking for people when the war came to an end. Lists of the missing were posted everywhere. Jozef searched for the comrades he had allied himself with in the labour camp. He was pleased to discover that Tomasz and Radoslaw had survived the war and were being billeted in neighbouring towns. Their special bond was reignited when they met up again in Italy. The three men remained best friends for the rest of their lives.

Having failed to find Ivan and Vladik, they feared the worst. After much searching, they eventually learned that Vladik had been killed when he single-handedly stormed a strategic German location during the fighting in Piedimonte. A couple of Nazi officers and several German paratroopers were slaughtered when Vladik stealthily advanced to their position and opened fire on the unsuspecting foes' hidden location. He died when the Germans returned fire. However, Vladik had managed to thwart a German counterattack on the Polish position, thereby allowing the Polish tanks to break through the German line. He died a war hero. His courageous act earned him the special Polish Medal of Valour, posthumously. His body lay in the Polish Cemetery at Monte Cassino.

The men were never successful in finding their comrade, Ivan. Jozef suspected he may have disappeared in action with the underground resistance fighters in Poland. Tomasz preferred to think that Ivan had survived and found his way back to his wife and child in their homeland. Radoslaw tended to believe that Jozef's assumption was more on point.

In the United States, General Lee, Commanding General of the American Forces in the Mediterranean Theatre, endorsed a bill that was introduced to Congress. It would have given the men of the 2nd Polish Corps and their families special immigration rights, allowing American citizenship to the men General Lee called gallant soldiers. Unfortunately, the Secretary of State did not allow the bill to be passed. The British government then reluctantly felt an obligation to take in the refugee Polish soldiers who had valiantly fought alongside them from Palestine to Italy. At the end of October in 1946, the 2nd Polish Corps, 3rd Carpathian Division, was transferred to the United Kingdom to join a resettlement corps and train for entrance into the civilian workforce.

Sadly, Jozef had to say farewell to Rosa and her family, who had treated him so kindly during his eighteen-month sojourn in Italy. Rosa had lost her youngest son to the fighting in the Northern Apennines, and now felt as though she were losing the son she had replaced him with. She sobbed bitterly at Jozef's departure.

Jozef also had to part ways with his lovely Maria, whose heart was broken. They had become close during his time in Italy, but Jozef had never thought to marry her. He did feel affection toward her, but memories of Lilyana back in Poland still haunted him and prevented him from making a total commitment to Maria. There was never a day that passed when Jozef did not ponder whether his first love had survived the tumultuous conditions back home. He could not help but wonder if she was still alive. Although it was impossible, his deepest desire was to see Lilyana again.

***

The Polish servicemen and women who did not return to Poland landed in Scotland, and they were transferred to various military resettlement camps around Britain. Being stateless, they carried the green passport of the United Nations Refugee Organisation with them.

They were not met with a friendly welcome from the British people. Many veterans from the United Kingdom had also returned home from the war seeking employment. Many Brits tried encouraging the Poles to return to Poland. It was obvious that the British people did not want the Poles there. Many Polish veterans felt unwelcome and uncomfortable in Great Britain, and they encountered many inequities there.

Polish refugees were debriefed and seriously discouraged from talking with the British people about their experiences in the Russian labour camps and the war. The British government feared offending Russia. Poland's significant contribution to the war effort was largely understated, and the British government also downplayed the gravity of the Katyn Forest massacre. Polish veterans were directed not to wear their war medals out in public. General Anders was not even invited to participate in the Grand Victory Parade that was held in London, although many other Allied countries that had fought alongside the British against the Germans were included. The 2nd Polish Corps had played a major role in the war as a division of the British 8th Army, but they were denied representation in the parade and celebrations. Several members of parliament signed a letter that was published in a London newspaper disapproving of the way the Poles were treated. The letter indicated how many Polish soldiers had died in the battle at Monte Cassino and northward up the Italian coast in consecutive battles, and during the arduous fighting in the Apennines. Polish forces had faithfully fought under British command across the Middle East and Italy, and Polish pilots had shot down many German planes over Britain in their allied cause. It didn't seem to matter that the Poles were the ones who had deciphered an early version of the German military Enigma machine and passed on information to the British about methods of how it was being used. This had enabled Britain to crack German codes, which Winston Churchill would later say had given them the means to win the war… yet the Poles in Britain were overlooked and treated badly.

General Anders lived the rest of his life in England, believing himself to be a Pole in Exile. He vehemently opposed Communism and deemed the Communist government of Poland to be illegal. He worked with the Polish Government-in-Exile in London and with refugee and charity organisations. The provisional government in Warsaw stripped Anders and many other officers of their Polish citizenship. They accused Anders of carrying out harmful activities to the Polish State. Anders died in 1970 and, as requested, was buried with his soldiers at the Polish Military Cemetery in Monte Cassino, Italy. In 1989, a free democratic government was formed in Poland under Lech Walesa, and the title of Legion of Honour was bestowed on General Anders posthumously, along with his Polish citizenship being reinstated.

Wojtek, the Polish Army bear, arrived in Scotland with the Polish servicemen and women, and he became very popular with the locals. After demobilisation, he was given to the Edinburgh Zoo, and remained there for the rest of his life. Former Polish soldiers often visited with him at the zoo, and sometimes they tossed him cigarettes to eat as he had done in the army. Wojtek was a guest on British television several times. He died in 1963, at the age of twenty-one.

***

Jozef enlisted with the Polish Resettlement Corps to serve in the United Kingdom and was initially housed at

Hodgemoor Camp in England. As he assimilated into British society, many good memories were made at Hodgemoor. Far away from the oppressive labour camps in Siberia and the turbulent war years that followed, he and his comrades had time to relax and blend into the fabric of post-war Britain. The men attended English classes, learned English customs and practised living like British people did. They worked on local farms, played football and attended religious ceremonies together. In their barracks, they cooked and ate meals, played cards, smoked and drank, and freely bellowed out old songs remembered from their homeland. In the evenings they went to the cinema to watch films in English, and they attended dances at local venues that were organised for the Polish veterans.

It was not long before some of them found girlfriends from the surrounding towns. They began to spend a lot of time with the English ladies. The British women helped them adapt to the English way of life and to learn the language. Many of the Polish soldiers married young British ladies and remained in the United Kingdom for the rest of their lives, raising families.

Jozef, Tomasz and Radoslaw were gradually demobilised until their release from the Polish Army. In December 1947, Jozef was honourably discharged on absorption into industry in England. After living in the camps of the Polish Resettlement Corps, many Poles settled in the London area and were conscripted as European Volunteer Workers. Jozef and his comrades remained in Northern England, where they gained employment as labourers with a local construction company. The three friends shared accommodations at a boarding house, and they resided there for almost a year. Toward the end of 1948, they moved to southern England together, where job opportunities looked a little more promising. They settled in a rooming house at Clacton-on-Sea.

Being more proficient in the English language now and feeling confident in his new life among the British people,

Jozef worked as a chef in a large restaurant by the ocean that attracted a large tourist crowd.

While in Clacton, Tomasz quickly found a steady girlfriend named Vivian. She continually tried to set up Jozef and Radoslaw with girls from among her large circle of friends. On the weekends, Vivian would arrange dates so all of them could go out together.

In December 1948, a Christmas dance was organised for the Polish veterans in Ipswich, a relatively short distance north of Clacton. Tomasz and Vivian planned to go, and they encouraged Jozef and Radoslaw to accompany them. Jozef hesitated, knowing that Vivian would invite one of her loud, brash woman friends to come and hang on his arm all evening. It took a lot of coaxing, but finally Jozef gave in to Tomasz and Vivian's constant begging, and he agreed to attend the dance.

Radoslaw did not seem to mind escorting Vivian's lady friends out on dates, and he was anxious to meet whomever she had paired him up with. On the day of the dance, Jozef regretted his decision the moment they stepped onto the train to Ipswich. An overbearing woman, attired in a very provocative dress, clung to him, smelling very strongly of some sort of perfume that she rubbed all over his neatly pressed suit. Her face was thick with makeup, and she kept her ruby red lips seductively close to Jozef's face throughout the entire train ride north. She cackled in a loud voice, drawing a lot of attention, and she talked incessantly about nothing. It was going to be a long and miserable evening.

Later at the dance, Jozef's date insisted he dance with her to all the tunes being blasted by the live band on stage. She embraced him tightly, her voluptuous breasts resting just below his chin, threatening to smother him. He had no interest in this flamboyant, loud-mouthed woman, and eventually she came to see that he was not the sort of escort she had anticipated being matched with. When she finally released Jozef from her clutches, she went to speak with Vivian, and was overheard complaining about her choice of date. Before long, her loud chortling could be heard coming from the other side of the room, where she had managed to attract a couple of young Polish men with her sensuous innuendo.

Relieved to finally be free of the aggressive woman, Jozef went outside to light up a cigarette. There, he met several other veteran soldiers who had served in the 2nd Corps under General Anders. He joined in conversation with them. They spoke about their current lives in England and referred to prospects they hoped to achieve in their new country. They avoided talking about their war experiences, but they did refer to their lives back in Poland during pre-war times. They mentioned whereabouts they had come from, and how much they missed family and home.

After Jozef had mentioned he was from the village of Stolpce in Eastern Poland, one of the soldiers alluded to the fact that a young Polish girl who frequently attended these Polish/English dances was also from Stolpce. He said he had not seen her at the dances lately since one of the officers from his division had started dating her. He could not remember what her name was.

Jozef was intrigued. He asked whether the young lady had arrived in England with the Women's Auxiliary Service group from the 2nd Corps, but the soldier said he did not know much about her. Jozef pushed for more information, but the soldier could only tell him that the Polish girl lived with relatives somewhere in Ipswich. Then the conversation took off in another direction while the veterans continued chatting.

As the night wore on, Jozef could not help dwelling on what the soldier had told him. He wanted to know more. Did the young lady have any knowledge about the current conditions back home in Stolpce? She might know what had happened to Jozef's family, or perhaps she might know what had become of Lily and her parents? He wondered if he might know this girl from his hometown. After all, Stolpce was not a very big place. He desperately wanted to speak to her.

Manoeuvring his way through the haze of thick cigarette smoke and a wall of bodies swinging to the music, Jozef asked around about the Polish girl, but his inquiry failed to produce any more answers.

The train ride back to Clacton proved to be a miserable experience that cold and snowy night. Jozef wanted to be left alone with his thoughts, but Vivian's friend was all over him trying to steal hugs and kisses he was not willing to offer.

***

1949 came and went quickly. Jozef had abandoned all hope of finding out more about the Polish girl from Stolpce. He attended several dances at the Legion Hall in Ipswich with Tomasz and Vivian that year, and he asked several patrons about the Polish girl. A few of the regulars knew who he was asking about, but said they hadn't seen the young lady in some time. She had a boyfriend now and was no longer attending the dances on a regular basis. Strangely, nobody seemed to remember what the Polish girl's name was. Nevertheless, Jozef continued to enquire about her whenever he went to the Ipswich dances. If there was any way to connect with someone from his home village who could possibly offer news about his family or his beloved Lily, he was anxious to do so.

Tomasz and Vivian were married in a small church at Clacton-on-Sea early in 1950. Jozef and Radoslaw attended the small wedding and served as Tomasz's groomsmen.

A Valentine's dance was to take place in Ipswich the following week. It was promoted as a major event with a famous big band coming from America to perform. Because it was to be bigger and more elaborate than usual, Jozef hoped the young Polish girl from Stolpce would attend and he would have an opportunity to speak with her.

When Jozef arrived at the dance with Tomasz, Vivian and Dorothy, whom Vivian had paired Jozef up with for the evening, they found the venue crowded and bustling with activity. Young couples, both English and Polish/English, gathered to celebrate new and developing relationships in a world of newly revived freedoms. Jozef attempted to be polite to his date, while at the same time trying not to encourage her in any way. He would have preferred to stand on the sidelines, observing and chatting with fellow veterans, but Dorothy hauled him out onto the crowded dancefloor time and time again. As the night wore on, Jozef became increasingly annoyed because he had not had an opportunity to look for the Polish lady from Stolpce or ask other patrons about her. Dorothy aggravated him further with her idle chatter and obnoxious laugh. She clung to his arm as though he were her personal trophy. He felt uncomfortable with the unwanted attention she attracted. The girls from Vivian's group of friends were far too loud and shamelessly forward for Jozef's taste. He could only dream about one young lady… his beautiful, humble Lily back home in Poland.

FIFTEEN
WHEN DREAMS COME TRUE

Lilyana and Gita were in a tizzy getting ready for the Valentine's Dance. Gita had come to the Prawoslaws' house so the two girls could curl each other's hair and prepare for an evening of fun and dancing at the Legion Hall. They had not gone to the Polish/English dances in some time, but tonight's Valentine's Day celebration promised to be extra special, with the Richard Wagnor Band from New York City performing. They loved dancing to the big band sound and could not wait to get there.

They found the dance hall more crowded than usual. It seemed that every young adult in Ipswich and the surrounding area had come out for this special event. Stefan and Patryk escorted Lilyana and Gita among throngs of people chatting, smoking, drinking and moving rhythmically to the beat of the music. They anticipated an entertaining evening. Aleksander had tagged along in the hope of finding some pretty English girls to dance with. He had grown into a fine young man who was particularly charismatic with the ladies.

***

The dance was turning out to be the usual disappointment for Jozef. He sat with Dorothy, who prattled on endlessly about nothing. Every so often he would smile or nod his head, trying to be polite and feign interest in what she was saying, but he really was observing the people and the activity around him.

Jozef couldn't help but notice a young Polish man sitting at the next table who had a real way with the women.

He had been dancing with a young lady who brought him back to the table where her cluster of girlfriends was sitting. All the ladies at the table seemed to know the young fellow. They were a lively bunch, joking, teasing, drinking and having a jovial time together. Every so often, one or more of the girls at the table would haul the young man out onto the dancefloor to dance with him, while those remaining at the table cheered him on. Jozef noticed that the Polish man was particularly good at jitterbugging and swing dancing. The young fellow's charm and good humour kept all the women captivated. Jozef admired this man's dance skills and his affable charisma; he had always been shy and awkward around women when he first met them.

A short time later, an English girl came by with her Polish boyfriend in tow. She wanted to introduce the boyfriend to the others who were sitting at the table. Obviously, she knew the women there, and she seemed familiar with the young Polish chap as well.

"Hello, Alek," she said. "Nice to see you here. We haven't seen you in a while."

The man stood up and offered the lady his seat at the table.

"Always the gentleman!" she remarked as she took his place.

"My cousins were coming to the dance tonight and invited me along," Alek said. "So, I thought I should come out and say hello to all my beautiful English lady friends."

There was a round of laughter that went up from the table as the young ladies giggled, pretending to be embarrassed, and accusing Alek of being a smooth-talker.

Alek winked at the Polish man whom the lady had just brought to the table. Then, stretching out his hand in gentlemanly fashion, he shook the man's hand and introduced himself.

"How do you do, sir? I am Alek. Alek Prawoslaw."

Jozef interrupted Dorothy in the middle of whatever she was saying.

"Did that man say his name is *Prawoslaw*?" he asked.

"Huh…? What's that, love?" Dorothy asked, not having a clue what Jozef was referring to.

Jozef got up from his chair and approached the young man named Alek. He was not sure if he had heard it correctly, but he wanted to know if the man's surname really was Prawoslaw. He had to ask… And if Alek *was* a Prawoslaw, Jozef needed to know if he knew of a Lilyana Prawoslaw, related or not. He refused to lose sight of Alek… Alek Prawoslaw? He would not let the young man go back out onto the crowded dancefloor with his lady friends before he'd had a chance to speak with him.

Poking Alek gently on the shoulder, Jozef said, "Excuse me. I do not mean to interrupt, but did I just hear you just say your last name is Prawoslaw?"

Alek turned around and looked at Jozef as though sizing him up.

"Do I know you?" he asked with a friendly smile.

Jozef grinned back and replied, "No. I believe we have never met. But I could not help overhearing. It sounded like you said your name is Prawoslaw. I am looking for somebody with that last name, and I am wondering whether you might know her."

"Oh?" Alek responded. "Who is it you are looking for?"

"I knew a girl named Prawoslaw back in Poland," Jozef continued. "We went to school together in Stolpce."

"Stolpce!" Alek echoed. "My family's farm was just outside of Stolpce!"

Jozef's heart skipped a beat. How many Prawoslaws lived around Stolpce? Not many. This young man *must* be related to Lilyana!

"Do you know Lilyana… Lilyana Prawoslaw?" Jozef managed to blurt out.

"She is my cousin," Alek informed him.

Now Jozef's heart beat so fast, he felt it would pop right out of his chest. He broke out into a sweat and his hands began to shake.

"You say she *is* your cousin? Does that mean Lilyana is still alive? Are you in touch with her? How is Lily doing?"

The desperation in Jozef's voice let Alek know his cousin Lilyana meant something special to this stranger.

"May I ask who you are?" Alek inquired.

"I am Jozef. Jozef Nowakowski from Stolpce."

Suddenly a bell went off inside Alek's head. He had overheard Lilyana talking about a Jozef Nowakowski from Poland with Gita a few times, and judging by the way she spoke about him, Lilyana seemed to have quite a shining for this Jozef Nowakowski. Now it was Alek's turn to become electrified.

"Not only I am in touch with her," Alek exclaimed, "but she and I live with our cousin, Tadeusz Prawoslaw, here in Ipswich!"

Jozef was thrown off balance for a minute. He had not contemplated hearing anything so unexpected and thrilling. He did not quite know how to respond. He stood dumbfounded for a moment. Then it occurred to him... the Polish girl from Stolpce that the soldier had told him about last year. It must have been Lily all along!

Before the reality had time to totally sink in, Alek was grabbing Jozef by the sleeve and pulling him through the crowd as he explained, "Lilyana is here at the dance tonight. I will show you where she is. I know she will be happy to see you again!"

Jozef remembered that he'd been told the Polish girl from Stolpce was dating a Polish officer. Perhaps she was married by now. What a disappointment it would be if he finally found his Lily only to discover she was already spoken for!

With Dorothy hanging onto his other sleeve, befuddled and struggling to keep up, Jozef asked Alek if Lilyana was married. When Alek answered no, hope sprang eternal inside Jozef's heart. Then Jozef suddenly saw Lily standing with some people not far off as Alek dragged him and Dorothy closer.

Alek called out to her, "Lilyana! Look who I have found here at the dance tonight!"

She turned, and in that instant, Jozef and Lilyana's eyes locked onto each other. They were swept away in a quiet moment of recognition. A look of shock came over Lilyana's face. She stood perfectly still a short distance away, appearing more beautiful than Jozef remembered. Curly, auburn tresses framed her lovely face. She wore a gorgeous, blue satin dress that complemented her beautiful eyes. There was an innocent countenance about Lily that separated her from the other ladies in the dance hall that evening. She was an exquisite vision of beauty and grace. Jozef's heart skipped a beat. He felt the blood rushing away from his head, and he had to steady himself lest he pass out cold on the floor.

"*Lilyana*!" Jozef whispered under his breath.

He fell into a trance-like state. The world around him came to a sudden halt. He no longer heard the music beating out loudly from the band nearby. The movement of young couples dancing to the rhythm slowly abated into a hazy background and disappeared. All sense of time and place vanished. Jozef stood alone as he drifted away on a cloud of pleasing memories. He remembered the last time he had seen Lilyana. They had had such a wonderful time together on the banks of the Neman River that day. He remembered holding her hand as they strolled past a succession of rowboats drifting along the water. It had been a beautiful day, with the azure hue of the sky reflecting blue on the surface of the river. Jozef remembered that the trees in the nearby woodlands were dressed in varying shades of green, and only a hint of breeze ruffled the tall grasses that grew along the riverbank. It had been a perfect day. He had proclaimed his love for his darling Lily that afternoon. Little had he known that Lilyana's father had been preparing the Prawoslaw family to leave the country, and even Lily was unaware that she would be forced to go the next morning. A short time later, the Soviets had marched in and occupied

Eastern Poland. The trajectory of their lives had been altered forever. Jozef had believed he would never see Lilyana again.

She stood by, equally mesmerised. The colour drained from her face. Lilyana felt weak at the knees and gasped at the magnitude of the moment. Jozef was as attractive as she remembered him being. The look on his face spoke volumes to her. Their mutual attraction drew them closer together. Neither one would ever remember having moved from where they were standing, but magically they found themselves face-to-face, staring into each other's eyes.

"Is it really you, Jozef?" Lilyana murmured.

"Lilyana… Lily!" Jozef exclaimed. "I thought I was dreaming. This is too good to be true! You really are here. It is you!"

They fell into each other's arms with a passionate embrace. They clung to each other for the longest time as tears of joy overwhelmed them. It was a poignant moment felt by all who were there to witness it. Jozef and Lilyana knew in their hearts that life's circumstances would never separate them again. Their reunion was destiny. It was God's will for them to be together. They had survived the atrocities of war-torn Europe to fulfil this moment they both had dreamt about for years. Their lives had come full circle. Together they were to share a future filled with love and gratitude. Contentment and new adventures lay ahead. They could not ask for anything more.

***

Lilyana's beau, Stefan, reluctantly let her go. He was fond of her, but it was obvious that her heart belonged to Jozef. Stefan knew he could not compete. Now he understood why she had seemed aloof toward him at times. Stefan would eventually marry an English girl and live happily in England.

Jozef moved to Ipswich and secured a job as a welder in a foundry down by the docks. Tadeusz, Paulina and the Prawoslaw cousins liked Jozef very much. They got to know him quite well during Lilyana and Jozef's months of courting. Many an evening was spent in their front room talking Polish as they reminisced about things in the home country during better times, before World War II came and changed everything. Jozef was often invited to dinner with the family, and Aleksander would ply him with questions regarding action Jozef had seen in the Middle East and across Italy, invoking memories Jozef would have rather forgotten. Aleksander idolised the young man Lilyana was to marry. He looked to Jozef as a war hero having fought for their homeland during his service in Anders' Army, and he could not have been prouder to have played such a major role in bringing Lilyana and Jozef back together. Tadeusz and Paulina looked to Jozef as a valuable addition to their family. Lilyana received their blessing when she married the love of her life.

The long-awaited nuptials took place at All Saint's Church in October 1950. Tadeusz would escort Lilyana down the aisle as Paulina cried tears of joy in the front pew. They had accepted Lilyana as their daughter, and they could not have been more delighted to see how happy Jozef made her. They knew Lilyana and Jozef's union was meant to be. It was a beautiful wedding attended by all the family and many close friends.

When they were first married, they rented a house together with Gita and Patryk in an older section of Ipswich. After little Anna was born to Lilyana and Jozef in 1951, both couples moved to the new, post-war council houses being built in the Chantry Estates. They rented homes next door to each other. Baby Sonya arrived in 1953, followed by Cristofor in 1955, while Gita and Patryk welcomed two little daughters into their family. Jozef was delighted to have a son to carry on his family name, having lost touch with his lineage in Poland, but life was difficult in post-war Britain, and he and Lily wanted something more for their children.

SIXTEEN
ANOTHER NEW START

In 1956, Jozef and Lilyana made a crucial decision and emigrated to Canada. Tomasz and Vivian had moved there in 1954. Radoslaw had met and married an English lady named June, and he and his new wife had followed Tomasz and Vivian overseas in 1955. His comrades had written letters to Jozef and Lily encouraging them to come, insisting that Canada was a land of great opportunities. They said job possibilities were abundant, life was good on that side of the Atlantic, and the future for the children appeared to be more favourable there. It was the latter assertion that finally swayed Jozef and Lily's commitment to go.

With wavering hearts, Tadeusz, Paulina and all the cousins in England said farewell to Lilyana, Jozef and the children at the port in Southampton. It was early November when they boarded the small, dilapidated ship that was to carry them across the North Atlantic to Canada. Paulina insisted that the old troop ship was not seaworthy enough to safely transport them through the notoriously rough waters.

It would prove to be a difficult journey from start to end. They were only one day out into the Atlantic when the ship developed mechanical problems and had to weigh anchor. They bobbed aimlessly on the ocean waves for a full day and night while the ship's mechanics worked to repair the engine. Lily and Anna became seasick early on, and the food on board did not agree with baby Cristofor. He was unwell throughout the voyage.

Mid-Atlantic, a late seasonal hurricane, Greta, swept across the ocean. Again, the ship had to weigh anchor, allowing the eye of the storm to pass ahead of them. It would become the largest hurricane ever recorded in the North Atlantic, with fierce winds creating huge waves and massive swells. The ship was caught up in Greta's peripheral fury. Everybody was ordered below deck while the ship groaned and heaved against the anger of the storm. Little Cristofor screamed and wailed while the storm raged on. At the height of Greta's fury, the small vessel was pressed down deep into the rolling waves, tipping from side to side, pitching back and forth. It fought to remain afloat for two days before the journey could resume. For Lily, it was reminiscent of the treacherous voyage across the Arctic waters during the war years.

A bleak horizon greeted them above deck afterwards, as grey ocean waves beat against an endless, dark, cloud-filled sky. Being November, it was cold and damp on deck. Many passengers were as grey as the sea, having succumbed to the vigorous motion of the North Atlantic.

The little ship survived the arduous voyage, and finally limped into harbour on Canada's eastern shoreline two weeks later. Lilyana was happy to set foot on solid ground. Several months afterwards, the old, dilapidated ship sank off the coast of Ireland. Paulina had been justified in her assessment of the ship's seaworthiness... or lack thereof.

***

The family's early years in Canada would prove difficult as many adversities presented themselves along the way. However, Jozef and Lily were hardworking people. Having lived through the worst of World War II in Europe, they had learned how to be resourceful and resilient. With indelible persistence they managed to eke out an existence and remain steadfast in their pursuit for a better life. They were not intimidated by the squalid conditions of the shacks they found themselves living in, nor were they deterred by the constant illnesses of their children, who contracted every malady imaginable. Jozef had to work two or three jobs at a time to keep up with rent payments, to pay bills and to put food on the table. The first five years in Canada were a true testament to Jozef and Lily's strength and endurance.

Tomasz and Vivian, and Radoslaw and June, were like surrogate uncles and aunts to Anna, Sonya and Christofor, and their youngsters were like cousins to them. All the children were close in age and enjoyed playing with each other. Tomasz and Vivian had two daughters. Radoslaw and June had a daughter and a son. At Christmastime, they would gather at one or the other's home and celebrate the holiday together. Gifts would be exchanged, and then the men would eat, drink, play cards and lament over things lost in the past. The women would prepare meals (including a lot of traditional Polish fare), do dishes and chat for hours. It was always special getting together during the holidays. Every summer, they would gather at the beach to swim, fish and picnic in the lovely provincial parks along the local lakes. The children spent endless hours frolicking about in the sand, water and surrounding grounds, creating happy memories to carry into their future.

In 1961, Jozef and Lily managed to convince their bank manager to approve an application for a mortgage on their first house purchase. They succeeded in relocating to a lovely, three-bedroom home in a nice, quiet residential neighbourhood, moving to Port Credit, Ontario. The children felt as though they had moved into a mansion by comparison with the shabby hovels they had lived in during the early years in Canada. Lily worked a part-time job as a cashier in a local grocery store to help make the mortgage payments every month.

Jozef and Lily welcomed another little son, Gregori, into the family in 1965. Through their hard work and perseverance, Jozef and Lily made a good life for their family, eventually becoming naturalised Canadian citizens and calling Canada their home. They fell in love with the land: the endless lakes, rivers and streams, the dense forests, the mountains, blue skies and the wild, untouched spaces. In many ways, Canada's wilderness reminded them of their native Poland. They instilled in their children an appreciation for Canada's spectacular landscapes, its variable climate, its extraordinary diversity, and for the freedom they found there. All four children would be cognizant of the fact that liberty is a blessing never be taken for granted.

***

For many years, Lily had encouraged Jozef to try reconnecting with his family in what had now become Belarus. He mailed off a few letters to the post office in Stolpce, hoping that his correspondence would be forwarded on to his family, if they had survived the war and were still living in the area. The letters were returned to him unopened. In 1967, Tomasz, who had recently divorced from Vivian, went back for a visit to his family's farm, which was situated in an area that remained part of the Polish Republic, close to the Belarussian border. While there, he managed to slip across the border into Belarus and personally hand-deliver a letter that Jozef had written to his family. The letter was addressed to Jozef's Uncle Pawl, who resided on the outskirts of Stolpce. Uncle Pawl brought the letter to the remaining Nowakowski family members in Belarus. All of them were overjoyed to discover that Jozef was alive and living in Canada. For twenty-seven years they had assumed he was lost to a Siberian labour camp, or to battles in the frontlines of war.

In 1968, Jozef received a letter from his brother, Tobias, in Belarus. It was received with great joy and celebration. Reconnecting with his family after so many years, and with so much turmoil separating them—it seemed like a miracle. Although heavily censored by the Soviets, Tobias' letter informed Jozef that his mother and his siblings were alive in Stolpce. Jozef replied to the address Tobias indicated in his letter, being extremely careful with his choice of words as he realised the Russians would screen everything he wrote. There could be no mention of anything political or religious. He could only relay basic news, and not make it seem as though he was living a better life in Canada than his family was in Belarus, or his letter would never pass the Soviet censors.

In time, more letters were sent back and forth, and several black and white photos were exchanged. It was amazing to see how much of a family resemblance Jozef shared with his brothers. Receiving an envelope in the mailbox with the address printed in Slavic script, postmarked from Belarus, was always cause for excitement. Jozef would learn that his older brother Lukasz was married with five children, having four daughters and one son. His sister Katerina was married and had three sons. Tobias was married with a son and a daughter. Sister Zofia was married with two sons and a daughter. His youngest brother, Marek, the brave little rebel, had married, but he had been killed in a tragic accident at the factory where he worked, leaving behind his young wife and two small children. Sad news arrived in 1983 when Jozef's mother, Emilia, passed away at the age of eighty-six, and again when Lukasz unexpectedly died in 1987. Zofia would pass away from heart failure early in 1990.

***

Lily had always wanted to contact her cousin Dimitri and Uncle Viktor in Russia, but she knew better than to try and send any correspondence. It would raise suspicion and put them in a compromising position if the Communist authorities discovered they were in contact with a former Polish citizen who now resided in a capitalist country. Nevertheless, she often thought about Dimitri and Uncle Viktor, and she prayed they were living happy lives. Then, in 1970, she received an interesting package in the mail. The postmark indicated that it had been sent from a lawyer's office in Leningrad, later to be renamed Saint Petersburg. It appeared to be very official and was addressed to Lilyana Prawoslaw/Nowakowski. She realised somebody in Russia must have been tracking her to know she was married with a new surname.

Lily waited for Jozef to return home from work before she opened the parcel that day. She was afraid to see what it contained. They opened the box together, curiously peeking inside. A legal letter lay on top of a small package wrapped in plain, brown paper. The letter was written in legal Russian language, causing Lily and Jozef to dig deep into their long-lost translation skills. They recalled enough Russian vocabulary to understand that the letter was informing Lily of her Uncle Viktor's death. At Viktor's request, the lawyer had been instructed to forward the contents of the brown package to Lilyana after his passing. Lily gasped at the revelation of her uncle's death, and she bemoaned the fact that she had never had the opportunity to reconnect with him and Dimitri.

Jozef encouraged Lily to open the brown paper and see what her Uncle Viktor wanted her to have after all the lost years between them. A brief note written in very broken Polish in Viktor's handwriting rested on top of a book inside the paper wrapping. Lily read the letter aloud and learned that the enclosed item had belonged to her Aunt Anna, Viktor's wife. Her uncle believed it should be passed on to Lilyana, because Anna would have wanted her to have it. With shaky hands, Lily carefully lifted the book from the wrapping paper. A lump immediately formed in her throat, and she could do nothing to stem the flow of tears that ensued. It was Anna's Polish Bible, well-used, and marked throughout with Anna's personal notes written in Polish in the margins of each page. This was a treasure beyond anything Lily could have imagined her uncle giving her. She ran her hand over the leather-bound cover and carefully leafed through the pages. There was a faint hint of the familiar perfume she remembered having detected among her aunt's personal effects at the chalet in Russia. Memories from long ago that had been tucked away were reignited.

She recalled her cousin Dimitri's ability to recite certain passages from the Bible in Polish as Anna had taught him. She wondered how her aunt had managed to keep her Christian faith alive and pass it down to her son amid their atheistic life with Uncle Viktor in Russia. Had Anna secretly taught these things to Dimitri when Viktor was absent from the home, or had Uncle Viktor been able to overlook this injudicious conduct because he'd loved her so deeply?

Lily pressed the Bible close to her heart and continued to read the remainder of Uncle Viktor's letter. She let out an audible gasp when she learned that *"Dimitri died an honourable death, killed in battle fighting to liberate Leningrad from the Nazis many years ago."*

She fell against Jozef's chest with sobs of sorrow for the loss of Dimitri and her Uncle Viktor. When she finally managed to reconcile herself to the sad news, Lily spoke of all that her cousin and her uncle had done to ensure that she, Aleksander and Larissa were given safe passage out of the Soviet Union during that very turbulent time. They had taken chances to extricate the three Poles, who they only knew because of Anna's family connection to the Prawoslaws. They had put their own lives and positions in jeopardy while carrying out their plan so thoughtfully, even when they were agonising over the dire situation in Leningrad, where the Yatskayas and Valentina were during the siege. It was a story of sacrifice and courage.

There was no doubt in Lily's mind that her cousin had fought valiantly to rid the city of Nazis, and to rescue Valentina and his family from the German blockade. Had Valentina and the Yatskayas survived? Lilyana remembered hearing about the horrific circumstances in Leningrad following the war. The Germans had encircled the city and held it for more than two years. Hundreds of thousands of people died in the city, mainly from starvation and hypothermia as no supplies could be brought in. By time the siege ended, hardly anyone remained in Leningrad. Dimitri became one among millions of Russian soldiers who were wounded, captured, killed or missing in action during the long fight to liberate his beloved city. Lilyana felt it was unfair that a good man like Dimitri had not lived to see the war end, to marry his beloved, to raise a family and finish his days in a more peaceful time.

That evening, Lily and Jozef walked to their local church. They knelt in prayer, saying words in memory for Uncle Viktor and Cousin Dimitri. Lily lit two candles to celebrate the lives they had lived. She owed her life and freedom to them. Had it not been for her uncle and her cousin, Lily's reunion with Jozef in England never would have happened. How different her life would have been had Viktor and Dimitri not interceded for her safety and wellbeing.

**

Lily often wondered what had happened to her dear friend Marta and the others from her dwelling who were left behind in Russia when the Yatskayas helped her and her cousins escape. Had they safely made their daring trek from the settlement to the outside world?

Many people searched for friends and family who were missing at war's end. Lily did pursue information she hoped to glean on the whereabouts of Marta Dobrowolski through the Red Cross and the Salvation Army, but nothing turned up. She would be left to wonder about Marta's fate.

Lily's search for her Uncle Jerzy and Cousin Wasyl never garnered any results either. Jozef reckoned they both had disappeared somewhere in the vast expanse of Russian wasteland.

**

Jozef and Lily remained close to Radoslaw, Tomasz, their wives and families in Canada as the years quickly went by. After Tomasz divorced Vivian, he married twice more, with each of his subsequent marriages lasting only a short time. His daughters preferred to remain with their mother. Over time, they would become estranged from their father. Tomasz was fond of drinking, and it would be the alcohol that sealed his tragic demise. He passed away with liver failure at the age of sixty-four. After a few failed attempts at becoming a restauranteur, he died a lonely, miserable man, mourning all the losses in his life that had been instrumental in driving him to drink.

Radoslaw lived to the age of seventy-nine. June, their children and grandchildren were saddened when he was struck by a truck on his way to a doctor's appointment on a snowy, winter day. He died as a result of his injuries. His family had trouble making peace with the fact that he had been through so much turmoil in his life, and yet it was a vehicle accident caused by a reckless driver that killed him in the end.

SEVENTEEN
THE LATER YEARS

Jozef and Lily lived in their Port Credit house for twenty-seven years. The children left as marriages and life happened. In 1988, Jozef and Lily sold the house and moved to North Bay, Ontario. It was in the north where they built their cabin home in the forest on the lake. They felt happy and fulfilled throughout their retirement years in the woodlands.

After the fall of the Iron Curtain in 1989, Jozef and Lily were finally able to return for a visit to their native land. They felt the need to make a pilgrimage to Belarus, their former Poland home. It had been fifty years since either one of them had stepped foot in pre-war Poland.

In September 1990, they arrived in Minsk and spent two days exploring the old city. Parts of it were as they remembered from their childhood, but much had been altered since the war. On the third day, they rented a small car and drove south-west into Stolpce. During that ride, memories of life in their thriving village came flooding back to them like they had only just left. However, Jozef and Lily felt apprehensive about what they might find there now.

A large sign printed in Slavic lettering appeared on the side of the road informing them they were entering Stolpce. Neither one spoke a word. It was as though the air had suddenly been siphoned from the car, and it was difficult to inhale. Jozef reached across the seat and held onto Lily's hand. She turned and gave him an encouraging smile. They did not have to speak to understand what the other one was thinking.

Jozef brought the car to a stop beside a fence that surrounded the small, wooden house where the Nowakowski farm once stood. It was remarkably different, but it was still the old farmhouse where Jozef had been born. Tobias had been able to take back part of the Nowakowski land under special restrictions following the war, and he lived in the farmhouse with his wife. His children had been raised there. The huge barn had been burned to the ground by the Nazis, and the outbuildings had been demolished a long time ago as well. What little remained of the family's huge acreage was no longer farmed. Much of the Nowakowski land had been severed and doled out to other families after the war ended. There was now a row of small houses stretching along the length of ground where vegetable and grain crops once thrived.

Jozef's sister Katerina and his brother Tobias were the only immediate family members remaining when he and Lily visited the farm in 1990. A large family reunion was organised by the extended family, and relatives from far and wide attended the special celebrations at the old homestead. It was a joyous gathering that went on for days as family members came and went. With fifty years of catching up to do, the chatter, tears and mutual exchanges of news and photos were endless... and everyone wanted to have a photograph taken with Jozef and Lily.

When things eventually settled down, Tobias and his wife, Elena, and Katerina and her husband, Rolf, took Jozef and Lily to the cemetery where Jozef's mother, brothers Lukasz and Marek, and sister Zofia were laid to rest. It was a sombre morning when they knelt and prayed before the family gravestones that were not far away from the farm. For Jozef, it was a moment of closure. At the age of seventy, he was finally able to say goodbye to those family members he had so violently been ripped away from fifty years ago.

Early one morning, while Lily still lay asleep in the old farmhouse, Jozef ventured outdoors and looked across the barren field where the family barn and outbuildings had once stood. He closed his eyes, and in his mind's eye, images from the past were reignited. He saw young

Katerina walking between the long lines of wheat and oats as she brought a bucketful of cold water to her brothers working the land on a warm, summer day. In his vision, Tobias and Marek were play-fighting among the rows of crops as they often did as young lads. It brought a smile to Jozef's face when he envisioned little Zofia dwarfed among the tall plants, with her chubby cheeks and curly hair wet from sweat as she struggled to bring a large jug of water out to the field for her brothers. Jozef imagined the barn where it used to stand, housing Borys the ox and Matylda the horse. He remembered the chickens scurrying around and pecking at the ground. He saw his mother standing in the doorway of the farmhouse, beckoning for the boys to come in for dinner. Emilia always had an apron tied around her waist and a smile on her face as she welcomed her boys in from the field. Those days were filled with happy memories of growing up on his family's farm... days so long ago now.

Jozef knew this would be the final time he'd stand on the land the Nowakowskis had farmed for generations. He breathed in a deep breath and let out a lonesome sigh. He tried hard not to recall that devastating wintry morning in 1940 when he was falsely arrested and taken away by the NKVD. So much had happened between that time and now.

He had always been haunted by the recollection of little Marek calling out to him, "*Return to this land and plant again one day, Jozef!*" He felt compelled to ask his brother, Tobias, if they could go into town and purchase some onion bulbs. He was finally able to return to the Nowakowski farm, and he needed to plant something there as he'd promised Marek he would do, all those years ago. It really was a token gesture now, and with autumn closing in, bulbs were the only type of plant that could be seeded this late in the season. Even though he would not be there to see a row of onions sprout up from the ground next spring, Jozef knew that Marek would somehow know he had returned to the farm and planted again.

Lily sensed the emotional strain Jozef was experiencing as he reconnected with his family and their farmland. As for her, there were no relatives she knew of who remained alive in Stolpce, and no gravestones to visit for her mother or father who had tragically perished after the Russians marched in and destroyed their lives. Although no one remained for her to return to, her memories of that distant time were just as strong and solemn as Jozef's.

She and Jozef walked the old streets of Stolpce and visited the landmarks they had known as young people growing up in the village. Of course, things had changed drastically, and the place no longer felt like home to them. All the wooden houses that once lined the streets had been burned in the war, and newer buildings of brick and mortar had replaced them. A modern office building had been erected on the spot where Prawoslaw's Mercantile once stood. The Prawoslaws' luxurious house where Lilyana grew up had been demolished. The residential property had been divided among four smaller houses situated along the main road leading into town. Lily could not help but wonder what had happened to the family treasures her father buried in the back garden prior to the family's attempt to escape the country at the start of the war. It had been her father's intent to return one day and retrieve the valuables, but that was not meant to be. No doubt, the Russians had fallen upon the bounty of riches when they scoured the land and destroyed her family's home. All was lost to time and history now.

Jozef and Lily strolled through the old market square where life had once flourished with activity. It was quiet. Market days were not held there anymore. All that remained was a statue of Lenin with his arm raised in an authoritative stance in the middle of the abandoned square. A man walking his dog passed by, and he looked at them curiously.

They ventured over to the Neman River and walked along its banks. Sadly, the wooden bridge where they had shared their first kiss was gone. Two wooden posts marked the spot where the footings of the bridge once stood. The old tree that was witness to their budding love in 1939 no longer grew there. It had been replaced by a series of small shrubs entwined with flowers and a stone walkway leading down toward the riverbank. Despite the changes, Jozef felt nostalgic and leaned over to kiss Lily's cheek when they reached the spot where the bridge used to be.

"I love you, darling Lily!" he proclaimed with an impudent glance.

Laughing, Lily replied, "Love you too, my dear man!"

***

Katerina and Tobias described the atrocities that had occurred in their quiet little village during the war. It was a sorrow-filled history of brutality and horror inflicted on them by the Soviets and the Germans. None of the Jews remained who had made their homes in Stolpce prior to World War II. Few had escaped the Nazis' attempt at ethnic cleansing. Nearly all the Jews who were not transported off to the death camps had been rounded up and placed in the Stolpce ghetto behind the Russian Orthodox Church. The closing down of the ghetto had resulted in the Jews being taken into the forest over several days, forced to undress, and being shot into an open pit that had been dug there. Eyewitnesses who were hiding in the forest reported seeing the earth continuing to move after the bodies had been covered over. Many of the victims had not been killed but were injured and buried alive. A short distance into the woodlands bordering Stolpce, a large mound remained in a clearing where the massacre of the Jewish people had occurred. Tobias drove Jozef and Lily there to see the mass grave. A monument stood nearby, commemorating the tragic history.

Polish residents of all faiths and beliefs, in Stolpce and surrounding vicinities had been terrorised, tortured and killed between 1939 and 1945. Many were shipped off to the Soviet labour camps and settlements, never to be heard from again. Many were transported to the Nazi death camps. Katerina spoke of their many neighbours who had mysteriously disappeared in the night, causing torment and grief for their families and friends left behind.

Jozef's family had suffered greatly throughout the war years with all the maladies that the Polish people endured. Miraculously, they'd managed to eke out an existence and survive, but one particularly terrible day lived on in their memories forever. It was a fateful day in 1943 when the Nazis had marched onto their land and dragged Jozef's family members outside. His mother and siblings, Katerina, Tobias, Zofia and Marek, were lined up against the wall of the barn in firing squad fashion as the Germans prepared to shoot the entire family. This was common practice during the Germans' ongoing quest to exterminate all Polish citizens from the face of the earth. Emilia, Jozef's brave mother, got down on her hands and knees in front of the commanding Nazi officer and begged him to spare her children's lives. She told him to take anything he wanted from the farm, but *please, please do not kill my children!* After several torturous minutes, the officer kicked Emilia in the head with his heavy boot, causing her to fall over where she knelt. He ordered his soldiers to ransack the house and barn, leaving nothing unturned. As the family watched in silent terror, the German soldiers took away what little remained of their food, their supplies and all equipment from the house and the outbuildings. They did not leave until every window in the house was smashed, and the door was torn from its hinges. Everything inside was ransacked. Nothing of value remained. The soldiers even took the bucket in which the well water was drawn, and they burned the barn to the ground... but because of Emilia's quick thinking and impassioned plea, the family members were not massacred like so many other Polish people were.

Katerina and Tobias told Jozef and Lily many sobering stories of pain, hardship and desperation that people in the outside world would never hear because records had been destroyed before the Allies arrived at the end of the war to pick up the pieces. Stolpce was set ablaze, and many people were left only with the rags on their backs. Disease, starvation and hypothermia killed many more.

Hearing the horrific details, Lilyana again felt that twinge of guilt for having escaped from the bleak reality of those tortuous years. Survivor guilt would be like a badge of shame she would take to her grave, knowing how so many Polish people had struggled to hold on but were not able to pull through. Jozef tried to convince her that it was not so much about having survived the storm as it was about how the two of them had managed to persevere through all the turmoil and hardships. He declared their survival to be a victory of the human spirit.

**

It was a crisp autumn morning when Jozef and Lily left Stolpce with a final farewell to Tobias, Elena, Katerina and Rolf. Their emotional departure was accentuated with a clear blue sky and the trees surrounding Stolpce ablaze in a glorious profusion of bright reds, gold and orange. As they drove through the countryside, they passed by fields that had come alive with vibrant blooms. Verdant meadows were dotted with pink amaryllis, yellow freesia and red poppies. It was a beautiful sight, reminiscent of happier times spent growing up here before their lives were turned inside out.

They flew from Minsk to London, where they were met by Gita and Patryk, who drove them into Ipswich. Thirty-four years had passed since they were last together. Jozef and Lily would spend two weeks with the Prawoslaw family in England.

Tadeusz and Paulina had long since passed on, and Larissa had only lived to the age of twenty. Her lungs and heart had been too damaged for her to live a full and normal life. Lily and Jozef would visit their resting place at the Ipswich Cemetery, and pay tribute to their memory.

They stayed with Gita and Patryk in the home Lily remembered as being the safe house of refuge she had escaped to on Bramford Lane many years ago. A joyous reunion was celebrated there with all the remaining Prawoslaw family members. Gita and Patryk's two daughters came with their husbands, and all four of Gita and Patryk's grandchildren. Celina and her husband, three sons and daughters-in-law, and seven grandchildren attended. Yuri and his son and daughter came with their spouses and combined five grandchildren. Fredek had never married, but he attended the celebration with his long-time girlfriend.

Aleksander was delighted to see Lily and Jozef again. He introduced his wife, Kathryn, and his sons, Joe, Andy and Michael to them. All three sons had their wives with them, and a blended mix of Alek and Kathryn's nine grandchildren. Aleksander proudly boasted about Joe and Michael's lives as airmen with the Royal Air Force, and about Andy's participation in the British Navy. His boys had obviously taken after their father in their love of military forces and service to country. Lily had to smile when she noticed a few of Aleksander's grandchildren playing with little models of jeeps, army tanks, submarines, navy ships and military aircraft. It appeared that Aleksander's influence had a far-reaching effect.

It was lovely to spend time with family. Lily and Jozef were treated like royalty during their stay in Ipswich. They visited many of the old places and friends they remembered, and they enjoyed spending time with Gita and Patryk, whom they had always felt close to.

They were sad when it was time to leave. A quick lunch was shared at the airport in London, with all of them realising this would be the final time they would be together. Then, Lily and Jozef boarded the plane, carrying many wonderful memories with them home to Canada.

***

Shortly after Jozef and Lily returned to Northern Ontario, Jozef's health began to fail. He experienced a series of heart attacks, and by 1999 he was in total renal failure as well. He required kidney dialysis a few times each week at the hospital in North Bay.

Despite his deteriorating health, Jozef continued to amaze everyone with his strong work ethic. He insisted on continuing to toil in his magnificent vegetable and flower gardens around the cabin. On his better days, he and Lily would take long drives out in the countryside, enjoying the beautiful scenery and stopping for lunch at little, out-of-the-way restaurants where they typically shared soup and a sandwich. In winter, Jozef did not cease to shovel snow away from the deck, the driveway and along the pathway leading to the car for Lily, who now suffered with crippling arthritis in her legs.

Three of their children remained working and living in Southern Ontario, but they came for visits in the north as often as they could. Their daughter Sonya and her husband resided nearby, and they frequently stopped by Jozef and Lily's cabin to help them in any way they could. However, Jozef and Lily insisted on remaining fiercely independent until the end of their days. Jozef often said it takes more than a bad heart and failing kidneys to put an old soldier down.

In early 2000, Jozef ended up in the hospital following a massive heart attack. His frail, old body was decidedly weakened now. He and Lily both knew his days were numbered. Lily sat by Jozef's hospital bed in the afternoons while he drifted in and out of sleep. They did not talk about that autumn of Red terror in 1939, the turbulence and horrors of their past in the Soviet Union, or the fate of the Polish cause they had suffered through during the war years of their youth. Instead, they focused on all that they had been blessed with afterwards... their incredible reunion, their fifty happy years of married life, their four children and seven grandchildren, their lovely home and all the blessings in between. Jozef said it had been a good life they had shared. He willed Lily to carry on without him. Lily remained stoic for her husband, but at home, alone in the cabin, heartfelt tears flowed as she lamented the pain Jozef suffered in the hospital, with his life slowly slipping away.

When the telephone call came, Lily instinctively knew it was the hospital calling to inform her that Jozef was gone. She had only just returned home from the hospital, having visited with her husband that afternoon. Jozef had endured another round of kidney dialysis in the morning, and it had taken a heavy toll on him. He had been lethargic and somewhat unresponsive when Lily visited with him after lunchtime that day. She held his hand most of the afternoon, and before she got up to leave, she kissed his cheek, telling him to sleep well until she returned to see him the following day. With what little energy remained, Jozef had squeezed her hand and opened his eyes long enough to thank her for the wonderful life and all the love she had given him through the years. He told her he could not have asked for a better wife, or a better mother for their children. Jozef said he could leave this earth happy in the knowledge that he had been blessed to have shared his life with her lovingly by his side for the past fifty years.

Lily tenderly stroked his face and told him it was she who was the thankful one, for having such a hardworking and caring husband. She knew that Jozef was saying goodbye in his own special way, but she could not find it in her heart to reciprocate. She sensed this would be the final time they spoke. Her heart was breaking, and the pain was palpable. She leaned over and hugged Jozef for a long time until one of the nurses suggested she let her husband sleep. She gazed at the man who had filled her life with so much love and so many pleasant memories. He had made his peace. Already he had fallen into a deep sleep. Tears filled Lily's eyes as she left his side.

***

The funeral had been a celebration for the remarkable life Jozef lived. He had earned the respect and honour that was given him that day. Afterward, Lily had Jozef cremated, and his ashes were set free in the woodlands he loved so much. In her eulogy, Lily alluded to a sacred place beyond the forest and the lake, where she believed Jozef's spirit had been carried to on the gentle wind. Her words painted a beautiful picture of an unspoiled place robbed neither of magnificence nor repose. She referred to it as Jozef's final resting place.

Sadly, Lily passed away twelve months later from complications with pneumonia. She had been very dejected and lonely without Jozef. She needed to be with him. With every step she took, Jozef's shadow had been beside her. Many believed that Lily had willed herself to go to that special place where Jozef waited for her.

Jozef and Lily's children, Anna, Sonya, Cristofor and Gregori, their spouses and the grandchildren said farewell to Lily with a service much like Jozef's at the small chapel in North Bay. They knew Lily had appreciated the way it was done for Jozef one year earlier.

Lily was cremated and returned to the earth in the same manner that she had done for Jozef in the woodlands by the lake. A light breeze blew, causing her ashes to drift up and away. Her family knew Lilyana's spirit was journeying to where Jozef lay. They watched her ashes rising and falling as she danced joyously toward her beloved husband. They could not feel sad. It was what Lily and Jozef had wanted. Having endured much and loved purely, Jozef and Lily would come to rest together in that sacred place that exists, between earth and sky.

BIBLIOGRAPHY

An Army in Exile by Lt. General W. Anders, The Battery Press (Nashville, Tennessee), 1949, 2004.

The Brief Sun by Robert Ambros, 1ˢᵗ Books Library, 2002.

The Long Walk by Slavomer Rawicz, Lyons Press, 1956, 1984, 1997, 2006, 2010.

The Polish Deportees of World War II edited by Tadeusz Piotrowski, McFarland & Company, Inc. (Jefferson, North Carolina), 2004

Without Vodka: Wartime Adventures in Russia by Aleksander Topolski, McArthur & Co. of Toronto, 2000.

World War II by H. P. Willmott, Charles Messenger and Robin Cross, D K Publishing Inc., 2004.

World War II Chronicle, Legacy Publishing, Publishing International, Ltd., Library of Congress Cataloging-in-Publication Data.

A Forgotten Odyssey, documentary film written and directed by Jagna Wright, and produced by Jagna Wright and Aneta Naszynska (London, England), 2001.

5 - Pinsk Falls Under Soviet Occupation in 1939 – Soviet Occupation of Eastern Poland:

http://www.rymaszewski.iinet.net.au/5soviets.html

Stolbtsy:

http://tunicks.com/Stolbtsy.html

Gulag: Soviet Forced Labor Camps and the Struggle for Freedom:

http://gulaghistory.org/nps/onlineexhibit/stalin/crimes.php

Soviet Gulags:

http://www.spartacus.schoolnet.co.uk/RUSgulags.htm

The Road Through the Gulag:

http://www.sakharov-center.ru/museum/expositions/english/way-gulag/

Kolkhoz:
http://en.wikipedia.org/wiki/Kolkhoz

German Invasion of Russia:
http://ww2total.com/WW2/History/Chronology/1941/06/June-16-22.htm

World War II: Alliance:
http://www.loc.gov/exhibits/archives/worw.html

Wladyslaw Anders:
http://en.wikipedia.org/wiki/W%C5%82adys%C5%82aw_Anders

My Escape From The Soviet Union With General Anders Polish Army:
http://www.rymaszewski.iinet.au/6escape.html

The Polish Soldier: 2nd Polish Corps:
http://www.mpvone.co.uk/polish.2ndcorpus.htm

II Corps (Poland):
https://en.wikipedia.org/wiki/II_Corps_(Poland)

Wojtek (soldier bear):
http://en.wikipedia.org.wiki/Wojtek_%28soldier_bear%29

Allied Invasion of Italy:
http://en.wikipedia.org/wiki/Allied_invasion_of_Italy

Italian Campaign (World War II):
http://en.wikipedia.org/wiki/Italian_Front

British Eighth Army:
http://en.wikipedia.org/wiki/British_Eighth_Army

The Polish II Corps in Italy – Warfare History Network:
http://warfarehistorynetwork.com/2018/12/10/the-polish-ii-corps-in-italy

Anders' Army: The Eagles in Exile:
http://www.robertambros.com/andersindex.htm

Battle of Monte Cassino:
http://en.wikipedia.org/wiki/Battle_of_Monte_Cassino

The Battle of Monte Cassino:

http://historylearningsite.co.uk/first_battle_monte_cassino.htm

Monte Cassino – The Road to Rome (General Anders' Polish Army):

www.derekcrowe.com/post.aspx?id=41

Gothic Line:

http://en.wikipedia.org/wiki/Gothic_Line

The Katyn Wood Massacre:

https://www.historylearningsite.co.uk/world-war-two/world-war-two-and-eastern-europe/the-katyn-wood-massacre

Katyn Massacre – Polish history [1940] Britannia:

http://www.britannica.com/event/Katyn-Massacre

Yalta Conference – Summary, Dates, Consequences & Facts:

http://www.britannica.com/event/Katyn-Masacre

Lend Lease tanks and Aircrafts for Russia in WW2 1941-45:

http://ww2total.com/WW2/History/Production/Russia/Lend-Lease.htm

Arctic Convoys of World War II:

http://en.wikipedia.org/wiki/Arctic_convoys_of_World_War_II

A Tribute to the Merchant Seamen of World War Two:

http://merchantships.tripod.com/merchantseamentribute.html

Siege of Leningrad:

http://en.wikipedia.org/wiki/Siege_of_Leningrad

The Siege of Leningrad, 1941-1944:

http://www.eyewitnesstohistory.com/liningrad.htm

Polish migration to the United Kingdom:

http://en.wikipedia.org/wiki/Polish_British

Polish Resettlement Act 1947:

http://en.wikipedia.org/wiki/Polish_Resettlement_Act_1947

Our Family Survivors and Descendants in Post War Poland:

http://www.rymaszewski.iinet.net.au/8surviv.html

AUTHOR PROFILE

Olivia was born in England and emigrated to Canada with her family when she was a child. She developed a passion for writing at a young age and eventually earned a college diploma in Writing and Journalism. Her interests include reading, writing, nature and all things pertaining to history. She considers herself to be a student of life. She resides in Northern Canada with her husband and the youngest of her four children.

Olivia was inspired to pursue her pastime of writing by a quote from John Irving: "If you are lucky enough to find a way of life you love, you have to find the courage to live it."

Email: oliviawoods718@gmail.com

***

What Did You Think of *Between Earth and Sky*?

A big thank you for purchasing this book. It means a lot that you chose this book specifically from such a wide range on offer. I do hope you enjoyed it.

Book reviews are incredibly important for an author. All feedback helps them improve their writing for future projects and for developing this edition. If you are able to spare a few minutes to post a review on Amazon, that would be much appreciated.

Publisher Information

Rowanvale Books provides publishing services to independent authors, writers and poets all over the globe. We deliver a personal, honest and efficient service that allows authors to see their work published, while remaining in control of the process and retaining their creativity. By making publishing services available to authors in a cost-effective and ethical way, we at Rowanvale Books hope to ensure that the local, national and international community benefits from a steady stream of good quality literature.

For more information about us, our authors or our publications, please get in touch.

www.rowanvalebooks.com
info@rowanvalebooks.com

CPSIA information can be obtained
at www.ICGtesting.com
Printed in the USA
LVHW031028260521
688557LV00001B/220